Reluctantly Charmed

ELLIE O'NEILL

Touchstone

New York   London   Toronto   Sydney   New Delhi

Touchstone
A Division of Simon & Schuster, Inc.
1230 Avenue of the Americas
New York, NY 10020

Four lines from "The Stolen Child" by W. B. Yeats (1865–1939) are reproduced in *Reluctantly Charmed*, as are four lines from "The Famine Year" by Lady Jane Francesca Wilde (1821–1896), who wrote under the name of "Speranza."

First Touchstone trade paperback edition March 2015

For information about special discounts for bulk purchases,
please contact Simon & Schuster Special Sales at 1-866-506-1949
or business@simonandschuster.com.

The Simon & Schuster Speakers Bureau can bring authors to your live event. For more information or to book an event, contact the Simon & Schuster Speakers Bureau at 1-866-248-3049 or visit our website at www.simonspeakers.com.

Interior design by Jill Putorti

Manufactured in the United States of America

10   9   8   7   6   5   4   3

Library of Congress Cataloging-in-Publication Data is available.

ISBN 978-1-4767-5755-1
ISBN 978-1-4767-5756-8 (ebook)

For my parents,
Mary and Bren

"The world is full of magic things
patiently waiting for our senses to grow sharper."

1

A year ago no one had heard of me. That was before all this. Before a columnist in *The Irish Times* wrote that I was a twenty-first-century prophet. Before I was denounced from the pulpit by the Catholic Church. Before a small group in Dublin misinterpreted me and destroyed a landmark clock in my name. Before I was chased by paparazzi. Before I became the number one Irish search word on Google. Before Mam wanted a boob job. Before people wondered, I mean *really* wondered, "what if." Before anyone had ever really considered the existence of an invisible world.

I can hardly remember back that far. I try to, but my old life is getting hazy.

It all started on a Monday. My birthday.

The office had gone through the birthday rigmarole and surprised me with a Victoria sandwich covered in candle wax. The sugar addicts and the easily distracted design department half-heartedly mouthed the words to "Happy Birthday." One budding soprano stretched his neck and crackled through the high notes. I recognized him from accounts but couldn't remember his name.

"Thanks."

All eyes shifted from me to the cake.

"Let's eat."

I backed away and they dived in.

I'm not a fan of birthdays. It took Claire, the office manager, two years to find out my birthday date. And then it was accidental. The amorous Italian I was dating that summer sent me flowers. Carnations. He had busy hands, more suckers than hands. We'd be in a bookshop, and all of a sudden they'd be up my shirt and in my bra. He'd eat my neck as a first course in restaurants and snake his legs around mine so it was impossible to stand up. It was irritating. Anyway, Claire twigged when she saw the petrol-station flowers, and I've had three uncomfortable ten-minute work birthday parties since then and no more Latin lovers.

When the cake had been demolished, I slunk back to my desk and sank into my chair, happy to lie low in case they wanted a speech. This was unlikely; most of them would have learned my name for the first time when they signed the birthday card. I work with four people, am on nodding acquaintance with another ten, and have no idea who the other three hundred are.

"Happy birthday, Annie." Matthew winked at me as he wheeled over my guests-only chair. He was trying to be funny: my name is Kate, but I was a dead ringer for Little Orphan Annie as a child, with a shock of red hair, large blue eyes, and a smattering of freckles that twenty years later still haven't joined up. Birthdays were ruined for me by Annie, or rather by Mam's insistence that I mark my special day by singing "Tomorroooooow" to neighbors, drunken relatives, and postmen—anyone with ears, really.

"Funny. You are funny."

Matthew started whistling "The Sun Will Come Out Tomorrow," his eyes tearing up with amusement.

I hadn't been sure about working with Matthew at first. I think it was his name. Matthew, not Matt, Mattie, M, but the full-barreled shotgun Mat-thew. It's unusual not to shorten your name. It feels very grand and a bit unfriendly. It made him sound like an earl or a liquor. He's none of those things, but he is a little bit grand, I suppose, by Dublin standards. He carries a briefcase and always has a black umbrella, like a banker. He uses a money clip, a gold shiny one. He asked if I thought he was "an awful eejit for having one." I shook my head and declared, "No, maybe we should all have money clips." And that seemed to break the ice.

I started working at Frank & Peterson, an advertising agency, five and a half years ago as a junior copywriter. Five and a half years later, I'm still a junior copywriter. I don't know how to shout. When I get turned down for a pay raise, I say thank you. I once plucked up the courage to ask for a promotion, which I didn't get, but I did get put on the summer party fund-raising committee and somehow offered to babysit my boss Colin's kids. I panic in the face of authority, and even though Colin speaks like a Disney character and twiddles his mustache in a friendly fashion, I'm still intimidated by him.

That was all going to change this year, though. My birthday is my New Year's Eve. I make resolutions. This year I was going to get a promotion, a proper promotion with a pay raise and a new job title. For four days now, I had told the universe I was grateful. I embraced the power of now while still managing to feel the fear and do it anyway. I had repeated affirmations in my head like "I am a rich, successful copywriter who is moments away from a promotion."

The good news was, in spite of my self-help mantras, or because of them—I hadn't made up my mind—the promotion was looking like a possibility. Through a series of errors, Matthew and I had landed one of the biggest accounts in the agency, the Starshoot Chocolate account. So far, the client didn't like us or any of our ideas, but I was optimistic. I was always optimistic.

Frank & Peterson is a giant multinational advertising agency, one of the shiny corporate ones where decisions are made from a head office in outer space, based on gravity pull and lotto numbers. They colonized a small indigenous agency about fifteen years ago, introducing new jobs and a corporate language and ethos to which most employees were happy to be shackled. Corporate life has a lot of perks—good Christmas parties and an excellent dental plan. My teeth have never looked better.

The offices are on the top floor of a building in the financial district of Dublin. If this were any other city, F & P would be at a dizzying height, inducing wobbly knees and shortness of breath, but not in Dublin, where the hand of God rests firmly on the skyline to stop it from getting too proud. Modesty is a much-respected Dublin trait, in the people and in the city.

The office overlooks the River Liffey and its ancient bridges, gray and heaving under the heavy commuter plod. The IV drip to Dublin is the river. It splits the city in two and serves as our very own Berlin Wall. Northsiders and southsiders seldom see the need to cross over and mix with each other, and only bad jokes about passports and visa stamps unite the two sides. It used to be that the north side was poor and the south side was rich, but for the past few years the economy had been booming, so everyone was rich and the jokes weren't funny anymore. Life was plentiful in Ireland. We were riding the crest of a wave that wasn't showing any sign of crashing. Kids born in the 1990s couldn't remember life before BMWs, stone massages, and organic-coffee shops. The past few months there'd been rumors that the good times were coming to an end, but no one seemed to be paying any heed to the naysayers.

The north side of Dublin feels gritty and disheveled. A lot of the buildings are tired and need a reality TV makeover. The main shopping street, Henry Street, moves at a frantic pace: elbows are out, necks jut forward, and there's a sense of urgency that that coat will be 20 percent off for only the next two minutes. In contrast, the south side is lazy. Grafton Street shoppers move slowly down the burnt-orange brickwork, like cows out to pasture. Shopfronts are charming and freshly painted, maintaining the feel of an older, grander Dublin. It helps that Grafton Street is anchored by the beauty and dignity of Trinity College, which is hundreds of years old, and capped on the far end by Stephens Green, home since the seventeenth century to the friendliest ducks in Ireland.

I'm a southsider. I went to a south-side school and a south-side university, my ex-boyfriends have all been southsiders and most of my friends are, too. Except for Matthew. He's a northsider through and through. We're very proud that we've managed to crash through the barricades to become friends.

Matthew ripped open his 2,453rd Starshoot, the reason he'd put on seven pounds in the past month. He pulled on his nose. He has a big nose and big eyebrows, features that don't work in isolation but together are quite attractive, and short dark hair and lovely olive skin that you wouldn't expect to find on an Irishman (he reckons a Spanish sailor wandered into his gene pool many generations back).

"The caramel in these is too chewy. My fillings shake when I'm near one. Will we go with that? 'Rip the fillings out of your head with Starshoot.'"

He drew a line on a blank page and dramatically placed a full stop after it. "Starshoot, in association with the dentists of Ireland."

I long-blinked in agreement. "How are we going to crack this campaign?" I started chewing the skin around my nails, always a sign that I'm nervous.

A slow mournful creak distracted us. In our agency the

postman always howls twice. Dudley from dispatch was approaching with his cart. He could deliver the mail and cop a perve at the same time—it was award-winning stuff.

With a heavy sigh, and never taking his eyes from my chest, which isn't particularly flat or buxom and normally doesn't warrant many glances, Dudley did a three-point turn and parallel parked. "Happy birthday, Kate." White spittle gathered at the corner of his mouth. He gave a little giggle and wiggled his shoulders. "So, are you two, you know . . . ?" He raised his unibrow.

It's impossible for some people to understand that Matthew and I are just friends. We've never had a sneaky snog or a drunken fumble. There's never been any sexual tension between us, and neither of us is closeted gay. We really like each other but have just never fancied one another.

"Well, are you and Connie, you know?" Matthew had caught him out. Connie worked in the canteen and was 874 years old.

"That's disgusting." Dudley coughed and straightened up. "This came for you. It's registered. Looks important." He passed me a large white envelope, reversed his cart, and left, muttering "disgusting" under his breath.

"Oh, registered." Matthew looked delighted to have a distraction. "A birthday present?"

I did an I-don't-know face and ripped open the envelope, which, disappointingly, was not car- or house-shaped. Still, I felt giddy and then confused when I pulled a legal-looking letter out of the envelope. I cleared my throat and in a professional, BBC-newsreader manner turned to Matthew.

"'Dear Miss McDaid. You are invited to attend the reading of the will of Miss Kate McDaid in our offices on Monday, May 5, at nine a.m.'" I looked up over the heavy cream paper. "What? Have I died and nobody told me?"

Matthew looked as baffled as me.

"Is this one of those weird after-death dreams?" I said. "I don't remember a white light."

"What else does it say?"

"'You are cited as a benefactor in her will and are required to attend our offices for a reading of said will. Yours sincerely, Seamus MacMurphy.' How can I be a benefactor of my own will?"

Matthew reached over and grabbed the letter from my hand.

"It must be a typo or a mail merge gone wrong or something." I gulped loudly.

"Very wrong if it's killed you off," Mathew said. "There must be another Kate McDaid. It's not that uncommon a name. We could google her."

"We'd just be googling me."

"Facebook?"

"Me."

"You should ring this guy, Seamus MacMurphy. Find out if it's a typo."

"When did you get so wise?"

"*Cagney and Lacey* reruns."

I laughed and picked up the phone. This had to be a typo.

"MacMurphy Solicitors. How can I help you?" The woman on the other end of the line sounded startled, as if the phone had woken her from a deep sleep.

"Can I speak to Seamus MacMurphy, please?"

"I'm afraid Mr. MacMurphy isn't available. Can I take a message?"

"Well, em . . ." How do I say this? *I've been invited to my own will reading?*

"I just got a letter and I'm invited to the reading of a will tomorrow and I don't know who the person is who died. Is that normal?"

"Your name, please?"

"Kate McDaid."

There was some paper rustling on the other end of the line. "Yes, Miss McDaid. You are invited to the reading of the will of Miss Kate McDaid." She paused. "Oh, same name."

"Yeah, that's why I was wondering if there's an error or a typo?"

"No, no typo." Her voice lowered. "We've been waiting for the reading of this will for quite some time. There's a real buzz in the office about it."

"About the will?"

"Yes. We've had it in the office for over one hundred and thirty years," she whispered. "It's one of those we never thought would come about." I heard a door banging behind her. She cleared her throat. "See you at nine a.m. tomorrow. Thank you." And she hung up.

I turned to Matthew, excitedly. "The will is over one hundred and thirty years old. This other Kate McDaid died back in 1880 or something. How did she know to invite me now? And why? Who is she?"

Matthew looked at me, chewing pensively. "I wonder if she had any money."

"And I wonder if any of it is going to come my way."

2

I am an only child from a long line of only children. Except for me there have been only male children in my family, like there is a direct line to the Chinese government, *one boy child only for you*. It's not normal to be an only child in Ireland. Four kids is average; five is not unusual. It's a sliding scale, depending on your parents' commitment to Catholicism and therefore aversion to contraception.

Catholic Ireland is alive and kicking. Chances are if your mother does the flowers for the local church every Sunday, there could be anywhere up to ten kids in your family. Growing up, friends' parents viewed me with great sympathy. "Poor Kate, all on her own," they'd say in hushed tones, as if I'd been left orphaned and limbless. Another lament was: "She'll never learn to really fight"—a required character trait in Irish society.

Being an only child has never been an issue for me. I've always had my parents' undivided attention, which is a good and a bad thing rolled into one. Being an only child also gave me an overactive imagination, when I was younger. I lived in a world of my own, filled with make-believe creatures and talking trees. But to be honest, while it never bothered me growing up, I would like a big family of my own someday, a gaggle of snotty-nosed, red-haired, freckle-faced urchins who learn to fight and play with one another. I want a full clan, a bursting-at-the-seams warrior clan.

And *because* I'm an only child, my birthday is a big event for my parents. I should qualify that my mother is a woman, just in case that isn't clear from the Chinese thing. They get really excited about it—overly excited. I've sat through the story of my delivery, including a full reenactment of labor pains, umpteen times. "And the doctor said, 'It's a redhead!'" Mam and Dad shout in unison.

This is played out every year in a little Italian restaurant in Sandycove run by an Irish couple with bad sun-bed tans. Dad always orders steak and chips, and none of that "fancy pasta stuff," which he pronounces "pazza." Mam drizzles olive oil over everything "in a Mediterranean fashion" and, after a glass of Chianti, pushes her cleavage closer to the waiter, who she says has Omar Sharif eyes.

This year was different, though. It wasn't just about me and encouraging Dad to try tiramisu. This year, there was another Kate McDaid at the table. Dad had also received a registered letter.

"She could be one of the McDaids of Clare. That's where we started, but a lot of them went on to America during the potato famine in the 1840s. She died over one hundred and thirty years ago, you said."

I had repeated my conversation with the secretary over 130 times.

"I'm flummoxed," Dad said, smoothing down a few wispy bits of hair on the top of his head.

"Your great-grandfather . . . Wasn't there something funny about him?" Mam jabbed at the air aggressively.

"If you call dying at the age of twenty-two funny." Dad jutted his jaw out, and Mam rolled her eyes. Ever since he'd retired last year there'd been a lot of that—backchat, the teachers in school would have called it. Mam had taken to phoning me a couple of times a week to discuss, through a series of sighs, "your father." Apparently he had insisted on wearing his old brown cords to Wanda Simpson's dinner party; he was always tinkering with his car and refused to buy a new one, even though they were driving the oldest banger on the road; and he spent an inhuman amount of time on the toilet. I stayed quiet and refused to take sides. As in any great war, sometimes you just have to sit it out.

"All I know about are the men—there were only men. There have only ever been men in my family until you came along."

Mam and Dad studied the letters intently, flipping them over, looking for a hidden clue.

"Well, there has to have been a woman somewhere." Mam was tetchy. She's organized, documented, highlighted, practiced. This would never happen on her side of the family. "You could take a look in the national archives."

"Ah, here comes the Brit in her," Dad tutted. Mam's grandfather had been English, and this apparently accounted for a lot of her faults, including, at times, not getting the joke, even when the joke was bad and didn't have a punch line. "If we're going back over a hundred years, sure, we could be hitting the famine, when your people raped and pillaged this country. There'd be no documentation, no paperwork telling you who was born. Weren't they dying by the millions, and those that weren't dying were off on the famine ships to America, to try and survive? Nobody knew who was coming or going."

Mam gave him a cold stare from under her eyelashes. "I will not be blamed for the famine."

The famine is a seminal event in Irish history. When it occurred in the 1840s, Ireland was still ruled by our neighbors, the English, and as a result of the potato crop failing all over the country and the refusal of the English to do anything to help us, one million people starved to death and another million—the lucky ones— emigrated to America.

I took a long drink of wine. "I guess we'll find out about it all tomorrow. Can you come, Mam?"

She nodded and we made arrangements. Later, I had my second birthday cake of the day—black forest gateau—like it was the eighties all over again and I was reliving my childhood.

The office of MacMurphy Solicitors was a sighing, creaking old Georgian building. Georgian architecture is a remnant of English rule over Ireland. They left us with grand and imposing squares in Dublin surrounding well-manicured gardens and beautiful rosy-brick houses that quietly whisper of a more genteel time, when the English wore top hats and *clip-clopped* with gold-tipped canes down cobblestone streets, ignoring the Irish peasantry. Most of the Georgian architecture (but not all, like the offices of MacMurphy solicitors) has been restored to its glorious heyday.

I locked my bike to the rusty railings and quickly surveyed the street for likely thieves. My bike was my trusted steed: I cycled everywhere. I wasn't a Lycra-clad cyclist, more like a spinning-around-like-a-whisk-in-a-bowl, leisurely, A-to-B pedaler. It was the easiest way to get around Dublin—everywhere is within a three-mile radius and flat. When I was feeling adventurous, I could even cycle in heels.

I tripped up the flaking steps. The hall door jammed as eight inches of ruffled carpet tried to straighten itself out on the other side. I squeezed in.

Mam and Dad were perched uneasily on two wobbly plastic chairs. Dad waved excitedly as if I couldn't see them, the only people in the room. They both gave my hand a little squeeze hello. They were dressed for a funeral or a job interview—gray and somber. I wondered if I should have worn something other than skinny jeans and wedge heels, something that said more solicitor's office than pub after work.

A wrinkled, gray-haired woman came around the door. She belonged in this building. "Mr. MacMurphy will see you now. First door on the left up the stairs," she wheezed.

Seamus MacMurphy looked like he'd administered a number of short, sharp electrical shocks to himself just as we'd pushed the door open. His hair was spiked like the top of a palm tree, and he bolted up out of his chair as we entered. He took long enthusiastic strides across the room, resembling a young skinny-legged and long-necked flamingo.

He shook our hands, tucking his shirt into his belt with his left hand as he did so. "Please, please. Sit, sit," he said, gesturing with a friendly smile to a number of armchairs, all collapsed and threadbare, before returning to his seat behind a mahogany desk stacked high with brown tea-stained files. The walls of his office seemed to be falling in on top of him; every picture was hung at an angle. "Did Patricia get you tea? And biscuits?"

We all nodded to say she had, even though she hadn't.

"Great, good." He rummaged headfirst in a pile of papers, then looked up, smiling. "I'm a bit unorganized, you know yourself."

We made noises to concur. We knew ourselves.

"But I tell you, we've been awful excited about this."

I suspected he'd be excited about a lot of things.

His face was flushed and smiley. "We've a couple of cases like this from the old office." He spoke from the back of his throat in a thick, west-of-Ireland accent. "It's been in this office for one hundred and thirty years. We'd check in every year to see if it was viable or not, and it wasn't, until your big day yesterday." He looked at me, grinning with every tooth exposed.

My big day yesterday.

"Where was the old office?" Dad asked.

"Ennis, Clare."

"I thought as much." Dad sat back in the armchair, his chest puffed out with pride, having solved stage one of the mystery.

"We shut up there years ago, moved to Dublin, but we carried a lot of the business with us. We've been on the go since 1800. That's why we have a lot of these old files." MacMurphy lifted up handwritten pages with long elegant inky swirls as proof.

"Sure, I might as well just get on with it," he then said matter-of-factly. "Is that all right with you?"

We nodded, but my head was stuck in the washing machine drum, going around and around. *My big day yesterday.*

"So, the will of Kate McDaid." He glanced at me over his glasses and chuckled. "Same name. It was written on October 30, 1878. The deceased requested certain conditions. This isn't that unusual—it happens—and back then most people wouldn't have made wills, and they wouldn't have understood the process. They made up their own rules, especially if there was money involved."

We started to shuffle in our seats at the sound of coins dropping into a piggy bank. "It's the criteria in this will that are slightly unusual, but, sure, we'll figure it out." He faced his two palms toward us as if we were protesting and not dumb-struck. "I should mention that parts of the will were in Irish, but we've taken the liberty of translating them into modern English. It's easier in this day and age."

He began to read. " 'I, Kate McDaid, of the village of Knocknamee, County Clare, being of sound mind, bequeath my entire estate to the firstborn female in my bloodline, Kate McDaid, on her twenty-sixth birthday.' "

My neck did a sharp click backward. That had to be me. The firstborn female in my bloodline. Me.

Mam and Dad leaned in.

"Is that me?" I shouted, sounding like I was seeing my new face after plastic surgery.

"Yes, let me see now," Seamus said. "Kate McDaid would have been your great-great-great-grandfather's sister."

That's a lot of greats.

"Me. Me? But how did you . . . ? How did you know who I was? Where I was?"

He grinned. "Oh, it wasn't easy. We hired a private investigator to track you down."

A private investigator? Visions of a man in a trench coat ducking behind newspapers and tiptoeing around Dublin flashed before me. I hadn't seen anyone. Had Kojak been following me around, sucking on a lollipop, and I missed him completely?

"But that's not possible."

"It is. We do it all the time."

"And my name? You knew my name?"

"Well, yes. It's in the will." He laughed to himself. "Good guess, I suppose."

This was all feeling very strange. I felt my breathing quicken. I was nervous.

Seamus MacMurphy studied the pages in front of him. " 'I, Kate McDaid, the Red Hag of Knocknamee, on this the 30th day of October, 1878, aged eighteen years and upward, hereby bequeath my entire estate to my beneficiary in title by name Kate

McDaid, who shall be a direct descendant of my family line, provided that she lives to her twenty-sixth birthday and that she fulfills the conditions in this will.'" He cleared his throat and looked up. I noticed his eyes narrow. "Now, here are the conditions. You don't get the estate unless you publish some letters."

"Letters?"

"Well, one letter and Seven Steps. She explains it all here. May I?" He coughed quietly, and started to read the pages splayed out in front of him.

As a girl, the fairies came to me; they whispered in my dreams and left songs in my head. I went to the glen and found them there. We danced and played. They took me into the fairy realm and showed me their life of joy. A life with no possessions and no want. They lived in harmony with the earth. Never again would I know such happiness.

But before the bloom was on me to enter womanhood, a sadness overcame the good people, and they told me of a terrible fate that stood in front of us all. Mortals had stopped listening to them, had forgotten their existence. Only the children, who never had the ears of the adults, could hear the fairy folk. The adults had filled their lives with noise and loud voices. They stopped listening to the breath of the wind, the pulse of the soil, the roar of the ocean. They built on fairy paths, tore through whitethorn bushes, forgot to speak to the trees or ask for a fairy's blessing. People had forgotten their need for the fairies, that we share the earth, that we must work together to keep her happy. If we don't, we all suffer.

The fairies gave me the gifts of healing and spell making. When I had the ways of a woman, they became invisible to me. Adulthood is filled with obligations and distractions. My purity was left in childhood. I have made many mistakes that have cost me dearly, and I have angered them.

The good people visited me for a final time in my dotage. They have given me a chance of redemption. They have asked for my help. They are ready to show themselves to the world again. The fairies must be seen and must be heard once more for the sake of humankind. They whispered to me Seven Steps that must be taken by many Celtic souls in preparation for their revelation. They have given me the great honor of passing these Steps on to the world, but because of my mistakes I have failed them. All doors are shut to me now.

I have seen you coming, young Kate. You are the real witch. You will finish what I have started. You have been fairy-struck. You know the fairy ways, the healing power of the earth, the spells of the otherworld.

Publish one Step every seven days. Each Step must be performed in order. Beware the wrath of the good people; they are fair but can show great evil when wronged. They are waiting. *Go n-éirí an bóthar leat.*

"And then she signs it 'Kate McDaid, The Red Hag, 1878.'" Seamus MacMurphy fixed his stare on the page before him.

The room froze. My parents, statue-like, remained silent. I felt like a cement mixer had spilled its load into my head. My ears filled with a white noise. I'd never heard anything so utterly crazy in my whole life. Fairies? *I* had been fairy-struck? *I* was the *real* witch?

"I don't get it." My voice broke the heavy silence.

"It is a little unusual." The understatement of the year fell out of Seamus MacMurphy's mouth.

Red Hag, fairy-struck, good people. I looked over at my parents, confused.

"I'm dumbfounded," my always-vocal dad said, his tongue clicking in his mouth.

Mam threw Dad a disapproving look. "I always knew your side of the family were mad."

"God love her, she was away with them, wasn't she?" Dad said, with all the moroseness of a eulogy.

I eyed him in disbelief. How could he have adopted such a serious tone? I felt a spasm in my stomach and a nervous tremor itch through me. I was going to laugh. I bit my lip to stop myself. I held my breath and felt my cheeks fill up with air. My chest jumped. It wasn't appropriate. I knew it wasn't appropriate. I shut my eyes to stop them from watering. My head rolled into my chest and my hands raced to my mouth as I released a low giggle and a gush of air. *Stop it, stop it, stop it!* I thought.

"Ah, Kate," Dad said, but I could hear the laughter in his voice. I looked up, and a crooked smile crept over his face. His eyes were giddy. I didn't need the encouragement.

"She was nuts," I said, slapping my thigh. "Nuts. Dad, you had a nutter in your family."

"It's your family, too." His eyes were filling up.

"Loop the loop." Mam tapped her temple, breathing through her nose.

Seamus MacMurphy was flushed and cleared his throat repeatedly in an effort to settle us.

"Sorry, sorry!" Dad shouted too loudly, half laughing. "It's a bit of a shock."

"What a load of nonsense," Mam added. "But, tell me this." She leaned forward and put her hand on her chin, serious now. "What's the estate?"

Biting on his bottom lip, Seamus MacMurphy puffed out his cheeks. His head quivered from side to side. "I can't tell you, I'm afraid," he said somewhat uncomfortably. "One of the stipulations of the will is that the estate is only revealed when the Seven Steps and the letter have been published."

Crazy, I thought. *This is crazy. But funny, crazy.*

"What do you mean published?" I said aloud.

"Published."

"Like in a newspaper?"

"It doesn't stipulate the medium. It just says 'published,' so newspaper, book, magazine, Internet. Published in a mass medium and on the same day every week from the day you start."

"She doesn't ask for much," Dad snuffled out of the corner of his mouth.

"Okay, so what do these things say?" I asked.

"Well, you have to agree to do this before I can show you."

"Okay . . ." I looked over at Mam and Dad. "Yeah, I'll do it. I want to know what they say. Come on, you must be curious?"

"What if you're getting into something you can't control?" Mam was always practical.

"Hardly," I laughed, thinking how I had no control over anything in my life, anyway—a career in freefall, a nonexistent love life, warring parents—so what harm would it be to add one more thing to that growing list? And with that one throwaway comment, I pushed Play, and the wheels started to turn.

"If you agree to one, you agree to them all. And you have to publish that first letter, the one addressed to you, from the other Kate McDaid." I nodded at the lawyer, and he slid an inky scrawled envelope across his desk. There was a wax seal on it. It felt very *Dangerous Liaisons*. "This is the first. It must be published word for word."

Smiling, I picked it up with the kind of excited feeling you get before you go on the dodgems at a carnival. Giddy.

I broke the seal and pulled out the single page that was inside the envelope. I tried to focus in on the handwriting. It was shaky and old.

"Well, read it out, for crying out loud."

Step One

In the glowing green fields and shadowy glen,
Our laughs can be heard 'mongst women and men,
The whistle of gale carries our joyous song,
In the rustle of trees, we've been here all along.

'Tis in the hardness of rocks and corners we dwell,
We're whispered in songs and stories you tell,
Floating o'er you, we sing and we dance in the rain,
But through the darkness of shadows soar black wails of pain.

One of yours we've kept in the depths of our lair,
We took her long ago, the girl of red hair,
With our gifts, she returns with promise of light,
To guide the way out of your sickness of night.

Acknowledge the spirit that in nature lives,
Whistle to flowers, embrace how the fairy world gives,
If you still do not see us, our anger you'll know,
A cradle burned, a soul extinguished,
In the music it shall show.

I cleared my throat and looked around the room. "It doesn't sound too bad. I mean, it's a bit airy-fairy, heebie-jeebie, but it's not going to do any harm, is it?"

"I've heard of talking to plants, but whistling to leaves

sounds like a load of old nonsense to me," Dad muttered into his chest.

Quietly I reread the first Step. "I think it's grand," I announced. "It's a bit self-helpy—'acknowledge the spirit in nature.'" I could feel my inner hippy about to explode out of me.

"'If you still do not see us, our anger you'll know.'" Mam slowly shook her head and furrowed her brow. "Fire and brimstone—I think she got a few of her ideas from the Catholic Church." Her face fell into a creased look of uninterest. She shrugged her shoulders. "Not to worry, pet." She leaned across and rubbed my knee. "There might be a bit of money at the end of it, you never know."

I nodded. I guessed it would be great if there was money at the end of it, a surprise winning lottery ticket. But at that moment, I wasn't thinking about the mysterious estate. I was thinking that it was kind of nice to get a long-lost letter from an ancestor. Even if she was mad as a brush.

3

When I got to work I made arrangements with Seamus MacMurphy to deliver the six other Steps. He promised to post or deliver one each week for the next six weeks. I had to publish each one the day I received it.

Then I hit Google. I found lots of websites for fairies with magic wands and recipes for potions and spells. I searched Irish fairies and found pictures of leprechauns sitting on pots of gold at the foot of a rainbow. Kids' stuff. I googled Irish witches, confident my picture wasn't going to appear.

For the record, I knew I wasn't a witch—not a white witch, a black witch, a red witch, whatever. I'd never walked into a room and had an icy chill race through me and just known that I'd been there before. I didn't see dead people, nor did I want to. I didn't know any spells, although I'm sure if I did, they'd have come in handy. I needed caller ID to know who was on the phone. I'd never so much as meditated. I worked, rode my bike, watched too much TV, listened to music, and went to the pub.

I didn't believe in magic, in witchcraft, or in prophecies from another time. I believed I had an Aunt Kate who was a bit batty and lived in a time when every village had a witch and people talked to fairies. I couldn't even imagine what that must have been like. Confusing, at best—you'd never know who you were going to step on.

But I did like the *idea* of fairies, and guardian angels and cosmic coincidences. It was just really hard to believe in any of it when you couldn't see it. I'd read self-help and spiritual guidebooks—I was a normal twenty-six-year-old, after all. I was interested in understanding how things worked and how I worked. I looked to the universe for coincidences. I tried to understand why a butterfly flapping its wings in Japan meant free hamburgers for everyone in New York. I'd read *Buddhism for Dummies* (well, the bullet points). I'd been grateful for at least two days, thanked the floor for letting me step on it, the tea for letting me drink it, the door for letting me open it. It was exhausting, and at the end of it there was no check for five million euros (which, when you think about it, is a moderate sum when you potentially could request an infinite amount—an everlasting gobstopper amount). I'd tried to attract the man of my dreams by clearing space for him in my wardrobe and sleeping on one side of the bed, and had been a little bit shocked when he never materialized out of my wardrobe with a bucket of strawberry ice cream and a fistful of rom-com DVDs.

I knew a bit about fairies—every Irish person does. When Ireland was a rural community, about eighty years ago, most people believed in fairies, in spite of the fact that almost nine out of ten Irish people were Catholic. In fact, it's probably because Irish people are brought up with the Holy Ghost, the Virgin Mary, apparitions, and moving statues that it's not such a huge leap for us to give fairies the benefit of the doubt.

The majority of us *still* attend Catholic schools. This isn't necessarily a conscious decision by parents to rear their children with a Bible in hand. It's more dictated by convenience: Catholic schools are free and there's at least one in every neighborhood.

But it has guaranteed that every generation has grown up with a degree of Catholicism beaten into them. It's safe to say that we're "pick and mix" Catholics, though. We believe that the church at its core has a good moral message of love and compassion, but we can't be bothered with the strict rules it imposes, like abstaining from alcohol on Good Friday (which has become the biggest day of the year for house parties, because the pubs are shut).

We hang on to some of the Catholic traditions, though, and most of us will say a prayer when it's necessary: for sickness, lottery tickets, or new babies. And I know I'm not alone in making a discreet sign of the cross every time I pass a church—it's like giving God a little wink, wink, letting him know I'm still here and hedging my bets in case he's still there. And so, while most of the fairy stuff has died out, there's still a lingering interest, because the supernatural is so much a part of our culture.

I knew about fairies from my granny. When I was small, Granny would regularly take me out to the garden to hunt down the fairies. She'd peer into the thickest, most overgrown part of the garden, the spot where they would have plenty of hiding places. "They love young people," she'd say, pushing me forward, and I'd look hard, searching for a stripy sock or red jacket with gold buttons, straining my eyes until I was almost blind. But I never saw anything.

Most of the stories I'd heard about fairies involved large quantities of whiskey. They were stories about fairies playing tricks on farmers, moving gates in fields and stealing cows' milk. They were superstitious folklore, and they belonged to an older, backward Ireland.

Nevertheless, on my way to work the next morning I stopped at Tesco's and bought a plant—something yellow. I slid a saucer underneath it on my desk and positioned it as far away from the death rays of my computer as I could. And I whistled to it. *Job done*, I thought happily. Now I just had to publish the letter and first Step somehow.

After a small amount of consideration, I posted them online. I say that nonchalantly with a flick of my hair and a cool exhale of a cigarette, as if I just randomly threw the words toward a computer and nestled back into a cloud of cushions. It didn't happen like that at all; it was much more contrived.

Matthew and I were in AlJo's when he had the eureka moment. I wonder now if I led that conversation, steered it, but I've never been a great manipulator, so I doubt it. I'm an indecisive follower, the type of person who orders the same tuna, tomato, and lettuce sandwich as the person in front of them in the deli queue, even though I don't like tuna. It seems like the easy option at the time, but thirty minutes later, when I'm picking the tuna off the bread, I'm riddled with remorse.

We always went to AlJo's for lunch. Your feet got stuck on the linoleum, month-old crumbs festered in corners, and the coffee was bitter and too hot. Al or Jo acted like his coffee shop was a front for an Italian money-laundering operation, his eyes shifting uneasily to the back kitchen every time the door opened, as if Fat Tony and Knuckles were sitting there sucking on raw meat and respecting the family. You learned to ignore the handprint that came welded onto the white bread sandwiches and not think about Al or Jo's dirty fingernails.

"Stick the letter up on Jim's site." I promise that's what Matthew said. I remember because I scalded my mouth with hot tea when I heard Jim's name mentioned. I still have a tiny scar on my top lip as evidence. "Not Red Horizon, that other crowd he was with, Space Monkeys. I did their website. It's still live but nobody visits it."

I breathed in deep and tried to look casual.

"You could take over the site if you want, or just put up a separate page. Whatever you fancy. Or you could just start a blog. That's publishing."

"I've never done a blog. It might be difficult," I said, immediately making up an excuse, trying anything to be closer to Jim. "Would he know?" I asked, hoping for both a positive and a negative response.

"No, it's four years old, but I can run it by him just in case."

I tried to look like I was mulling the question over before enthusiastically nodding like a bobbleheaded dog in a car window.

Jim was Matthew's friend. They'd gone to school together and, in true Dublin style, had never managed to lose each other. Schoolfriends are always right around the corner in Dublin, winking at you from every pub you walk into, along with your college friends, your first kiss, and your worst one-night stand. A million people live here, but it's a ridiculously small town. I think if anyone ever carried out a survey, Dublin would unanimously be the worst place in the world to have an affair. People tend to stick to their own turf, so generations of families get knitted together and entwined in one another's lives. So if your wife or husband doesn't spot you jumping into a navy car and heading down a back road in the middle of the night to conduct your affair, your mother's friend from school has a daughter whose husband will.

I'd first met Jim about a year earlier. Matthew and I had gone for a postwork drink in a decrepit little bar near the agency with a heavy patterned carpet and couches with springs that poked into your bum. We were on Heineken number two, giving out about blockbuster movies (they have no heart—me; they don't need a heart, they have action—Matthew) when Jim walked in—no, swaggered, he swaggered in. With shoulders that filled the door, dark, curly hair that skimmed his T-shirt collar, and a four-step entrance: enter, breathe, survey the room, and pause to be appreciated. He spotted Matthew and without waiting for an invite pulled up a chair and ordered a whiskey.

When Jim talks to you, you're the only person in the room. He zones in and looks right into you. When he asks, "How are you?" he says it earnestly, like he really cares. When he goes to the bar to buy a round of drinks, he puts his hand on your shoulder and insists you stay for another one. He nods hello to the barman and the barflies, and returns to the table with their stories. Strangers talk to him, open up to him. He has an easy manner, he's relaxed and charming. It's almost impossible not to fall under his spell. It helps that he's devastatingly handsome, with long, heavy black eyelashes that always look wet, like he just got out of the shower, and dark eyes, dark hair, and a thin white scar running across his chin that he got falling off his bike when he was a kid.

The first time I met him I was mesmerized. Within twenty minutes of his arrival our table of three had grown to six as people gravitated toward him, and by the end of the night the barman had found an old guitar, put it in Jim's lap, and the entire pub was demanding that he sing. He didn't need any persuading. Jim is the lead singer in a band called Red Horizon. A lot of guys in Dublin are in bands, chasing U2's shadow, but not all of them can sing like Jim, gravelly and with so much soul it leaves a dusting of goose bumps on your skin. When you develop an infatuation for someone, you always find a reason to believe that this is exactly the person for you. It doesn't need to be a good reason—in the long run, always being the center of attention is the kind of thing that would drive you insane, but in the haze of infatuation it's just the thing that you've been searching for all these years. When we said good-bye that night, Jim squeezed his arms around my shoulders and locked me in. "Matthew's so lucky to have a friend like you."

I was hooked. I started fishing. Over the next few weeks I pestered Matthew about him. Where did he drink? Kehoe's. Did he have a girlfriend? Matthew didn't know. (How could he not know?!) Where did he live? Rathmines. My friends started to get annoyed when my suggestion for every Saturday night was (surprise, surprise) Kehoe's or maybe dinner in a cute little restaurant in Rathmines. They'd roll their eyes and tell me to give up the ghost. "If he's interested, he'll find you," was my best friend Fiona's wise advice as she sucked on a cigarette outside McSorley's Pub in Ranelagh, half a mile from Rathmines. "And I'm sick of drinking in the suburbs. I'm all in favor of you getting together with this guy, but it's like a fecking treasure hunt every week. Just e-mail him. Why don't you ask him out?"

She was right, but I was nervous. He might say no. So, instead of taking the direct approach that might have saved a lot of time, effort, and irritated friends, I joined the Red Horizon e-mail list, and went to see them play. I took Lily with me, my other best friend, a hopeless romantic who, like me, thought that maybe Jim was just a bit shy. He wasn't. When the gig was over and we were hanging at the bar watching as the venue emptied out, he came over and planted a giant kiss on my cheek. "It's so good to see you, I can't believe you came. It's so great for us to have support." Blushing, I told him how great the band was and what a great singer he was. He looked straight at me and smiled, then invited Lily and me to the pub next door for a drink. We skipped in, Lily whispering in my ear, "You are so in there. He's gorgeous!"

We had a lock-in in the pub—doors shut, lights off outside,

and full secret party raging illegally inside. A lock-in is probably the most exciting thing that can happen to an Irish person. It's a guaranteed singsong, and heavy drinking until six in the morning. There were tequila slammers with slices of orange, because the bar had run out of lemon, cocktails, pints, singing, a bottle of red wine at one point, and definitely a rum and Coke. They were celebrating; Red Horizon had just been signed to support some Swedish rock band on their tour in Sweden. They were leaving three days later.

The whole night Jim sat pressed up against me, his thigh rubbing mine, his arm draped behind me on the couch, his hand occasionally skimming my knee. I knew things were looking good, so when he turned to me and said, "Maybe we should go and get some coffee in my flat?" I wasn't remotely surprised. I knew what was coming. There was no coffee. There were clothes frantically cast off and scattered on his bedroom floor. There was kissing much sweeter than I'd expected, and there was the gentle swirl of his fingertips that I melted into in seconds.

I woke before him the next morning on the far side of the bed, duvet up to my neck, my brain seized by a cloudy hangover, a million thoughts trickling through. I'd slept with Jim on the first date. I know, I know, not always the smartest move if a girl really likes a guy. But I had met him before, so technically it wasn't a one-night stand. Was it? Of course it was, what was I thinking? Should I wake him up? Should I get up and put on one of his shirts and go cook breakfast and pretend that I'm in *Sex and the City* and I do this kind of thing all the time? Should I tell him I don't normally do this kind of thing? Should I tell him I like him? I should probably wait for him to tell me first. Oh God, what if he didn't like me? What if this was all a mistake?

Just as I was thinking about chocolate, he stirred, brushed

his hair out of his half-open eyes, and smiled slowly. "Morning. What are you doing over there?"

I crossed the bed in a nanosecond, and he snuggled into me, twirled my hair, and kissed my neck. We chatted about music, or at least he did—I was very busy concentrating on the fact that I was in bed with a gorgeous man. I nodded and occasionally said words like *electronic, downloads,* and *Arctic Monkeys,* and worried about the remnants of last night's makeup on my cheeks. I pretended I didn't have a hangover and heard myself laugh slightly hysterically at a joke he told. I was very proud that I didn't make any declarations out loud. I was confident I could play hard to get if you took away the sleeping together bit. I grinned like an idiot when we walked to the bus stop, my hand wrapped up in his, aware of how we might have looked to any passersby—just a normal couple who had fallen out of bed after a great night on the town. Happy. He was handsome, and she was a bit bedraggled but looked like she might scrub up well. At the bus stop he put my number into his phone. "I'll call you, babe, yeah. You're beautiful."

I stared at my phone for three days, and it was working, because I checked repeatedly. He was going to Sweden, like I knew he would, and he was going without me, like I hoped he wouldn't. Which was silly, I knew it was silly, but when you're staring at your phone for three days, your mind starts to wander, or at least mine does. I couldn't help but think that maybe he'd call and get me over for a weekend, or a week, or a month. I could take leave from work and go on tour forever. Told you it was silly.

Fiona told me to turn off my phone. "He might not call. He's in a band. You had groupie sex. He's gone to Sweden. Don't beat yourself up over this."

But it was more than groupie sex, I knew it was. A week later

there was a text message: "Sweden rocks. Hope you're good, babe."
And that's how it played out, a text here and there, mainly about
Sweden rocking. And then nothing, and then three months later I
heard he was back in Dublin and had a Swedish girlfriend. I never
saw her, but in my head she was an uber-female, six foot, tanned,
leggy, blond. She was Swedish—are they ever anything else?

That was a year ago. I've banged into him a couple of times,
Dublin being Dublin, and he's hugged me tight and asked me
how I am. And I've felt weak and stung every time.

But I'm not pining for him. I haven't spent the last year pathet-
ically looking at my phone or thinking of him constantly. But for
me, he is *that* guy. The one who pops up now and again. The one
who flashes back. The one I've tried to forget about but found
his smile tattooed on the inside of my eyelids. The one what I've
embarrassingly googled a lot, and facebooked, and when I hear
his name spoken I still blush. He's the one whom I can't help
wondering about. He's my *what if* guy, and I can't shake him.

And then Matthew had this great idea to stick the letter and
the Steps on spacemonkeys.com and, true to form, I agreed to go
along with it.

As I said, Space Monkeys were Jim's band before Red Horizon—
Celtic rock meets R'n'B. Seriously. They were terrible. Even Jim,
with his charisma and sex appeal, couldn't save songs from lyrics
like "I want to make love to you to the beat of the bodhran drum."
Their website was a couple of pages, neon-colored, with flowers
and a hippy-dippy theme. Matthew took one look at my puzzled
face and tried to explain that the band had requested those colors
and they were nothing to do with him or his web-design abilities.
He was right about the lack of visitors: the last entry had been four
years ago. *Blondie18: OMG Jim you are sex on legs.*

And so on a Tuesday afternoon in the first week of May,

Matthew and I posted the letter and the first Step online. I stood behind, peering over his shoulder, doing backseat typing.

"My granddad talked about the fairies." Matthew smiled back at me. "He was from a farm in Galway. He died years ago, but I remember he used to always leave a bit of milk in the end of a glass for the fairies, and he'd never finish his food, he'd leave a few bits. He said you had to keep them happy." He shrugged his shoulders.

"Looks like they were easily pleased with just a few leftovers."

"Yeah, I dunno. Some of that stuff is kind of nice. Thinking that there's something else out there, that maybe it isn't just this."

"Do you believe it?" I asked cautiously, and as the words slipped out of my mouth I knew I was unsure as to which way I wanted him to respond.

"In fairies?"

Slowly I nodded and bit my lip apprehensively.

"Don't look so worried." He laughed at me. "I dunno, a lot of it is kids' stuff now. The tooth fairy, leprechauns." He shook his head. "But it didn't start off like that. It used to be adults who were talking to fairies, like my grandfather."

"And was he a bit gaga?"

Matthew did a look of mock disdain and grabbed his chest dramatically. "How dare you think that my ancestor could be gaga."

"You know what I mean."

"No, honest, he was fine. Still doing *The Irish Times* crossword every day until the end. I think it was just different then. There were more ghosts in corners and banshees wailing. Everyone went to mass because they were scared they'd end up in hell. It's not surprising they believed in fairies."

"But now, like, you don't believe in them now?"

"They're a nice idea, but they belong to another generation. A generation long dead." He smiled at me. "Don't worry about this stuff. It's harmless. You're not performing any crazy sacrifices or weird religious things. Come on, she wants you to whistle to flowers. It's grand."

"Yeah, you're right. It is grand."

"Anyway, we've done our good deed for the day. Coffee?"

I jumped up. "I'll get it. I was going to swing by Marjorie's desk to pick up that show reel."

I was happy to step away from the fairy chat, which was making me feel uneasy. Besides, Matthew made horrible coffee.

Marjorie was three years younger than me, two years qualified, and one step away from robbing my job out from under me. She made no secret of her ambitions. Her steely determination would have been admirable if it was not in direct competition with my own meekly disguised self-promotion. She sat on the same floor as Matthew and me, but a few departments over. Her back was poker straight, she was neatly pulled into her desk, her sleek blond ponytail contrasting sharply with her all-black leggings and figure-hugging polo neck, highlighting her curves that often caused the cessation of work in the all-male production department, much to her delight.

I idly approached her before picking up and absentmindedly fiddling with the stapler on her tidy desk. "Hi, Marjorie. How's it going?"

"Kate. Good, yes." She eyed me perkily. "Busy, busy."

"Tell me about it," I lied.

"I've been put onto the porn account," she said quietly, puffing out her ample chest, her eyes shifting narrowly from side to side.

"There's a porn account?" I asked. F & P is a huge company, and if I was honest, I didn't know what half the accounts were. They were split between departments and disciplines, so I shouldn't really have been surprised that there was an account I didn't know about. But porn . . . I sat myself down on a vacant seat and pulled in beside Marjorie.

"New to the agency, Internet-based." She nodded knowingly.

Marjorie didn't normally lead creative accounts. Normally, she assisted.

"Are you taking the lead on this?"

"I'm ready for it, Kate. Anyway, it's not something that you and Matthew would be interested in."

"Porn?" I shook my head. "No, I wouldn't imagine."

"I'm a good fit for it. I told Colin you wouldn't be interested."

"Okay," I said, immediately thinking that was weird. I wouldn't be interested in a porn account, but I didn't need Marjorie to vet my work. Still, Colin was so busy these days, he would have been happy that she volunteered. And yet it seemed strange.

"The client," she lowered her voice even further, "Hugh Delaney, is a most hateful man."

"Well, you're never going to expect a porno guy to be nice, are you? I'd imagine they're lowlifes, scummy types? Is he all string vests and medallions?"

"He is . . ." She paused, blushing slightly. "Absolutely hideous. Repulsive, even."

"Really?"

"Seriously awful. Stinks of aftershave, looks like he has a hairy back, bad teeth. A horrible, horrible man."

"He didn't ask you to star in one of his movies, then?" I laughed.

She ignored me. "He has terrible manners. He's so gruff and rude, and he doesn't seem to appreciate the way the agency works. He called our planning report a load of bollocks."

I bit my lip to stop a smile creeping in. Planning reports often *were* a load of bollocks, but it was a case of the emperor's new clothes—not to be mentioned aloud for fear of discovery.

"He comes to meetings with this big, hairy, flea-riddled, filthy dog, and he's filthy, his jeans are dirty, he wears these muck-laden boots. He calls everything 'shite' or 'bollocks.' He really is difficult."

"He sounds pretty horrible, dirty *and* dirty. Porn, eugh . . ." My face crumpled in disgust. I was still wondering how F & P had let a porn account slip into the building. They'd pitched for the Church of Ireland last year. It was an unusual fit.

Later I quizzed Matthew about it. He wasn't much help, other than telling me with a wink that the client was supposed to be a wanker but he didn't know much else.

I had bigger fish to fry than porn, anyway. Two days later, Matthew got a phone call, one that made him drop his briefcase and race to his computer. He tapped on his keyboard with a look of intense concentration.

"You're not going to believe this!" he shouted from his desk to mine.

"You cracked the Starshoot campaign?"

"Seriously, you're not going to believe this."

I'd never seen Matthew so animated. I rolled my chair over to his desk, forcing him to budge up his armrest.

"Seriously."

"The drama! What?"

He gestured toward his computer screen. Spacemonkeys.com was up in all its neon glory. It was the Kate McDaid page. There were comments posted on a message board underneath the letter.

Grrrril_n_boil: wow this is v interesting. Who is Kate mcdaid?
johnnyBgd: Whats with custodians of mother earth???? Who
　　are???? The fairies?
Herman: I whistled at a flower, it whistled back.

Anna_89: whats this got to do with Red Horizon? Where's
    Jim? Jim I love you

Richie_84: The fairies used to take people for 7 years and send
    them back to their village with powers.

Grrrril_n_boil: Good people = FAIRIES. Any ideas?

johnnyBgd: I thought fairies were evil. Are they still around now?

Anna_89: jim is not a fairy

Marie2x: looking fwd to the next one kate—what else do u know?

I felt a pain in my chest. They were talking about me. These
people I didn't know were talking about me. My mouth went
dry, and I struggled to breathe. I felt sick. *Go away,* I thought.
Please, go away. I looked at Matthew. "I thought you said there
was nobody on this site."

"There wasn't. Jim just called to ask what was going on."

Oh no, not Jim. "I thought you cleared it with him."

"Forgot."

Jim had one of those e-mail notification alerts set up for any
messages on spacemonkeys.com. He'd forgotten he had it until
a few days earlier. Red Horizon had a radio interview at the beginning of the week, and he'd mentioned that he used to be in a
band called Space Monkeys. A few diehards googled him. That's
how quickly it happened, how quickly it took off, and that's
probably when I should have pulled the plug. Only problem was,
now Jim was involved.

4

Matthew and I got to Grogan's at seven thirty. Jim had invited us to a Red Horizon gig there. Grogan's is a tumbledown, creaky pub like an old man with a broken back and knobbly fingers who keeps dirty gold under his mattress. It's down a back street in the city center, where it's been for a hundred years. Dublin is full of old pubs laced with heavy carpets and sticky furniture. They're permanent fixtures in the city. New bars (not pubs) opened and closed every few months within meters of them. They were polished and shiny, with white walls and gleaming mirrors guarded by menacing bouncers with necks as pink as pigs. Now that the Celtic Tiger was roaring like a crazed animal, there seemed to be no end of money to be spent and money to be made. Bars were being redone, and marble and crystal glassware was everywhere. Dublin competes with itself all the time. It feels like it should move on and look modern, but it doesn't really want to.

It was rumored that U2 had played Grogan's back in the seventies, but every pub started that rumor. I wasn't sure why Red Horizon were playing there—I thought they were bigger than that. Grogan's hosted the faded stars, the has-beens and the never-beens, not the up-and-comings. Red Horizon felt like a band on the cusp: DJs name-dropped them, they were featured on the back pages of music magazines, guys with long fringes wore their T-shirts. Once in an interview, Ronnie Wood from the Rolling Stones had mentioned them. "Red Horizon, they're good," he'd said. He was drunk at the time, but still, it was impressive. They were almost there.

An Asian woman with a strong Dublin accent, dropping her *t*'s and elongating her vowels, pretended to name-check us on the door. She didn't even have a list. We marched on in. It was no longer unusual to see Asian people in Dublin, but fifteen years earlier we'd been a nation of freckled-skinned, frizzy-haired individuals, thanks, probably, to an enormous amount of inbreeding due to strict immigration controls. Back then, any pillowcase-wearing member of the Ku Klux Klan might have arrived in Dublin, excited about the rumor of an all-white society, a true Aryan race, only to shake his head in despair when the reality of a really bad-looking nation peered back at him. Thankfully, the gene pool is being rapidly diluted, and soon we'll no longer have to give christening gifts of sunblock to babies.

There were about sixty people inside Grogan's that night, busy for a Thursday. Ten were standing at the bar, all men cradling pints. Engaged in thoughtful conversation, they shuffled slowly from foot to foot. The band was vacuum-packed onto the stage. I say stage, but it was really just a step that put them a good half an inch higher than us mere mortals.

The pub smelled of clashing perfumes and furniture polish. The all-female audience on the floor swayed from side to side, their shiny hair flickering in the dim lighting. Chests heaved in unison—*Look at me, Jim, look at me*. I slid into the mob and caught the rhythm. *Look at me, Jim.*

Jim was wrapped around the microphone stand looking pained, his face creased with intensity, as if he was desperately trying to remember his pin number. "Yooooouuuuuu—always youuuuuuuuuu." His hair was damp with sweat, and as he ran his hand through his flattened curls the mob took a sharp intake of breath. His top lip curled into a controlled smile; we were in the palm of his hand. He shook his shoulders free and started tapping his foot. We did likewise.

I was still on the Red Horizon e-mail list. I never canceled it. I knew when they were touring, enjoying summer weather, or hopping on a Bus Éireann bus to Portlaoise. I didn't read the e-mails most of the time—I knew *that* bus had left the garage. But this time it was different, because the generic e-mail had been followed by a personal e-mail from Jim. It felt like I'd been hit by a brick in the face when his name popped up. Why was he e-mailing?

From: Jim@RedHorizon.ie
To: Matthew@FandP.com; Kate@FandP.com
Subject: Tonight's gig
Hi guys, really hope you can make the gig tonight, was hoping to grab you for a pint after??? J

I immediately forwarded the e-mail on to my best friend, Lily and Fiona, for advice. What was going on?

Lily came back first.

From: Lily@BT.ie
To: Kate@FandP.com; Fiona.Finnan@vined.ie
Hmmmm, I dunno. What does he want? It's been too long to try and spark anything up. Maybe he wants to be friends???????

From: Fiona.Finnan@vined.ie
To: Kate@FandP.com; Lily@BT.ie
No guy wants to be friends with someone he's slept with!!!!

BUT Paul in here is friends with his friend Alan and he just e-mailed him and guess what . . . The Swede isn't around anymore. Broke up a while back. You never know, K, he could be looking for a repeat offense? Good luck. X

I'd worn a pair of killer heels, pinned my hair up high and let some loose curls fall around my face, and put on a puffball-style black dress that was too short for me and definitely too short for a backstreet gig.

The crowd was clapping loudly. Relieved and happy, Jim threw his head back, smiling. "Here come two of my friends. Late." He grinned into the mic. "Matthew, and Kate McDaid."

He said my name like you'd give directions to a Japanese tourist—loud and clear. There was a hush, a few seconds, a murmur. I heard a rumble. "Kate McDaid, Kate McDaid" bounced across the room. I felt my chest cave in and my shoulders bend. What?

Matthew, seeing me flounder, pulled a barstool under me, and I sat crouched.

"What was that all about?" he whispered in my ear.

I shook my head. What *was* that?

A few hours later, I was four beers in and feeling normal again. Red Horizon had packed up their equipment and there was only a sprinkling of golden-haired groupies left. Jim joined Matthew and me at the bar. He was glowing, high after performing. He hugged me again. *Damn you and your hugs*, I thought. *If you didn't hug so great I might have forgotten about you a long time ago.* But I lost myself to it, and then crossed my legs and stretched my back out at the bar, trying hard to differentiate myself from the groupies in the room.

"Good gig, man, good gig." I had to stop myself from laughing out loud at Matthew's Californian surfer-dude act.

"Thanks, yeah. We were a bit off half an hour in, but I think we recovered." He nodded toward the barman and ordered a whiskey and lemonade.

I sat on my hands, trying hard not to stare at his profile.

He swirled the ice in his whiskey and turned his shoulders into me. "How are you, Kate?"

"Good," I squeaked.

"Mad stuff going on, hey?" He fished into the pocket of his tight dark denim jeans and pulled out some printed pages, which he laid flat on the bar counter. It was the letter.

"Yeah, sorry about that. I didn't think anyone was on that site. Look, I can take it down, put it up somewhere else. It has to be published, but it doesn't matter where." I could feel an apologetic ramble taking over.

He stopped me. "Don't take it down. Actually, I wanted to know if I could put it on the Red Horizon site as well? This is good stuff. There's a buzz."

"You think fairies and a potentially mad self-proclaimed witch is a good buzz?" I eyed him in disbelief.

"Hey, look, if it gets people talking, sends them to our site, you bet I think it's a good buzz. I'm all over this—fairies, witches, whatever." He winked at me. "Look, I'm sorry. I thought I'd have more time, but there's a thing I've gotta go to. Kind of last minute." He glanced at the adoring groupies who had reapplied lipsticks and readjusted hemlines and looked about ready to pop in his direction. He drained his drink. "So, it's cool if I put it up on our site?"

I nodded, stunned. And he disappeared into a mist of groupie hairspray.

✦ ✦ ✦

Work the next day was . . . infuriatingly confusing. First, I received an e-mail I wasn't expecting.

From: Jim@RedHorizon.ie
To: Kate@FandP.com
I've got an interview with a journo at lunch tomorrow, we're going to AlJo's. Could I buy you a coffee after? Say 1:30?
J x

Was it a date? It sounded like a date. Was it a friend date? We'd never been friends.

And, secondly, I met the porn client, and he left me reeling. He was as hateful as Marjorie had described. I didn't know who he was, initially. Dudley had called me down to dispatch to pick up a set of advertising-award DVDs sent for me. By rights he should have delivered them, but, as he'd told me on the phone, he "just couldn't be arsed." So there I was, slipping into the empty lift, when a deep gravelly shout bounced in my direction, causing the hairs on my arms to stand up like soldiers.

"Hold the lift."

A *"please" would be nice*, I thought as I scrambled around, looking for the Open button.

The man startled me. It wasn't the sheer size or handsome presence of him—because he was handsome and he was huge, six foot plus something or other, with shoulders that grazed opposing walls—or his dirty blond hair that looked unkempt and unstylishly spiked on top of his head. No, it was his eyes. Gray and stormy like the Atlantic Ocean. He held me in his gaze for several long seconds, knowing, probing, penetrating. And then he seemed to shrug it off with a blink and a long stride, as he heaved himself into the lift, looking anywhere but at me. In one movement he stretched his arm across, and I saw how his gray knit sweater pulled against his muscles. I also saw that his light denim jeans were dirty but nowhere near as filthy as his boots, which were positively caked in mud. He hit the Open button again.

"I'm . . ." I could feel myself blushing because (A) he was so handsome, and (B) I was talking in the lift, which is something that never ever happens. ". . . going to the basement." I pushed the B button, in spite of the fact that his finger was still firmly positioned on the Open button.

"One minute," he mumbled softly into his neck.

"What?"

"Hold." And looking anywhere but at me, he gestured outside, as though he was waiting for someone to arrive. And so we stood, and stillness filled the lift, and silence bounced between us, and I listened to his breathing (hard and fast), reviewed his profile (chiseled), complexion (pale with pink cheeks), smell (he smelled of the sea), and prayed for some elevator music to relieve the tension.

"Maybe they're not coming," I braved, an eternity later.

"He's coming." And he finally looked at me—sternly.

"Okay. It's just that I've got to get to the basement, and I've a meeting . . ."

His look stopped me from talking anymore. It was cross and determined. "He's coming. You don't need to be in such a rush," he responded with a warm and singing west-of-Ireland accent.

"Well, I do. I've work to do," I said, suddenly affronted.

"I'm guessing the world won't end if you're a minute behind schedule."

"You don't even know what I do. Maybe it would end." I crossed my arms belligerently. He might have been tall and handsome, but he didn't know me to judge the uselessness of my job.

"This is an advertising agency, not the UN."

"That doesn't mean that what I do isn't important."

"I never said it wasn't." He smirked slightly, and a dimple imploded on his left cheek.

"Christ, you're condescending," I said in an uncharacteristic burst of aggression.

"I'm not. I just—" He furrowed his brow and his voice grew softer. "Here he is."

And then a small gray horse, a small smelly horse in the shape of a dog so tall it skimmed my waist, bounded into the lift.

"Good boy, Setanta." He crouched down to the dog, an Irish wolfhound, and rubbed his head affectionately. "I wouldn't leave without you." He threw me a smile, teasing.

Setanta's brown eyes looked up sadly at me from beneath his gray bushy eyebrows.

"Sorry," I said to the dog. I'm a sucker for sad eyes.

As the lift started to descend, a penny in my brain proceeded to drop. The porn client! Marjorie had said he had a dog. But he wasn't "repulsive." He was knee-shakingly handsome. Even if Marjorie and I had differing parameters of what was attractive, I was pretty sure that this guy was undeniably handsome. Even if you didn't fancy him, you would still have to recognize his attractiveness. Why had Marjorie said he was repulsive? Maybe it was the porn thing—*that* was repulsive. Eugh. How gross. Porn. Images of blow-up dolls, greased bodies, and filthy old men playing with themselves flashed before me. And there I was in an enclosed space with him. Eugh.

He cleared his throat and, in a heavy country accent, said softly, "I didn't mean that the work here isn't important . . ."

My moral compass was pointing straight toward fire and brimstone and the path of the righteous Jesus. "It's a lot more important than your work," I muttered very quietly to myself.

"Sorry?" He looked at me, confused. "I didn't catch that."

"Nothing." I pursed my mouth and shook my head disapprovingly, in the manner of a disgruntled fifties housewife seeing Elvis dancing with swinging hips for the first time.

Ding. The doors opened, and I marched out with my head held high, shaking my hair free, victoriously. Porn nil, Kate one.

✦ ✦ ✦

I was meeting the girls that night for sushi. We regularly met on a Friday night to let off steam. We were all on diets and sushi practically burned the calories off the bottle of wine we'd drink with it.

On this particular occasion I needed their advice. I trusted them—Fiona the practical and Lily the romantic. The three of us had met in college, accidentally walking into the wrong lecture in the first week of first year. Lost on campus, we found the bar and crashed a freshers' week free-drinks reception. Within forty minutes we'd formed our own relay team for a beer and crisps race. We came in last, but we did it with a lot of laughs and a lot of spills. Nothing cements a friendship like freshers' week. Over the years we'd done what really true friends do for each other: held hair back, wiped up the tears, borrowed and lost each other's clothes, laughed, agreed that no men were worth it, lied for each other, and held disastrous dinner parties.

That night, we never got to talk about Jim. Fiona stormed in, her pale skin red with anger and her dark hair flapping behind her like a cloak. She was raging. She had a work drama of high importance.

Fiona worked for an investment banker. She'd started on the phones part-time through college and in the past eighteen months had made it onto the trading floor. This was all she'd ever wanted. She put in long hours, sacrificing her family and social life. "I'll fall in love when I'm forty," she'd say. "I don't have time for it now. Now I work."

A few months earlier her team had been restructured and she got a new boss, a woman whose main agenda was to save money and make cuts. The rumor on the trading floor was that Ireland was ripe for a recession, and it was only a matter of time before the whole country fell. The banks would be the first to be hit and needed to make a preemptive strike. The boss was looking for slipups as an excuse to fire people.

That day Fiona had slipped up. It was minor. She'd misfiled a docket. But she knew what it might mean for her career, and she was angry at the injustice of it all.

Lily and I swooped in supportively and ordered more wine to help her figure out a plan of action.

"I've worked all through Christmas for the last two years, for God's sake, and they're going to fire me over this."

"You don't know that yet. Nothing has been decided."

"Pass the wine," she said, looking exhausted.

We talked well into the night and left the restaurant when the stools were upside down on tables. We hugged good-bye at the corner of Georges Street, and Fiona marched off, feeling slightly more prepared for her counterattack the next day.

I, on the other hand, felt completely unequipped for my meeting with Jim. I spent half the night willing myself to sleep, and the other half obsessing over conversation possibilities. I regretted that I was only a third of the way into *Calm from the Inside Out: A Self-help Mantra for All.* I got up at four a.m. and tried on three different outfits, settled on one, and then, overcome with exhaustion, fell asleep in it.

5

I felt completely exposed and unprepared as I pushed open the door of AlJo's in my second-best outfit—skinny jeans tucked into brown knee-high boots, a blue cowl-necked satin shirt, and heavy gold hooped earrings. *Relax*, I told my leaping stomach, *it's just coffee.*

AlJo's was particularly greasy that day. You had to chew the air on arrival to get it into your lungs. Jim and a blond woman were in deep conversation, leaning against a wall under a picture of Pope John Paul. Ratzinger hadn't made it into AlJo's good books just yet.

Jim looked up and waved, and I felt that familiar pull toward him. He had a black leather jacket on and a streak of stubble across his jaw that I wanted to reach out and touch. He introduced me to Maura Ni Ghaora. He used her full Irish name. I thought only TV weathermen and people opening pubs in New York used their Irish name. All Irish people have them. Mine is Cáit, which you need a lot of spit in your mouth and sandpaper in the back of your throat to say correctly, when it sounds like "Cwatch." Catchy, isn't it? I didn't see the point in using Irish names. They are impossible to spell and they made getting through customs difficult.

By using her Irish name, Maura Ni Ghaora was advertising that she was a fluent Irish speaker and could hold her own in ringlets and green velvet at a set dancing competition. The thing is, we can all speak some Irish; we learn it the whole way through school and graduate bilingual in swear words. We put it to great use when we're traveling—talking about foreigners with impunity is probably our only in-joke. Same goes for Irish dancing. It's drummed into us at school, and with a bit of arm twisting most Irish people can pound out a jig. Most of us keep our Irishness to ourselves, though. You never know when a fluent Irish speaker will upstage your pidgin Irish, or a River Dancer will emerge from the wings to step on your toes. Advertising it puts you in a whole other league of Irish—the Supersized Irish.

I smiled hello. Maura Ni Ghaora had a white-blond razor-sharp bob that shimmered in the fluorescent light of AlJo's. Her face was so tightly pulled that any remnants of what she might originally have looked like had long since disappeared under the plastic surgeon's knife. Her makeup was cemented on, except for her eyelashes, which were glued into an alert curl. It was impossible to put an age to her. Fifty? Thirty? Seventy? She was dressed immaculately in an Armani or some other tailored navy pin-stripe designer suit way out of my league that screamed money. Her shoulders balanced out a neat waist and pencil skirt, and it was all anchored by a pair of black heels to drool over—Prada, Louboutins—I didn't know, but I knew I was not in the company of Marks & Sparks sale items.

Maura moved to shake my hand, and I noticed that she was wearing shiny black satin gloves, evening-wear style, that went to her wrist, a sliver of which was exposed as fine-boned and lily-white as she reached forward. She wore a gold signet ring on her little finger, with what looked like a ruby in its center.

"Dia dhuit." Maura's voice purred with undertones of friendliness, but her sky-blue eyes were expressionless.

I raised my eyebrows at that one, and a knee-jerk reaction fell out of my mouth. *"Dia is Muire dhuit."* "God be with you" and "God and Mary be with you" are the literal translations of the Irish greeting and response—not something many people ever say or use.

"How great to meet *the* Kate McDaid." Maura smiled, revealing a mouthful of perfectly straight white teeth. I shot a look at Jim, who settled back into his plastic chair and shrugged.

"Hi," I mumbled, before starting to chew the skin around my fingernails.

"I was just speaking with Jim about how interesting this all is." Maura spoke slowly, choosing her words. "These Steps. This gift that you have. This insight into the fairies."

"Well, I don't think I have an insight into the fairies. I mean, I don't even really believe that there *are* fairies. I mean, I don't mind looking at flowers and everything, but I don't think you'd say that I had an insight." I was babbling incoherently.

"Shhhhhh." She patted down the air with her hands and closed her eyes. "You mustn't speak like that, Kate. They're listening. They're always listening."

I gulped loudly and then found myself apologizing to the empty space in the room. *Oh dear,* I thought, *this has been an unusual week, what with whistling to plants and now talking to thin air, hoping not to offend it.*

"This is all very new to me. I'm not sure what to think," I said. I was feeling muddled and confused.

"Did you ever get your fortune told?" she asked coolly, looking me up and down.

I shook my head.

"Horoscopes?" She clicked her fingers determinedly.

"Yeah, I read them all the time."

"Do you believe them?"

"When they say what I want them to say." I blushed and glanced quickly at Jim, thinking how, that morning, I'd read: "A person from your past has the power to dramatically alter your future. For the better."

"You can't see how your star sign works?"

"Well, it's written in front of me in a magazine."

"And what's this? This is in front of you." She produced a brown leather folder from her handbag and carefully opened it to reveal the Step and the letter, neatly printed out on cream paper. Certain words were highlighted.

"Here, you see." She pointed at words. "Young Kate. Red hair." She leaned across the table, staring intently at me, and musk-scented perfume wafted over me as she got closer. "It is you. The fairies want you. They're using you . . ."

"No," I interrupted. "No, no, no. I'm the same person I was last week. Honestly. I have not been fairy-struck. I mean, I think I'd know. It sounds painful."

Maura sat very still, staring at me for too long. I saw her hands clench, almost imperceptibly. "That's fine, Kate. I understand. You're not there yet. It will come. There will be an awakening for you."

"You're scaring me now," I said, only half joking.

"They are the keepers of great secrets and answers." She smiled at me, but I noticed her eyes wandering, as if she was looking for something or someone around me. "May I ask, has anything been different since the letter arrived?"

"No," I lied, thinking about how I'd said good morning to the plant on my desk, waved at a magpie without realizing, and was now about to have a cup of coffee with my *what if* guy. "All exactly the same."

"Strange. I would have thought there'd be a shift in some way. There will be. They're an ancient race. They don't step into our realm without there being disruptions." She looked at me calmly, her blue eyes unnerving me. "They have answers," she said again, lifting her hands, dreamlike, to her face and running the tips of her gloved fingers delicately around her eyes.

"Was there . . . ?" She breathed deeply then smiled tightly. "Was there any mention of Tír na nÓg?"

"Tír na nÓg?" The land of eternal youth. I remembered it from stories as a kid. If you went there, and you only got there through a wild adventure or if a fairy brought you, you never aged, you never died, and you lived a life of absolute pleasure. Only a few mortals had crossed into it, or so the story went.

She nodded.

"That's kids' stuff, isn't it?"

"Quite the opposite."

"Why would there be a mention of Tír na nÓg? No, there's nothing about that."

"If there is . . ." She sucked in a breath. "Could you keep me informed?" She flashed a wide smile and handed me a cream business card.

I took it, nodding and shaking my head at the same time. "I doubt there'll be anything about that here, but thanks."

Maura smoothed down her hair. "I should leave now. I have work to do."

She stood up and shook my hand again. "It's been an honor. Thank you so much, and look out for my piece in *The Times* the day after tomorrow."

"*The Times?*" *The Irish Times* is a serious newspaper that exposes corrupt politicians and budget deficits, and is the bible for Ireland's elite decision makers. I didn't even think it had a music section. I'd have thought music was too fluffy for it. I sat back down again. "I thought you were from *Hot Press* or *Music in Dublin*."

Maura shook her head and looked at Jim. "No, *The Times*. It's read by opinion makers. It has a lot of sway." She looked at me seriously. "I have the ear of many influential people."

I nodded.

"Your story is of great interest to some of these people. Powerful people. They'll be watching you, and they could be upset if this is not brought to completion."

I must have looked confused, because she quickly changed tactics and pulled an uneasy smile.

"It's just . . ." and she trailed off, deciding not to elaborate. "I'll leave now." And she nodded at me, as if she'd made her mind up about something.

Jim accompanied her to the door. I watched her glide out and immediately place a phone to her ear on exit.

AlJo slid over to the table, unshaven and sweaty. "She, eh, she won't mention this place, will she?" His eyes darted toward the back kitchen. "I don't want the publicity, you know?"

I told him I'd do my best to ensure anonymity. AlJo's could remain ours alone for a little while longer.

I picked up a saltshaker and put it down again. I was surprised that my hands were trembling. *Just relax*, I thought, *calm down*. I kept biting my nails and tried to dehunch my shoulders. What did he want? What was I doing here?

Jim came back to the table, grinning. He sat across from me and stretched his long arm over the seat beside him. He eyed me with the intensity of a Tom Cruise stare. "So, how are you?"

"Great, great. You?"

Now, if I'm honest, I expected the same response. Conversations in Ireland follow a certain pattern. There are no exceptions:

"How are you?"

"Great. You?"

"Grand."

"Any *craic*?" (*Craic*, pronounced "crack," is the Irish word for fun and not, as you might have thought, a highly addictive street drug.)

"Not much. Yourself?"

"Divil a bit."

"Nothing strange, so?"

"Nah, nothing really. You?"

"Well, now that I think of it . . ."

And then you're off. The conversation is officially allowed to start. Anything that moves at a faster or more aggressive pace is considered rude. Conversation needs to warm up and get slowly lubricated before the chat fires up. So I nearly fell out of my chair when Jim prematurely launched into the conversation.

"It's great, isn't it?" he gushed. "*The Times*? It's such great publicity for the band."

"Yeah, it's brilliant for you. Strange fit, though, *The Times*?"

"Publicity is publicity. She contacted me out of the blue on Tuesday."

The same day I posted the letter and the first Step, I thought.

"This could make such a difference to Red Horizon. We need the push." He was practically skipping in his seat.

"You don't think she'll mention me, do you?"

"Nah. You don't mind, do you?"

"Absolutely not."

"That was a good interview. She's a fan of our music. Often

the journos aren't, you know? They just get sent out by their editor and they're not into it. But she's into it."

"She didn't look like one of your typical fans." Maura's ice-cool demeanor, her age, her suit . . . Normally Jim's fans are hysterical seventeen-year-old girls, looking to whip off their clothes to show him their tattoo.

"We're such a diverse band, our fan base is that broad." He held his arms out wide to emphasize "that."

"That's great," I said, trying to sound like I could be a supportive girlfriend to a rock star if the opportunity arose.

"Yeah, it is great."

And then there was a pause, a heavy silence. We both looked around the room. One question swam uneasily around my mind. What did he want?

"We, em . . ." Edgy, he looked over my head, out the window, peered into the back kitchen at the mafioso. "We need the publicity. We're in a bit of trouble with the record company, you know?"

I didn't know. And I definitely didn't know what this had to do with me.

"They don't think we have the edge anymore. They're downgrading us. Which is bollocks." He clenched his fists. "We're just starting, you know?"

There was no skin on my fingernails left to chew.

"This stuff. These Steps." His head was turned to the side, and he was straining his eyes to see the far wall. He tapped his foot. "They could help us. It's new, it's an edge, it could be something different. Nothing might come of it, but, at the same time, something might. I mean, you see Maura, she's into it. Kate, can you help us? Help me?" He stopped. He shifted in his seat and turned toward me.

Breathe and pause. I sank a bit. I felt that heavy weight of being let down, disappointed once again by the dating merry-go-round. He didn't want me. He wanted fairies, he wanted publicity, he wanted his band.

"Sure," I said quietly.

"I mean, you wouldn't have to do anything. Just, you know, keep putting them up on our site, and like, if it's okay with you . . ."

I nodded in agreement, not even knowing what he was going to ask.

"If it came up in interviews, I could mention it?"

I was still nodding.

"And maybe you could, you know . . ." He said "you know" a lot. I didn't know anything. ". . . tell me about Kate McDaid?"

I knew he wasn't talking about me. "Em, well . . ." My voice was soft and quiet. "Thing is, I don't know anything about her. You know as much as I do."

He looked at me, disbelieving.

"But my dad is investigating. We're trying to find out more." I eyeballed him and held his gaze.

He smiled. His shoulders dropped and rested back against his seat. "Thanks." He took a quick gulp of his coffee (black, two sugars). "Matthew's okay, yeah?" He was moving the conversation back into more normal territory, away from fairies and failing rock bands.

"He's great. We're working on a campaign that's slowly going belly up—Starshoot. You know the chocolate bar?" Why was I talking about this? I should have been talking about music and bands and him. Me and him. Could there be a me and him? Could I make a last-ditch attempt at a me and him? Should I even try? My gut instinct told me to walk away from this. He was not interested.

His eyes glazed. "Sure."

"Well, it's going pretty badly, and we have this terrible client. It's all a bit of a nightmare." Still I couldn't stop. I should stop. Stop talking about this.

"Sure."

"He's German, and all German-like." Did I think I was cracking a joke? What was that? What's "German-like"?

"Sure." He finished his coffee. "Kate, I've gotta shoot. Got a rehearsal this afternoon." He stood up, leaned across the table, and put his hand on my shoulder. He looked into my eyes. "Thanks, thanks for everything."

"Sure," I croaked.

He swaggered toward the door. Just as he was about to push it open he turned around and shouted: "That color blue really suits you."

And in an instant, I felt the same way I knew my mam would feel if she ever managed to meet Julio Iglesias. Magical.

Don't Look Back in Anger

by Maura Ni Ghaora

In the far field of my grandfather's farm in Gweedore, Donegal, grew a fairy thornbush. It was a whitethorn bush that flowered in the summer and withstood the winds of winter, a whitethorn bush that was said to be the home of a fairy, a mischievous fellow who was not to be disturbed. As children on summer visits, my brothers and I would dare each other to touch it, to see if we could see him. We never did.

Years after, my grandfather died and the farm

was sold. A small housing estate was built, and, despite local protests, the whitethorn bush was cut down. The fairy lost his home.

In the very spot where the whitethorn bush once grew, a man from Dublin opened a shop, and in a town with next to no crime that shop was robbed, its windows smashed. After eighteen months in business, the owner was declared bankrupt. Now the shop stands vacant. The locals say the fairy has a new home.

In my column I write about a New Ireland, a progressive, successful country where people drive shiny new cars and buy homes that their parents would never have dreamed of owning. It's a country that nurtures talented young people and artists before projecting them onto a global commercial stage. This New Ireland doesn't look back, because we've been led to believe that there's nothing there worth looking back *for*. Look back and you'll find hundreds of years of oppression and misery, the famine, poverty, and emigration. Why should we dwell on our past?

Recent events have made me think that perhaps it *is* time to look back. Have we been wise to ignore our rich heritage of Celtic mysticism and spirituality?

A few days ago, I was preparing to interview Jim Johns, the lead singer of Dublin band Red Horizon. As I always do before an interview, I researched my subject online. On Red Horizon's website, I found something that caused me to think again about our old Celtic beliefs.

Jim's girlfriend, Kate McDaid, has recently inherited a series of letters apparently given to her deceased ancestor, also called Kate McDaid, by the fairies.

Not a lot is known about the earlier Kate McDaid, other than that she lived in Clare in the 1870s and was a self-proclaimed witch. She also claimed to have the gift of healing and spell making, and knowledge of another world, a world inhabited by fairies. She believed that fairies and humans needed to interact, for the good of nature, our planet, and ourselves.

In her will, Kate McDaid bequeathed the Seven Steps, as they are referred to, to her descendant, Kate McDaid. The earlier Kate hoped her young descendant would inherit her powers, and asked her to share the Steps.

The living Kate McDaid published the first of the Steps on Red Horizon's site last week. The other six Steps, which are to be published in sequence, hint at a fairy awakening that would benefit us.

For some reason the older Kate McDaid could not fulfill these Steps within her lifetime. In her first letter, she states that many Celtic souls need to take part, so perhaps she was never able to get the requisite number of helpers. Maybe, because she was believed to be a witch, no one would listen to her.

Reading that first Step has, for me, opened a door to the past, to an old Ireland. There was a time when witches, druids, and fairies walked among us; when mothers dressed their baby boys as girls for fear that a fairy would steal them; and when people heard warnings of imminent death from the cry of the banshee. To my grandfather, fairies and banshees were as real as his grandchildren. Now I wonder where they've gone. Why did we close our eyes and stop listening? Is it possible that they're still here, right beside us but in another realm, knocking on our door? Is it possible there might be a modern witch among us?

The first Step asks us to acknowledge nature and the fairy spirit within it, to whistle to the flowers and to pause and admire the beauty of the natural world. What harm is there in taking half a minute out of our busy lives to stop, to pause and appreciate, to know that we are all of the same earth, that we work together? Do it. You'll be happier for it.

Red Horizon play Whelan's on Wexford Street, Dublin, Friday, 10 May, 8 p.m. Tickets at door.

6

I'll be honest with you. It's not ideal to be outed as a modern witch in a national newspaper. But I couldn't wipe the smile off my face. "Jim's girlfriend, Kate McDaid." Me. Jim's girlfriend. Being called a witch paled into insignificance compared to the dizzy heights my imagination could go to now. And, anyway, Maura Ni Ghaora didn't directly point the finger at me in terms of being a witch. It was implied—I got that bit—but there was no direct accusation. Whereas "Jim's girlfriend" was pretty much stated as a fact. So I took the whole witch thing very well.

The article was hidden on page seven of *The Irish Times*, a small column on the left-hand side in the bit of a newspaper nobody reads. Or so I thought. I laughed down the phone when Pauline Glynn rang me. Our mothers had played hockey together for years, and I was regularly updated on Pauline's successes, marriage, child, major career in RTÉ—Ireland's national radio broadcaster—and her big house in Killiney, one of Dublin's most affluent suburbs. I took great comfort in the fact that she had a really big bum. Slim everywhere else, but a ginormous bum. It was good to know that you couldn't have it all.

"Is it you, Kate? In the paper? The fairy stuff?"

"Hi, Pauline. Yeah, it is, yeah."

"It's fascinating."

"Well, I don't think I'd call it fascinating . . ."

"Hmmm, look, I recently got a big promotion. I'm now head of production on the *Tom Byrne Show*. It's a huge position."

"Congratulations."

"This is exactly the kind of thing our listeners would love, this step into another world, this mystery. Will you come onto the show? Talk to Tom?"

"What?" If I'd been standing, I would have fallen over. "No way. I'd sound like a lunatic. I'm not going on national radio to talk about fairies. I don't know anything about fairies."

"Well, you must know something? It's in your blood."

"No, no, honest to God. This very distant relative was a bit mad. I'm not going to embarrass myself on the radio talking about her and fairies. No way."

She was quiet for a moment. Thinking. "Well, if I can't persuade you . . ." She sighed heavily.

"No, you can't."

"How are your parents?"

"The same. Yours?"

"Same. I see you have a new boyfriend."

And I couldn't help myself. The immature twelve-year-old came bursting out of me, the one who always heard about Pauline's excellent exam results and tennis trophies. "He's in a band, you know, very successful, very, very handsome." And the minute I said it I felt stupid and petty.

"Right. Okay, look, if you change your mind, you know where I am."

And that should have been the end of it. But it wasn't. Forty minutes later, Mam was hollering down the phone to me. She couldn't believe I'd said no to Pauline, and her mother was such a good friend to her, and this was no way to treat your friends. I furrowed my brow at that one—they were more rivals than friends. The conversation went downhill from there.

I told Mam there was no way I'd hang myself out to dry on radio.

"Well, that's just fine," she said. "Your father and I will. Pauline says they'd rather have you, but they'll take us."

I tried to talk her out of it. I really did, but she was adamant. Mam was, if nothing else, a good friend.

My parents' media debut was on a gray shivery Irish spring Monday with winds howling and rains spitting. Maybe it was because it was cold and I needed to hibernate, but I slept in that morning. I leapt out of bed half an hour late, ran to the kitchen, and turned on the radio.

Not only had I missed most of their interview, I was going to be late for work.

". . . so tell me, was there ever an inkling that she was different?" Tom's familiar morning voice caused me to cock an ear in his direction, busying myself around the kitchen. Surely I had time for a quick coffee?

And there it was, a quick breath—no sound, just a sharp intake of breath that I recognized immediately. Mam.

"Ah, *different* isn't the right word, Tom. She was always special. She's a very special girl. They said I couldn't have children, you know, so for us she was special, a miracle. And when she was born, didn't the doctors say, 'It's a redhead'? Not a boy or a girl. A redhead!"

I stopped. I felt my grip tighten around my coffee mug as I tried to breathe, my feet anchored to the kitchen floor. *Stop talking about me*, I thought. *Stop it.*

"And of course, red hair has always been associated with mysticism in Ireland."

"Very interesting, Teresa." Tom Byrne did sound interested.

"Tell him about her imaginary friends." It was Dad.

"She did, Tom, she had imaginary friends as a girl. We thought it was just because she was an only child, Tom, but I suppose you never know."

"Do you think she could have been communing with the fairies, even then, as a young girl?"

"You never know."

I dropped my coffee mug. It shattered into smithereens, and a dark pool that looked like blood slowly crept around the soles of my shoes. Edging in closer and closer to me. I turned and ran shoulder first into the bedroom and, falling on the bed, reached for my phone. I scrolled down until I found "M" for Mam. The call went straight to a chirpy voice-mail message. "D" for Dad was the same. They had their phones turned off.

Stunned, I walked into the kitchen and wiped my sweaty damp hair off my forehead.

Tom was still talking. ". . . I know my gran swore by it. She'd never have thirteen people at a table. Noel and Teresa McDaid, thank you for coming in. You've given us all food for thought. And please, visit us on rte.ie for a link to the Step, so you can see for yourselves what we're talking about."

"Thanks, Tom."

That was me off-balance. My parents were on national radio talking to Tom Byrne about me and my imaginary friends who may or may not have been fairies. Nobody read a page-seven column in *The Irish Times*, but *everybody* listened to Tom Byrne.

My heart flip-flopped the whole way to work. Once there, I fixed my stare on the floor, only looking at coworkers from the knees down. If I couldn't see their faces then they couldn't see mine and they couldn't ask me about fairies. I almost slid under my desk and waited for someone to say something, to throw a pointy hat in my direction or shuffle by on a broomstick. But nothing happened. Phones rang, keyboards clicked, and my coworkers moved around as usual, the scent of toner trailing behind them. Nobody had been listening, or, if they had, they hadn't put the pieces together. Kate McDaid is a common name, after all. It could have been anyone. I let out a deep breath, felt my shoulders fall and relax and my stomach slowly unravel. It was just a normal day in the office.

Then Marjorie flew toward me at torpedo speed, her face a lopsided mix of bubbling excitement and sadness.

Oh God, she knows.

"Did you hear?" she whispered into my ear, overenunciating her words.

"I heard," I said, immediately feeling depressed.

She twirled behind her and grabbed my guests-only chair. Wheeling it almost on top of me, she sat down with a heavy sigh. Now we looked like Siamese twins.

"It's just so sad."

"Sad? Well, if you mean pathetic sad, yeah, I guess."

She let out a little squeak and, even though it seemed impossible, leaned closer. "They say drugs might have been involved."

"What?" I nearly fell off my seat. "Drugs?"

"I know." She sucked in her cheeks. "What a tragedy. He was only twenty-eight."

"No, my dad is at least fifty-eight."

"What? Drake Chandler. I'm talking about Drake Chandler. What's your dad got to do with him?"

"Drake Chandler, the lead singer of Burning Cradle? The emo guy? What about him?"

Her whole body erupted. "You mean you don't know? You haven't heard?"

"Well, like, I know who he is, obviously, who doesn't know

about Drake Chandler? Didn't he start off that whole emo movement? He's responsible for all those teenagers wearing black eyeliner and all that hard rock music."

"He's a god." Marjorie hung her head dramatically. "He *was* a god." She cocked her eyebrow to see if the change of tense had registered with me.

I nodded, encouraging her to spill the gossip that was moments from gushing out anyway.

"He's dead. He was found dead a few hours ago in his mansion in Seattle. It was suicide. Such a tragedy. And the saddest part is, he'd been dead for a few days, swinging from a chandelier. It's so horrible."

I nodded in agreement, picturing his handsome face, which I always knew would have been even more handsome if he'd wiped off some of the makeup. But that's just me—I'm not into makeup on guys.

"It's all over the Internet. Everyone's saying that the signs were there. The lyrics in his songs were so dark—he was crying out for help." Marjorie furrowed her brow, as if she could have—maybe even should have—been the one to help him. For a moment I thought about celebrities and how they become so familiar you think you know them and could be the one to connect with them.

"That's really sad," I said. "All his fans are going to be so lost without him."

"Look." She pointed to a large-screen TV in the corner of the office. A small group of guys from the art department were huddled around it shaking their heads in disbelief. The TV was flashing images of Drake Chandler and his house, his band, Burning Cradle, and a depressing shot of a stretcher with a body covered in a white sheet.

I shivered. "Terrible."

"I'll let you know if I hear anything else," Marjorie said, standing up from my desk and quickly moving over to the more informed group at the TV.

It was definitely sad—a sad way to end a life.

I waved to Matthew. He picked up his phone and nodded toward mine. This was pure laziness—he sat a few feet away.

"Morning."

"Hi. Mad about Drake Chandler, isn't it?" he said.

"I know, really sad."

"He finally did what he was singing about."

"Looks like it."

"Did you hear about the note?"

I looked over at him and saw him unwrap another Starshoot. "No. There was a suicide note?"

"Yep. Looks like you're not the only one going on about the fairies."

"What? You're joking." I cradled the phone to my neck and started typing frantically: "Drake Chandler suicide note." I clicked onto cnn.com, and there it was. "Have you read this?" I said into the phone.

"Not all of it."

"'Too much, too fast, the impossible is now. I took this world and lived with it, but it wouldn't let me. They wouldn't let me. I've been in a dark place for too long, and now I need to see the light. The fairies are finally letting me dance with them. *To the woods and waters wild, with a fairy hand in hand/For the world's more full of weeping than you can understand.*'"

"Drugs?" Matthew looked over at me, nodding.

"Looks like it."

"You don't think there's anything . . ." He paused. "Your fairies? His fairies? That stuff in the first Step, that line about 'our anger you will know, a cradle burned, a soul extinguished, in the music it shall show'? Ah, it's probably nothing . . ." He trailed off.

How was I supposed to answer that? "I don't know. It's unlikely, when you think about it. He's a rock god superstar, and he's in America. Surely it's a different caliber of fairy. How could he have anything to do with the Seven Steps? *And* he was on drugs."

"Yeah," Mathew said quietly. "He had Irish ancestry, though. I remember reading about it before. He used to talk about it in interviews."

"I don't know. What am I supposed to think?"

He paused. "They say fairies play tricks. What if your aunt foresaw this? What if enough people, enough Celtic souls, didn't do the first Step, and that's why he died? The music was extinguished."

"He committed suicide. How could the fairies have done this? He left a note." My heart was thumping loudly in my chest. "Fairies? Come on, Matthew."

"You're right. It's drugs."

"Drugs."

I didn't know until a while later that Drake Chandler's suicide note quoted the Nobel Prize–winning poet W. B. Yeats, who had spent years in the west of Ireland immersed in fairy culture, exploring and absorbing Irish folklore. It wasn't the first time I wished I'd listened more in school. And I should have listened to Matthew then. Because it was the first sign that there was something more to the Steps. But I suppose I didn't want to hear it, I didn't want to know, and I didn't think. I didn't think. It seemed impossible. I never thought there could be a connection. Why would I ever think there could be a connection between me and Drake Chandler? Him, a world-famous rock star, and me, a junior copywriter in a Dublin ad agency? I couldn't make sense of it, not then, anyway. That came later.

7

"How's the Starshoot working out for you?" I said down the phone. I looked across at Matthew, raised my eyebrows, and smiled. It was Tuesday morning and I was due to post the second Step that afternoon.

"Delicious. I think I'm addicted. We have to do something, though. The Little Prince wants a work-in-progress meeting soon."

The theme tune to *Jaws* exploded in my mind. My promotion, my future pay raise, my career, all depended on Günter Lindz. A client with so much attitude, the office had nicknamed him "the Little Prince."

I nodded, hung up, and tried to think about chocolate, nothing but yummy chocolate. But it was tricky. Starshoot is a really nice chocolate bar, packed with nuts, caramel, some crispy bits, and crumbly chocolate. It's been around since the seventies. It's the kind of chocolate bar your granddad would shove into your pocket as you said your good-byes, and you'd find it later, warm and melted, and lick the insides of the wrapper. It's a fuddy-duddy chocolate bar, old-fashioned and outdated. Old people dunk it into their tea. No one under fifty eats it. Ever. But now, the Little Prince wanted young people to suck on it with lattes, he wanted to see it fall out of the pockets of supermodels and hear it name-dropped by IT people. Unfortunately, there were already seven other bars in the market that had the exact same ingredients and were seen as cool and hip. So there was nothing to say about Starshoot other than it was a very nice chocolate bar and your granddad loved it. "Starshoot—a nice chocolate bar for pensioners." We had a problem, and we knew it.

People like Matthew and me, who come up with ideas in an advertising agency, are known as "creatives." I don't think even van Gogh had a title so grand in his lifetime. It's a misnomer. There's very little real creative work involved in our jobs. Instead, it's about selling. We're supposed to package a product in such a way that the consumer feels that they need it, that they have to have it, that it *completes* them. We try to start that itch for a new pair of shoes, that longing for a perfume that conjures up images of the south of France and Marilyn Monroe, that desire for the mascara that will make you a better person. The product should feel like completion, if only for a nanosecond.

At least, that's what we're supposed to do. Matthew and I work as a team. Officially, I write the words and he draws the pictures, but our roles often blur into one. Like with Starshoot—we were trying to come up with a *big idea* like "Just do it," "Because I'm worth it," "Melts in your mouth, not in your hand." We needed a concept, a slogan or a thought that would create a need in every chocolate-craving hipster. And we were struggling, so much so that a little niggling voice in my head was telling me we might be out of our depth and not up to the task.

We'd landed the Starshoot account by accident. We'd been working late one night, slaving, whipped and loin-clothed, over a particular telco leaflet. The office was a ghost town: the foosball tables had stopped clicking a few hours before and the

Nigerian security guard had done one patrol, drunk a coffee with us, and gone on to his other moonlight job at the bank next door. We had a nine a.m. meeting with Colin to "whip and skip out the good stuff." But there was no good stuff: there were more pictures of phone cords, electrical plugs, wires, speakers, a maze of telecommunications. Then there was a *bang, wallop* in reception, followed by the familiar clopping sound of our short-legged boss.

Wobbly, Colin saw us at our desk and ran over, panting. "Thank God you two are here! I need a creative team. Now." He ran his hands through his shoulder-length hair. "Günter Lindz from Chocolatez has just called. He has an emergency briefing on Starshoot. He's on his way in. You two are going to have to take it." As the words fell out of his mouth the smell of desperation filled the air. His eyes started to crack, fizzle, and pop with panic as he realized just who he was asking to take this briefing—a junior copywriter and a junior art director. Colin quickly scanned the office, hoping that a janitor, Chinese phone guy, Nigerian security man, anyone other than Matthew and I could step in.

"There's no one else here, Colin. And we'd love to take the briefing. We love chocolate." Matthew had spoken in the manner of an eight-year-old girl twirling her dress.

Colin had looked defeated. "Okay, okay," he'd whispered, dry-mouthed.

That was weeks ago and we'd made no progress.

I pulled out my notebook, wrote "Starshoot" at the top in neat capitals, and carefully drew a large question mark underneath. Now I was getting somewhere.

My phone buzzed. Marjorie.

"Kate, can you spare five minutes?"

"Have you more on Drake Chandler?" Although I suspected not—her voice was slightly elevated, more business than gossip.

"No. Could you pop into meeting room four, please?"

"Meeting room? Oh no, do you have a client there? Can you not ask someone else to do it? I'm just about to dive into some very important work."

"It has to be you. Colin wants you here." She sounded very annoyed. "It'll only take five minutes."

As I tapped on the door of meeting room four, I decided to only feign objection if they sent me out for eclairs. Really, Dudley should have done those kind of jobs, but I supposed I would go if I got an eclair, too.

Marjorie nervously swung the door open. I peered past her. Hugging the red Formica meeting table were two guys from the online department whom I half recognized, as well as Colin, who was nervously twirling his mustache, and the porn client, dressed in a baby blue T-shirt, his arms outstretched and resting on the backs of the chairs beside him, as if he was too large for just one seat.

The porn client's gray eyes fell on me, piercing, studying. The giant shaggy dog plodded over to me and stuck his wet nose into my hand, nudging me into the room. Maybe the guy doesn't recognize me from my outburst in the lift, I thought, deliberately avoiding looking at him.

I turned to Marjorie, every inch of my freckled skin blushing. "Yeah?" I whispered meekly, conscious of my breathing and the porn client's eyes.

Marjorie swung her arms toward me, presenting me like a shiny car on a game show. She turned to the room. "This is Kate."

"Hi," I said, studying the tiled floor, refusing to look up at him.

He pushed back from his seat and crossed to me in a heart-beat, extending his hand. "I'm Hugh. Nice to meet you . . ."

I threw my hand out and slowly raised my eyes to him. And he smiled. It was one of those rare smiles that seemed to face the whole world for an instant and then concentrated on me, seeming to understand me—only the best me, or the best impression of me. It was as if he knew me. His face was creased and the smile lines around his eyes made him look rugged. ". . . for the first time." His hand was rough and mine felt weak and lost in it.

"And you."

He smiled at me again, and my heart fluttered a little too fast.

"Soooo . . . ?" With her swinging arms, Marjorie created shapes and shadows around me.

"What are you doing?" I asked out of the corner of my mouth.

She tightened her lips. "Just wondering if you could be a fit? For Hugh's site?" She swung her ponytail and absentmindedly checked her pink nail polish. "I mean, you've got that real Irish look. I mean, it wouldn't be you—you're not a model, obviously." She stared me up and down judgmentally, causing me to pull on my navy V-necked sweater and hitch up my jeans in one clumsy movement. "But I wanted Hugh to see the look that Colin and I have been talking about—the freckles, the red hair—to see if it could work for the face of the site."

"The site? The p—" My mouth hung open in shock.

Marjorie stepped in front of me. "I . . . I . . . don't think this was a good idea, Colin," she said a little too loudly.

"No. This is a bit too strange." I looked over to Colin for support.

He quickly jumped to my aid, me the self-conscious show pony. "Marjorie, that's fine. Kate, you can go, thanks for coming in. Sorry for disturbing your morning. This wasn't a good idea. Thanks, Kate."

Stunned and confused, I headed out the door.

"I think I've just been auditioned for a porn site," I hissed at Matthew as I passed.

Back at my desk, I opened a bar of Starshoot to help calm myself down. "I don't know who's worse: Marjorie or Colin?"

"What happened?" Matthew shouted, only half interested.

"You don't want to know."

But *I* did, and an hour or so later I quizzed Marjorie. "Seriously. What was that about?"

"Like I said, the Irish thing. They're based in the west. I thought it could be a fit—the red hair, your look?"

"You should have warned me." I was sounding really very cross with her.

"Oh, come on. It was just a moment of inspiration, a creative blast. He's a difficult client. I had to think on the spot. Don't get up on your high horse about it, Kate. You should be flattered."

"Flattered?" High-pitched and slightly hysterical, but definitely not flattered.

"Well, *I* would have been. It's not happening, anyway."

That's a relief, I thought, *whatever "it" was.*

"Hugh thought you weren't right. Said you were too 'natural-looking,' which basically means you're not model material, but we knew that."

Too "natural-looking"? What was that? Too fat? Too red-faced? Too frizzy-haired? "Natural-looking" was never a compliment. That man was infuriating.

"Don't do that to me again. I'm just glad I don't have to work with him. He's an arsehole."

"Arsehole," she said in agreement.

Which was how I was feeling about Marjorie at that moment.

My angry thoughts were interrupted by Dudley, who, oblivious to all nerve endings, whistled to the tune of his creaking cart.
He idly wheeled through the office to the sound of nails running
up and down a blackboard.

Colin stopped him by placing his two hands on the front bas-
ket and eyeballed him. "For the love of God, stop, for the sake of
the children."

"I just have to deliver this to Kate."

"Take it by hand, for all our sakes."

Dudley tutted loudly and reached into his cart, almost top-
pling over with the weight of a giant purple orchid. He swayed,
continuing to whistle until he got to my desk and plonked the
plant down.

"There you go now. Very nice. Who's it from?"

I couldn't hide my excitement or my smile, even though
Dudley's presence always guaranteed extreme irritation. My eyes
widened and I felt a surge of giddiness as I bit my bottom lip apprehensively. Could it be Jim?

"That's my business, Dudley." I tried to sound cool and collected. Other than from the sucker-handed Italian, I'd never received flowers at work before.

"Is it Matthew? You two are always chatting, all lovey-dovey."
Dudley's eyes were tiny slits, and his underbite looked even more
pronounced, if that was possible.

"No." I reached for the card and ripped it open.

Kate,

So lovely to meet you last week. I'm working on a follow-up
piece for *The Times*. I've started looking into the life of your

aunt. You might be surprised at what I've found. I'd love to talk
to you about it.

Maura Ni Ghaora

Maura gave her phone number and an e-mail address.

My heart sank. There were quite a few people I'd hoped the
flowers might be from, but Maura Ni Ghaora wasn't one of them.

"They're from a friend, Dudley. All right?"

"Tsk, tsk. The attitude on you!" He bobbed off, walking with
his neck first, and I picked up the orchid in its pot.

"Dudley!" I shouted after him.

He screwed his heel into the ground and spun around, looking
at me goggle-eyed.

"You never said hello," I said, dismayed.

"Hello, Kate," he said, rolling his eyes.

"Not to me, to the flower. It's upset. You never said hello."

"To the flower?"

"Yes, to the flower," I replied with great determination. As I
held the orchid in my hands I could sense a feeling of distress.
It was all out of sync, upset, and that upset *me*. I can't explain it
other than to say that I absolutely, positively had to fix the situation. There was no way I couldn't address this. And I didn't care
that it seemed a bit weird—well, more than a *bit* weird.

Dudley looked at me and his expression changed. He chewed
on his underbite nervously. "Hello, flower," he said quietly.

I smiled back happily at him, immediately feeling better.
"Thanks, Dudley."

He shuffled off, looking anxiously over his shoulder.

The orchid was beautiful—majestic, heavy-headed, almost
sad. I put it beside my yellow plant and marveled at how the
flowers complemented and blended with each other. I quietly

whispered hello to the orchid and introduced them. "This is yellow plant. Yellow plant, this is orchid." And then I thought that maybe I'd gone mad. Seriously. I was talking to flowers, giving them feelings, and I'd made Dudley greet one. Flowers! Weirdly, it did make me feel better, though. There couldn't be any harm in it. Who knows? I really wasn't sure what to think.

I wondered what Maura Ni Ghaora had uncovered. I had already googled life in Ireland in the 1870s, and from what I could gather it was bleak and shoeless, an era that could foster madness, maybe even encourage it. It didn't sound romantic and magical at all. I doubted that Maura Ni Ghaora and I would see eye to eye on that.

It was Tuesday, so I was due to post the second Step. There were 157 comments on the first Step now, which seemed like a lot, most of them misspelled or abbreviated. Nearly all were okay, though. They were about hugging trees and giving nettles and ivy a big thumbs-up, stuff that I was half into doing, anyway. The one thing I didn't like, and it was the thing that was driving a lot of the comments, was the connection to Drake Chandler. The words of the Red Hag (I couldn't really stomach thinking of her as "Kate McDaid"—it was too strange) were being interpreted as a prophecy. Visitors to the site had posted messages that she'd foreseen Drake's death, and that his suicide was a direct result of not enough "Celtic souls" greeting nature and acknowledging fairies. These grieving fans of Drake Chandler, desperate to make some sense of a tragic death, were becoming avid fairy followers.

And now the second Step had arrived. Seamus MacMurphy had hand-delivered it, calling in on me at work. I'd told him just to send it by courier, but he insisted, claiming he couldn't wait to see what was inside the envelope. His long limbs folded into my guests-only chair, and he rubbed his knees excitedly like a kid on Christmas morning. "This is funny, isn't it?" he said, letting down his lawyer's guard.

I broke the wax seal and read aloud.

Step Two

When grief burdens your shoulders and
you can take the pain no more,
When the ghost of loss is in you and
heavy clouds blacken each shore,
May a soft wind whirl these words around
and reach your depths of sorrow,
As sure as storms turn into calm,
there will be hope tomorrow.

We have seen it with immortal eyes,
your hurt, your woe and pain,
The circle of life continues,
as before and will again,
Go forth alone to nature, walk in her woods,
cherish healing seas,
Whisper your heart's desire, clear your head of noise—
we will listen and we will please.

The world is full of more joy than
you can now understand,
Feel us with you, take our message—
we are holding your hand,

With the gifts that we have given,
watch for those who cannot see,
Their mouths are struck with sores,
for no cure can there be.

Seamus looked at me disappointedly, like Santa had forgotten to bring his Scalextric set again. He shrugged his shoulders. "Walk in the woods? I thought there might be a bit more hocus-pocus."

"Let's wait and see. I have a hunch that the hocus-pocus is only just starting."

8

I was meeting my parents for tea. Not tea as in the English version of supper, but for a cup of tea.

Tea is Ireland's other religion. Most of the world associates Irish drinking with alcohol, but our first love is tea. It's the cornerstone of every Irish home. We drink more tea per head than any other nation, even India. The biggest insult an Irish person will give to another Irish person is to invite them into their home but not offer a cup of tea. You might as well stick a knife in them.

Mam and Dad wanted to meet in the Shelbourne. That really tipped me over and poured me out. The Shelbourne is the poshest hotel in Dublin. It overlooks the ducks on Stephens Green, and you could happily lie down on the plush-carpeted stairs and fall into a deep slumber for a thousand years. You can see your reflection in the polished flowers, and it's rumored that geisha girls wash the sheets with their own tears. It's all heels on marble and the gentle tinkle of chandeliers. I was very happy to go along.

I cycled over from my flat off Camden Street. At the Shelbourne, the doorman's eyes shot down his long pointy nose when I asked him where I could park my bike. His elegantly gloved fingers gestured toward a murderous-looking alley, where,

I suspected, he wanted to get rid of me, my bicycle-clipped jeans, and my luminous armbands.

These jeans cost 180 euros, I wanted to shout at him, and I have a very nice top underneath my waterproof jacket. Cycling is not about fashion! But then I thought I'd look like a nutter, screaming at a doorman in the Shelbourne while wearing a helmet with "go faster" stripes painted on the side.

My parents were lounging in a window seat in the bar. Dad was dressed in a brown woolen shirt I didn't recognize. His arm was casually draped over the back of the couch, and Mam was bent forward, talking on her phone with a look of concentration on her face. She had on a baby-blue jacket tied in a tight bow at her neck.

I eyed their tea enviously. I needed a cuppa—I was stressed. I'd picked up four phone calls that day that I'd thought I'd never receive: two from newspaper journalists, one from a magazine, and another from a radio station. They all wanted to interview me, to ask me some "top-line" questions. I didn't know how they'd gotten my number and I was reluctant to speak to them. I knew how things could be twisted. I'd turned my phone off early in the afternoon. I needed a plan before I spoke to these people. The second Step had been live for only one day and already they were excited. I had to work out what to say.

"Hello, celebrities."

Dad jumped up and gave me a bear hug, then ran to the bar, shouting that he'd get me a cup. Mam made a just-a-minute gesture, poking her index finger in the air. When she'd finished her phone call, she leaned over for a tight squeeze across the shoulders.

"Mam," I said, cutting straight to the chase. "I didn't appreciate your talking about me on the radio. And anyway, I didn't have any imaginary friends when I was younger—well, I mean, I did, but no specific ones. I had a healthy imagination."

"I don't know about healthy. You had Paulie with the hat and Susie with the big bum."

"That was Samantha from down the road."

"Ah, sure. I can't be expected to remember everything," said the mother of one child. "But you did have imaginary friends. You were always off in your own world down the garden, talking to yourself."

"That's what only children do, Mam. It's not revolutionary. We're making up our own brothers and sisters, and it's not for radio."

"Exactly," she said, ignoring me. "They have imaginary friends. You had a lot of them, though. One specifically that you were very fond of, a male, I think. At one point your father and I thought about sending you to a doctor, a head doctor."

"Seriously?" This was the first I'd heard about it.

"Yes, we did, but then all of a sudden you didn't have him anymore. You started palling around with the kids on the road, and sure, that was the end of that."

Dad plonked a cup in front of me. "Did she tell you about the TV?" He eased himself into the couch.

Mam picked up the teapot and started to pour. "We're naturals." She beamed at me with pride.

"Natural what?"

"Talkers? Media types? Sure, who knows. Anyway, it's all a bit of gas."

"What's the TV?" I asked, amused.

"TV7." Ireland's poor-cousin TV station. "They want us on their breakfast show on Friday. Can you believe it? It's only a two-minute slot, but who knows where we could end up." Mam's voice was shrill, and she clenched her hands into tight fists, her eyes wide with expectant fame.

"Are you going to do it?"

She nodded wildly. "Of course. This is the most exciting thing."

"What are you going to say? Don't talk about me," I said with as much authority as I could muster. And then I started to laugh. This really was very funny. My parents were going to be on TV. Never in my life had I ever thought they'd end up on TV.

"Well, the same stuff as we said to Tom, I suppose." Tom Byrne was now "Tom." "Sure, we hardly mentioned you. Anyway, come on, why don't you do it with us? They'd love to see you."

I squirmed in my seat. The thought of going on national TV and talking about fairies and witches, neither of which I knew anything about, just didn't appeal. "Well . . . and don't take this the wrong way, because if you want to do it, you should, but I just think I'd look like a bit of an eejit."

She nodded matter-of-factly. "You know, that's the great thing about being older. You lose all that . . ." She waved her hands at me. "All that self-consciousness. You just don't care what people think anymore. Your father and I are going to have fun doing this, and we haven't had fun in a long time." She looked serious, but quickly changed her tone, readjusted her skirt, and took a sip from her teacup. Smiling, she added: "They're interested in your great-great-great-grand-aunt Kate, so we'll tell them about her."

"You don't know anything about her."

They quickly flashed eyes at each other, a nanosecond of a glance. Dad piped up: "Well, I got in touch with my grand-uncle Willy's second wife, Audrey."

Willy had scandalously married a woman fifty years younger than him, promising to leave her a fortune in his will. There was no fortune—she ended up nursing an old man with no giant check at the end of the rainbow. But she made up for it with her second husband, a property tycoon from Belfast. I didn't know she was still alive. She must have been about a hundred.

"She remembered Willy talking about a Kate. It was near the end, though. He wasn't making much sense. Audrey didn't pay much heed to it; he was also singing rebel songs and claiming to be Napoleon at the time. He said his grandfather had a sister, a woman so evil Audrey said his face had washed pale talking about her. That's why he wouldn't be buried in Clare. He was scared she'd come for him." Dad shook his head slowly. "Load of nonsense."

"How come you never knew about her?"

"Well, from what Audrey said, it sounded like they were all a bit scared of her. No one wanted to mention her."

"Why? Did you ask her why?"

"Of course I did. She didn't know." He looked down at the table. "I never thought there were any women on my side of the family. And there you have it."

"Evil." I furrowed my brow. "I never got the impression that she was evil from any of this stuff. A bit mad, maybe, but not bad."

"Well . . ." Dad was starting to look bored. "She was alive a long time ago, and you know some people thought fairies were evil because of the tricks they'd play. So if they thought she was in cahoots with them, you could see how people might think she was evil, too."

"Do you know anything else about her?" I asked, interested.

He and Mam both shook their heads. "Look, all this stuff is probably a load of claptrap, especially the stuff about you. Who knows if there's any truth in the fairy stuff? There might be a half-truth here and there, there might be something—I'm not discounting it—but the bottom line is that people are interested in fairies, in witchcraft and whatever, and your mother and I have decided that, if we can, we're going to have some fun with it. We're going to enjoy it. And if people want to talk to us on TV, well, we'll go. When would we ever get to go on TV?" Dad laughed at the sheer lunacy of it all.

I nodded. I couldn't argue with that, and we all sat back and relaxed into the salubrious surroundings. Soon we decided to move on to the heavier stuff. I jumped up before Dad could to get to the bar—he'd bankrupt himself on the rounds system one of these days. Two gin and tonics later, Dad was starting to mumble about the cost of drinks and I was looking for my jacket to leave, when Mam grabbed my leg excitedly. "Jim? Who's Jim? I can't believe I forgot to ask you."

I blushed like an eleven-year-old in the school yard who's just realized she doesn't hate boys. "He's a friend. That was a typo in the article. The journalist got it wrong."

"Really?" Mam said, never taking her eyes from mine. "Your father and I are going to buy his record and see what kind of a fellow he is. See if he's good enough for our Kate."

"Honestly, he's just a friend." *Oh my God*, I thought. Mam and Dad would probably become Red Horizon groupies. Things were getting weirder by the minute.

Around nine I cycled home. I lived on the south side of the city center, on the first floor of a converted house. Even though my flat was small, I loved the color and bustle of the neighborhood, which was dotted with settled immigrants and friendly old Dublin families. I couldn't imagine living anywhere else.

It was a lovely bright evening, a sign that summer was knocking on the door of spring. And yet the Irish weather never fails to disappoint. It still managed to rain. There were sheets of it crashing off my face, and my sodden jeans were creaking with every turn of the pedals. I humped my shoulders over the handlebars and went as fast as I could, thinking about how great it was to see my parents so happy. It had been a long time since they'd been so giddy and full of life. Maybe, as Mam said, it was just a bit of gas and these Steps would give us all a bit of a laugh over the next few weeks. I hoped so.

In spite of the rain and the arthritic damp that was seeping through my clothes, I felt upbeat when I pulled into the front garden of my flat. I got off my bike straight-legged—I'd need a WWF wrestler to help get me out of my jeans—and started to chain my bike to the railings, thinking, as I fumbled for the key, how I'd have to talk to my landlord about cutting back the overgrown creeper. It was coming at me, reaching for me from every angle. Then I felt a spasm in my back. I was being watched. You know the way you just know, the way your primal instinct kicks in?

Firmly clutching my bike chain in my hand, I swiveled around and manically scanned the overgrown bushes for a shadow. I could hear my own breathing, which was confusing. I heard a rustle in the leaves and, with a fright, jumped backward about twenty feet, straight into the next day's rubbish collection. Cushioned by the wet, oozing black bags and almost suffocating from the smell of putrid onions, I involuntarily flailed my arms and legs in panic. My kicking split the bags and I saw a packet of pasta and a can of Coke break free.

"Are you okay?" The quietest voice I'd ever heard whispered from over my head.

I screamed and tried to kick, liberating some Daz Automatic and Walkers crisps.

"I'll just be over here if you want some help," the voice squeaked before a shadow moved back into the garden.

I rolled out of the rubbish and with great difficulty attempted every yoga position I'd ever read about to try to stand up while still clutching my weapon of mass destruction.

"I have a weapon," I shouted into the blackness.

"Okay," came the response.

The shadow moved to the path and into my line of vision. He was tiny, wide-faced and anorak-wearing, with a side parting that must have been the envy of every Ken doll. He didn't look like a mugger. He was firmly clutching a book with one hand and waving like a three-year-old on a merry-go-round with the other.

"Hi," he shouted.

"What are you doing here? Who are you?"

I straightened up, confident that with a Chinese burn and some serious ear tugging I could outwit this mouselike mugger.

"My name's Simon. It's a great honor to make your acquaintance," he shouted from the path with a nervous stutter. "I'm the chairman of the Seven Steps Fan Club."

Those last few words hung in the air between us. Silence. "The fan club members have some questions for you that we hope you could answer? For example . . ." He started rummaging through his book, flicking furiously through the pages. I couldn't hear what he was saying over the rain.

"I can't hear you. Did you say questions?" I screamed.

"YES."

I waved at Simon to come into the garden. He looked like he'd be eye level with my belt, so I didn't think I had anything to worry about.

He shuffled in nervously. "A great honor," he said, thrusting his wet hand toward mine.

I gestured toward the rubbish and my now filthy hands. He nodded like he understood and quickly produced a pen and scribbled something into his book.

"Did you say fan club?" I asked, hoping I'd misheard him.

He nodded. "We have some questions for you about the Seven Steps."

"Who are you?"

"Simon Battersby."

"Yes, but who are you?"

"Well, I'm thirty-four. I'm a chemical engineer. I live in Dublin, and I think that the Seven Steps are going to save us all."

"Save us? From what?" I looked at him with a mixture of shock and sympathy. "Come on—the Red Hag, fairies, it's a load of nonsense," I said. "Have you ever heard anything like it before?" I laughed.

"Yes, yes. It's written right here." He flicked through his book and landed on a printout of the first Step. The page had been decorated with neon colors and pictures, just like on the Space Monkeys' website. Rain was bouncing off it, and he tried to shield it with his hand. When that didn't work, he dug around in his pocket and produced a clear plastic folder that he placed over it.

"But I wrote that. Well, Great-great-great-grand-aunt Kate did."

I thought he must have been deaf, because he was nodding with such enthusiasm. "Well, the Red Hag also featured in the eighth quatrain of one of Nostradamus's predictions, except, of course, he referred to 'the great Red one.' Oh, and earlier in the seventh quatrain, when he spoke of 'a sect and the wise red-haired one.'" Simon flipped the pages in his scrapbook and showed me a double-page spread of diagrams and charts.

I nodded slowly. Was it just me or had everyone gone mad? "This is ridiculous," I said.

He flipped his book again and scribbled in it.

"Ridiculous."

He looked at me straight on. "I get it. Yes."

Weirdo.

"Drake Chandler, his first song, his first hit, he referred to a duplicitous red-haired lover." He smiled at me knowingly. "There's a few too many coincidences, if you ask me."

I didn't ask you, I thought.

"How many people are in this fan club?"

"Just me at the moment."

I breathed a sigh of relief and turned on my damp heel. "Good night, Simon Battersby. Try and stay in from the rain."

"Kate, Kate. One more thing."

The urgency in his voice made me spin around.

"The journalist, the one who's writing the articles. She's not on your side. Don't trust her. I've come across her before on another project. She likes the darker side of the supernatural."

I shook my head. As if I was going to take advice from the stalker in my garden.

"Good night."

I ran all the way up the stairs, slipped out of my clothes, and took a long hot shower, letting any thoughts of the Seven Steps Fan Club's one and only member slip down the drain.

9

I'm always willing to try the latest fad. I was an early adopter of leggings, and I can put forward a balanced debate on the pros and cons of the Atkins diet. If people are talking about it, I'm going to try it. And so on Thursday morning before work I decided to "go forth alone to nature" and complete the second Step.

I found myself climbing onto a rock on Bray strand and looking out to sea. The Step's instructions were to "cherish healing seas." And so I sat. In fact, I probably shouldn't have chosen Bray as a destination to commune with nature, because it's a seaside town, and kids' screams reach a whole new decibel of excitement, fueled by cotton candy and sticks of rock candy. The seagulls only accept chips dosed in curry sauce, and will squawk about it until they're served up just as they like it. Tickets for the big wheel and the dodgem cars come with strobe-light warnings: may cause seizures, death, and/or deafness. But it's only a few train stops away, and the fairies just mentioned nature in general. No specifics. So, nature with the incessant *ker-klunk* of fifty-cent slot machines was probably okay.

The rock was cold and sharp and very uncomfortable, and I wasn't too sure if I should be touching it with my hands. Did I need to make actual contact with the rock, or was it enough just to be sitting on it and feeling its damp sharpness soak through my jeans? Then I focused on "clearing my head of noise." This wasn't easy either, because all I could think was: *Clear my head of noise, clear my head of noise, clear my head of noise.* It was a lot of noise bouncing around in my head. And there were other voices popping in, too. *What am I doing sitting on a rock in Bray? If someone I know sees me, they're going to think I've gone mad. Maybe I have gone mad. Should I be listening for fairies? What would they sound like, anyway? What am I doing? Shhh, I should be thinking about nature. Shhh, focus on clearing your head of noise—I need to empty out my brain.*

And then I was on a loop back to square one, desperately searching for silence. And how long was I supposed to sit there for, anyway? Until I felt a tingle? I was already tingling—well, shivering. I took the shiver as a prompt to ask for my heart's desire. I had to think about that: "my heart's desire." *Be realistic*, I thought. I desire, and have always desired, money, nice clothes, a smaller nose, hair with less frizz, an Hermès handbag, and a labrador puppy with big chocolate-brown eyes whose hair doesn't molt onto the couch. But I'm no fool: I've read fairy tales. I know that you never, ever wish for material possessions. You wish for the intangible: love, health, joy. And so I did—I wished for a love that would make my face ache with smiles, a healthy body whose lungs filled up with fresh air, and a joyful skip in my soul. And as I slid off the rock, my jeans damp and an icy tremor in my bones, having not seen or heard a fairy, I felt jolly. Honestly I did. I think taking a minute or two, or five, out of your day to sit on a rock on the beach—to listen to the sea gurgling, in between sirens and fighting seagulls, to think about things that make you happy—actually makes you feel happy.

I didn't feel like I'd had a fairy experience—not that I'd know what a fairy experience would feel like—but I did have a smile on my face as I bought my train ticket from the stationmaster.

He collected my coins with dirty fingers, rubbing them on the arm of his navy jacket. "You look happy."

"I am," I said.

"You must have gotten lucky last night." He flicked the ticket at me with a knowing wink.

"Pervert!" I shouted, grabbing the ticket. I pulled my cardigan tight around me and marched up the platform, back to real life with a whack, thud, wallop.

When I got back to the office, I kept my early-morning expedition to myself. No one needed to know that I'd been sitting on a rock. At my desk was a sack full of kitty litter, a mountain of cat food, and a giant Irish wolfhound. The kitty litter and cat food I could explain: I'd agreed to babysit Colin's cat. His oldest son was suffering from allergies, and while he was getting tested the doctor recommended removing the cat. I'd offered to take Mister Snoop Doggy Dogg, who was going to be delivered to my flat that night.

The wolfhound's chin was perched expectantly on my seat and he wiggled his eyebrows as I approached.

"Setanta? What are you doing here?"

He shimmied under my desk in the manner of a shrug and proceeded to curl into a ball, a big ball, and pretend to be asleep.

"I know you're pretending."

He opened and shut one eye.

"You can stay if you're quiet."

He leaped out and furiously wagged his tail, rubbing his wet nose into my hands.

"I said, be quiet!" Laughing, I scratched behind his ears, and attempted to push on his back to get him to sit. "Where's your horrible master, hey?"

He flicked his head to one side, studying me. Then he sat and rested his head on his paws. Eventually, he lay down.

Quite liking my new work partner, I slid into my seat. But already my mind was turning to my expanding workload.

"Ka-a-a-ate?"

I looked up. "Hi."

Marjorie slowly crossed the office, a pink cashmere vision in a tight, striped pencil skirt and 1950s heels straight out of *Mad Men*.

A cloud of perfume billowed around my desk as she pulled up. "What's he doing here?" Her eyes narrowed, and her neck jutted forward an inch, betraying her casual tone of voice. Marjorie always seemed to be looking for a weakness to pounce on to shamelessly promote herself upward.

"Setanta is working on the Starshoot campaign," I said, sticking my neck out as far as it would go.

"Well," she smiled sweetly, self-consciously holding her finger up to her mouth, "that's fun." She gritted her teeth. "I thought you might be struggling. It's a big challenge. I'm available any time if you need some help."

"Thanks so much." Butter wouldn't have melted. "We're doing fine."

"Well, you know where I am." She spun around like whipped cotton candy.

I had noticed her lipstick was smeared and I could have sworn she had the beginnings of a cold sore. It was the first time I'd ever seen her makeup slightly askew.

* * *

After work that evening I went to the cinema with Lily to see an independent French film. It wasn't the kind of film we usually went for, but Lily had a crush on a guy at work who was all about French films, museums at the weekend, and goatees. She had already preplanned her morning coffee conversation, when she would mention the film to him, ever so casually, to illustrate that she, too, liked French films, could visit museums at the weekends, and appreciate goatees.

As it turned out, neither of us could understand what was going on, and we spent the first twenty minutes nudging each other, whispering things like "I don't get it. Who's he? Did he do it?"

Afterward, as we made our way through the lobby, stuffed to the eyeballs with popcorn and Maltesers, we tried to work out how Lily could possibly talk intelligently about a completely incomprehensible film. "What about the lighting at the opening credits?" I was trying to be helpful. "You could say it was moody and symbolic."

"Hmm," she said thoughtfully, slowly twirling her fingers through her blond curls. Lily has the most amazing hair, perfect white ringlet curls that make her green eyes sparkle. She's the kind of girl who always gets a second look from guys, and she wasn't used to not having her crushes reciprocated. "I might just use words like that—symbolic, poetic, difficult."

"That could work."

We shuffled on in silence.

"He sounds difficult," I added truthfully.

"I know. But he's cute."

"That is difficult."

We nodded in agreement, both understanding the complexity of liking a good-looking man.

"I know the goatee thing and the museums and the fact he has a blog is a bit odd, but I do like him." Her face looked hopeful. "I just can't get his attention. It's like I'm jumping up and down in front of him and he can't even see me." She shook her head.

I cleared my throat and mulled it over quietly. *How can Lily get Goatee to fall in love with her?* Suddenly I began to see how this love match could ignite. I felt excited and unbelievably sure that I had the answer. I was having a moment. It was like when you play Trivial Pursuit and a question on sport comes up or, worse, a question on golf comes up. And not only have you never watched golf, you don't know who plays it or how they play it. You have a vague idea that they wear baby-pink argyle socks pulled to the knee, but that's the extent of your golf knowledge. And then what should be your worst nightmare happens: you're asked who won the 1980 PGA tournament. And it's for a piece of cake. And you just know, hand on heart with 100 percent certainty, that it was Jack Nicklaus. You've probably never said his name out loud before in your life, but you know it's the right answer. Well, that's how I felt about Lily and Goatee: I knew I had the right answer.

"Did you ever make cookies?"

"What?"

"Well, you said he drinks coffee. Why don't you bake some cookies and bring them into work?"

"Because I've never baked anything in my life, and this is not the 1950s."

"No, no, hear me out. Bake cookies with lots of sugar. Make sure you put vanilla essence in them and a sprinkling of ginger and some rose petals. Grind it all up. I know it sounds weird, but it'll work. Think of him while you're baking. Shape one of the biscuits into an image of your face, and when he bites into it, stand right in front of him, and say: 'You love it, don't you?' You have to say the word *love*, and he will, Lily, he'll see you and he'll fall in love with you on the spot."

She started to laugh. "You're so funny. Is this some love potion?"

"I think it's more of a spell." I smiled. "I must have read it in *Woman's Own* or *Bella* or something. But I know it works—in fact, I'm 100 percent positive this will do the trick, Lil."

She laughed. "Are you using your magical witch powers?"

"Obviously. The witch powers that I got from a magazine."

She shrugged. "It would be rude not to try. I've tried everything else: new haircut, cleavage, perfume. No harm in a little baking."

"That's the spirit." And we laughed happily as we pushed through the exit doors. Outside, there were a good few people hanging around, waiting for the next film, smoking.

Lily fumbled in her oversized handbag for cigarettes. Triumphantly, she pulled out a pack of Marlboro Lights and then cursed her lack of a lighter.

"Back in a sec," she said before trotting off to a group lost in a cloud of smoke.

I rocked back and forth on my heels, waiting. And then the strangest thing happened, and it happened with such clarity, it was as if it was in slow motion, and I felt my heart leap out of my body with shock.

Bright lights started flashing, and I heard clicking.

"What the hell?" I looked to my left. Two men with cameras were snapping furiously, their long lenses poking in my direction.

Shocked, I repeated myself: "What the hell?" Instinctively, I threw my hands up to my face to avoid the attack. Whir. Click. Flash.

"Kate, look this way."

The men were shouting at me in loud, overbearing voices. "Kate, do you have any fairies with you now?"

The cinemagoers looked over at me, straining their necks to see what the commotion was. "Who's that?" I heard someone mutter.

Flustered, I stumbled backward.

"Fuck off!" Lily screamed at the top of her lungs. She waved her cigarette in front of her like a sword, stabbing the air between us and them. Swiftly, she looped my arm in her own, and with speed and precision, as if she'd run from paparazzi all her life, she bundled me into a taxi and slammed the door behind me before shouting, "Go! Go! Go!" at the driver.

Still in shock, I pulled out my phone and texted Lil: "Thanks. How mental was that?"

It felt weird, wrong, that somebody would take my photograph, and those lenses felt very intrusive. It felt like an attack.

Back home, I paid the taxi driver the outrageous fare of twenty euros and marched up my path, still shaking slightly. As I put my key in the door, I noticed a package on the step addressed to me. I picked it up and ripped it open. A book, a giant hardback entitled *Ye Olde Book of Spells.* Confused, I opened it. Scrawled on the inside cover was a message from Simon Battersby. "The Seven Steps can save us all. Your friend, Simon."

Save us all from what, Simon?

I stomped upstairs, threw the book on the hall table, and changed into my blue brushed-cotton pajamas, thinking all the while, *Tomorrow will be a better day.* Only it wasn't. It was worse.

10

It was Mam and Dad's TV debut. They were on the breakfast show with Mark and Sinead from 7:26 to 7:28. I flicked the telly on with great trepidation, knowing they could be seriously loose cannons. Dad had his cord suit on, and Mam a floral dress that I recognized from last summer and her berry lipstick newly applied. They were grinning, then laughing and interrupting each other as they animatedly waved their hands around.

"How do you feel about these Steps?" Sinead moved in closer to my parents on the brightly colored couch, chummily sipping from a cup of tea.

Dad's voice dropped to a serious tone. "There's something in them, Sinead. A message of grave importance. We can't ignore it."

I threw my eyes up to heaven. He was playing to the camera.

Sinead pursed her lips and nodded like a wise sage. "It's true, the answers to our future often lie in our past. We just have to look to our history. Society often repeats its own actions."

The answers? To what?

I flicked it off, just as they were cutting to a pig festival in Ballinspittle. A journalist in wellies was drowning in eight feet of muck.

When I arrived at work, Setanta was waiting for me. He was

becoming a permanent fixture under my desk, where he'd lie at my feet, resting his chin on my knees or burrowing his head into my hands. He turned up about twice a week—the rumor in the office was that Hugh Delaney's creative work wasn't going well. Colin and Marjorie were hosting twice-weekly work-in-progress meetings with him, something that never happened—the work was clearly bombing. I was happy when Setanta was there. I enjoyed his company and chatted away to him and Matthew in equal measure, convinced I'd draw inspiration from one of them. Matthew was fond of him, too, and said I was being really mean when I deliberately moved the box of Starshoots out of Setanta's reach. The dog kept turning up anyway, in spite of the lack of treats. But he seemed to have an in-built beeper: at certain times he'd just up and run, as if chasing a rabbit, but I knew it was because Hugh was leaving the building.

On this particular morning, though, Hugh came looking for Setanta. He marched through the office, feet stomping, arms swinging, stressed-looking, blond hair ruffled and spiked, calling out like he was in the middle of a field, oblivious to the fact that in an office the highest decibel of conversation is a loud whisper. Hugh didn't fit in an office. His presence somehow made everything around him seem more artificial: the Formica chairs, electronic keyboards, plastic tables, fluorescent lightbulbs. He looked like an oak tree straining for the sunlight; he obviously needed the outdoors to breathe. It was like a survival reality show, nature struggling against corporate city life.

"Ah! He's with you." Hugh smiled a dazzling smile, all white teeth and twinkly eyes, and fell onto his knees to come eye level with Setanta, who was ecstatic to see his owner.

"Are you being a good boy?" Hugh said in a gushing cartoon-style voice, to which Setanta responded by violently wagging his tail and jumping up to him.

Laughing with that dimple exposed, Hugh looked up at me. "Is he bothering you? Will I take him?"

"No," I said adamantly. "He's great. I really enjoy having him around."

"It's strange. He's not normally very friendly. He's usually stuck to me like glue." Hugh rose to his full height, all long legs and shoulders, and looked teasingly at me, a cheeky grin on his face. "I wouldn't want him disturbing your important work, now."

I won't rise to him, I thought. "That's okay. He helps me with my important work. He's quite inspirational."

We both looked down at Setanta's wide-eyed expression and the plastic bone he'd spent the last few hours chewing on. He wasn't exactly a likely muse to my creative ambitions.

"I talk to him," I qualified, blushing a little bit. I looked directly into Hugh's gray eyes and somehow felt the sway of the Atlantic Ocean. I was thirsty, parched. His presence dislodged me.

Hugh nodded and responded softly, "So do I. He's a great listener."

"Nonjudgmental . . ."

We both laughed. And once again I thought how handsome he was, how masculine he looked with a shadow of light-brown stubble brushing his jawline.

"He loves the gossip," I said.

"Ah, he's an auld pet." He bent down to pat him. Suddenly his head came up, his eyes on me, making my color rise, as if somehow he could hear what was really going on in my mind. But all he said was: "He keeps secrets well."

"I suspect he'd turn me in for a can of Pedigree Chum."

He grinned at me with an honest, open smile. "He'd never do that to you."

"Let's see." I laughed.

"Nah, he's always nice to the pretty ladies."

And suddenly a switch flicked and I could feel my blood boil. Pretty? "Don't you mean 'natural-looking'?"

"What?" His eyebrows creased.

I took a deep breath and swiveled my seat back to my computer screen. *Remember what he does*, I thought. *Porn. I shouldn't even be speaking to him. What would my mother say?*

"I have work to do," I said sternly out of the corner of my mouth.

"Of course." He looked at me, puzzled, no doubt, that my friendly demeanor had changed so quickly. "I didn't mean . . . Right." He seemed to stretch a little and become even larger. "We'll be off, so." He rubbed his hands down the front of his jeans. "Right." He turned. "C'mon, Setanta. Bye, Kate."

"Bye." I sat seething, watching him lumber through the office, his shoulders hanging low and his boots stamping, as Setanta loped along beside him. Infuriating.

I turned to Matthew to see if he'd heard the conversation, but he was intently staring at his computer screen. He looked stressed, his face pinched. Chubby but still pinched. His eyes looked serious.

"I don't think you're going to like this."

I sat down and tried to brace myself for whatever he was going to say.

"There are two things. Well, there are three," he said.

"I'm ready for it." I closed my eyes, prepared for the reckoning.

"There's this." He produced a newspaper from behind his back and handed it to me. It was open to page ten. There was a large photograph of me from the night before—those paparazzi fellows worked fast.

I examined it closely. In the photo I looked pale and had a double chin. *I thought these things were photoshopped.*

I stretched my neck self-consciously and felt my eyes widen as I read the caption: "A quiet night at the cinema for Kate McDaid. Kate, who publishes the Seven Steps, is being hailed as a modern-day witch. She's put a spell on us, that's for sure."

The breath was pulled from me. My head started to spin.

Matthew quickly handed me a glass of water.

I took a sip. "There's my picture, and they're calling me a witch. They are seriously calling me a witch."

"How did they know you were there?"

"I dunno. They were just there when we came out of the cinema. They pounced. It all happened in about twenty seconds." I took a deep breath. "The other two things—does it get worse?" I half laughed.

"No, that's the worst." He picked up the paper and flicked back a few pages. "But that Maura Ni Ghaora has written another article. It's not too bad, but she does mention you again."

A blur of black-and-white print swam in front of me. I'd read it later. He was right: it did feel tame in comparison to a color photograph.

I drained the glass of water. "And behind door number three?" I smiled at Matthew.

"The Little Prince wants a work-in-progress meeting this afternoon. He's flying in from Stuttgart."

OH NO!

"No warning. No nothing."

Matthew shook his head. "We've got four hours."

"Shit." All thoughts of fairies, paparazzi, or TV-star parents fluttered from my mind.

"We'd better—"

"I know. I've booked us a room."

I scooped up pens, paper, notebooks, markers, and crossed the office floor with Matthew, aware that my brain might explode at any point. *Chocolate, chocolate, chocolate. Think, think, think.*

"Need any help?" Marjorie piped up from across the office. She pushed herself away from her desk, ready to run toward us.

"Got it covered, thanks, Marj," Matthew shouted back.

Marjorie shuddered slightly.

Matthew smirked over at me. "She hates Marj," he whispered.

"You know where I am," Marjorie said, looking hopeful.

He gave her a thumbs-up sign. "Hope the cold sore clears up soon."

She quickly put her hands to her mouth and sat down.

"She must have kissed everyone in the art department *and* the studio. The whole ninth floor has cold sores. It's like an epidemic," he muttered to me.

Or a spell, I thought. *Their mouths are struck with sores, for no cure there can be.* I shivered slightly.

Once we were in the conference room, I pulled out my markers and got to work. STARSHOOT, I wrote in block capitals across the giant whiteboard. Then I stood, mouth pursed, looking at Matthew.

"Right. Good start." His face was pulled so tight, he looked like he might snap.

"Right." And we stared at each other for a long time.

"Em . . ." Matthew clicked his fingers in the air. He looked like he was getting something. "No. It's gone."

"What was it? It doesn't matter if it's not right. We have to start," I said, watching the straws I was clutching slip through my fingers.

"Starshoot—packed with crumbly goodness." He shook his head. "Told you."

"I'll write it up. It's a start. But we can't lead with taste—seven other bars on the market taste the same. We've got to think life-style, trendy, cutting-edge." I started scribbling on the board, re-lieved to see the white space filling up.

"The chocolate of kings." A half smile crept across his face. "Pr-Princes. Little Princes."

We'd already put a number of slogans and ideas before the Little Prince. "Live it. Love it." Or my favorite: "Choose joy. Choose Starshoot." He'd knocked back all of them for one reason or another. It had begun to feel like we were no longer targeting the youth market but the Little Prince market, and we only had one consumer to please.

"What do Little Princes like?"

This was how Matthew and I worked: we joked, we played, and somewhere along the line we pulled an idea out of the hat. Normally.

"Shoes with heels, silk scarves." Matthew was doodling while he was talking, drawing a caricature of the Little Prince with a huge head. "German sausage." He raised an eyebrow and I laughed.

I started to sing "These Are a Few of My Favorite Things" in the style of Julie Andrews. "Saunas and schnitzel and bad Europop . . ."

"Mercedes and bratwurst and Hasselhoff . . ."

"Ah," I interrupted. "They love him."

"Still?"

"Didn't he single-handedly end the Cold War?"

"I know he sang on the Berlin Wall when it was coming down."

"That's proof enough for me that he's in the hearts of the peo-ple. He's an honorary German." We both laughed.

"He does transcend generations, but could he sell chocolate to the Little Prince?" Matthew's laughter was verging on hysteria; his eyes were watering.

We dismissed the Hoff and came up for air three hours later. We had a few ideas, none of which felt right, all of which confirmed my doubts that we weren't up to the task.

We headed for AlJo's greasy arms and two comforting bacon sandwiches. Within seconds it felt like old times, as we sniggered behind plastic menus, debating the merits of egg mayonnaise sandwiches and cinema popcorn.

"What's going on with you, Matthew? I never even told you that I liked your new T-shirt," I said, feeling every inch a bad and distracted friend as he sat up proudly.

"This *is* new. A lot of my clothes have shrunk in the wash," he said with a sly smile, patting his new chubby belly.

"Those damn washing machines."

He went quiet and started shifting uneasily in his seat.

"You okay?"

He nodded, but chewed his lip so ferociously I knew he couldn't be. A nerve rash crept up his neck. He took a deep breath. "I have a confession." He looked down at his sandwich.

"Okay," I said, feeling anxious. "Is it something bad?"

He nodded. "I just need to tell someone. I'm so ashamed."

I took a deep breath. "It's okay, Matthew. You can tell me." I hoped I sounded genuine, but the truth was I didn't know if I really wanted to hear his confession. He looked guilty. He looked like he'd really done a bad thing.

He mumbled something into his sandwich before taking a giant bite out of it.

"What?"

He said it again, a similar mumble.

I burst out laughing. "God, Matthew! For a moment there I thought you said you'd signed up for Internet dating."

His whole body exploded into a nerve rash.

"Nooooo. What? You have?"

"I'm so ashamed." He threw his two hands up to his face and rocked to and fro.

"But that's . . . Why? Why would you do that?"

Matthew was a good-looking guy. He was an extrovert, he was funny, nice. Why in the name of God would he be online?

He shrugged and sighed heavily. "I'm at work all the time, all my friends are in couples. I've no wingman since Tom hooked up with that Aussie chick. I've spent my last four Saturday nights in playing Nintendo. I get set up with the same girls again and again. I keep thinking about phoning exes because I'm bored. Something had to give." He looked defeated.

"But the Internet?" I shook my head in dismay.

"I know. I'd heard of a guy in America who met someone . . ." His voice trailed off weakly.

"America," we whispered in unison. Knowing full well what that meant. Online dating works in other countries. In Ireland it's viewed as being for the truly desperate, for those who have failed in normal social settings, for those people who are truly so unattractive that even the drunkest man/woman in the bar won't take them home at the end of the night. It's a public hanging. Anyone can find you on it: schoolfriends, your mother, grandmother, teachers, boss. They can all look at your profile online and wonder to themselves what happened to you along the way that you couldn't get laid the way other normal Irish people do, with alcohol and witticisms.

"Okay," I said, trying to gather my thoughts. "Is there anyone nice on it?"

He looked like he'd burst into tears. "I accidentally clicked into my cousin's profile."

"Oh dear God, this is worse than I thought." Ireland being

Ireland, you're going to know someone on the site, but a cousin? Oh, that took it to a whole new level.

"I'm supposed to go on a date next week. A date." He said the words deadpan. I understood. Irish people don't date. We don't know how. We go out in groups, drink, and maybe by the end of the night kiss someone who either made us laugh or looked good. Numbers are exchanged, there's an avalanche of text messages, and eventually there's a meeting a week or so later somewhere loud, where there's dancing, and all you can really hope for is that they're not really bad-looking and they were funny, but either way there'll be alcohol by the bucketload to dull all senses. Sobriety kicks in about six weeks along, when a decision is finally made as to whether or not there's a relationship worth pursuing. That's how we date. We don't sit in coffee shops and ask each other about five-year plans or family situations. We get drunk and hope for the best.

"Who is she?"

"She looks pretty, but—" He shook his head. "She said LOL in her e-mail and she used those wink things." He took a sharp intake of breath.

"It's a whole new world."

"I never thought I'd end up on the Internet." He looked so sad, my heart broke a little.

"Hey, you're just trying it out. It's not forever." I hoped I sounded supportive.

"I know. It's tough out there."

I wanted to tell him he was a great guy, and there was a great girl out there for him, but that would have sounded too clichéd and corny, and not like anything I'd ever say to him. So instead, I talked about work. "We should head back to the office to get ready for a true Starshoot whipping."

"Will we pray to your aunt?" Matthew asked.

"Great-great-great-grand-aunt. And not funny."

Half an hour later we stumbled into the boardroom. It was fully prepped as per the Little Prince's demands: scented candles (vanilla only), sparkling and still water (no ice), lemon cordial in a glass jug, one elevated chair with two cushions, and five Bic pencils positioned on a clean notepad. Just the way Daddy liked it.

The Little Prince stomped in, the sound of his Cuban heels clicking ahead of him. Colin wobbled behind, chewing gum and looking anxious. The Little Prince definitely appeared taller. He was wearing a pinstripe suit, which I knew could give the illusion of height, but I could have sworn he just skimmed my elbow last time we met, and now he was hovering around my shoulder. His hair, blow-dried into a Texan bouffant, did add a good two inches to him.

He didn't say hello.

We made greeting grunting noises at him. Colin leaned over the table and started to apologetically pour water.

"It is best just to proceed."

More nodding, more grunting.

I rarely spoke at this type of meeting, overwhelmed by awkwardness, nerve rashes, and perspiration. Public speaking is not my forte. So we'd agreed that Matthew would present the concepts. He stood up, creaking his chair, and rearranged the notepad in front of him. He explained that we hadn't had much time, it was early days—all the usual excuses. Then he produced our first concept: a kind of Calvin Klein black-and-white ad with whispering supermodels, very moodily lit, using words like *fusion*. The Little Prince said nothing. The second concept, which was a bit like a shampoo ad—sunny meadows, frolicking, laughing, glinting—was met with stony silence. By the third concept, the Little Prince's cheeks had entered the seventh stage of fuchsia. The fourth was greeted by a sharp intake of breath. Colin eyeballed Matthew and quickly shook his head, warning him to finish the presentation now. Matthew slyly hid concepts five and six under his notebook and sat down.

"Zis is all you can give me. Zis sheet." The Little Prince slammed his hands flat on the boardroom table.

"Okey-dokey. It's early days. These are not completed concepts." Colin whistled.

"I understand zis," the Little Prince raged. "But there is no idea, no heart." For the record, the Little Prince spoke like that, like a fake German, even though he *was* German. It was like he'd just watched four World War II movies back-to-back, wearing knee-high boots with Alsatian dogs snapping at his heels.

Again we nodded enthusiastically and agreed. I felt about two inches tall, like I could squeeze into the Little Prince's pocket. He continued to berate us, to kick us up and down the meeting room with his Cuban heels. He was shouting about firing the agency, the talentless agency. Layoffs and breadlines flashed in front of my eyes.

Then, just when I thought I couldn't take any more humiliation, wallowing in the depths of despair, I blurted out, "David Hasselhoff." The room went quiet as all heads turned toward me, surprised that I, the meeting mute, had spoken. It was like I was hovering over myself; it was an out-of-body experience. I cleared my throat. "David Hasselhoff"—was I really going to say this?—"is sitting on a star in space, and he takes a bite out of a Starshoot and he literally explodes into space, becoming one of the stars, and maybe, like, his face is on the stars. An actual *star* shoot. And the line, the line is . . ."

I was reaching. I turned desperately to Matthew for help.

Matthew cleared his throat and calmly turned to the Little Prince. "The Hoff has it. Do you?"

Colin stepped forward, about to gag me. Matthew put his hand to his mouth in absolute shock at what we'd just said, at what we'd just presented.

"Hasselhoff?" The Little Prince's eyes narrowed. He looked interested.

"The Hoff." My voice was high-pitched and shaky.

"You could have somezing here." He looked at his watch. "I have to go. I have to catch a flight back to Stuttgart." He said "Stuttgart" like there was too much spit in his mouth. "I'll be back in a veek. Vork on ze Hasselhoff concept."

He pirouetted out the door, and we slumped onto the table.

"David Hasselhoff!" Matthew looked like he'd been hit by one of those red lifesaver thingies they carry in *Baywatch*.

"What a bad idea. I'm so sorry." I felt faint.

"Well, well, do you know, it doesn't matter anymore. We just have to make this work. The agency needs this campaign to work—budgets are low. If he wants David Hasselhoff, we'll get him David Hasselhoff." Colin looked decidedly optimistic, and there was a postmeeting expression on his face that I didn't recognize. He was either having a minor stroke or there was a smile curling on his bottom lip. "Really, it is important we get this right. Good work."

11

Listen

by Maura Ni Ghaora

Come away, O human child!
To the waters and the wild
With a faery, hand in hand,
For the world's more full of weeping than you can understand.
"The Stolen Child"
By W. B. Yeats

Twice a month a Chinese woman sticks needles into my face. I pay for her services. I have a bad back, and I believe that acupuncture helps relieve muscle pain. It is an ancient Chinese tradition that I, and millions of other people around the world, believe in. It is not, however, endorsed by doctors or recognized as a science. All I know is that when the pins are removed and I get up off the table, I feel good.

How is it that we can embrace one ancient tradition and ignore others? Why is it okay to get acupuncture or reiki or to use crystals to heal a broken heart, but it's not okay to talk about the possibility of other worlds and of spirits? Why do we roll our eyes cynically when someone mentions the banshee? Why are we so quick to dismiss Irish stories of warriors and fairies and magic places? This is our tradition, our cultural heritage, and I believe that there is a place for this mystery and richness in our modern society.

In summer, my grandmother always left the front and back doors open. The house had been built on a fairy path, you see, and they'd agreed to let my grandmother stay on if she'd let them run through. There was a fairy doctor in her village, a man who lived on the *sliabh* (mountain) and walked with a limp. He knew fairy cures. He spoke with fairies and regaled the villagers with tales of the fairy world as they'd fill his cup with *poitín*. There were stories of men falling in love with the fairy queen, of her great beauty, of eternal youth, of hurling games that lasted for days and wars that raged under cover of night. Beautiful stories of far distant lands, of love and hope and passion, a world few are lucky to glimpse.

Over the generations, fairies have disappeared from view. Content in our material lives, we have broken the dialogue we once had and built a wall between our two worlds. We have cluttered our heads with ideas and notions and alienated our senses, emotions, and purest thoughts.

But at last we've been given an opportunity. Some≠how, the fairies have decided to reopen dialogue with us. They've asked for our ears, for a

chance to commune again, for a chance to be still
and to feel. If there is a drop of Irish blood in you,
listen to Kate McDaid. Listen to the Seven Steps.
Clear your head of thoughts, and feel their message.
They are listening, too.

I finally got around to reading Maura Ni Ghaora's article. It was
pretty tame stuff, all things considered. But since it had been
published, she'd been ringing me and leaving lots of messages, all
hinting that she had information about the Red Hag.

I'd promised myself I wouldn't call her back. But it was Friday
night, four days before the third Step was due to be published,
and I had no plans. I was lying on my bed in my pajamas, with a
face mask on and some deep-conditioning treatment in my hair,
and I was bored.

So I crumbled and called her. The curiosity had gotten to me.
I couldn't say no to Maura Ni Ghaora.

Afterward, as I hung up the phone, I realized that the conversation hadn't gone according to plan at all. I really needed to
learn to take more control of situations. Maura Ni Ghaora was
on her way over.

I had just enough time to wash my face and pin up my hair before the bell rang. Still in my pajamas, I opened the door. Maura
Ni Ghaora stood on the step with her back to me. She swung
around in a dramatic twirl, her platinum bobbed hair flying. She
wore a camel-colored floor-length coat that encircled her protectively. Her sculpted, perfectly made-up face, frozen in time,
broke into a grimace. "Kate, how wonderful to see you." She held
out a gloved hand—white leather this time. She was wearing the
gold signet ring on the little finger of her left hand.

"I brought some wine."

She glided into my flat, which suddenly looked sad and impoverished next to her glamour.

"How very bohemian." She spoke softly, running her gloved fingers over a scarf that doubled as a throw. I'd bought it in Penneys for €2.99 two years earlier. She removed her camel coat, which looked like it cost more than all my furnishings put together, and revealed another killer power suit. This one was dark green, nipped at the waist, with a pencil skirt—timeless.

Maura perched herself on the edge of my sofa, looking distinctly uncomfortable, while I meandered around the kitchen, hunting for clean wineglasses. I was still wondering whether I'd made a mistake inviting her around, but she had information and I was curious.

I handed her a wineglass. It was cheap and clunky and looked like a foreign object in her gloved hand. She placed it on my wobbly coffee table.

"This is a lovely neighborhood," she said awkwardly.

"I like it here. I've been here awhile."

"There was a pub we used to frequent around here a long time ago. Flannery's? It's gone awhile. You wouldn't remember it."

I smiled. I'd heard about Flannery's. It had been a notorious hangout for Irish politicians, gangsters, and businessmen, a place for cutting deals and passing brown envelopes under tables. It had been shut at least thirty years.

"Back in the heyday with Liam and Brick," she said softly to herself, but I caught it and couldn't resist.

"Liam and Brick?"

"Like I said, it was a long time ago." She batted the air with her hands and shuffled uneasily in her seat, nervous that she'd spoken out of turn.

Liam and Brick were infamous, probably Ireland's shadiest

characters. Liam McCarthy was the leader of a political party that eventually got into government. Brick was a gangster renowned for kidnapping and dismembering people. Liam's friendship with Brick was a badly kept secret. If Liam didn't get what he wanted, Brick got it for him. They were shady company to keep. I was both surprised and intrigued that Maura had known them.

She closed her eyes and took a deep breath. When her eyelids flickered open, those startling blue eyes were focused on me. "What do you know about your aunt?"

"Not much."

"She was from Knocknamee, wasn't she?"

She spoke with such certainty that it was more of a statement than a question. I nodded, amazed that she knew. It was close to the only piece of information that I had managed to keep to myself.

"Knocknamee is considered by those in the know to be a place of great importance to the fairies. It's a place of great natural beauty and is their most western point in Ireland."

She spoke slowly, her words measured, as if this was a rehearsed speech. "That is the closest point to their home, Tír na nÓg." She shivered slightly and looked at me searchingly. "Is there anything else? Anything you haven't revealed?"

I shook my head. But I could see she didn't believe me, that she didn't trust me.

"Nothing?"

"No."

"No mention of Tír na nÓg?"

Again with Tír na nÓg, I thought. This fairy tale she seems so interested in, this mythical land of youth and warriors. Why?

"Knocknamee has been on the map as a place of importance to the fairies for a number of years, but not publicly, if you understand what I'm saying." She attempted to raise her eyebrows, but her forehead was so frozen nothing much happened. "People who have an interest in the other world know of its importance. There's a village next to Knocknamee called Feakle, which is a publicized place of folklore." She gave a low laugh. "It's also on the map. It was home to Biddy Early, Ireland's most notorious witch."

Biddy Early. The name sounded familiar. "That's the name of a pub in Kilkenny."

"The witch came before the pub."

"In fact, I think there's one in Boston, too."

"There are pubs all over the world named after her." Maura looked annoyed that I was sidetracking her. "She's one of Ireland's most famous female characters. A witch, but a white witch."

"They're the good ones, aren't they?"

Maura nodded.

"Biddy Early had been taken as a child. The fairies often took people for up to seven years, and then would return them to the mortal realm with powers or gifts. They gave Biddy Early the Bottle." Maura looked at me as though I should know what the Bottle was.

I shook my head.

"The Bottle was a crystal ball of sorts, revealing the past and the future. People came from all over to discover their fate, and she was never wrong. When she died in 1874, the Bottle disappeared and was never seen again.

"Biddy Early and Kate McDaid were from neighboring villages. The fairies would have allowed only one witch or healer per village. They would have known each other—there's no doubt about that. And Kate McDaid would have been envious of Biddy Early and the Bottle, that I'm sure of. There's only ever been one Bottle in Ireland's history. A number of witches but one Bottle."

"So they knew each other? Back then, witches were into social networking?" I laughed at my own joke.

Maura didn't. "Biddy Early was a white witch. She used her powers for good." Smiling, she shook her head. "Your aunt was not so revered. She was more of a wicked witch."

I laughed again. Wicked witch—it was too funny.

"They probably clashed. They both had similar powers but used them for very different things. I've found an old rhyme that children used to sing there." She cleared her throat, and in a beautiful raspy tone that bounced off the walls of the flat and caused shivers to run down my spine, she started to sing:

> *Grab your silver and gold,*
> *Run fast through the fields,*
> *She's left her big house on the hill,*
> *The Red Hag is coming, she's coming, she's coming.*

> *She'll eat out your young,*
> *Burn down your house,*
> *Steal your cattle with fairy might,*
> *The Red Hag is coming, she's coming, she's coming.*

"She doesn't sound very nice. The fairies? Are they nice?" I shuddered.

Maura paused and leaned toward me. "The fairies are ultimately good. They play tricks, yes, sometimes very cruel tricks, but it's only when they see something happening that's wrong, or something they deem to be wrong. They want to be acknowledged in our world. They know, as we should know, that it makes for a better environment."

I swallowed hard, not sure where to look or what to think. I shook my head and snapped back into reality. "Maura, you speak like the fairies are real, like they actually exist."

She took her gloved hands up to her mouth and pressed them tightly against it, almost biting back words. Then she took a deep breath. "Of course they exist," she whispered.

"Back then, maybe—the idea of them, in the past, maybe. But now? Seriously?"

Maura sucked in her cheeks, calming herself, and pursed her lips tightly in restraint. "They are alive in our recent history. In 1999, Clare County Council stopped work on a bypass, a motorway that was already in production and costing the state hundreds of thousands of pounds, because the road would go right through a fairy bush that would have to be cut down. The locals petitioned against it. Everyone knew that the fairy would cause accidents on that road."

I sighed.

"In the 1950s, Walt Disney came to Ireland covertly, before he made *Darby O'Gill and the Little People*. He traveled the length and breadth of the country looking for a leprechaun to take home with him."

I laughed a little too heartily, considering the look of disapproval Maura gave me.

"Kate, you need to understand the importance of the position you're in. The fairies need you. You must believe in them for them to accomplish their plan."

"Their plan?"

She nodded calmly. "There's a plan. There's always a plan."

"Always?"

"Kate, you're not their first. They've been around longer than us." She held her gloved hands together in a prayer-like pose and pursed her lips again, pausing for a moment, thinking. "I can help you, Kate. I understand the fairies."

Why would she possibly want to help me? What's in it for her? I wondered.

She smiled an elastic-band smile, and an icy chill raced up my spine. "There are many important people interested in your succeeding at your task, Kate."

Like Liam and Brick? Gangsters and murderers? Something about her left me in no doubt she was somehow connected.

"It's in all our interests that the fairies' needs are met."

Was this a threat? It felt like a threat. It wasn't so much what she said but how she said it. There was a warning tone in her voice, even as she delivered her message with a smile.

Distracted by the wails at the window, I moved across the room to let Mister Snoop Doggy Dogg in. With just an inch or so of the window pulled open, he pounced and hissed his way to Maura's feet. His shoulders jutted forward, his tail pointed to the ceiling, and every hair on his body stood at high alert. A low growl that I could feel in the pit of my stomach erupted from him.

Maura was paralyzed in fear. Her hands gripped the side of the sofa and she squeezed her eyes shut. She was whispering something in Irish over and over again.

"Snoop!" I screamed, clapping my hands for attention. Crossing the room, I scooped him up and waited for my familiar touch to calm his body, which was rigid and ready to attack. I marched him into the kitchen and, despite his whining protests, shut the door.

"I'm so sorry. He's normally really well behaved."

"I didn't know you had an animal." Maura ran her gloved hands up and down her legs. "I'm not good with them."

I passed her the untouched wineglass. "He's normally a real pet. I don't know what got into him. Are you okay?"

"I'm fine." I noticed that beads of perspiration had appeared on her top lip. Her cool demeanor had been rattled.

"I should leave. I have encroached enough on your hospitality." She grabbed her coat and swung it majestically around her shoulders.

"You're welcome. Thanks for all the information." I started to walk her to the door.

"And Kate." She twirled back. "You can trust me."

Maura's conversation had unhinged me slightly. Who were these important people? Why did they care about the Steps? She definitely seemed to have a lot of knowledge about the fairies, but, in spite of her request, I didn't know if I could trust her. Was she one of the good guys? I couldn't tell.

Nevertheless, I slept soundly and peacefully that night and had the most wonderful dream about a beautiful village full of laughter and joy, surrounded by green hills and patchwork fields. Maura must have planted it in my head when she was talking about Knocknamee.

Considering all the wine I'd drunk, I didn't feel one bit hungover when I woke on Saturday morning. Like a cat in the sun, I stretched out, long and lazy, thinking about my day ahead. No plans, nothing. I had a glorious day of lounging and faffing, with the hope of some Gruyère cheese on pepper crackers along the way.

Spurred on by a rumble in my belly, I picked yesterday's jeans off the floor and threw on a hoodie, wishing I could disguise the deep-conditioning treatment I still hadn't washed out of my hair and thinking, not for the first time, what a shame it was that Western women hadn't embraced the burqa. Hood up, head down, I grabbed my bike and cycled the two-minute downhill slide to Kumar's, my corner shop.

There are a good few Indians like Kumar in Dublin now. They arrived a few years ago, opening petrol stations and corner shops. Their heavy singsong tones are now laced with soft consonants and a lilting brogue. Kumar was staring goggle-eyed at *Sky News*, muttering to himself about "this country." He always had a lot to say about "this country." Taxes, crime, poverty—you go in for a Lucozade Sport and you come out with a manifesto.

I was going to get some really bad food—maybe some nachos and a pizza and even some chocolate ice cream—and I wasn't going to feel one bit guilty about it. I got lost in the multicolored aisles, and soon my arms were weighed down with bad food choices.

"Hey, Kate. You are celebrity now, no?" Kumar's thick Indian accent peppered with brogue fell heavily on the floor. The tips of his fingers were gently rubbing an angry-looking cold sore on his bottom lip.

"What?" I tottered up to the cash register and laid out my fat feast in front of Kumar's excited face.

"Yes, look. You are celebrity."

He flicked through the pages of *Heat* magazine and landed on the "Spotted" section, where readers sent in photos or info on mundane celebrity sightings: "Cliff Richard spotted buying three oranges in Marks & Spencer's." And there I was, next to an ad for ringtones. It was a photo of me freewheeling through the streets on my bike, looking like I hadn't a care in the world: "Spiritual guru Kate McDaid spotted cycling through Dublin."

I grabbed the magazine off Kumar and quickly closed it.

"Why you celebrity? You do *Big Brother*?"

"No. It's a mistake."

"No, no mistake. It's you. Look." He grabbed the magazine back from me and thumbed through the pages, only to leave fingerprints all over my face.

"Okay, not a mistake. A misunderstanding. How much?"

"You celebrity." He smiled proudly. "You celebrity in my shop. I put your picture here." He pointed to a spot just over the Marlboro Lights.

"I'd say about twenty euros, would you?"

"No, it's twenty-two fifty-four."

"You did that without a cash register!" I said, more shocked by Kumar's adding-up skills than by seeing my picture in *Heat*.

"Ha, ha. You tell your celebrity friends."

I handed over the money, laughing, and left the shop with my two bags of saturated fats.

My bike was gone. I'd left it resting against the shopwindow. I hadn't locked it because I was only going to be two minutes. I *was* only two minutes.

I raced back inside. "Kumar! My bike's been nicked!"

"From my shop? No, it's impossible." Kumar shook his head in disbelief.

"It's not. It's gone."

"This country."

"Well, yes, this country. But my bike! What'll I do?" Unfamiliar with crime etiquette, I was feeling flustered.

"We'll call the guards. This is a celebrity crime."

The guards are the Irish police. "An Garda Síochána" is their full Irish title, meaning "guardians of the peace."

"Don't mention the celebrity."

"Privacy. I understand." He narrowed his eyes and picked up the phone.

Two cups of tea later a burly guard clutching a notebook in his sausage fingers and wearing a serious face inched into Kumar's shop. His ruddy cheeks, duck-footed gait, and wide-eyed stare betrayed his county of origin, even before he lost his vowels to the back of his throat. He was from Cavan, a landlocked county renowned for its squat natives with tight Achilles tendons and high-color complexions. I tugged on my hood, hoping that every bit of my deeply, deeply conditioned hair was hidden.

"So, you say your bike was stolen?"

"It was stolen."

"Where was the vehicle parked?" He rocked back and forth on his heels.

"Outside." I pointed to the window.

"Locked?" He raised his eyebrow and looked at me from under his guard eyelashes.

"Well, not actually locked . . ."

He snapped his notebook shut. "What did you expect?" he said with a sigh.

I shrugged, defeated.

"She's a celebrity," Kumar piped up, pointing a finger at me accusingly.

"Really?" The Cavan guard's eyes lit up.

"Yes, look." Once again Kumar produced *Heat* magazine and pointed to my photo.

"Hey, you're that New Age witch or something, aren't you?"

"No," I said, tired.

"Yeah, you are. Kate McDaid!"

I closed my eyes. "I am Kate McDaid."

Kumar was jumping up and down with excitement.

"I've heard of you. Yeah, yeah." The guard's cheeks were flushed. He turned to Kumar. "Could you excuse us for a minute? Police business."

Kumar backed away deferentially and busied himself in the frozen foods section.

The Cavan guard leaned into me. I could smell coffee on his breath. "Do you do healing?"

I shook my head and said I didn't do anything. He continued as if he hadn't heard me. "It's just, I have a problem, you know . . . down there." He looked at his crotch and, just in case I hadn't fully understood him, pointed his notebook in the direction of "down there."

"I don't, em . . . No, I don't." I was embarrassed for him.

"I can help you with the bike if you can help me."

"It's your job to help me with the bike."

"Ah, you know what I mean." He looked at me, exasperated. "It might be these new uniforms, they're awful tight, and some funny material—they irritate the area. Even in my normal clothes now . . . I'm hoping it's not permanent."

"Forget the bike." I grabbed my shopping, thanked Kumar, and left.

A Cavan accent called after me as I trudged down the path. "Does this mean I can't be cured? What'll I do?"

I looked back over my shoulder at his worried face.

"Go see a doctor."

"Thank you, thank you. I will. That's exactly what I'll do," came his jubilant response.

I headed for home, his cries of gratitude fading into the background.

12

It was lunchtime on Monday and I felt like a drink—a giant glass of chilled Chardonnay would have gone down a treat. But I wasn't meeting the girls until seven that night, so it was going to be a long afternoon. The third Step was due to be published the next day, and I felt edgy about it. But it was too early in the day, and the week, and not appropriate to drink in the office. So I decided to settle for a cup of coffee instead, and maybe I'd crack into a Starshoot.

Our communal kitchen—one sink, draining board, kettle, mini fridge, microwave, and permanent note from reception about tidying up your *own* mess—was busy with the lunchtime kerfuffle. I hung back until everyone had cleared out, then set to work on the business of making coffee. Then in he came, filling the room, a room which I would have thought clients weren't supposed to enter.

"Kate." He looked shocked to see me.

"Hi, Hugh." We locked eyes before I quickly looked away. "You're in the office a lot these days?"

"I know." He threw his eyes up to heaven. "As if I haven't better things to be doing. Marjorie keeps getting me in to review, review, review. Twice a week it is now."

"I guess they want to make sure they get it right for your first campaign with the agency." I stirred the milk into my coffee. "I'll be out of your way in one second. Is Setanta not with you today?"

"No, my brother's visiting. I thought Setanta could keep him company." He hung his head. "I miss him, though."

I smiled. "He's too big not to miss." I stirred my coffee some more. "Would you like a cup?"

"Oh, no, thanks. I'm a tea man, myself." He grinned. "Coffee's a bit city for me. I'm from the west." As if I wouldn't have guessed by the jumps and lilts of his accent. "I'm all out of sorts in a big city."

I rolled my eyes at him, laughing. "Dublin's hardly a big city."

"It is for me." He scrunched his face up. "I can't stand the cars, or the noise. Can't wait to get back to the wide-open spaces." A dreamy look washed across his face, peaceful, and then he snapped back into action. "Could I ask you something?"

I swallowed hard, nervous. *What could he possibly want to ask me?* I nodded.

"What do you make of these?" Out of the back pocket of his jeans he produced some pages and laid them out on the draining board. He rubbed his fingers over the paper creases, smoothing them out.

I stepped forward, aware that his arm was millimeters away from grazing mine, and focused hard on the pages in front of me, trying to keep my breathing regular and quiet.

Logos, pages of different-colored logos.

"They're for the site. I don't know which one I should pick."

"Do you like any of them?"

"I think they all look the same."

I looked up at him and laughed. "Seriously?" The pages were covered in shapes and colors as different as fire and ice.

"I don't understand this stuff. Colin and Marjorie like this one." He pointed to an orange and blue combination that fuzzed on the outline. "But I don't know." His hands were dirty, and, seeing that I noticed, he self-consciously thrust them into his jeans pockets.

"Well," I said, more serious now, recognizing that he genuinely didn't know what to do. "A logo represents your brand, and what your company is." *Porn, porn, porn* flashed through my head; I shook it. "Your logo will be the most visible part of your organization, more so than a TV ad or a press campaign. The logo is an instant identifier for your customer, so you need to choose something clear and identifiable."

"Right." He nodded, staring at me, interested.

"You've got to be able to reproduce it across all mediums, too, so that's important to bear in mind. It should look good really small or really big."

"Right."

"And the colors will become your brand. They'll be your walls, your floors, your building."

"Right, so which one do you like?"

I hunched over the draining board, studying the pages in front of me. He inched slightly closer to me, breathing, looking, smelling like the sea, his elbows white against the board edge and his whole body angled forward.

I couldn't focus. I shook it off and pointed at a red and black design like a bull's-eye. "This one."

He ran his tongue across his lips and nodded. He wasn't looking at the logo; he was looking at me, expectantly. "That's the one, then."

"No, no. Look, I don't know anything about your business, thank God," I said, snapping back to reality and taking a step back into the kitchen. "Maybe this one is totally inappropriate, not that appropriate really is your business, let's be honest." I was rambling now, nervous words tumbling out of my mouth. I could feel my color rise. I didn't know if it was because we'd just had a normal polite conversation without any disagreements, a conversation that was beginning to feel flirtatious, or if it was the way he was looking at me, but I suddenly felt light-headed and in a spin.

"No, no, this is great. This will work great. Thanks." He took a step closer toward me. I could feel his breath, see his chest rising.

"My work mightn't save the world, but neither does yours, no siree." My voice was high-pitched now. I felt jittery and panicky. "In fact, you might be the ruination of it." I waved my arms around as I twirled toward my coffee cup, which I grabbed and half spilled in one gesture. There I went again, but it was true, and I had to remember whom I was talking to, and, yes, he might have a smile that caused me to wobble, but he represented all things wrong, and anyway, everyone said he was hateful. Why was he being so nice to me now, then? Oh, my head was spinning.

"What?" His arms rose up on either side, looking like he might catch me from falling.

"I should go."

He shook his head, looking puzzled. "Okay."

I ran away from the porn guy, coffee cup in hand, not knowing which one of us was crazier, but knowing that seven o'clock and a glass of white wine couldn't come soon enough.

I met the girls in some Mongolian restaurant in Temple Bar. We wouldn't normally go to Temple Bar, Dublin's cultural quarter. The cobblestones catch in your heels, and it's full of English stag parties over to get drunk, puke, and get laid, in that order. But apparently you could cook your own meat in this restaurant and choose from an all-you-can-eat buffet. I thought it sounded like a lot of work.

Fiona's older and married sister, Anne-Marie, was joining us, which meant one of two things: she'd either bore us to death with how happy and fulfilled her children made her, or drink us to death with how depressed and trapped her children made her. It was a toss-up. When I spotted her tired eyes and pasty skin, more pronounced because her dark hair was pulled back tightly off her face, I knew it was the latter.

The restaurant was really buzzy for a Monday night, with people shouting over each other to be heard and big gangs of friends laughing and shaking off the weekend. It put a spring in my step. I could forget about fairies, witches, porn sites, and handsome rock stars.

Anne-Marie hugged me hard at the table. "I promise I won't talk about the kids, I promise. It's just so good to be out. Do you want a cocktail?"

Everyone was in great form. Lily pulled on her blond curls and reapplied her lipstick. She was beaming.

"Hello? Cat? Cream?" Fiona eyed her suspiciously.

"Ahhh!" Lily gave a short scream. "Guess who asked me out."

"No way." Fiona slapped her hand onto the table. "Mr. Goatee?"

"I baked the cookies, and he ate them."

"Cookies?" Anne-Marie raised her eyebrows.

"Yeah. Kate read an article in a magazine, some old love potion." Lily grinned.

"Really?" Anne-Marie asked. "So what was it?"

Everyone inched in closer to the table to hear Lily's story.

"A love potion. You have to bake a cookie and give it to the man you love or fancy. And last Thursday I decided to go for it, so I googled a cookie recipe. Do you know you need a special tin to cook them in? I went to four different shops. I haven't baked since home economics classes at school. I still had the instruction booklet for my oven *in* my oven."

"I wouldn't have a clue how to work my oven, either." Fiona shook her head.

"Really? But you do all those multimillion-dollar deals?" Lily asked.

"Them I can do. An oven, not a clue."

"Well, one day when you're an old married woman like me . . ." Anne-Marie smiled at her.

"Never going to happen, Anne-Marie. My oven is going to remain unused. Anyway, Lily, domestic goddess, tell us what happened."

"So I started baking with all the stuff you'd said, Kate, the vanilla and rose petals. I quite enjoyed it, actually. I started laying all the mixture out, and then there was the one that I had to make into the shape of my face. I didn't really know how to do that but I used some raisins for eyes, rose petals for lips and oatmeal as hair. I was feeling very inventive and creative."

"Very 'Mary Make and Do.' What's with the face, though?"

"All part of this love potion. I did feel a bit strange doing it, but I do really like Mr. Goatee." Lily smiled, embarrassed, but we all nodded it away, aware of the lengths we'd all gone to for men we really liked.

"At work at eleven, I sent an e-mail around the department saying there were freshly baked cookies in the kitchen. Everyone made a scramble for them, as they always do, including Mr. Goatee. I hung on to my face one and then pretty much cornered him between the kettle and the microwave. When I think about it, I was really quite pushy." She bit her lip remembering. "I held it up in front of him and said, 'Here, take this one.' I think he was surprised. He didn't say anything, but he had an expression on his face that wasn't great, kind of 'You're a crazy, weirdo baker lady.' But then he bit into it, and I said it." She took a deep breath. "I said: 'You love it, don't you?' and his face . . ." She beamed. "It softened around the edges and he locked eyes with me. It was a nanosecond but it was all there. And about an hour later, he marched up to me and asked me out to dinner on Tuesday."

"That's so exciting! I knew he'd ask you. He just had to see you." I smiled.

Anne-Marie clapped her hands together, delighted. "I love all this magic!"

"I know," Lily said. "And the best thing is, when he asked me out he had that puppy-dog face, you know the one guys get when they like you, when their eyes go really big and their mouth kind of hangs open? He had that."

"That's not the look of like. That, Lily, is the look of love," Anne-Marie said.

"Thank God you read that magazine article," Lily told me. "You can be a bridesmaid at our wedding."

We all smiled, excited about Lily's romance, and filled up our wineglasses to toast it. Then I turned to Fiona. "And what's going on with you, my lovely?"

"Work dramas," she said. "Don't want to talk about it anymore. It's my free time. They will not get into my free time."

We nodded in agreement, knowing we would probably get around to talking about it after a few drinks, but we'd let her ignore it for now.

Fiona eyed me. "You look great," she said.

I smiled. I'd dipped into the remainder of my pay packet and bought myself a Karen Millen dress as a little pick-me-up. It was yellow silk, and it felt feminine and dressy.

The wine was flowing and soon we'd discussed the looming economic crisis, which we all agreed we were bored to death of; a new yoga teacher on Harcourt Street, who was said to be revolutionary; and Fiona's work (I knew she'd crack). Apparently she was to be brought in front of the board to defend her error. She didn't have a defense. She knew she'd messed up. She could only hope that her flawless track record would be taken into account. She was very angry about the injustice of it all.

We were all a bit tongue-tied. Fiona had poured her life into her career, and the possibility of it being snatched away was unthinkable. We talked it through as best and supportively as we could, but without much solid advice.

Eventually, the conversation slipped back to idle gossip about mutual friends who were buying houses out in the country, much to our absolute bewilderment as city girls. And I thought about Hugh Delaney and how a peaceful look had washed over his handsome face as he talked about the countryside.

"Why would you do it? There's no cinema, no restaurants, and you have to drive for hours to get to an airport to get out of this country." Lily shook her head in dismay.

"And there's the muck . . ."

"And there's the locals. They'd all be in your business. Small-minded and superstitious."

Anne-Marie nearly spat out her drink. "Superstitious. God, I haven't asked you! What's this about the fairies and witches?"

Lily and Fiona threw each other a glance, a brief moment that I caught. I looked at them, confused. I knew them so well that I could see immediately they'd been talking about me, about the fairies and witches.

"What?" I ignored Anne-Marie's question, and directed mine at the glance between them.

Fiona looked uncomfortable. "We, em . . . We just . . . we think there might be something in them."

"What?" I was shocked.

"You. We think there might be something in this for you." Lily stared at me, nodding her head. I realized that this was a rehearsed speech.

"Is this an intervention?" I laughed.

"No." Fiona looked serious. "But the fairies, they were real. My aunty used to wash the steps of her house down so the fairies had somewhere to sit when they were passing through."

"Oh, come on," I said, exasperated. "Is this like Bono? The way everyone in Dublin has a Bono story—went drinking with him, danced with him, mother embarrassed him. Does everyone have a fairy story now? We never talked about fairies before, ever, and now all of a sudden they're everywhere."

"Well, a lot of people do believe in them," Lily said, sagely.

"I'm not saying I don't believe in them or, rather, in the possibility of them—I can't make up my mind. I mean, one part of me thinks there's always a possibility of there being something else out there: ghosts and spiritual connections and maybe even fairies, I don't know. But then, another part—the part of me that throws away books like *The Alchemist* halfway through—can never believe in palm reading or tea leaves. That part of me thinks that this is a load of nonsense. Honestly."

Lily shook her head at me disapprovingly. "That doesn't sound very open-minded."

"Look, the truth is, this ancestor was probably completely nuts and wrote these Steps herself. It's interesting in terms of exploring my family history, but the other stuff is probably just folklore."

I tucked into my steak, shaking the conversation off as best I could.

Lily and Fiona looked at each other again.

"What? Come on, out with it."

Fiona cleared her throat. "Well, ultimately, this letter and these Steps are pointing to you. Potentially, you might have some kind of insight or something."

"What a joke, right?"

"Well, not really, no." Fiona shrugged her shoulders.

I put my knife and fork down, getting ready for my next speech.

"Sometimes you know things, things we don't know, we couldn't know," Fiona said.

"What? What are you talking about? I don't know anything. I've never known things. Oh my God, are you saying what I think you're saying?"

"No. I don't think so. No." Fiona was going bright red, struggling to get the words out.

Lily took over. "You asked me if my uncle was sick the day before he was diagnosed with cancer . . ."

"That's because I was watching a film and the guy in it looked like your uncle and he was sick. It was just a scattered thought."

"Sometimes you finish my sentences," Fiona said.

"I've known you for nearly ten years. Lily does the same."

"No, you do it more."

I sighed. This was ridiculous.

"At my movie night last month you knew I was going to show *Point Break*."

"Fiona, if you'd ever get over your obsession with Patrick

Swayze's back we'd watch something other than *Point Break* or *Dirty Dancing* at your movie nights. It was a pretty safe guess."

"What if this is a thing? You can't ignore it," Fiona pleaded.

I exhaled heavily, thinking how I wished I could have a cigarette, even though I smoked only on rare occasions. This felt like an opportune time to wave a cigarette around. "Okay. Let's say I have a gift. That somehow I am some type of clairvoyant or fairy whisperer—whatever. Wouldn't I know? Surely I would know. That's what being a psychic is—you know things. And I don't. And let's say I have a gift. Why would I be a junior copywriter five years on? Surely I'd have the intuition or whatever to have nailed every campaign that came my way? And surely I'd have more money than I have and fewer credit cards, and I'd have a nicer wardrobe. And I'd know who stole my bike. And, and, and . . ." I was swirling my glass of wine around. "I'd be dating hot Hollywood stars."

"The hottest," the table echoed in unison.

I finished off my glass. Speech over. "I don't know anything. Don't look for something that isn't there."

We fell into an uncomfortable silence.

"Yeah, I suppose," Fiona said reluctantly. She smiled. "But, for the record, you do have a nice wardrobe."

We laughed. The moment had passed, but I felt uneasy. If my best friends were asking these kinds of questions, what else was out there? Was this what people were thinking? Should I be thinking this? Was there something there?

"Oh, you don't know how lucky you are," Anne-Marie piped up. "Worrying about being a witch and about your wardrobe. My one-year-old has cried nonstop for twenty-four days. He can't stop crying. And now I'm going to start crying because I'm exhausted. I haven't slept; he hasn't slept. I've done everything. I've brought him to the doctor; I've bought every rocking machine you can think of. Short of drugging him, I don't know what to do." She threw her hands over her face and heavily rested her elbows on the table.

Fiona slowly moved the bottle of wine away from her and we all nodded sympathetically as a few small sobs escaped.

"Did you put a bit of whiskey in his bottle?" Lily offered, followed by an explanation. "Mam said it worked a treat for us."

The sobbing mother nodded. "Tried it. It gave him the hiccups. He just cried more."

"What about baby yoga? I've heard that's a great relaxer," Lily said earnestly.

"Tried it. Yoga, Pilates, massage, swimming classes."

"TV?" Fiona piped up.

"His best friend is Thomas the Tank Engine. I've tried."

We all studied the table, clueless in the ways of motherhood.

I moved some steak around my plate and sighed. *What can Anne-Marie do to get her baby to sleep through the night?* And then it came to me, a eureka moment. I sat up tall and smiled from ear to ear. "I've got it. Problem solved. Did you ever get some fresh lavender and rub it on his sheets, and then take a spoonful of chamomile and sugar, and put it in some warm milk, and then let a few feathers, preferably white ones, hang over his bed to catch the bad dreams? And air out his pajamas in a southwesterly gale. That'll work. He'll sleep divinely for you."

The table got whiplash as all heads spun toward me in a perfect silence. I continued to tuck into my steak.

"Excuse me? Lavender? Southwesterly gale? Feathers?" Lily spat the words at me.

I shrugged. "Yeah," I said with my mouth half full. "I think Mam told me about it. That stuff really works. He'll be grand." I quickly buried my head in my glass, realizing what I'd just said. Feathers? Southwesterly gale? These words just flew out of me. Where were they coming from? How did I know these things? Even I had to admit I sounded crazy and not just a little bit witchy.

"It's probably the milk and sugar that does it. I think Mam threw the other things in for good measure." I tried to sound nonchalant and not mildly freaked out.

"Are you sure you didn't read it in a magazine article, next to a love spell?" Lily looked nervous and anxiously clawed at her neck.

"No. I'm pretty sure it was Mam."

I hung my head. How did I know these things? What was going on? And what else did I know? I'd have to watch what I said from here on in.

13

Step Three

We are the laughter left in rooms,
the echoes of your sound,
We are a web of drifting mist
that works its way around,
We are the flowers' mingled scents
and wind beneath birds' wings.
We are all that is light and floating
with the calm air as she sings.

Yours is a borrowed world,
an island in our own,
We pull the strings that make you rise
and point you the way home,
We send you thoughts throughout the day,
instinct that guides all that you shall do,
We whisper ideas into your head,
and watch them work on you.

Listen for your fairy name,
you have known it all along,
We know your true path from birth,
and have battled to sing your song,
Do our wishes and take heed, if not,
your money's lost and your houses they fall,
Remember her red-golden sunset
costs nothing at all.

Her green hills are endless with rainbows that bend,
Tears of joy you should shed for the beauty she lends.

Third week, third Step and, if I'm honest, I found this one creepy. Let's say I had bought into everything up to this point. I really didn't mind greeting nature, sitting on rocks, asking for my heart's desire. But this Step felt like a shift. The poor old Red Hag must have been really losing her marbles when, pretending to be the fairies, she wrote this one. The implication was that, somehow, fairies were pulling the strings in our lives. That we were merely playing out a game they were controlling. That the ideas in our heads were theirs, that they nudged our instincts. (I wished they'd nudged mine better when I went to Kevin McLear's birthday party the previous December and wore a pink off-the-shoulder dress that clashed with my purple eye shadow and green shoes. The pictures still haunted me on Facebook.) That they had a plan mapped out for our lives to be a part of nature, to benefit us, them and the earth.

My office phone rang, distracting me from staring at the third Step on my computer screen. Mam. "Darling, you're not going to believe it. This fairy name thing, I swear you had one when you were a little girl."

"Mam, are you looking at the Internet? That went up only two seconds ago! Anyway, it's Tuesday afternoon. Don't you have yoga?"

"I skipped it today. Your father and I need to be constantly updated, in case the media hit us up for another interview."

"Of course."

"But Kate, you did have a fairy name. Well, I didn't think it was a fairy name back then, but you said that your imaginary friend, the one you had when you were around five or six, whose name I can't remember, had given you a name. Do you remember it? I can't remember for the life of me what it was. But you asked us to call you it."

"No, Mam, I don't even remember having an imaginary friend."

"You did, for a long time. Hang on, I'll ask your father." I heard her shouting into the kitchen.

"Princess Fi Fi or Frou Frou. Your dad says it was definitely princess something or other. Does it ring a bell?"

"No."

"Well, think about it, you never know. I swear, the more I read these Steps, the more I'm enjoying it. I'm going out to the back garden now to ask the fairies what my name is. I hope it's something exotic. Will you come around for dinner tonight?"

"Great. Love to. Talk to you later." I hung up.

A fairy name? I'd had a fairy name? Of course I hadn't! My parents were just excitable. And while an imaginary friend did seem the type of thing an only child would conjure up, I had no recollection of having had one.

"Smutty Farlane is my porn name. I wonder what my fairy name is?" Matthew was wearing a zipped-up navy Adidas tracksuit. It wasn't like him to be so casually dressed at work, and I could see his briefcase peeping out from behind his desk. *Unusual fashion statement*, I thought. Chewing on a Starshoot, he walked over to me with a big smile on his face. He stopped to pat Setanta, who was eagerly sniffing the ground for some Starshoot crumbs.

"Don't let him eat chocolate," I said firmly to Matthew.

"I know, I know. He's watching his figure."

And I don't want his infuriating owner giving out to me, I thought, wondering where Hugh was and why I hadn't seen him around for a while.

Online, comments were slowly trickling in about the third Step. Matthew and I watched as bloggers' names that were now very familiar to me popped up each time I hit the refresh button.

> GR8tim: I've always felt a connection to the name fiachra—I
>   wonder if that's my fairy name
> Seocha: listen quietly and they'll tell you
> DDdddrink: I knew I should always listen to my instinct
> Banananas: that's your gut talking

Matthew sighed. "These people are so strange."

"What I don't understand is how they don't question this. Why aren't they on there saying it's a load of crap?"

"Because they're weirdos," Matthew said, looking at the screen in confusion as more and more posts filled the page. He took another bite of his Starshoot and chuckled to himself. "You know that baby thing, or birth, there?" He pointed at the line *We know your true path from birth* on the screen. "I remember hearing something about that. That when a baby is born there's a race between fairies as to who gets to be the baby's guardian." He exploded laughing. "You should see your face! You think I'm one of those weirdos. I'm not. I'm just telling you that I remember hearing something about it. Google it."

"I can't be bothered." Bored, I clicked into my e-mail.

To: Kate@FandP.com
From: Jim@RedHorizon.ie
Subject: Music
Kate
What do you think of our new song?
Click here to hear it.
I'll give you a shout this afternoon.

J

I clicked through the link, halfheartedly put in my earphones, and pressed Play. Deep beats trembled, and Jim's voice echoed softly around strumming guitar. The song had a haunting melody, and Jim's voice rose and fell. "I knew when I read the letter, and learned the Seven Steps," he sang.

I hid a smile behind my hand. What was he playing at?

"What's up?" Matthew budged down to my level. I removed my earphones and handed them to him. He put them in his ears and listened. His eyes widened and the smile slipped from his face.

He popped the earphones out. "I don't know, Kate. What's he up to?"

"What do you mean? It's funny. It's sweet, and it's a good song." I hoped I sounded annoyed because I felt annoyed. What did Matthew mean by "What's he up to"? I angrily strummed the tops of my fingers on my keyboard. *Click, click.*

"Okay," Matthew said carefully. He opened his mouth to say something else but then changed his mind. Pulling over a chair, he sat in beside me. I was still tapping on my keyboard, breathing sharply.

"I know what he's like, Kate," he said softly into his chest.

"What's that supposed to mean?" I spat the words out.

"Nothing." He stared ahead of him. "The music, that's his life. He'll do anything for it."

"Hmmphh."

We sat in silence. Well, he sat in silence. I sat in a huff. Matthew was raining all over my parade. It was bad form. Of all people, he should understand. He should be happy for me. I had a gorgeous rock star looking for my attention. This kind of thing never happened to me.

"Hmmmphhhh." I pursed my mouth and glared at Matthew.

Colin wobbled past and gave us both two thumbs-up. "Any word on our *Baywatch* friend?" he shouted.

"Getting right on it," Matthew shouted back before dropping the remainder of the Starshoot into his mouth. "Do you want to get back to it?"

I nodded reluctantly, and we slipped into the black hole of work. David Hasselhoff was proving difficult to pin down. For me, celebrities lived in magazines or on *Entertainment Tonight*. If they were real people, which I doubted, they were the closest things to fairy-tale characters we'd ever know. If David Hasselhoff did exist and wasn't just a computer-generated lifeguard, then surely he was like Rapunzel, imprisoned in a high tower away from mere greasy-fingered mortals, people who might cast a shadow across his blue eyes. Cushioned on mountains of gold, massaging his chest hair, the Hoff could not possibly be contactable.

Which he wasn't. I'd already tried several times. Now I tried again, and started calling some new numbers I'd got off the Internet, numbers in L.A. Even saying "L.A." gave me goose bumps. It made me feel like I was closer to *them*, the Hans Christian Andersen creations.

"No, but thanks for calling," the receptionists would twang down the line from sunny L.A.

"Could you give me a contact number for his people?" When talking to foreigners, I always felt like my accent was overpronounced, that I sounded like an Irish cliché with a bowl of potatoes and a pint of Guinness in front of me. In fact, that day, I was looking very city chic and sophisticated, more like espresso coffee and paninis, I felt. I was wearing a flowery skirt (since my bike had been nicked I was wearing a lot of skirts) and a nice black wraparound top. I was looking officey, not *Riverdance*-y, but my speech was a lilt of slurring *t*'s and colloquialisms like "sure, not to worry," "that'll be grand," and "hope the day is good for you."

Twenty-two calls in, I could feel a "top of the morning" about to slip out of me. Then I hit the jackpot—an intern receptionist. She sounded so young—I could hear her braces cluttering her mouth in her speech. "Uh, who? Mr. Hasselhoff? Oh, that guy . . . Uh, sure, I have his number, I think."

I nearly felt bad, nearly. I was sure she wasn't allowed to just give out numbers. Accepting it would be unethical . . . and then I wondered who else she might have. Would it be really wrong of me to ask for Brad?

Turns out what she gave me wasn't the Hoff's number after all, it was his PA's, PA's, PA's PA or something—she was so far removed from him I wondered if she'd ever even seen a red swimsuit.

"So it's for a chocolate bar?" It was the first time ever, I presumed, that the PA had gotten her mouth around the word *chocolate*.

I gave her the pitch, trying to sound as enthusiastic as possible.

"Are you Irish? Oh, David loves the Irish. But he prefers, like, the Germans, uh-huh?"

"That's great. Do you think he might be interested?"

"No."

"Not at all? Are you sure?"

"Uh-huh."

"Really?"

"Yah. David is clean-living. He doesn't eat refined sugars so, like, he won't be interested in this."

"Could I send on details of the script and the shoot anyway?" I pleaded.

"Sure. But it probably won't get in front of him."

"Please."

"Uh-huh."

I e-mailed it through, pinging it into cyberspace with my fingers crossed and making a silent wish. At least it had left my desk. At least now it was sitting in the recycle bin of somebody else's desktop.

There was an atmosphere in the office that day. It felt like we were about to pitch for something big; there was a rumble, an energy, that something was about to happen. People were fidgety, and I couldn't help thinking that it had something to do with me. Had everyone seen *Heat* magazine? Was it common knowledge that I was in supposed cahoots with the fairies? Were there fairy and folklore stories on the tips of everyone's tongues here, too? Or was I just paranoid?

I happened to walk past the Glorious MD, All Must Bow at His Feet, as he was posturing outside his office. His PA, who seemed to be permanently affixed to his ear, looked at me and then whispered to him. And, for the first time in five and a half years, he threw a chin nod, the equivalent of a papal blessing, toward me.

I didn't respond. I positioned my own chin even farther into my chest and scurried on. As I passed by my work colleagues, I saw the neon glare from spacemonkeys.com flickering on computer screens. I didn't have the courage to look up to see who was reading what, and who might be looking at me strangely come the next day.

When five o'clock came around, I was just happy the workday was over. I put on my coat, slung my handbag over my shoulder, and sidled up to Matthew. "I'm going to head out. Going for dinner at my parents' house." I started to walk away and then quickly turned back. "Is it just me?"

"Hmm?" Matthew looked up from his desk. He looked half asleep, and his green eyes were misting over.

"I just feel like everyone's looking at me. Are they? Or am I just paranoid?"

"I haven't really noticed. They could be, I guess."

"I knew it." I tightly clutched the strap on my handbag. "They are. The Glorious MD gave me a chin nod."

He grinned. "You're in, so."

"This could go weird."

"Relax. Maybe they've heard about the Hoff, and they think you're cool now or something. Or maybe they dig fairies. So what if they're looking at you? Suck it up."

He rummaged around the masses of paper on his desk, doodled something on a sticker, and stuck it on a Starshoot bar. "Here. For the bus trip."

I shoved it in my pocket.

Later, while sandwiched between a group of schoolgirls playing Ne-Yo on their mobile phones and screaming at the top of their lungs on the top deck of a yellow number-8 bus to Sandymount, I felt peckish and whipped out the Starshoot. "SMILE," Matthew had written on the sticker next to a picture of a smiley face. Maybe Matthew was right. Maybe I did need just to suck it up. I could never stay mad at him for long—he always did make me smile.

I was looking forward to Mam's cooking, but I also wanted to ask Dad a few questions. Something had been jarring with me about Maura Ni Ghaora. Who was she? Why was she so determined to stay close to me? What did she have to gain? I was suspicious about her background, too, especially since she'd mentioned Liam McCarthy and Brick. I knew Dad was interested in that era—and I thought he might know more about them than I did.

Just as I got to my parents' front door, my phone rang. Jim.

I took a moment to steady myself before I answered. "Jim. Hi." I sounded wobbly.

"Kate, yeah. All good?"

It is now, I thought. "Yes, grand. You?"

"Look, there's a launch for our new song on Thursday night. No biggie, quiet enough. Can you come?"

"Eh . . .'"

"With me, like, my, you know . . ."

Date? Was he really asking me this time? "Yes. Sounds great. I'm in."

"Cool. I'll send you on the details. Good chat."

And he was gone. I was wide-eyed and startled when Mam swung open the door.

She'd cooked lasagna. Dad was grumbling because he wanted potatoes with it. She was refusing.

I kicked off my shoes and collapsed onto the couch, feeling giddy and expectant after Jim's call. I flicked through the newspaper, half expecting to see something written about me. There wasn't anything.

"Are you looking for your picture?" Dad winked at me. He was sitting in his spot, a battered armchair molded to his shape.

"No," I lied, wondering why I was a bit disappointed that I

hadn't seen my photo in there. What was happening? Was I beginning to enjoy this stuff?

"No mention of the Red Hag today. We've already been through it."

"Maybe that's the end of it."

"Maybe." He nodded. "I'd be sorry if it was."

"Really?"

"I would, yeah. It was a great laugh being on the telly. All the lights. The paycheck didn't hurt, either. Some of these media people have more money than sense. Everyone saw us. The phone hasn't stopped ringing with relations from Kerry and Donegal pretending they want our autographs now."

We both laughed at that. The Irish attitude to fame—drag you down before you get too big for your boots.

"They must be calling you, the media people?" Dad said. "Why don't you do something? I bet there's money to be made in some of this for you, too. Your mother and I are taking what we can."

I bet there is, too, I thought. "I don't know, Dad. Then what happens? Do I become like one of those people who do reality TV and for the rest of their lives when they walk into a pub other people think they know them from somewhere? Only for me they'll realize they know me from the fairies, and they might think I'm a witch, because who knows what would stick? And I'll never get a date, and it's hard enough being single here, anyway. I don't know."

"Maybe you're thinking about this too much. You've always been an overthinker."

"Thanks for the diagnosis." I changed the subject. "Dad, Liam McCarthy: what do you know about him?"

Dad nestled even farther back into his armchair and gave me the rundown on Liam and Brick. Apparently Liam had died, decrepit and bankrupt, back in the early eighties, aged in his early eighties. Brick had been about ten years younger, Dad thought. He'd disappeared around the early eighties, too. Liam was a criminal, but he never served time in prison, in spite of many investigations. Brick was a psychopathic killer who had masterminded kidnappings and murders and tortured gang members— terrible crimes often in the name of a confused justice, gang against gang, drug lord against drug lord, with Liam and Brick winning every time. Dad reckoned that Brick had had an undercover army that carried out his every request. They were always one step ahead of the law, and, together, they'd dominated the headlines and terrified regular Irish people for years.

"Liam was a *me feiner*," Dad said, crossing his legs. *Me feiner* is an Irish insult meaning "self-server," someone interested only in his own gain. "He pretended to be a politician, 'of the people by the people,' but he was only out for himself. Like a lot of them, I suppose. But he was different—he was a dangerous fella. All smiles and then he'd throw a dagger in your back."

"You mean all that stuff with Brick?"

"Now he *was* dangerous. How they didn't catch that bastard. Should have locked him up and thrown away the key."

"He must be dead by now, though."

"Ah, he'd have to be. He just disappeared into thin air, though, when Liam McCarthy died. He was at the funeral, or the wake, and then that was it. Gone."

"How come the police never got him?"

"It's hard to tell. There were a lot of rumors that Liam McCarthy was paying them off, and then when he got into power, he managed to publicly distance himself from Brick, but privately they were still in cahoots. Another corrupt politician, hey?" He laughed to himself. "They're all at it."

Dad hauled himself out of his chair. "I've got a book about

Liam somewhere. But where . . . ?" He began to riffle through the bookshelves behind him.

I wondered how and why Maura had known them. I supposed she could have come across them in her job as a journalist, but the timing was curious, I thought, because if Maura was Liam and Brick's peer, she was a lot older than I'd ever guessed. *A lot.*

"Here it is!" Dad shouted, like he'd found gold. He pulled the book off the shelf and handed it to me proudly.

I flicked through the pages to the pictures in the center of the book. Liam McCarthy had been a tall, handsome man in his day, but became white-haired and bent over as the years passed.

"Can I borrow this book, Dad?"

Dad nodded. "He was a bit of a ladies' man. Never married, which was unusual for a politician, not even to pretend to have a normal family life."

I wondered whether *that* was the connection with Maura. She could have been a girlfriend of Liam's.

"There were always rumors about him around religion, too. He'd be photographed going to mass and all that, but some said he was in a group that was into all that dark arts stuff—sacrificing animals and praying to the devil, that kind of crap."

"Really?"

"Rumors. You know, he wasn't a popular man. I suppose they'd start rumors about anyone. But there was a club in Dublin—the Hellfire Club. People said he was a member of that." Dad drained his glass and looked sadly at it.

"What was the Hellfire Club?"

"The Hellfire Club was an old ruin of a house on top of a hill in Dublin. The story goes that it had been built on a cairn, an ancient passage grave, in the 1700s, and that it was haunted. It had been burned down several times, and adopted by satanic cult groups over the years for devil worship. It was full of old rumors and scary stories."

A shout came from the kitchen. "Do you want to eat out there or in here?"

"I'll eat anywhere so long as there's potatoes."

"You'll go hungry, so."

"It's fine, Mam. We'll come into the kitchen. Come on, Dad." I put the book in my bag, then grabbed Dad's arm and heaved him out of his chair.

In the kitchen, Mam was on the phone, bent over, listening intently. Her cheeks were brimming with air and conversation was moments from erupting.

"Uh-huh, uh-huh."

We sat at the table, watching her attempt to rein in her excitement.

"Yes, yes. Well, she's here now. Uh-uh. I'll ask her." She straightened up, and the veins in her neck jumped out. "Kate. Is your phone off?" She started pointing to her own phone. "The producer of *The Nightline* wants to talk to you."

"*The Nightline?*" I said in disbelief. "Prime-time TV. Seriously?" *The Nightline* is *the* Irish television show. It's current affairs, it's entertainment, it's the cornerstone of Irish cultural life and has been for the last thirty years.

Mam thrust the phone into my hand.

"Hello."

"Kate, wonderful to speak with you. Anna Clarke, head producer on *The Nightline*." The voice was plummy. "How's your diary, Kate? We want you to come onto the show to talk about fairies." I wasn't being asked, I was being summoned.

"I don't know. I'm not really sure." A million thoughts raced through my mind, but I stopped at one that I couldn't answer:

Why would I do this? It might be fun for two minutes, but there's the rest of my life to think about. "No. I don't think it's for me. Thanks for asking, though."

Mam's face dropped. She shook her head at Dad, who was rolling his eyes to heaven and mouthing the words "Do it."

"Anna, does it have to be me? My parents are as much involved in this as me, and you know they already have media experience."

"Yes, we have seen them. But we'd prefer you. After all, you're the redhead everyone is talking about."

"Well, I really don't want to go on TV, but they will. And they're in the same gene line—Kate McDaid was related to my dad, too." I paused, waiting for her to respond.

"You're definitely not interested?"

"Definitely not."

Another pause. "Put me back on with your mother."

I gave Dad the two thumbs-up. His smile was so wide it almost wrapped around his face.

Five minutes later, Mam hung up. She let out a little scream. "They want us. Well, really, they'd like you, but they're going to take us. *The Nightline.* Can you believe it? There's a wardrobe to choose from; they're putting us up in a hotel. A hotel! Your father and I haven't stayed in a hotel since Ruth Murphy's wedding. It's so exciting."

"It is, Mam, it's great. But just maybe be prepared that it could all fall a bit flat. I mean, it's prime time. The viewers may not be interested in fairies and witches." I hated being the voice of reason, but someone had to warn them.

"She didn't think so. She thinks this has global appeal. Global. She mentioned that guy who died—what's his name? The singer who wore makeup, all black? A lot of loud guitar sounds? Drake someone or other."

"Drake Chandler, Mam." I felt like a teenager with an uncool mother.

"They think the old crazy witch predicted his death . . ."

The two of them were whooping and dancing around the kitchen, laughing and swinging.

"We'll never have this chance again!" Dad spun Mam around to some imaginary music in their heads.

"And you know what?" Mam's voice was soothing. "If the Seven Steps fall flat, they fall flat. At least we'll get to stay in a hotel."

Suddenly I felt worried. I wasn't worried about the Seven Steps falling flat. I was worried about them taking off.

14

Three nights later, Mam looked nervous under the glare of the TV lights. There was a slight downturn at the side of her mouth that gave it away. That, and the fact that she introduced herself to *The Nightline* host Patrick Molloy by saying: "I'm a bit nervous, Patrick." She pulled uneasily on her jacket, a tight-fitting orange bolero whose color matched her eye shadow. There were smiles all around. Dad casually placed his arm across the back of the lemon sofa, ready to take whatever they threw at him. He was a seasoned professional—no bright lights or TV cameras could distract him.

A few miles away I was standing in my sitting room, full makeup on and hair blow-dried to within an inch of its life. My date with Jim was later that evening, and I was too uneasy to sit down in case I accidently pressed my hair to the back of the couch and ruined it. I was jittery with nerves about the date, and watching my parents on TV triggered joy and dread in equal measures.

Patrick Molloy faced the camera as it zoomed in, a serious look on his face. I noticed immediately that he had a cold sore, a scab protruding from his bottom lip that no studio makeup could hide. He looked uninterested and slightly bored. "Admittedly, the mystic world has never really interested me much, but one of our researchers here recently discovered what she feels is a mystical phenomenon: the Seven Steps. Many of you may already be familiar with the Seven Steps, following the recent tragic death of rock star Drake Chandler, the lead singer of American band Burning Cradle." Patrick hung his head low. "Part of the mystery surrounding Drake Chandler's death is that it seems to have been predicted by these Seven Steps, which were written some 130 years ago but have only recently come to light.

"To date, three Steps have been revealed. Here to tell us more about the Seven Steps are Noel McDaid and his wife, Teresa, the descendants of the self-proclaimed witch Kate McDaid, who died back in 1870."

Patrick Molloy slowly walked toward an armchair and folded his long limbs into it.

"Thanks, Patrick," Dad piped up, sitting forward on the sofa. "I'd just like to say that we're no experts in witchcraft or fairies. In fact, we only learned about Kate McDaid—well, the other Kate McDaid—a month ago."

"Of course, your daughter, Kate, actually inherited these Steps, and is thought to have some mystic powers herself. To have been fairy-struck." There was that word again. Mam raised her eyebrows and inched toward Dad on the couch. I inched uneasily backward in my sitting room, away from the television set, wishing and willing Dad to cut this conversation short and not bring me up again.

"That's right, Patrick. She's a very special girl."

That's enough to have me burned at the stake, I thought. *Well done, Dad.*

"To be fair, this is all new for Kate, too." Mam's voice was shaking slightly. "But if I could go back to the Steps, I think that they're causing a stir, and people are interested in them because of their simplicity, the pureness of their message."

"What do you think might be the repercussions of not fulfilling these Steps?" Patrick Molloy butted in.

"We don't know yet. But I recommend that everyone, or rather anyone with a drop of Celtic blood in them, does as is requested. We know from history that fairies can turn when provoked." Dad turned to Mam and deadpanned: "Isn't that right, Petaled Lightfoot?"

"It is, Tickled Warrior," Mam responded, blushing. She looked across at Patrick. "We've adopted our fairy names, as requested in the most recent Step."

Patrick nodded, but a flicker in his eyes betrayed his skepticism. *He thinks they're mad*, I thought.

"And these fairy names? How exactly did they come to you?"

"The back garden gave them to us."

"The back garden?" Patrick raised an eyebrow.

"Yes. We did as we were told." Dad smiled. "We have a beautiful garden, so we went out there, surrounded ourselves with nature, breathed it in, and asked the fairies to whisper our names. And they did."

"Just like that!" Patrick sneered.

"Just like that." Mam and Dad grinned back. I had to laugh. Their enthusiasm for the Seven Steps was infectious. And I believed them. I bet they did go out to the back garden, and, as well, I bet they took photographs of it that they might try to sell. They were getting very good at spotting opportunities.

Patrick sighed and shook his head. "In terms of repercussions, this storm that's threatened in the most recent Step, this battle for the home—I've heard that it could be interpreted as the current economic crisis. What are your thoughts on that?"

"It could be, yes," Mam piped up. "But it also could be a literal storm. Last week, in the southwest of Ireland, there was a terrible storm. Floods and gale-force winds caused electricity blackouts and ruined a few homes when the River Shannon burst its banks."

"Do you think that could be the wrath of the fairies? That they feel not enough people are recognizing their existence?" Patrick couldn't hide a smirk.

"Yes, I do," Dad responded, deadpan. "More people need to do what the fairies ask. There are actual physical repercussions for not taking part." He turned to face the cameras directly and stared down the lens. "It's only a few minutes out of your day. Talk to nature, ask for your fairy name, be grateful, and you'll see—good things will happen to you." He smiled a warm, friendly smile.

And I couldn't help myself—I was grinning back at the screen. I wondered how my life had gotten to that point. That, on a drizzly summer's evening, I was hovering in my sitting room with a cold cup of tea in my hand, watching my parents on *The Nightline* talk about fairies.

Patrick then introduced a fairy expert via satellite from Middle Earth. Thomas Cox looked like a stretched leprechaun, with a dark, matted beard, crooked teeth, and giant googly eyes. I guessed they'd found him in a joke shop or a Kinder Surprise egg.

Thomas was very excited about the Seven Steps. "We have to accept this for what it is: a message from the good people one hundred and thirty years ago asking and allowing us to interact once more." He took in short, sharp breaths, trying to control his excitement. "This is monumental in our research. We've always known that the west of Ireland is rich in mystic ways and fairy folk."

"Can people really believe in fairies and witches?" Patrick quizzed him.

Thomas Cox rubbed his beard, pensively. "It's a well-known fact that the Irish have a long tradition of spirituality and mysticism. And, unlike any other culture, there are actual firsthand accounts of experiences with the good people—the fairies. It's not just folklore." He wagged a finger. "We have firsthand accounts from people living today who say they danced with the fairies or their grandfather was cured by a white witch."

"So, what's the history of Irish fairies?" Patrick asked, struggling for facts.

"Well, the ancient Irish peasants often considered them to be fallen angels. That in the great war between God and Lucifer they were indecisive, and fell neither on the good nor the bad side, so it was agreed they could inhabit the earth forever, as gods of the earth. Yes, yes, gods of the earth. They were originally known as the Tuatha Dé Danann, fairy people who ruled Ireland in 1700 BC." He paused for dramatic effect. "Through the years, many poets and mystics have felt that, behind the visible and what we know, there are chains upon chains of conscious beings who are not of heaven but of the earth. That this visible world is merely their skin."

The camera flicked back to Mam and Dad, who were nodding furiously in agreement with leprechaun man. Had they known this stuff? Or had they decided it looked good to go along with this deranged man, who looked like a fairy himself?

"So if fairies are immortal, which we have been led to believe, the fairies that are trying to communicate with us now are the original Tuatha Dé Danann?" Patrick asked.

"Yes, and their base, if you'd like to call it that, is Tír na nÓg, the land of eternal youth. This is the true fairy realm, where they never grow old, never die, never want. Where they only pursue pleasure in whatever form they choose."

"Sounds nice."

"Well, unfortunately, it's very difficult for us mere mortals to enter. You need an invitation from a fairy, and to get that you need to have done them a good turn. Some mortals have entered, but it's not easy. There are, of course, stories of wild adventures that have led to the shores of Tír na nÓg."

"So Ryanair don't fly there, then?" Patrick's joke fell flat with his guests.

Stealing the moment, Mam leaned forward, her hand hovering inches over his knee. She paused and looked straight down the lens. "We don't know the truth here. We're exploring our family history, too. We're blowing the cobwebs out of the attic, and we've been shocked. Shocked but proud. Proud of our heritage."

There were grunts of approval all around.

They said their good-byes. Patrick looked relieved as they disembarked from the sofa. Part of me was glad to see someone with such obvious skepticism. There seemed to be a lot of acceptance of these fairies and not enough questions asked.

I turned off the telly and felt my shoulders relax. I waited for my phone to buzz with a text message from Mam. It flew in, three minutes later.

"Patrick is even more handsome in the flesh. We're having a ball. Xx"

Good for you, I thought. But, at that very minute, I had far more serious matters to attend to. My date with Jim was happening in two hours. I had goose bumps, jelly legs, and butterflies in my stomach.

Don't worry, I got it. I knew why Jim had asked me along—I was good publicity. But there was still a part of me, a *big* part of me, that wondered if there was anything between us. It was worth a shot, but I'd had a lingering sense of dread all day. I could feel a cramp rumbling in the pit of my stomach, and I'd had a headache hammering at me all afternoon. Call it instinct or call it being an experienced dater—somehow I knew I should have said no. But I just couldn't stop myself. I wanted to play it out, and so I didn't listen to my gut, I just went for it.

I wore the yellow silk dress with gray wedge heels that would have me tottering close to eye level with Jim. I knew my hair and makeup were good. I felt physically prepared, but mentally nowhere near where I should be. I ran through hundreds of imaginary conversations with Jim, varying from the hugely romantic "I've been a fool all these years. Let me dedicate my life to you" to the hugely silly explosions of giggles and "I've never enjoyed myself so much with anyone" to the bizarre "Sometimes I have to wear talcum powder under my leather trousers" (his, not mine). I was going to throw my head back and laugh, be carefree yet enigmatic, the kind of girl who enters a room and people wonder who she is and what her story is. I practiced my enigmatic face, but I just looked distressed, so I decided that maybe the whole witchy thing might give me an air of mystery, an air of "who's that girl?"

Unfortunately, *everyone* knew who that girl was. The launch, which Jim had described as just being a small affair—twenty or thirty people and maybe one journalist—was anything but. The event wasn't, as expected, in the back room of a dodgy pub. It was in Chandelier, the front room of a high-end Dublin nightclub.

Standing outside, waiting to give my name to the buck-toothed perma-tanned blonde on the door, I peered past the red satin curtain. There were plush velvet couches, cushions with tassels, and chandeliers dripping from any available ceiling space. The girls were skinny and fake-tanned, tapping false nails on champagne glasses. The guys used a lot of hair product and knew exactly how to catch the light on their cheekbones.

"Kate McDaid," I said.

The buck-toothed blonde's jaw dropped. "Oh, my God! This is fabulous, just too fabulous! Wait here!" She reached out and clutched my arm. Eyeballing me, she picked up her phone. "Yah, yah, she's here. Get him out."

I tried to shake free. "Em, can I just go inside? I'm supposed to meet someone."

"Jim, yah. He's on his way." I felt her nails dig deeper.

I nodded, wondering how she knew and wishing she'd stop staring at me.

"Sorry." She let go of my arm. "I work for Sony. I'm, em, a bit of a fan of yours."

"Of mine?"

"Well, you know, the fairies. They're just fascinating. You know, if you need representation, I know a fantastic PR person who'd just love to get their teeth into this."

I looked at her buck teeth and shook my head. "I'm fine, thanks. I don't need anyone's help."

"Wow! That's so interesting, and so humble of you!"

"No, no."

She nodded excitedly. "Honestly." More nodding. "Have your powers kicked in yet?" she asked in all seriousness.

"No, but that's because I wear a vial of kryptonite around my neck to repel them."

She nodded again.

Oh God. Where's Jim?

His hair was curled to perfection, unruly and not *too* styled. His broad shoulders towered over Miss Buck Teeth and me. He was wearing a black T-shirt that was stretched tight across his chest and a leather string necklace tied around his neck.

"Hi!" He dipped down, lightly kissing me on the cheek. His skin was clear and smooth; he must have just shaved. He straightened up and hooked his fingers into his brown leather belt. "You look nice."

"Thanks," I said, unable to tear my gaze from him.

"Are we good to go?" He looked at Buck Teeth, who was as starstruck by Jim as I felt, her mouth hanging open and her eyes moments away from rolling out of her head. He was so beautiful, so mesmerizing.

He turned to me and I tried to breathe, I really did, but my breath was catching.

"I'm sorry. I tried to call you earlier." He threw his arms up in the air. "This was Sony's idea. They're pushing the boat out. You don't mind, do you? I mean, it's only for tonight, and, hey, there's free drinks in it."

"Not at all, it'll be fun." I tried to throw him a dazzling smile.

"Half an hour and it'll be all over." He held out his hand and I slid mine into it.

Buck Teeth pulled back the curtain, and the flashing lights catapulted off one another and into my eyes. I felt my heart jumping, I was so scared. There was no end to the lights: I was blinded by their flashing and bouncing. The only thing guiding me through was Jim's hand in mine. As in a near-death experience, I knew to just keep walking toward the light. I cowered behind Jim's arm, concentrating on putting one foot in front of the other.

"Kate, Kate!" Voices shouting my name came from every direction. "Over here, Kate! Give us a smile!"

"I hate this," I whispered at Jim's arm.

He bent down to my face, exposing all his teeth in a huge grin, waving furiously at the crowd with his right arm. "Isn't this brilliant?" He took a deep breath and looked euphoric. His beautiful face was alive with the reflecting flashbulbs.

"Brilliant," I said, every inch a startled rabbit. My hand gripped his tighter and I tried to smile, but it felt more of a grimace.

Jim contorted his body into shapes and poses, turning toward the lights, basking in them. I felt my shoulders cave in on me and my neck retracting. I was so uncomfortable. How did celebrities do this? I saw pictures of gorgeous people on red carpets all the time, looking like rays of sunshine. I'd flick through magazines thinking, *Ooh, I'd love to have a go at that, to prance in front of the cameras, beaming with a well-practiced hair flip.* I've imagined what I might say: "This old thing? Just threw it on," or how my hair might be coiffed and how my mouth would pout. How calm and still and ethereal I would be. And now here I was, stomach sucked in so hard I was dizzy, regretting not having worn full-body Spanx, trying to smile without making my eyes look too squinty, and focusing hard on dehunching my shoulders and stretching my neck so I didn't have a double chin. And then there were my shoes. They were so high. One wobble and I was wiped. I was hating every second of my red carpet debut.

"Kate, Kate! Come on, Kate! Look at Jim. Yeah, that's it. Look like you're really in love. That's it."

Jim let go of my hand and wrapped his arm tightly around my shoulders, squeezing me into his chest. "Hey, lads, we're just good friends." He smiled broadly.

"Yeah, yeah, Jim. We've heard that one before. Give her a kiss." I felt myself stiffen under his arm. I wanted to kiss Jim, but not like this, like a show pony, with cameras flashing and men shouting.

"We're just good friends," he gushed again, winking at the cameras.

"Kate, Kate!"

It was Lily. What was Lily doing there? I could make out a shadow waving ten feet behind the photographers. The shadow pointed toward the end of the red carpet and a break in the barriers. I gently pushed free from Jim's embrace and, wearing a frozen smile, took the two steps toward the barrier. Lily, in a bright green T-shirt, looked as distressed as I felt. She held out her hand and quickly grabbed me, pulling me away from the flashing bulbs and plush red carpet. She threw her arm around my shoulders and guided me to the back of the room and through a door, which she slammed behind me. Now we were in a small empty room. Lily sat me down on a large couch.

"Are you okay?" Her eyes were full of concern. "You looked like you were dying."

"I think I was. Did you see that?"

"It was awful."

"Hell. That's hell."

"Take a deep breath."

"What are you doing here?"

"Mr. Goatee. He's into Red Horizon. Here, I'll get you a glass of water." She turned around and pushed through the door toward the bar.

I was trembling. I wrapped my arms around my middle. I was having flashbacks of necks straining and eyes on stalks looking at me. Hopefully, Lily would hurry back.

With the buoyancy of a puppy, Jim bounded into the room. Shiny-faced, he jumped from foot to foot in front of me, every inch of him bubbling over with excitement. "Wasn't that such a rush?" He bent down and grabbed me by the shoulders.

"Hmmm," I lied.

"Man!" He punched the air and let out a woohoo, like a frat boy with a free keg.

Lily reappeared clutching a glass of still water. She gently slid it into my hand. "Jim." She looked stern.

"Great to see you, Lily, brilliant. I've got to run. We're playing the song in five." He bent down again and this time he kissed me full on the mouth, making a large *mmmmwa* sound. He stepped back, touching his chest, smiling. "See you later." He winked and bolted through the door.

I took a deep breath and ran my fingers over my lips in shock before settling back into the couch. Lily collapsed beside me, and we exhaled in unison.

It was starting to sink in. I had celebrity status—there was no denying it anymore. I was out there. "I don't know if I'm cut out for this life," I moaned.

Lily smiled at me mischievously. "You were a natural." Her eyes filled with water and her cheeks exploded into apple shapes as she started to laugh.

"Ah, come on." I playfully slapped her leg. "Not funny."

"Your face!" She was laughing really hard now. "Talk about a deer in the headlights!"

"Shut up." I started to laugh, too, happy that everything was normal again.

"I'll never forget your expression."

"Yes, yes." I laughed even more, trying unsuccessfully to take a sip of my water.

"Your face."

"I get it. Where's Mr. Goatee?"

"At the bar, he banged into his sister, I'll let him at it." She nodded.

Red Horizon started to play. Lily and I crept back into the front room and found a dark corner where no one could see us. I looked toward the stage. Jim had wrapped himself around the microphone stand and was lazily running his hand up it. He closed his eyes, stretched his neck to the side, pouted his lips, and paused for appreciation. There must have been eight hundred people in the room, male and female, who wanted to sleep with him at that very moment.

And then it came to me in a flash—one of my inexplicable eureka moments. "Princess Lo Lo Ki Ki. That's the name, Lily. That's what I wanted everyone to call me. I remember now."

"Now? You remember now? Is that your fairy name?" She looked at me, confused.

"Must be the music," I said, unsure. Again, I wondered how and why these things kept popping into my head. What was going on? "It's not a great name, is it? Lo Lo Ki Ki."

Lily shook her head, smiling.

That was my name. I had wanted everyone to call me by it. That's what Mam was talking about. I remembered I was wearing my favorite Teenage Mutant Ninja Turtles T-shirt and roller skates and I was demanding that Mam and Dad call me Princess Lo Lo Ki Ki, announcing with all the might of a seven-year-old that I had arrived. I guess I wanted a nickname at the time. I must have made it up, I thought. I definitely didn't remember anyone giving it to me, certainly not an imaginary friend and especially not a fairy. I was pretty sure I'd remember that—wouldn't I?

15

"Show her." It was Saturday morning, the morning after the Red Horizon song launch, and I hadn't even shut the door to my flat—the latch hadn't even clicked. Simon Battersby was now accompanied by a band of merry men, which numbered four equally anoraked individuals, and they were sitting on the brick fence of my garden. One was lazily kicking the dirt at the foot of the old oak tree. Its leaves had changed to full spring bloom, unlike the anoraks, which were worn day in, day out. With military precision they jumped up when I appeared. One, the one I would fondly nickname "Dweeb Number Three," shouted: "Show her!"

Who's her? I wanted to ask. *The cat's mother?* But I thought better of it. They'd probably get excited at the mention of a cat, it being a witch's best friend and all that. And Lord knows, this troop didn't need any encouragement. They seemed to have set up camp at the front gate, without having actually set up camp, unless they'd managed to unfold a tent and slide it into a pocket moments before I came down the stairs. They were loitering like a bunch of wide-eyed priests lost in the lingerie section of a giant department store.

Simon was fiddling with a flask of tea, and I suspected he had something important to tell me about stars aligning or the ancient Irish translation of a specific word used in one of the Steps. But instead he wanted me to meet his band of Anoraks. He spoke softly as he gestured around the group, introducing his men by rank and fairy name. There was Treasurer Oisin Snowdrop, Chief Investigator Fionn Toadstool, and a Fairy Doctor, Oak Dust.

I raised my eyebrows, thinking they'd all be a lot happier playing at *Lord of the Rings*. Collectively, Simon told me, they'd named themselves "the Followers of the Seven Steps," but I knew I wouldn't be able to think of them as anything other than "the Anoraks."

"Show her." Dweeb Number Three elbowed Simon quite forcibly in the gut, propelling him to the front of the group. I wondered if Simon was being made to talk to me not because he was the chief, or whatever his title was, but because I suspected none of them had actually ever spoken to a girl, and their blushing and stammering might overwhelm them and hinder their investigation.

"There's this." Simon turned his head away dramatically and held out his arm, rigid as a pole. A newspaper was swinging on the end.

I walked the few steps toward him and took it from his hand, shaking my head from side to side, surprised at how weary I felt about the media.

"We did not endorse this," he said into his shoulder.

I read the headline out loud: "Are the Seven Steps a Secret Cult?" Then I laughed—I couldn't stop myself. The paper had photographed the Anoraks, listed off their titles, and attempted to decipher so-called codes they were apparently signing to one another. One was Simon blowing his nose. Unfortunately, there was also a giant photo of me, looking more curly-headed and freckle-faced than usual. I looked at the Anoraks and shrugged. "I know, it's not great having your photo taken when you don't know about it."

"This is not a cult," Simon said.

"Well, honestly, Simon, I don't know what this is. I don't know what you're doing here."

"We're here for you."

"Yeah. You see, Simon, that's just a bit weird." I kept shaking my head as I handed him back the paper before turning sharply to the guy on Simon's left. "Will you stop writing? Please." That was another thing they were doing: scribbling down every word I said. It was ridiculous. "Seriously, guys!" I slapped my hands on the side of my legs in despair. "I'm going to the shop."

"Well, there are some of them around as well."

"Who?"

"The photographers. They were here earlier."

I released a slow groan. The paparazzi again. They seemed to be turning up everywhere I went, clicking, whirring, snapping. They'd photograph me twirling my hair, walking, sitting; I didn't have to be *doing* anything. They'd started selling the photos to some newspapers, magazines, websites. And then some journalist or other would study it and decide that my expression was "happy," "sad," "wistful," "witchy." My clothes were analyzed: I was a fashion leader, and a fashion disaster. The day before, I hadn't noticed that I had a hole in my dress—it had been snagged on the corner of a table. One website said it signaled "the depths of my depression," and another declared it to be "a new fashion trend inspired by fairy weaving."

The thing was, I had as much of a celebrity obsession as anyone. I bought celebrity magazines, subscribed to celebrity diets, and laughed at their religions. I loved it when they got skinny, and I loved it even more when they got fat. Their lives are a soap opera, a dramatically beautiful one with an implausible script, but I never expected to have a supporting role in it. I wasn't qualified to be a celebrity. I didn't sing, dance, or act. I didn't do anything, and yet I was occupying valuable movie-star space, places where bona fide members of celeb-ville should be denying plastic surgery, considering foreign adoptions, and praising their speedy metabolisms. I was baffled. Maybe there weren't enough celebrities to go around? Maybe that's why they had to turn me into one?

"I'll be quick. I just want some orange juice," I muttered to myself and started off down the path.

Four steps later, the Anoraks were still there, shuffling behind me.

"What are you doing?" I asked.

"We'll come, too," Simon said to the ground.

It's a free country, I thought. *Unfortunately.* I couldn't tell them they couldn't go to the shops. Kumar would probably be glad for the extra business. I felt my shoulders tense up but continued to march on, now shadowed by the Anoraks. Not for the first time I cursed whoever had nicked my bike. If I'd had my bike, I'd have been down and back to the shops and the Anoraks wouldn't have been able to follow me. Instead, there I was plodding slowly through a suburban neighborhood—me, the Anoraks, and the paparazzi.

Two weather-worn, fat-bellied, heavy-footed photographers circled me. They chirped like hungry birds, calling my name and asking what I was doing.

"Going to the shop to get some orange juice," I responded flatly.

"Is that a clue, Kate?" Simon piped up.

"Clue to what? WHAT?" I quickened my pace, wondering

if I should turn back. But I could see the fluorescent lights of Kumar's shop, and, anyway, I shouldn't have been intimidated. I wanted orange juice.

Kumar greeted me like I was a delivery man giving him a discount. He was delighted I'd brought along six other people, four of whom were expressing an interest in his dairy fridge.

He wrapped his arm around me, enveloping me in aftershave, and told the paparazzi to take a photo. "I'll hang it here," he said, pointing to the spot over the Marlboro Lights that had once been blank but now hosted a collage of images of me, underneath a giant sign that said, "Kate McDaid, Best Customer."

"Ahhh, Kumar." I looked at him, exasperated.

He grinned, squinting his eyes. "Very good for business."

"Can I just get some orange juice?" I muscled my way down the aisle, conscious that two other shoppers, clutching their frozen pizzas, were staring at me. Cameras were clicking, whirring, flashing. I quickly grabbed a liter of something that had an orange on the front, threw some money at Kumar, raced out of the shop, and ran, something I haven't done since school hockey classes. I ran all the way back to my flat, propelled forward by wheezing paparazzi and asthmatic Anoraks. With lightning speed, I put the key in the door, slid through, and slammed it with gigantic force. I stayed fixed on the spot, waiting for my breathing to level out. My hands were shaking and there was a tremor in my legs, but I wasn't sure if it was just from having exercised. *This is madness*, I thought, *absolute madness*.

I decided I had to replace my bike—I knew I could outride these guys. I got onto eBay and searched for secondhand bikes in Dublin. Much to my surprise, up popped my trusty old steed. I hadn't known bike thieves were so Internet-savvy. Then I saw that the starting bid was 300 euros, and I practically fell off the sofa. I'd bought that bike three years earlier for forty euros from a guy in a tracksuit with HOUSE OF PAIN tattooed on his neck. He'd treated the whole thing like a drug deal, looking over his shoulder, sniffing suspiciously, in spite of the fact we were in his bike shop. I doubted that he'd given me the deal of the century and that somehow my bike was worth a lot more than I'd paid for it.

Then I saw the item description: "Kate McDaid's bike. A modern-day witch's broomstick. Get it now." They'd also included a photo of me on the bike that looked like me on a bike and not a witch on a broomstick. Two hundred and forty-seven people had bid.

I reached for my phone. "Can I speak to Garda Fitzgerald, please?"

"One moment, please."

"Hello." It was Garda Fitzgerald's voice.

"Hi. This is Kate McDaid. You're investigating my bike that was nicked from outside Kumar's corner shop on Camden Street."

"What? Sorry."

"My bike was stolen."

"No, it doesn't ring a bell."

I sighed heavily. "I'm Kate McDaid, the spiritual guru."

There was silence on the line. "Is this about my problem? Do you know something?" Garda Fitzgerald whispered at last.

"No. It's about *my* problem. My bike."

"I can't talk to you about this here."

"Do you want me to come into the station? I have information."

"No! God, no. I'll come to you. I'll be there within the hour." And he hung up hastily.

I wondered to myself what the Anoraks and the paparazzi would make of a guard turning up on my doorstep. It might put them off or cause them to scatter. *This could all work out very well*, I thought, smugly.

Garda Fitzgerald arrived twenty minutes later. His feet were polar opposites as he duck-walked up the path past the Anoraks and the paparazzi with an air of importance and busyness. The buttons on his uniform caught the light and reflected the flashlights of the paparazzi, who were pelting him with photographs and questions.

He blushed from ear to ear as they asked him what he was doing. "Police business," he shouted at the top of his lungs, so that even Mr. O'Brien four doors down wouldn't question his presence.

He wanted five sugars in his tea. Red-faced, he sank into my sofa and undid the top two buttons of his jacket. Beads of sweat popped onto his forehead.

"Will this be painful?"

The cup wobbled in my hand, splashing some milky, sugary tea onto the carpet. "What?"

"The healing."

"What?"

"The healing for my problem, you know, down there." He looked at his crotch.

I handed him the mug, shaking my head. "I want to talk about my bike."

"And then will you heal me?" He pursed his lips in concentration.

"Okay," I said, deadpan, realizing that it was probably the only way to get his attention.

He sighed with relief.

I showed him the bike on eBay and the bids.

He looked stern, nodded, and took many notes.

"So what'll we do?"

His nodding turned into a shake. "I'll pass it on to the Internet fraud squad. It's out of my hands."

"But it's there, look. It's in your hands." I pointed at the screen.

"No, no, it's on the Internet. Nothing to do with me. I'll make sure somebody looks at it." He flipped his notebook shut. "You can trust me."

I put my head in my hands, feeling exhausted. "I just want my bike back."

"Right." He stood up. "Should I take my pants off?"

"Excuse me?" I straightened up.

"For the healing? On or off?"

"On, for the love of God!"

"Right."

There were a few seconds' silence as I raced through my brain for options. "How can Garda Fitzgerald relieve his itchiness?" I said to no one in particular. And there it was again. It came to me in a heartbeat and I knew it would cure him. "Eh, combine the skin of an apple, a warm egg, four teaspoons of nutmeg, and some boiling water. Plant a tree for regrowth, symbolizing a new beginning to your life. Drink the mixture for three days, and on the third day you will be healed."

"I will?"

"Yeah," I said, shocked. Where was all the hocus-pocus stuff coming from? I was getting good under pressure at making things up.

"That's amazing."

"Mmm."

"And it will definitely cure the . . . ?" He shifted uncomfortably on his feet.

"Mmm."

"Thank you, thank you."

Garda Fitzgerald skipped down the path. The new jolly policeman even stopped to chat to the Anoraks.

"Don't forget about my bike!" I screamed after him through the open window.

He waved back, instantly forgetting.

I put on a tracksuit and threw myself onto the couch. This had taken a turn for the worse. Now, I felt under house arrest.

16

Step Four

Your mansions are her fields, your shelter is her trees,
Her music is the wind playing harp strings on the seas,
She gives to you her light, her green and her earth,
Nature is the one thing of true lasting worth.

You shatter blue skies with fire and smoke,
And do more wrongs to her than seasons evoke,
Devil's Bit is cluttered with your long roads that bend,
Trees torn from the earth—you take beauty that she lends.

Be careful, work together, don't choke her fair land,
Feed from her, plant for her—you must understand,
Watch where you tread, your footprints don't fade,
Through the years man will weep
for mistakes that you've made.

We ask you to make us a home in your lair,
With flora and fauna, where nature is there,

For those Celtic souls who don't listen, who refuse,
Come sneezes, wet eyes and tongues they can't use.

✦   ✦   ✦

I was about to post the fourth Step and I was a complete and utter nervous wreck. It had been only four weeks since I'd first heard of the Seven Steps, but things were escalating fast. I felt torn. Part of me wanted to pull the plug, to put an end to the freaks outside my door. But another part, my parents' daughter's part, wanted to see how this was going to play out.

Still, the attention was really getting to me. Initially, I'd laughed it off, but now it felt—I don't know—more sinister. People seemed to believe in fairies. Really believe. They believed these Steps were from another world, and if that was the case, which it seemed to be, they believed that I had a message for them, that I was different from everyone else, that I was some type of a key to unlocking this other place. And while it's nice to be told that you're special by someone other than your parents, it didn't ring true for me. I was sure that I was not the person everyone wanted me to be.

Journalists, TV producers, and marketing consultants were ringing me with questions. What were my thoughts on global warming? If I was an animal, what animal would I be and why? Did I see dead people? How big are fairies? Was I interested in endorsing a face cream?

I stopped asking how they got my number. Nothing felt private anymore, nothing belonged to me. I was becoming public property, or rather an image of me was, the one in newspapers. That person was suddenly in the public eye. But that person, the witch, the one they really wanted to see, was not Kate McDaid, junior advertising copywriter and biking enthusiast.

I had no control. If I tried to answer their questions, if I said "I don't drink coffee," they'd twist it into "Kate McDaid refuses to allow toxins to enter her body. She lives a life as pure as the fairies." I stopped talking to all of them as soon as I read the headline "Is Kate an Alien?" in *The Mail*. There was a photo of me looking up to the sky. I couldn't win.

Drake Chandler's suicide note hadn't helped. That sounds a bit callous of me, doesn't it? But I couldn't help but think if he hadn't died, if he hadn't sung those tormented songs, if he hadn't taken truckloads of drugs and written about the fairies in his suicide note, there wouldn't be nearly as much interest in me and the ramblings of the Red Hag. Maybe Simon Battersby and the Anoraks would have appeared—they loved a good conspiracy— but the other stuff, the bigger stuff, the papers, the paparazzi, the celebrity, would it really have happened if Drake Chandler hadn't mentioned fairies? And no matter which way I reread that first Step, I really felt that it was too much of a leap to read his suicide into it. As far as I was concerned, the Red Hag had not predicted his death. His death was not caused by people not recognizing the fairies. It was caused by drugs, it was very sad, and it was suicide.

I also felt sure that the cold-sore epidemic was a natural occurrence. That type of thing happened all the time. One person got a cold sore—everyone got a cold sore. It was a coincidence that the people around me who were inflicted were nonbelievers.

There hadn't been a storm, as predicted in the third Step, not one that I could see, anyway. Yes, there'd been an economic crisis, and yes, houses were being repossessed. But I didn't know whether that could be classified as an actual *storm*.

The Friday after I'd posted the fourth Step, during *The Nightline* on RTÉ, Patrick Molloy had stuttered and stumbled through the first hour of the show before being overcome with what could only be described as a seizure of sneezes. Live on air he found himself unable to speak, his eyes red and runny, his body convulsing in spasms. For the first time in the history of RTÉ, the show was stopped halfway through, and a film, *Weekend at Bernie's*, was broadcast instead. Obviously Patrick had had a cold coming on—first a cold sore, then a fit . . .

It was the same with the ninth floor at work. Half of them were off sick, overcome with what they described as hay fever. Kumar at the corner shop told me proudly that he'd run out of tissues. Even his four-box supply in the storeroom had sold. Could it be hay fever? Was it yet another coincidence?

Since I'd been publishing the Steps, I had definitely been appreciating nature more and I regularly gave Mister Snoop Doggy Dogg an extra tickle under his chin, and I loved having Setanta snuggled at my feet at work. I also occasionally found myself looking out for the elusive Hugh Delaney, but sightings in the office had been scarce in recent days. My heart had felt full, if that made any sense, since I'd sat on that rock and felt joyful. So I was convinced that there was no harm in the Steps themselves. It was just the furor they were causing that bothered me.

Then I was asked to be the keynote speaker at the European Convention of Witches. The invite told me that "I was not alone." I have to admit, I was almost tempted to go. Curious maybe more than tempted. What could possibly go on at a witches' convention? Would it be like a cookery class, where they swap spells and potions? Did they wear black hats, paint their skin green, and put warts on their noses? Would it be like a Halloween party? I had to remind myself that these were grown-ups, and then I just felt weird, and politely refused their invite.

I laughed at it all with my friends. We bought the papers and pored over them, flicking through them furiously for photos of me, cringing in unison at bad journalism and headlines: "Witches in Stitches," "When Irish Eyes Are Spellbinding," and, my favorite, "Fairy Fearful Forecast." But I worried. Now and again I'd look up and notice a glance, a signal. Fiona and Lily would laugh too loud, their smiles would be too wide, the headlines were "too funny," "too ridiculous," "such lies." And I knew my friends had doubts about me. Well, maybe not doubts—nothing as concrete as doubts—but a suspicion was chipping away at the back of their minds.

Meanwhile, Mam and Dad were enjoying their fifteen minutes. They'd hired an agent, Harry McMahon, a skinny bleach-haired man who air-kissed and proclaimed Mam to be a "genius." Dad let me know with a wink, a nod, and a downturned wrist that Harry was, you know, "one of them." Dad was sure he'd never met a gay man before (I didn't have the heart to tell him every sixth guy he'd ever met was probably gay) and he was pleasantly surprised by how well they got on. Harry informed me that theirs was a star on the rise, and if he could only get his hands on me, who knew where we could go as a family. "Think the Osbournes or the Addams Family," he repeatedly said to my stubbornly shaking head. Harry was securing and locking down any deal he could, and, as a result, Mam and Dad were making money. In the previous four weeks they'd made more money than Dad's pension brought in in a year. Dad was now the face of a massage chair, a website that traced your family tree, and denture glue, and he was in talks to write a DIY book about car maintenance. Mam loved the guest appearances, and was turning up at the opening of every envelope, waving and smiling for the cameras. She was starting on the audition circuit for reality TV: *Celebrities on a Farm, Celebrities up a Mountain, Celebrities in the Kitchen.*

Together they were the face of Tan-a-lot, a self-tanning gel: "No streaks and an instant sunny glow in thirty seconds."

Unfortunately for Dad, though, Mam was spending the money as fast as it was coming in. She said she'd waited her whole life to shop without looking at the price tag. She refused the advice of fashion professionals, believing she had her own personal style nailed down, a bit like Kate Moss. Only when you saw photos of Mam in magazines, Kate Moss wasn't the first name to pop into your head: Liberace or Cher circa 1995 was more likely. Patterns exploded all over her: paisley, floral, spots—every combination that never knew it was a combination. I watched with trepidation as her hemlines got shorter and her necklines lower. Her ears began to droop under the weight of heavy yellow gold, and her wrists looked pained, adorned as they were with stones the size of small islands. She was contemplating a boob job and I had visions of lads' mags knocking on her door for a discreet photo shoot, which absolutely terrified me.

Dad still wore his cord suit with suede elbow patches, although Mam had somehow persuaded him to get auburn highlights. He stroked his remaining few wispy bits of hair and told me quietly that he was scared the dye would sweat out and he'd end up with red streaks down his face. Dad was thinking of upgrading his car, but he suspected correctly that the neighbors probably weren't gossiping about his battered old banger anymore.

But they were happy. They held hands and flirted with each other. Dad would proudly wrap his arm around Mam's shoulders, and she'd cuddle into him, giggling. While other couples their age were gardening and joining bridge clubs, Mam and Dad were skipping up red carpets and practicing their poses for photo shoots. If the Seven Steps had achieved anything, they'd brought happiness and passion back into my parents' marriage, and for that I would be forever grateful—and embarrassed, if Mam didn't sort out her wardrobe soon.

People were crawling out of the woodwork: teachers from school were e-mailing, ex-neighbors were dropping in, and guys I'd dated who had never called me back suddenly found my number again. I didn't know what any of them wanted. It was like they were reaching out, trying to catch the celebrity, so when they were nursing pints in the pub on a Friday night they could tell the drunk beside them that they knew Kate McDaid.

By the time I published the fourth Step, trying to maintain a normal life had become increasingly difficult. Work was a nightmare—not the actual work, which was coming together quite well, but the office itself. I was now the coworker everyone wanted to know. Conversations would stop if I was within ten feet of a group, and heads peeped around watercoolers and laptops to stare at me as I walked by. My desk area was a thoroughfare for gawpers nudging each other and saying, "That's her, that's her," while I'd sink lower and lower into my chair.

And then there were the gifts. Bucketloads of gifts had begun to arrive, some days three or four, one day fifty-four. Flowers, iPods, shoes, handbags, foot spas, chutneys. Gifts from journalists, producers, or product manufacturers who wanted me to be photographed wearing or using their stuff. It was exciting, initially: every day was Christmas Day. But then there was just so much of it, and there's only room for so many wallets/key chains/ bicycle pumps in your life. So I gave a lot of it away. Not all of it—obviously, I kept the handbags and shoes—but the jams and aftershaves were up for grabs. The accounts department met me with hands hanging and a greedy glint in their eyes as I handed out baskets of fruit and iPhones. The design department sent me an angry e-mail, saying they felt that accounts were getting all the best gifts and that they were second on my list. Unwittingly that week I started a turf war.

Dudley was the biggest benefactor of all. His child-catcher cart was brimming over with presents daily, and some days he'd just call me from reception, listing off the items and telling me which ones he wanted. By rights, I thought, the design department should have been sending *him* angry e-mails.

The day after I posted the fourth Step, I was desperately trying to forget everything and just focus on work. Matthew and I had to go to a meeting and ended up being away from the office for maybe two hours.

While we were out, Setanta came visiting, as he always did. Seeing we weren't there, he did what any dog would do: he dived headfirst into the box of Starshoot chocolates on the floor by Matthew's desk.

When we got back from the meeting, Matthew went to see the design department. I returned to my desk to find Setanta flat out on a bed of half-eaten Starshoot bars. He was struggling to breathe, his tongue hanging lopsided out of his mouth and his eyes flickering at half-mast.

My heart stopped. "Setanta!" I dropped to my knees and put my hands under his head. "Oh, God. Please be okay," I said aloud. "Please be okay." His breaths were short and sharp, and his whole body was straining to keep breathing.

I grabbed my phone. "Marjorie. Get Hugh. It's Setanta. He might be dying."

Before I'd even hung up, I could feel Hugh's presence hurtling toward me. In a moment he was at my side. He slid to his knees and cradled Setanta in his arms, his face red with worry and anger.

"What the hell happened?"

"I . . . I dunno."

"Jesus Christ!" He picked up a handful of the Starshoot wrappers that littered the floor. "What the fuck were you thinking?"

He rose to his feet. Setanta, sick and panting, somehow looked small in his arms.

"I didn't, I—"

"He's a dog. He can't eat your type of food. What the hell is wrong with you?" His eyes narrowed, and he looked at me with pure hate.

"He . . . Oh, God, I didn't mean—"

"Save your pathetic excuses. You people haven't a clue." Hugh glared at me like I was the creator of all evil, the keeper of a pitchfork and horns. He nuzzled his face into Setanta's and whispered in his cartoony voice: "It's okay. You're going to be okay. I'll save you." Then he turned and ran, disappearing with such speed I began to think I'd imagined the whole scenario.

Later, I tried to get Hugh's number from Marjorie, but she point-blank refused to give it to me, saying it was inappropriate for me to have dealings with her client. So I got it from Colin, who couldn't have cared less.

I called Hugh that evening, praying with all my might that Setanta had made a full recovery. Thankfully, he had. But it didn't stop Hugh from chastising me like a naughty child. I took my punishment and apologized profusely. I was just happy Setanta was okay. He needed a few weeks of rest and relaxation, so Hugh was taking him home. Hugh was sick of Dublin and the people here, he said.

I took that to be a direct dig at me. The man was infuriating beyond belief. He never failed to find an opportunity to insult me or belittle me, and yet he was the one working in the porn industry. How he could get so high and mighty flabbergasted me.

But there was something about him, something that, in spite of everything, I liked and admired. The way he cared for Setanta, his ruggedness, even his dirty boots. There was something about him that was so different he stood out. He didn't try to be anyone he wasn't. He didn't play any games. There was an honesty about him that was refreshing. Unfortunately, I'd probably never see him or Setanta again. It was a thought that, if I was honest, quite depressed me.

Colin had an idea about David Hasselhoff and the Starshoot campaign, and I agreed to do it if he absolutely 100 percent agreed to promote me after the ad was shot. I don't know where I got the courage to ask him for the promotion, but I knew I had to—it was one of those now-or-never moments.

We were at the end of a pier about to jump off, but we couldn't do it without David Hasselhoff, who, it just so happened, was impossible to get hold of. We'd tried every angle we could think of—fan sites, stalker sites, medical sites—nothing was working. The PA's PA's PA's PA in L.A. had never returned my call—that had gone nowhere. It was time to jump.

Colin sat me down, running his fingers through his shoulder-length hair. He was embarrassed to ask me, he said, twiddling his mustache. "But you need to use your celebrity to reach out to another celebrity. That's how these things work."

David Hasselhoff wouldn't have heard of me, I argued. Colin said that it was worth a try, that we were at the end of our collective tether. We had to get him on board, which was why he'd offered me the promotion.

I thought about it for a while, weighing up the options with Matthew over an egg salad sandwich at AlJo's. I really wanted that promotion—I *deserved* that promotion. So, I did it. I called Mam and Dad's agent, Harry McMahon, and asked him to use his agent network to find the Hoff and tell him that the witch Kate McDaid was looking for him.

Fifteen minutes later, the Hoff called me direct.

"Kate McDaid. *The* Kate McDaid?"

"Is this David Hasselhoff? This is great."

"I can't believe this is Kate McDaid!"

It went on like that for quite a while, both of us saying each other's name. I was so excited, you'd think I'd won a full house at bingo. The legendary David Hasselhoff was talking to me. I felt myself bowing slightly on the phone to him. He'd heard about the Steps from an Irish friend in L.A. He told me that he was Irish on his great-grandfather's side.

He was so nice. He said our idea for the campaign was *awesome*, and he sounded so believable that for a moment I thought it was. He agreed to everything. Because of his tight filming schedules for *America's Got Talent*, he could give us only twenty-four hours of his time. That was all. I knew we could work around it. He asked very politely if we could send him some samples of Starshoot. I'd looked nervously over at the four or five bars at the bottom of what was once a five-hundred-pack box under Matthew's desk and scribbled down a note to ask the Little Prince for more. I told the Hoff that I'd firm up the details and call him back as soon as I could.

After he'd hung up, Matthew, Colin and I high-fived one another. We were *The A-Team*, we were amazing, we were advertising stars. It felt great. Matthew and I were finally going to get a campaign out the door. And I was going to get promoted. Things were looking up.

We sent out the bat signal and arranged for the Little Prince to come into the office the following day. I couldn't wait to see the look on his face. Only when I did see it, it wasn't what I expected at all.

✦   ✦   ✦

As per usual, the meeting room was fully prepared for the Little Prince's arrival with the sparkling and still water, double cushions on one of the seats, sharpened pencils, and scented candles. His Cuban heels announced his entry, and we stood to attention. His face looked softer, his hair flatter, and he bowed his head as he came through the door. *He must really love David Hasselhoff,* I thought.

Quietly, he shrank down into his seat.

"We have great news." Matthew stood tall, pulling excitedly on his nose. "We have managed to secure David Hasselhoff for the Starshoot commercial."

Silence.

I anxiously chewed my fingers.

"He's a big fan of chocolate and can't wait to endorse Starshoot."

Silence.

"He has agreed to do the commercial."

Silence.

"It's great news."

Matthew sat back down.

The Little Prince slowly looked around the room, before fixing his gaze on Matthew. "Can you please leave us?"

Matthew looked at me, and I shrugged in response. "Okay," he said, and left the room looking confused.

The Little Prince turned his eyes to me. I could see they were moist, like he might cry. His face was sad and heavy. "I know who you are."

I blinked, hoping to indicate that I, too, knew who I was.

"I know vot you can do." Somehow I didn't think this was going to be about my amazing advertising abilities. "Ve have people like you in my country—gypsies and ze like."

"Oh, I'm not a gypsy. Never even wear my hair in plaits."

"Vell, a vitch, votever. My point is, I know vot you can do. I know how you got David Hasselhoff to agree. He is a superstar, a music genius, a god."

"He is. He is, indeed," I replied with great enthusiasm. "He's also a very nice man."

"But you have done somezing." The Little Prince wagged his finger at me.

"I made a phone call." I shifted nervously in my seat.

"No."

"Yeah."

"No. You have put a spell on him."

I laughed.

"Zis is great chocolate. I know zis is great chocolate." He started to beat his chest. "But zis is not the chocolate of a god."

"I made a phone call. He likes chocolate."

"*Nein.*" He pursed his lips and sternly shook his head.

"It's business."

"No. Zis is magic."

"Well, why did you agree to let us go down this route if you thought he would never do it, if you thought we couldn't get David Hasselhoff?" I was surprised at how forthright I was being with the Little Prince. Clients with their tightly gripped purse strings are meant to be cushioned and marshmallowed, told happy endings. Not questioned—never questioned.

"I never thought you vould get David Hasselhoff. I vas going to fire ze agency. I vanted to fire ze agency, but now they have you and vitchcraft."

"They always had me."

"Not like zis." He sighed heavily.

"Don't fire the agency," I pleaded. "People will lose their jobs."

"Vell, now if I fire ze agency, you vill put a spell on me."

"I won't put a spell on you," I said, thinking I would if I could. "Look, let's just put this all behind us. It's all going to be over in a few weeks, anyway. David Hasselhoff is coming in a couple of days. It's going to be a very successful campaign. We should celebrate."

"And you von't put a spell on me?"

"Well, you're not going to fire the agency, are you?"

"No."

"Okay, then, no spell."

Did I just negotiate a deal over a spell? What was wrong with me?

The Little Prince flicked his hair into its natural bouffant. He pushed back his chair and hopped down.

"I vill see you at ze shoot."

And he smiled. I could have sworn he smiled.

17

"The Seven Steps" was the number one downloaded song during the first week after release. It was on a loop on the radio and people were humming it in the streets, tapping it out on their bus journeys. It was huge. Red Horizon was huge. Jim was doing interviews constantly. I'd hear him on the radio, see his handsome face on the telly. He was asked about our relationship a lot, and he'd respond with the stock answer that we were "just good friends." I'd blush. I didn't really know if we were even friends, let alone good friends.

So he surprised me on Friday evening after work. I was feeling under house arrest, with people constantly camped outside my flat. It was miserable. And then Jim's text came and my heart skipped a beat.

was wondering if I could come over? Jim

Come over? Come over this second? I quickly scanned my flat. It was a mess. There were mountains of Sunday papers on the floor—not great, considering it was Friday. There were only certain parts of my couch that you could sit or lie on without getting a spring in your back. The carpet definitely needed a clean and, more importantly, so did I. I texted back immediately:

Great. Wld be lovely to see u. come over in the next hour? Kate

c u thn

I spun myself into a tornado of activity. Cleaned the flat, cleaned me, changed the sheets. (Who knew? Something could happen. Did I want something to happen? Better to be prepared.) I had a lightning shower, shaved my legs, threw on my favorite BCBG dress—green, to the knee, chiffon, and definitely a bit over the top for a casual call-in, but this could be more than casual.

Twenty minutes after the last text, the bell rang, leaving me no time to pick up the papers off the floor or call Fiona for advice. My face burned up and my heart pounded out of my chest as I went down the stairs. *Be cool, be cool, be cool,* I repeated to myself, then tripped on the edge of the carpet at the bottom of the steps.

I took a deep breath and opened the door about half an inch, hoping Jim would know to scurry in quickly to avoid the pesky photographers hanging around outside. He obviously didn't know, though, because he pushed the door wide open. Behind him, there was an aviary of chirping paparazzi flashing and snapping. They seemed to have multiplied overnight. All I could see was Jim, his big smile, and what looked like a halo of light behind him.

"Hi." He smiled and I melted. He reached in around me and gave me a long, tight hug. It felt wonderful. It would have felt even more wonderful if we weren't being watched by fifteen overweight men. I moved back in off the doorstep, pulling Jim with me.

"Do you want to . . . ?" And he gestured with his head toward the photographers pushing the door open more. I shook my head and shut the door tightly behind us. Alone at last.

"I brought food," he announced, holding up a plastic takeout bag. "Hope you like Chinese."

"Brilliant, I love it." I bit my lip, hoping I wouldn't explode there and then.

We traipsed up the stairs to my flat.

"I see you've built your shrine. 'We ask you to make us a home in your lair.'" He pointed at the hall table, which was heaving under the weight of gifts I'd received.

"I didn't build a shrine," I said, exasperated. And then I looked at it, looked properly at it, and what I had thought was a mess of books and knickknacks, some flowers, candles, even a jar of jam, had somehow formed a C-shape, almost like an altar. Mister Snoop Doggy Dogg was curled up underneath it. He'd been sleeping there a lot, and I'd just thought it must have been a heat trap, a cozy corner. Now I wondered.

"I didn't think I'd built a shrine," I said quietly. I was feeling a little weirded out. What was happening?

"Not much of a housekeeper, hey?" Jim was standing in the middle of the messy sitting room.

"I'll get some plates and glasses."

I went into my equally messy kitchen and rummaged around. "I don't know where all those photographers came from. There's normally only two," I shouted.

"Mmmm."

I reappeared with a bottle of wine, two glasses, and a corkscrew. I handed the bottle and corkscrew to Jim, apologizing. "I'm really bad at opening bottles. I normally just try to get the screw-top stuff but . . . em."

He took it from me and, in one gesture, popped the bottle open. He sat down—I guessed that because he didn't flinch it wasn't on a spring—and poured two large glasses. I busied myself in the kitchen and brought out the takeout.

"Thanks for this," I said, setting two plates down on my

wobbly coffee table. "I can't go for takeout—it's impossible with all the people outside. Well, there's normally only six, including the Anoraks, but that's enough."

He nodded. I sat down opposite him in my one rickety armchair. He started shoveling the food into him. Minutes passed. Was he not going to talk? Were we just going to be silent? Maybe he was really hungry? I chewed slowly on my chicken sweet and sour, trying to think of conversation topics.

"So, the song, the song is doing really well?"

He nodded.

I stared at my plate. "It's great for Red Horizon."

Another nod. When had he turned into a mute?

He finished his food, pushed his plate away, and grabbed his glass of wine. His eyes ran around the flat, spotting, no doubt, every piece of dust and unfluffed cushion.

"It's messy. I didn't have time to clean."

"Mmmm."

I couldn't swallow the sweet and sour, and pushed it away.

"You look great." I don't know where that came from—it just came flying out of my mouth. I guess it was all I'd been thinking about, really. He did look great. Dark denim jeans, his curly hair just tipping the back of his blue T-shirt, clear and fresh skin. Delicious.

He smiled for the first time since the doorway. "Yeah, thanks." He patted his jeans. "I've got my pockets stuffed with Zovirax. I think I'm getting a cold sore."

I froze. Jim. A cold sore. Was he a nonbeliever, too?

"If you put some lemon, St. John's wort, and ginger in river water, drink it four times a day, and sleep with some rose petals under your pillow, it'll be gone in two days." Oh, for the love of God! I'd never said the words "St. John's wort" before in my life.

Jim looked at me strangely. "Thanks," he said and, ignoring my remedy blurt, quickly continued, "You know, so much of this business is about image. What you look like will sell the song. I'd say it's fifty-fifty—the music and the image. If you look at previous rock 'n' roll stars—for example, Jim Morrison, who I've tried to model myself on in some respects, but not entirely—if you look at his image, it was all cultivated and pronounced . . ."

He was off and I couldn't keep up. Image, him, his face, his looks, more about Jim Morrison, something about Oasis, and a lot of harsh words about the industry. I kept nodding. Occasionally, I made a sound in agreement, but mainly I nodded.

Eventually, Jim stretched out his legs and reached in his pocket for a pack of cigarettes. I must have made a face, not because I'm antismoking, particularly, but because I didn't know he smoked. I thought I knew everything about him. How had I missed this important detail? It must have registered with him because he walked over to the window and pushed it open. He was still talking about Jim Morrison as he perched himself on the windowsill.

"Emmm." I kind of waved my hands around, noticing how dry my throat was. I hadn't spoken in about two hours. "The paparazzi can see you from the window. You might be better out in the kitchen. I normally keep the curtains closed."

"They don't bother me." He took a long drag on the cigarette and blew smoke out the window in their direction.

"Right."

I poured myself another glass of wine. Jim hadn't touched his drink for hours—he hadn't stopped talking long enough to take a sip. Now he flicked his cigarette out the window and, leaving the curtains open, started to pace the room.

"You're so lucky, you know, that you're not in this industry.

You're in, ah . . ." He looked at me confused, as if he didn't know where he was for a moment. "In, ah . . ."

"Advertising. I work with Matthew." Did I need to introduce myself? I looked at him with a frown.

"Matthew, yeah, yeah. Good guy, good guy. He can sing, too, you know. When we were at school, we were in a band together. But he just doesn't have it. You know, *IT.*" He tightened his two fists.

"I didn't know Matthew could sing." I laughed, imagining my friend onstage. He'd probably be good, confident, but he was not a limelight guy.

"He didn't have it."

"Well, I don't think he'd want to be a pop star." I didn't like Jim talking badly about Matthew. Matthew, who wouldn't say a bad word about anyone.

"I'm not a pop star." He glared at me. "It's rock, baby, rock 'n' roll."

I felt so uncomfortable. No matter what I said, pop star, rock star, it was wrong. I was wrong.

There was silence again as he continued to pace the room. He fell back onto the couch and picked up the remote control. "Does this thing work?" He flicked on the telly and channel-hopped for about three minutes before settling on a Channel 4 countdown, *Top British Children's Programs of All Times.* It was on number 58.

"I love this stuff. Yeah," Jim said.

I wasn't sure if that was a question, if I was being asked whether I wanted to watch the show, or if it was just agreed that this was what we'd be doing. I said nothing, just shoved a prawn cracker in my mouth, delighted that the awkward silence had now been filled by bubbly Blue Peter presenters.

Another two hours later, as it was approaching midnight and

the number 1 slot, Jim started to get fidgety. He kept looking over and back at me, as if he had a twitch in his neck. Flick, flick, flick. As the credits began to roll, he turned toward me and, deadpan, without raising an eyebrow or breaking a smile, he swung his flicking neck toward my bedroom door. "So, do you wanna . . . ?"

I didn't need to take a moment to consult my inner fairy guide or to stop and listen to my instincts. I stood up and smoothed down my dress. "No. And I think maybe you should go, now," I said calmly. "I'm tired and wouldn't mind hitting the hay—alone."

Jim bolted off the couch, looking slightly shocked at the rejection, possibly his first. "Right, right," he said in a panicked voice. He quickly picked up his jacket and threw it over his shoulders. He leaned in to give me a kiss on the cheek, but I dodged him.

"Do you mind seeing yourself out? I don't fancy all that camera clicking again."

"Right. Thanks for a great night," he shouted over his shoulder as he headed down the stairs.

I felt really disappointed by the whole evening. Disappointed that I'd let it happen, that Jim was such a letdown, that the *whole evening* was a letdown. And I couldn't help but wonder how a night in the company of Hugh Delaney would have gone. It wouldn't have been awkward; he was so comfortable in his own skin. He wouldn't have played to the paparazzi. Could he cook? I didn't know. I'd probably never know, considering he thought I'd poisoned his dog. I decided I should probably stop thinking about Hugh, as I doubted very much he was thinking about me.

"Good riddance," I hissed in the direction of the door. Out of the corner of my eye I saw a little flicker over the hall table, the area that Jim had called a shrine, like a piece of paper flapping in the wind from an open window. I swear I felt a whisper—I don't think I heard it, it wasn't a noise or a sound, I *felt* it.

To bad rubbish.

I spun around, scanning the room. "What?" I spun again. "Who's there?" I could hear my breathing, excited, nervous. "Who's there?" I shouted again. "Show yourself!"

But I didn't mean it. I didn't want to see anyone or anything. I backed into a corner, focusing on the area the whisper had come from, then slid to the ground, staring intently, watching, waiting. Was I watching for a fairy? I think I was.

18

Maura Ni Ghaora was late. I ripped my paper napkin into tiny balls, making a small field of snowballs around my knife and fork. The waitress gave me a disapproving look, so I quickly ordered a glass of wine. I didn't really want it, but as a former waitress I know how annoying it is when a table orders water. Especially tap water.

I'd turned up early for my lunch with Maura. Now that the paparazzi were increasing in number, my escape route from my flat had become more complicated and took a lot longer. I'd had to change taxis three times on the twenty-minute journey to the restaurant, and I was beginning to feel like a CIA agent, hopping cars and looking over my shoulder. It all took so much planning. In the end, I'd arrived twenty minutes early, so I'd asked for a table at the back, where I sat, uneasily watching the door for cameras.

It was Saturday, three days before I was due to publish the fifth Step. Maura had said she had more information for me. In other words, she'd dangled the carrot and I'd reached. She seemed so mysteriously connected, and her unquestionable belief in fairies made me feel that she might have answers for me.

I looked around the restaurant. There were heavy linen

tablecloths, shiny glasses, baskets of bread rolls, and tall leather chairs. A woman wearing a large black straw hat had been staring at me since I came in. I kept trying and failing not to look back.

"Kate." Maura extended a gloved hand regally and slid into the chair opposite. She idly flicked some nonexistent dandruff off her dark gray suit and twirled the ruby signet ring on her left hand. Her hairline was slightly askew, and I wondered for the first time if she could be wearing a wig. It was difficult to know. Her hair looked so perfect, but maybe that was what was wrong. It was *too* perfect.

"Are you well?" she inquired. "How is everything?"

A wave of emotion caught me off guard and I felt tears pricking behind my eyelids. I blinked them back, realizing just how on edge I was. I was stressed and worried. Not happy.

I buried my head in my glass and nodded frantically, hoping she'd take that for an *all's well*. I knew only too well that Maura wasn't remotely concerned with how I was and was merely passing pleasantries.

A waitress appeared. Brushing the snowballs under the table, I took a long sip of wine and ordered the chicken burger. Maura ordered a small green salad.

"It seems that your relationship with Jim is progressing?" Maura's bulging cheeks bulged even farther as she forced a smile, clearly feigning interest in my private life.

The memory of Jim's swift exit the night before caused my face to turn bright red. "No, it's not what it looks like."

"That's not what it says online."

"Well, you can't believe what you read online."

"What about the pictures? Coming out of your flat? Can we believe that?"

I shifted uncomfortably, remembering. "There were pictures

of that?" Of course there were pictures of that. Why was I surprised?

"Are you finding the paparazzi difficult?" Her catlike eyes narrowed.

I shrugged, hoping to appear nonchalant, not sure what Maura's angle might be.

"I could have them removed."

"Not necessary. I'm fine." I wasn't sure how Maura could have things "removed," and once again I wondered about her connection with gangsters. Could she be dangerous?

I decided to get things back on track. "So, you said you had information? Dug up any old corpses?"

She smiled and played around with the leaves on her plate. "Funny you should mention it, because there isn't a corpse."

What was she talking about?

"No corpse, no grave, no record of Kate McDaid's death."

"Ah, would you stop. That's awful. She is dead, isn't she? That's how this whole thing started. Her will. She's dead."

"Yes, I think we can take it for granted that she is dead. But there is no record of her death and no place of burial."

"Was that normal?" I asked, thinking that maybe back then there were so many people they just fell into ditches and died and no one missed them. I hadn't paid much attention in history class.

"Not really, no. Wakes were big affairs back then."

I looked at her blankly.

"When people died, they'd lay out the body in the front room for three days, and relatives, neighbors, friends, enemies—pretty much anyone and everyone in a fifty-mile radius—would stop in to pay their respects. And they'd grieve, they'd drink and cry, and sing and dance. Nobody bottled up their feelings—they'd come for miles to cry, and many came for miles to drink, and it lasted day and night for three days."

I nodded. "It was all a bit of a party." I was familiar with the legendary shenanigans at Irish wakes.

"So most deaths during that period were registered. But not hers. It is unusual."

"Well, who would want to go to a witch's wake? They were all probably delighted to see the back of her."

"But wakes were about making peace with the dead, too. Forgiveness moved the person on to the next life. They often attended, you know."

"Who are 'they'?"

"The fairies." She looked at me over the rim of her water glass, waiting for a response. "They'd often attend wakes to see the person off."

"Did they not get stood on, being two inches high?" I was making a joke, but she just looked at me, unamused.

"Everything is capricious about them, even their size. They take whatever size or shape pleases them."

"Lucky them. They can wake up a size eight."

Her expression changed and her voice hardened. "Kate, you seem to find this to be a joking matter."

"No, no. It's just how I deal with things. I joke. Badly, it appears."

She straightened up in her seat and resumed normal conversation. "There is a family burial plot."

"Really? I'll tell Dad. He'd be interested."

"Well, it's just the one grave: the mother, father, and brother, who must have kept on the family line. There is room on the tombstone for a fourth person, but, like I said, she's not there."

I asked whether she thought it relevant that there was no grave.

"No grave, no body. I don't know. I'm just trying to build up a picture of who she was."

"Why?"

"I believe this is important." She looked me straight in the eye. "This isn't just your family history, Kate. This is our collective history. We need to understand why the fairies chose your aunt. What is their intention? What is their plan? We have no records of her."

"We?"

She smiled thinly. "We . . . Yes, we wish for the fairies' plans to come to fruition."

"We?" I asked again.

She shook her head, dismissing me.

Maura was irritating me now. Her self-assured look, her cockiness, the way she was playing me, insinuating she knew a lot more than I did. I mean, she probably did, but she could have at least let me in on what she was after. Still, two could play that game.

"I've thought about not posting any more of the Steps," I said. I waited to see her reaction.

Her eyes widened in shock, and she nervously clutched her neck. "You can't do that! You owe it to us, to all of us."

"But I'm getting sick of it. It's blown out of proportion. I'm not who you think I am."

"You can't stop now! There could be side effects. You might be who they think you are." Her gloved hand crawled across the table and grabbed hold of my wrist. She dug her fingers into me. "You must finish this."

I shivered. I put my knife and fork down and pushed my plate and her hand away.

"Apologies," she said quickly. "I'm very passionate about this. You've gone pale, Kate. Are you all right?" Her eyes narrowed.

I paused, wondering whether I should tell her. Tell her that, in spite of myself, I thought there might be something living on my hall table and that I'd stayed up half the night staring at it, waiting and watching for a fairy to appear. Tell her that I talked to plants all the time, and that I knew things I hadn't known before, such as cures for cold sores and restless babies. Tell her that I had a name, a weird name, possibly a fairy name. I shook my head, knowing that even the most cynical people would think these coincidences were stacking up.

"Don't give up on them, though. Finish it, Kate. You have to finish it."

I didn't tell her the truth, that I was nervous about finishing the Steps, nervous that they might drive me mad. Instead, I blurted out the reality of my current situation. "I'm followed by paparazzi everywhere I go. My bike was nicked and has appeared on eBay. People at work think I'm weird. These Steps have put me in a bad situation."

"You could have fun with them, like your parents are." She drained her water glass.

I shook my head. I couldn't see how this could be fun.

"This is important stuff."

And again I thought I might cry. What was wrong with me? I felt so exhausted, pulled so tight I was fraying at the edges. I looked at my empty plate and nodded frantically, blinking back the tears.

Her phone buzzed. I saw the name Frank O'Connor appear. She looked at it, then at me, considering whether or not to answer. She did, and spoke briefly in Irish. I couldn't understand much of what she was saying, but an occasional word flew my way: "having lunch," "her," "I'll call later."

"That wasn't Frank O'Connor, the head of the Gardaí, was

it?" It was a long shot. I was testing the water with her, seeing what her reaction would be. Frank O'Connor was our decrepit defense minister, who also served as the chief of police. He was at least two hundred years old, with a shock of white hair and skin more wrinkled than a rolled-up silk dress. He walked with a cane and a bent back and was known to be a fluent Irish speaker.

She nodded calmly, then added softly: "He follows the actions of the fairies closely."

I was amazed. "Are there more people like him?"

"The less you know the better, but you should know that things could become difficult for you if you decide to stop now. I'm on your side, Kate, but other people . . ." She glanced at her phone. "They might prefer to step in and hurry things along using any means possible." She raised a carefully penciled eyebrow at me.

The silence batted back and forth between us as I tried to digest what she'd just said.

She removed the napkin from her lap, reached across the table, and shook my hand. "Good afternoon, Kate." Coolly, she slipped out of her chair, paid the bill, and left, leaving me confused and scared. Why was she threatening me? Should I be worried?

Why were these people interested in the fairies? Educated people? Politicians? I couldn't understand it. How could things become more difficult for me? Weren't they difficult enough?

I started to exit the restaurant and was weaving my way out when the woman in the black straw hat rose to her feet with great effort, balancing by her knuckles on the table. She pointed a short stubby finger at me, her face flushing bacon-pink and her nostrils flaring to the size of a small fireplace. "Sh-sh-she's a witch!"

My head ducked down and my shoulders drooped six inches. *Get me out of here.*

"A witch!" She looked around to the other diners for support. They mumbled in response, all necks snapping rigidly toward me.

"Her! K-K-Kate McDaid." Her finger stretched out even farther.

A man behind her in a beige-colored suit sprang up like a jack-in-the-box. His eyes were wild. "It's her!"

My mouth was dry and my heart pounded. All I could see was the door. *Get out, get out, before they get you.* I fixed my eyes on the handle and ran toward it. Then I hurled myself through and quickly slammed it behind me. Trembling, I raced in the direction of the main road, waving my arms for a taxi. One screeched to a halt and I dived onto the backseat.

I was being hunted.

19

Step Five

We see a time of taken freedom
and sharpened, darkened skies,
The tears of men we know are coming,
and all will wipe their eyes,
We see a time of twisted fate, a time of broken glory,
It is your future, it is coming—we know this as your story.

We see a time of burning havens,
an air of fire that moans and sings,
We see a time of great unrest,
a time of strife and all these things,
We see a time when torment spreads,
and all else is out of mind,
A time of being shook by pain,
which makes you weep and makes you blind.

So in these doubtful waiting hours,
our lessons to you we teach,
We ask you to stop the time,

put ticks and tocks away from reach,
And know that we are old and young,
and this is how it's meant to be,
Not confined by clocks and tocks,
but living in peace as us and we.

The fifth Step had a tsunami effect. Videos appeared online of people holding hammers over watches and smashing them triumphantly. Bloggers left instructions about how to disconnect the clock on computer screens. The Anoraks lit a small fire in a metal bin and burned some calendars. A man was arrested on O'Connell Street for throwing stones at Clerys clock. (The Gardaí said he was "vandalizing a national monument." He said he was "doing the fairies' will." I wasn't sure how his defense would stand up in court.) Of all the Steps, number five resonated the most. Or maybe it was the cumulative effect—five is better than four.

I hadn't left my flat during the weekend before I posted the Step on the Tuesday, but I was told by reliable sources—my parents and Matthew—that out there in the real world there was a serious sense of anticipation, excitement, and energy on the streets. Seven Step parties were held for the big reveal, and groups on Facebook had organized events. Schools had held art competitions and posted the results online—brightly colored pictures full of leprechauns jiving and fairies sprinkling fairy dust on the streets of Dublin. Fiona had been approached to sell her story on "the real Kate McDaid." She said it was the best laugh she'd had all week.

People were wearing green T-shirts with SEVEN STEPS scrawled on the front. There was a YouTube video of a guy getting a tattoo of the words "Seven Steps" across his chest. What would his mother say? Ann Daly, the newsreader on the telly, made a reference to the fairies in an interview with Colin Powell. They'd been talking about religion. By all accounts, Mr. Powell remained stony-faced; thankfully, the fairies hadn't hit the political press. Every radio station played "The Seven Steps" constantly. Someone had bought the rights to use it for a coffee ad, so it was everywhere. So was Jim: while I ducked and dived he posed and strutted. The remaining members of Red Horizon faded into a smoky background as he strode into the spotlight.

I'd received requests for interviews from journalists promising to tell my side of the story and TV crews wanting to follow me. (I laughed at that one, where would they follow me to? The bathroom? The kitchen? I couldn't even go to the shops anymore.) The bloggers, the Anoraks—they all wanted me to speak. I was referred to as "elusive," "mysterious," "enigmatic." I said nothing because I didn't know what to say.

For the record, I don't own a watch, never have. I've been given watches in the past but always seemed to lose them. It's as if they just slide off my wrist. There were no clocks in my flat, and even the time setting on my mobile phone was wrong. There were clocks at work, obviously, and on my computer, but I didn't actually own a timepiece, so I didn't have anything to destroy, even if I wanted to. I knew Maura would say that my not owning a watch was no coincidence. Lily and the others would have probably exchanged "aha" glances about it, too. But I was hardly the only person in Dublin who didn't have any clocks. This was hardly proof positive of my special relationship with the fairies. That said, the coincidences were becoming impossible to ignore. And if someone like Maura—who was definitely a bit eccentric but also educated and intelligent—believed in it all, could that count for something? In all honesty, there was a part of me that couldn't deny the "coolness" factor. How fantastic would it be if there was a parallel world running alongside ours, with fairies and magic and all those fabulous things I'd believed in as a child?

But then the Anoraks would do something so ridiculous all ideas of coolness flew out the window. On the day I published the fifth Step, they held hands and, singing a song by Drake Chandler in homage to the fairies, they skipped around a bush in my front garden that I recognized to be a giant weed. These were grown men—albeit grown men in anoraks. These were the people who believed in fairies. They were seriously deluded, and I really didn't want to be part or, God forbid, the president, of that club. No, common sense would prevail. I was a logical, sane individual who worked in advertising, read diet books, and had unfortunate one-night stands with guys in bands. I was a modern city girl, and I had no time in my life or room in my handbag for little people.

By Wednesday, I was fully ensconced in captivity. Colin had thankfully given me leave to work from home; I think my presence in the office was becoming too disruptive. I kept the doors of my flat locked, and in between checking work e-mails, I summoned the spirit of Howard Hughes and obsessively cleaned all day long. I picked dust off the skirting boards with a safety pin and polished the walls in the kitchen. I even washed the sofa covers. I had chapped, flaking fingertips and raw nostrils from all the bleach. I was cleaning as a distraction.

Lily called. She was having problems with Mr. Goatee. He was in love with her, but while love should never normally be a problem, his love was verging on obsessive and she was getting freaked out. He was calling in to walk her to work every morning. He'd turn up with coffee; he'd text her and phone her. I argued that these were all nice gestures for a blossoming romance, until Lily filled in the details. Mr. Goatee had started waiting outside her flat an hour before she got up in the morning just in case her alarm clock didn't go off. He'd bring her four different types of coffee so she could choose what she wanted during the walk to work. He sent "I love you" texts seventy-four times a day. He called her, *and* he called her family to talk about her. He was, to put it mildly, acting like a man under a spell. Either that or he was an obsessive lunatic who, in the manner of a Lifetime movie, would at some point make figurines of Lily out of egg cartons and bottles of washing-up liquid before imprisoning her in his wardrobe because he loved her too much to share her with daylight. I suspected that the cookie recipe—could I call it a spell?—had done something to him.

By late afternoon I was starving. My spotless fridge had suffered a mass evacuation—it was dismal and empty. All that remained on the top shelf was a jar of marmalade, which was opened only when Mam called over for breakfast. I looked enviously at the cat food and Mister Snoop Doggy Dogg's overflowing kitty dish. After eight hours of hard-core cleaning, I knew exactly what I had to do. I had to ring Matthew.

I did, telling him I was hungry and agoraphobic. He laughed and promised to be over in a jiffy. *Brilliant*, I thought. I couldn't wait to see him, to relax, to laugh, to see his big smiling face and watch him rub his nose and tell bad jokes.

I looked at myself in the mirror. I was pale and hungry-looking. I pulled my hair off my face, brushed some bronzer on my cheeks, and changed out of my cleaning pajamas and into a pair of boyfriend jeans and a T-shirt.

I heard a commotion outside and knew he was nearby. I could hear shouts, panicked pleas, and high-pitched girlish shrieks coming from the mouths of middle-aged men with large cameras. I peeked through the curtains. A hooded and sunglassed Matthew was racing down the garden path in a flurry. I feared he might run straight into the ground. He had a heavy backpack on, and it looked as if the paparazzi were trying to grab hold of its straps. He shook them off like a wild horse and galloped right into the front door with a thud.

I leaped down the stairs to let him in.

Once inside, he pressed up against the closed door. "Jesus Christ!" he shouted. "Have you seen what's outside?" He bent over to catch his breath. "Bloody hell!"

I'd never heard him curse so much. I gazed down at his bent-over back, amused.

"There's so many of them."

I shrugged, feeling like an old pro.

"So many," he repeated to himself, talking directly to his shoes.

"Thanks for coming."

"Of course I'd come." He straightened up and pulled his hood back, running his hands through his tousled hair. "Wait until you see what I've brought." He kissed his fingers, the way he often did in AlJo's, imitating a stereotypical Italian waiter. "*Magnifico!*"

"Do you want a hand?" I gestured toward his backpack and the steep stairs, but he shrugged me off.

In the living room he shed his jacket to reveal his zipped-up Adidas tracksuit. He looked down apologetically. "Clothes keep shrinking," he explained.

I nodded, deliberately averting my eyes from his Starshoot midriff.

"This place is so clean! This isn't like you. Is that bleach I smell?"

With a proud sweep of my arms, I told him I'd done it all myself and had the bleach scars to prove it.

"Well, you've clearly done enough for today. So now, you sit down, Princess Lo Lo Ki Ki," he said with a sly grin. "I'm taking control of dinner." He guided me over to my own sofa and plonked me down. Within seconds, I had a glass of wine in my hand and the Killers were thumping out some dance beats in the background. From what I could gather, Matthew was thrashing the kitchen, beating up the counter with a variety of pots and pans. Now and again he'd shout out, looking for a masher or a sieve, and even once for a pestle and mortar. He was making a curry, a delicious-smelling curry that was making my eyes sting and my mouth water.

"We could have just got a takeaway, you know," I shouted to him.

"Not the same. It's tastier if you make it from scratch," he hollered back.

"I never knew you cooked."

"There are probably a lot of things you don't know about me." He was standing in front of me, looking right into my stinging eyes with a giant bowl of curry in his hands.

"I'll just chuck it here, yeah?" He put the curry bowl on the coffee table before running back into the kitchen. With a whack, bang, wallop, he produced more plates and dishes. The coffee table was on the verge of collapse, breathing a heavy sigh under the weight of Indian dishes.

We tucked in greedily. With every happy mouthful I complimented the chef. He bashfully accepted. And for the first time in a long time I completely relaxed.

After I'd finished, the food coma set in, so I snuggled up on the couch into a cushion. We started to chat about work and the upcoming shoot with the Hoff.

Matthew laughed. "I think the Little Prince will keel over

with a heart attack when he meets the Hoff. It's going to be hilarious to watch."

"I bet the Hoff is cool. I'll definitely get my photo taken with him for Facebook."

"I got hold of a really old *Baywatch* poster. He has big hair in it—it's brilliant. I'm going to get him to sign it."

"Brilliant." I smiled. "It'll be fun. Work, but fun work."

Matthew nodded enthusiastically. He paused. "So what do you make of it all? Honestly," he asked cautiously. He snapped a papadum in two.

I looked at him in disbelief: I couldn't believe he was still eating. I knew he wasn't talking about the Hoff anymore. And, to be fair, Matthew had been there at the beginning, when Dudley delivered the letter. He felt as much a part of this journey as I did.

"Well, I've been humming and hawing a bit about it all. Could there be something in it? Could fairies exist, or have they existed? Today I decided that it's just not possible. There is no earthly way that fairies can exist."

"You think that? Even now?"

"What do you mean 'even now'?"

"It's just that the Steps, they're good, you know? There's no bad messages in them. What's the harm, really?"

"Matthew, you just ran up my garden path for fear of being attacked by paparazzi. I'm under house arrest, watches all over the place are being smashed up, and people are calling me a witch."

"Oh yeah," he laughed, playfully throwing a crumpled napkin at me. "Aside from all that stuff."

"I can't believe in them. Do you not understand?"

"No."

"If I believe in them . . ." I couldn't believe it, I couldn't believe it, I was finally going to say what had been chipping away at me.

"If I believe in them, in the fairies and that my great-great-great-grand-aunt was a witch, then . . ." My mouth dried up. I swallowed hard. "Then *I'm* in it. I'm part of it. I'm a witch."

Matthew turned his face to me and sympathetically smiled. "Then you're a witch."

"You see? It's just too ridiculous." And we both laughed.

"What if . . . Okay, hear me out." He pulled on his nose. "What if you are? I mean, she saved all this for when you turned twenty-six. What if this is something that just comes on you?"

"Like puberty?"

"Well, hopefully not as bad as puberty," he joked.

"But it hasn't, and it won't," I said, trying to convince myself.

"Yeah, you're right. I'm just being stupid. None of it can be true. I mean, if it were true, you'd be riding around on a broomstick."

"And I'd be making spells to get food in—not having to make phone calls to you."

And then maybe I could add that spell to the list of other spells I seemed to be able to concoct. My mind turned to Mr. Goatee, which reminded me that Matthew was supposed to have had his first online date the night before. "Oh my God! How could I forget the date? Wasn't it last night? How did it go? What did you do? What happened?"

Matthew shook his head, laughing into his wineglass. "Let's just say I'm coming off that site. It's going to remain our dirty little secret."

"Come on. It can't have been that bad."

He raised his eyebrows at me. "It was."

"Information, please."

"Where do I start? She was more thirty-six than twenty-six, divorced and angry about it, had this weird snaggletooth that crept down her bottom lip, was blond in her picture but brunette in person . . ." He was laughing hard now.

"My worst online dating fears have come true."

"It gets worse. She went to school with my older brother, and went out with his best friend, Desperate Dan. You know, the guy who'd shag anyone . . ." His eyes were watering with laughter. "And, and . . ." He slapped his leg for emphasis. "She drank water all night."

I couldn't stop laughing, either. It was too bad. "Was it the worst night of your life?"

He nodded. "When she told me the company she works for had brilliant maternity leave, it put the stamp on the entire evening."

"When's the wedding?"

"July."

"She'll probably be knocked up by then."

"Hopefully. We want a large family." He collapsed on the couch amid peals of laughter. "Game over. I'm off that website. I'm going back to bad setups."

"Just stick to what you know—get drunk and pick up. These newfangled crazes like the Internet will never catch on." I drained my glass of wine.

Matthew cleared the dishes, not allowing me to get up from my sofa coma. He picked at the plates as he went along, chewing the remaining chicken curry and chatting about anything that popped into his head. We decided on a game of Scrabble. I always won, so I was delighted when he suggested it but also slightly suspicious that he was just being kind. He knew that a Scrabble win would make me happy.

Later, after he left, I decided on one more glass of wine, and I did something I'd been putting off since I'd met Maura for lunch. I googled Frank O'Connor, the defense minister, Maura's contact. I wanted to know if there was a connection, if he could really be interested in fairies.

Nothing I read online revealed anything extraordinary about Frank O'Connor's background. A civil servant career had led to a career as a politician, and he'd slowly made his way up the ladder. He was married, had two grown-up children and four grandchildren, was untouched by scandal, and, for all intents and purposes, had led a blemish-free career. I browsed idly through various pictures of him, not sure what I was looking for. Then one photograph caught my eye. It had been taken about five years earlier. He was handing an oversized check to a charity, and there on the little finger of his left hand was a gold signet ring with a large ruby at the center. My heart stopped for a moment in shock. I zoomed in. There was no doubt in my mind: the ring was just like Maura's. What did it mean? Had he given it to Maura?

Frantically, I attacked the shelves in my flat and found the book on Liam McCarthy that Dad had lent me. My heart was racing as I flicked through the pages to the photographs. They were old black-and-white photographs. Where was his left hand? Often hidden in his jacket or clasped behind his back. Where was it?

And then I saw it: a ring on his little finger that looked identical to Maura's and Frank O'Connor's. It must have been a secret sect, a cult. What were they doing? What did they want?

I stared at the photographs, not sure what to do next. I was nervous. Maura was right. They were powerful people and there seemed to be a lot of them, and only one of me.

20

It was Friday, the day of the shoot. We were hours into shooting but still David Hasselhoff hadn't arrived. His flight had been delayed.

I'd spent the night in the hotel near the studio. When I'd planned out my journey from flat to studio, taking into account the paparazzi chase, changing taxis, ducking and diving, it was going to take me about four hours. So I decided to get a head start on everyone and took off twenty-four hours before the shoot, winding down back alleys and speeding up motorways. I stayed in a Travelodge near the industrial estate in west Dublin where the shoot was taking place. It had cardboard walls, a sticky patterned carpet, and the lumpiest bed I've ever encountered.

I didn't get a wink of sleep, but I was on time for the six o'clock shoot. We were in a giant echoing warehouse, ten miles outside of the city, and there were wires and cameras everywhere. I was the first to arrive, and as soon as I stepped onto the set, the director press-ganged me into an intense conference about the script and lighting. When he let me go hours later, the Hoff still hadn't arrived.

I was only mildly concerned. He'd get there eventually—planes had to land at some point. In the meantime, there was a feast of breakfast delights to snack on: croissants, pancakes, fresh fruit, and stacks of bacon.

Matthew was glugging down pancakes with maple syrup. He didn't look up to say good morning.

I sidled up and shoulder-nudged him. "Hi."

He looked over and nodded. His mouth was full.

"No sign of the Hoff?"

He shook his head.

"He'll get here eventually."

A nod.

"The bacon's good."

A nod and a grunt.

There was no point talking to Matthew when there was food around: it always turned into a one-way conversation. "I'm going to chat with Colin."

Colin looked like he needed calming down. He was pacing up and down, buckled over like a perfectly shaped letter *r*, his eyes boring a hole into his shoes. His hands hung past his knees, fingers folded into a nervous fist. I could hear him chewing anxiously as I got closer. He was quietly talking to himself.

". . . of course he'll arrive. I'll just say he was late . . . of course he'll arrive."

"Hey." I shuffled beside him and automatically copied his pace. He straightened up slightly and seemed to snap out of his trance.

"Of course he'll arrive." He looked at me and I realized from his expression that this was a question.

"Of course he'll arrive," I repeated in a soothing fashion.

"It's a hundred twenty grand a day, a hundred twenty grand a day," he said into his mustache. "The agency will have to bury the costs, we'll have to bury the costs. How?" He turned on his heel and retraced his footsteps for the hundredth time. "How?"

I bit my lip and scurried along with him, conscious that anything I might say would probably be the wrong answer.

"Günter Lindz will be here soon. He wants to see David Hasselhoff. He wants to see David Hasselhoff." Colin stopped. Still talking into his mustache and looking at his shoes, he mumbled: "The agency can't afford this. People will lose their jobs if we don't get this campaign right."

I strained my ears to listen to his rantings. Job cuts would be disastrous. My job was the only thing keeping me going.

Colin picked up the pace. He was back to figures: "It's too much—a hundred twenty grand a day, a hundred twenty grand a day." He froze again, midtrot, and stopped talking.

I straightened up and offered to get him some breakfast, as if breakfast could solve everything.

"Oh, good, you're here," he said, seeing me as if for the first time. "Can you get an update on where David Hasselhoff is?"

Happy to be of any use in a crisis, I sped off to my lever-arch folder, stuffed with contacts for David Hasselhoff: PAs' phone numbers, agents' numbers, agents' PAs' numbers, airline details.

They nearly all gave me the same answer: David Hasselhoff was in Dublin on the set of a Starshoot commercial with Kate McDaid, a great personal friend.

Only the airline was more useful. The plane was currently circling Dublin, but bad weather meant they could not predict the landing time.

"But it will land, won't it?" I shouted into the phone.

"They all have to land." The woman laughed.

I sensed another potential problem. "It will land in Dublin?"

"All I can say is that the plane will land."

Oh dear, I thought, *oh dear*.

It was all hands on deck for the big day, so Marjorie was on the shoot. Her hair was pulled into a severe, headache-inducing ponytail that matched her black business suit and dominatrix-style heels. Her eyes darted around the studio, aware that an opportunity to shine might arise at any moment. "Kate? Any calls I can make for you?" she asked.

"Can you get through to a mobile phone on an airplane?"

She studied my face, her brain obviously scrolling through possibilities. "It's against the law to leave your mobile on on planes," she said, deadpan.

"I know, Marjorie. That's why we have a problem." I couldn't help but smirk to myself: the cold sore on her mouth had spread, erupting all over her bottom lip.

"It's not a problem, Kate. It's an opportunity."

"Marjorie, it's a problem." I rolled my eyes at her. Now was not the time for forced optimism. This was serious. No Hoff, no ad.

"We just see things differently, then," she said, before pirouetting off toward Colin, probably to tell him that we had "an opportunity" to tackle.

The shoot director was pacing in a somewhat jauntier manner than Colin, but looking equally nervous. He was wearing a beret, which I'd been assured was an ironic fashion statement, and a pair of large denim dungarees, the cuffs of which fell over his battered Vans runners. He'd spent the last four hours trying to shoot around the Hoff, which was impossible, considering the Hoff was in every shot. Every angle of the Starshoot bar had been filmed.

He and the crew were nervously chomping into Starshoots like greedy children, and had made an impressive dent in the latest pile of free samples.

I spotted Matthew slowly backing away from the breakfast buffet. He looked stoned and was breathing heavily.

I pounced. "Problem," I whispered out of the corner of my mouth.

He looked at me with glazed eyes.

"The Hoff is still up there circling and may not even land in Dublin. This might all need to be pushed back a day or a day and a half, but it costs so much money, and, anyway, he can give us only twenty-four hours for the shoot. Colin's seriously talking about job cuts."

The gravity of the situation woke Matthew from his food stupor. "What'll we do?"

Before either of us could answer we both jumped in fright at the sound of a door squeaking loudly, like fingernails running up a blackboard. A puff of stinging aftershave exploded and crackled into the room. We heard the confident *clip-clop* of Cuban heels on cement floor. And there they were: the Little Prince and his entourage, looking hungrily around the room, expecting to see their idol. They'd come by train from the north of Ireland, where apparently they'd spent the previous three days at a global chocolate conference titled "The Future of Chocolate—Berries!"

The Little Prince's gray silk suit reflected every glimmer of light in the room, creating a halo effect around his tiny body. He saw immediately that the Hoff was not present. Seeing Colin, who had creaked his back upward, the Little Prince headed for him like an excited torpedo. Colin broke into a grin that I recognized as pure panic and ran toward his client. They huddled together on the far side of the room, backslapping and guffawing. Shouts of "Good, yah, good!" bounced around the cavernous warehouse.

Matthew looked at me, worried. "I don't think he's told him, somehow."

"I don't think so, either," I replied.

The Little Prince was beaming from ear to ear, his face luminous with joy. He waved like an Oscar winner as he and his entourage exited. Matthew and I both gave him a thumbs-up sign, and then slapped one another's hands down immediately.

"What are you doing?" Matthew hissed.

"I dunno," I said, suddenly feeling ashamed and betrayed by my thumbs. "I just got caught up in the moment. He looked so happy. You did it, too."

"I was copying you."

"We're dead."

Colin, who had aged fifty years in five minutes, hobbled toward me, wringing his hands in despair.

"Do—do—do you have any news?"

"Emmm."

Matthew nudged me. *Just tell him.*

And so I did, and I watched a grown man cry. Big fat tears careened down the crevices of Colin's face. Somebody pulled up a chair and he collapsed onto it, the full extent of his devastation playing out in a series of whimpers and sobs. "Th-that's it. It's over."

I awkwardly patted his shoulder. "The Little Prince seemed to take it well. Very well, in fact."

Colin arched his back at me and rolled his eyes in disbelief. "I told him the Hoff was getting his makeup done in his dressing room. He's coming back to meet him in an hour."

Matthew and I looked at each other, scared.

"Maybe he'll understand," Matthew butted in.

"We're going to lose the account. We're going to have to cover the cost of the shoot. Jobs are gone, gone. There's a recession knocking on our door, and we're going to be one of the first to take the fall." His voice was high-pitched and squeaky.

The director and his crew had begun circling the crumpled Colin.

"Should we just pack up then, mate?" the director shouted across without an ounce of sympathy. "Suits me. We can go to the pub." There was a murmur of approval from the rest of the crew at the prospect of a pint at half-ten in the morning.

"I don't know. I don't know what to do." Colin sobbed into his hands.

Matthew, normally good in a crisis, pulled me out of the crowd and over to the side of the room. "What'll we do? We have to fix this," he whispered. "The promotion, maybe even our jobs, everything rests on this."

"I know!" My hands flew out, palms facing up to the sky. "But I don't know what we can do. What do you think?"

The crew had started to shuffle around the room. Some were putting on jackets and picking up bags, ready to bolt for the door as soon as they got the nod.

"Kate." Prodded by a poker, Colin rose up.

I looked over expectantly. Could he have a solution? I strode back to him.

"You could fix this." His eyes were clear and his nostrils flared.

I heard some members of the crew groan. They started taking off their jackets again.

Nodding, I agreed with Colin. "I could. I—I—I tried, you know? I rang Aer Lingus, and I got onto the Hoff's agent and his PA. If you can think of something else, I could get right onto it immediately." I was poised, ready to jump.

"No, no." He shook his head, his long hair waving ferociously behind him. "The other stuff."

I stayed silent, scared of what was coming next.

His eyes narrowed. "You could get him here."

"How? Even if I went to Germany or wherever he's going to land, we'd still be a day behind, and he's out of time. He has to go back to the States. It's all about time. I'd go if I thought it would help, but I don't see how that would make a difference."

"No, no." Colin waved his fingers in front of me. "The other stuff."

I sighed heavily. "Colin, there is no other stuff."

"Well, maybe there is. Maybe if you just focused, you know, really worked at it, maybe you could summon him here, or maybe you could stop time? The fairies, your people, they have some control over time, don't they?"

"Stop time?" I raised my eyebrows.

"Well, whatever it is you do . . ."

"This is what I do. I work here, in advertising. I can call people on the phone. I can't summon people and stop time." I couldn't believe what I was hearing. Colin believed I had magical powers.

"Oh, come on, that's bullshit." He looked angry. "Just try. Try and stop time."

I was totally taken aback. In five and a half years, I'd never heard him raise his voice, never seen his color go beyond a mild fuchsia. I'd also never seen him cry.

"Colin . . ." His name hardly came out of my mouth.

"The Little Prince said you can do it. He said the only reason the Hoff agreed to come was because of some spell. So come on, work that spell." The crew members were gathered around red-faced Colin, looking at me like I was a freak show, a real live bearded lady.

"There is no spell, Colin."

"Oh, come on."

"There is no spell, Colin." I spun around. "Tell him, Matthew."

Matthew, who had remained quiet during the whole transaction, stood two feet behind me, stony-faced.

"There's no spell, Colin. She used her influence. That's all."

"You see? I told you." My jaw jutted out defiantly. "I told you," I repeated for the benefit of the goggle-eyed crew, who were waiting for a genie to pop out of a bottle.

"Well, can't you just try something?" Colin clenched his teeth at me.

"Try what?" I shouted.

Matthew took a step toward me. "You know, Kate—maybe you could, maybe you could just try something."

"What, Matthew? You know I can't!"

"Maybe if you just tried." Matthew looked everywhere but at my furious gaze.

I wanted to punch him. I wanted to punch them all. How could they, how could they put me in this position? How could he? I looked at Matthew, and a gigantic wave of rage washed over me. How dare he!

"How could you?" I spat the words at him.

"Kate, it's our jobs. I don't want to lose my job. I love my job. I love working with you." He raised his eyes slowly and looked at me. "Maybe if you just tried to stop time . . ." His voice trailed off as he realized the mistake he'd made.

"How could you?"

Marjorie sprang into the center. "Maybe I can? Maybe I can?" She started spinning in a circle, like a deranged twister, waving her arms. Then she pulled her hair out of its ponytail and whirled it around furiously, shouting at the top of her lungs: "Hocus-pocus, diddly-ocus!"

The crew took a step back. Nobody knew where to look.

Slowly they inched away and dispersed around the room, leaving Marjorie wriggling and flapping on the ground like a fish. *"Abracadabra!"*

I turned to Matthew. "Hocus-pocus, Matthew." My eyes filled with tears, and my anger turned to sorrow and then a searing pain of absolute loss. I knew there was nothing else to say. It had all been said. I picked up my jacket, looped my bag over my shoulder, and, wiping my cheeks on my sleeve, I walked out.

21

In films, when an actor runs out of a room crying, she's always followed by someone. Then they have a fight, or some type of romantic declaration, there are more tears, maybe some shouting. But there's always a resolution after the crying.

It doesn't happen like that in real life. I stormed off the set, barely able to see through a mist of tears, banged every door behind me and stomped my feet and gritted my teeth until, finally, a blast of cool air hit me. I was outside. But there was no patter of feet racing after me, no shouts or pleas for forgiveness. There was no one.

As the final door slammed I found myself in the deserted car park of an industrial estate somewhere west of Dublin. The wind whistled past windowless cardboard-box buildings with sprawling car parks. There were no cars and no signposts. It felt like a corporate ghost town. I looked left and right. Nothing was familiar. I decided to go right, thinking there must be an exit somewhere or a person I could ask directions from. Five steps in, it started to rain, and heavy plops washed the tearstains from my cheeks.

There are moments in life when you're entitled to feel sorry for yourself. This was one of those moments. For starters, I'd probably just lost my job *and* my best friend *and* everyone thought I had superpowers *and* it was raining *and* I was lost in an industrial estate. *Poor me*, I thought. *Poor, poor me.*

But I marched on, trooper-like, past the cement boxes, scanning furiously for a person, a sign. And then one came. Well, it actually fell out of a tree and landed in front of me: a large black cat. He had clumps of fur missing and a lame back leg that he cocked haughtily in an effort to maintain some semblance of dignity. One eyeball protruded while the other eye was at half-mast. He looked like a lazy pirate. I wondered how he'd made it up a tree to fall out of.

"Where did you come from? Does anyone own you? Did the fairies send you? They seem to be popping up everywhere these days." I knew no one could hear me, except for the cat, obviously.

He cocked a ripped ear in response.

"Left, right, left, right. Where'll I go?"

Looking decidedly unamused, he turned around on his three good legs and started walking to the left. With no better options, I followed him. I followed him all over the industrial estate as he snaked around Dumpsters. He paused to clean his ears. I stood, waited, and then followed again. And after a while, after I'd stopped crying, soaked to the bone, he led me down a tight alleyway littered with rubbish bags, and at the end I heard the roar of angry traffic, and there in front of me was a monstrous motorway with cars like dangerous bees zipping past. I looked around for the mangy cat; he was sauntering off, his tail poker high. *Bye-bye*, I thought. *Now what do I do? Which way is home, Toto?*

I stuck my thumb out. Anywhere was better than here. If I went too far north, I could always turn around and go south. I just needed a car to take me to the nearest petrol station, so I could figure out where I was and then call a taxi. It would all be fine. I wouldn't think about what I'd left behind me; I wouldn't give it one more thought. Except I couldn't stop seeing Matthew's face and feeling betrayed. *Stop, stop, stop!* I pushed those thoughts away, closed my eyes tightly, and focused all my energy on the word *stop. Stop. Stop. Stop.*

A truck came to a halt. A monster truck. Had I just stopped a truck by thinking about stopping a truck?

A large, ruddy, pockmarked face edged out the window. "I'm going past town." His words were carried on the wind to me. He opened the door, handed me a sweaty palm, and pulled me up high into his monster truck. I fell into the seat, and a large molded casing surrounded me, like a Barbie Doll in a box. It smelled of vinegary pine freshener. The driver was wearing a patterned woolen jumper with triangles running across his middle in orange and blue—it was the Made in China squeaky wool kind.

"Howerya." He back-nodded his head, giving the standard Irish greeting.

"Grand, thanks."

"You were on the motorway."

I smiled back at him.

"Unusual to see a girl on the motorway." He moved the gear stick, and the truck let out a large hissing noise. "Into town, is it, so?"

"Thanks, yeah." Then I had a flash forward of what awaited me at home: cameras clicking wildly, shouting, pleas from the Anoraks, and no food in a cold flat that wasn't feeling like a haven anymore. My shoulders started to tense up at the thought of the race up my garden path. There'd be press everywhere. I chewed my fingernails, thinking hard.

"I'm on the road four days," he volunteered. "Four days on, four days off. I pick up hitchhikers now and again. Bit of company, you know yourself. I get sick of the radio. There's only so much Tom Byrne a person can take."

The truck chugged off, blending into the spaghetti lanes of cars. The red furry dice hanging from the windscreen mirror rocked hypnotically back and forth.

"I'm transporting frozen foods. Ice cream, pizzas, you know yourself. Sure, if you were hungry, we could defrost something." He let out a little chuckle to himself. "Shtick it on the engine, sure, it'd be cooked in no time." I got the impression he'd told this joke before. It was his, no pun intended, icebreaker, with hitchhikers. And it worked. I laughed. There was something fatherly about him, good-natured and old-fashioned.

"It's a great truck. Huge."

"She's good, all right. Not a bother out of her."

I stared out the window at the cars whizzing by.

He kept talking. "I used to transport live cattle, but I got sick of it. The mooing and the braying and the neighing out of them, you couldn't hear yourself think. So I said, I'm not doing it anymore. I said give me the dead things, and they did. Thanks be to God."

I decided he didn't need me to agree with him, he just needed someone there to absorb his sound. "I go across the country, collect the delivery in Dublin from a warehouse about thirty miles behind us and then it's straight all the way to Clare, deliver it to Aldi—you know, Aldi, the Germans—deliver it to them and then come back to Dublin. Spend the night and off again the next day. I'm probably driving about seven hours straight a day. I'd do more if they'd let me, but sure, it's all unionized and legalized. Sure, you can't do anything anymore."

"You go to Clare?" I straightened up in my seat.

"I do. Aldi in Ennis. The Germans."

I chewed my nails some more, thinking. I didn't believe in signs anymore. I didn't believe in coincidences anymore. I didn't think the universe was weaving a path out for each and every one of us—I thought it was too busy with battling aliens and galaxy wars. But if I did believe in coincidences and signs again, I thought this might have been one.

"Do you know Knocknamee?"

"Sure. Amn't I driving through it twice a day? We've been trying for years to get them to bypass it. You have to go right through the village. It's a tricky, small road. They'd plans and everything for a bypass, but every time it was about to go in, they objected, the locals. Sure, you wouldn't know what's going on there at all."

"So, you're going through it today?"

"I'll be there, all going well, in about three hours, I'd say."

I watched the raindrops trickle down the windowpane. "Do you think you could give me a lift there?"

"To Knocknamee?"

I felt my heart race. Knocknamee. This felt right. This felt good.

"Yeah, Knocknamee."

"Why would you want to go there? It's a tiny place."

"I've got family down there. It's about time I looked them up."

"Sure. Hold tight. We'll be there in three hours."

Four hours later, we were approaching Knocknamee. George, my truck driver, had regaled me with stories of his life with his wife, Mary, and their four kids. He told me Mary wanted him to stop driving and take a job with the council, but he was having none of it.

George stopped at the top of the hill to let me out. He gave me a quick hug and tried to thrust twenty euros into my hand for a cup of tea and a bite. I refused the money and told him to give it to his ten-year-old son, who was doing a skipathon the following week.

I was sorry to say good-bye to him, but he assured me there'd be a seat next to him for the trip back to Dublin.

I waved him off and took in the view of the village of Knocknamee. The sun was shining—during the trip across Ireland we'd outdriven the weather. I hadn't expected Knocknamee to be so beautiful. It was the stuff of dreams, and yet it felt familiar. The main street meandered like a peeled orange skin curling back on itself. Peppered on its curves were cozy thatched cottages, some hosting creaking iron signs swaying lazily: Guinness Is Good for You, *Oifig an Phoist*. Their straw roofs flickered in the golden sun.

The village was nestled at the foot of majestic sweeping mountains draped in green velvet, which guarded the place like a mother's protective hands. A giant shimmering Catholic cross perched on top of a church spire loomed proudly at its entrance. I breathed it in—the purity and sharpness of the air overflowed in my lungs. Beaming, I sprang down the hill toward the lovely village of Knocknamee.

I strode along the main street, drinking in the atmosphere. It was quiet. I came across a handful of villagers, old men stooped on a bench, flat caps shadowing their faces, tweed jackets capturing the heat of the day. I nodded in their direction, but they were too busy discussing politics or whatever to notice me.

The largest building on the street was Tyrrell's, a grocery shop at the front with a small pub tucked in behind. A bell rang announcing my arrival as I swung the door open. Dusty tins of

Batchelors Baked Beans adorned the shelves and pink inflatable armbands and buckets and spades littered the corners of the shop. A wire rack of neon-colored postcards swayed freely and bottles of TK lemonade balanced on newspapers.

A tall white-haired man watched me curiously. His belly rested on the countertop, and the buttons on his white shirt strained with his every breath. "Howerya."

I smiled. "Grand, thanks. Is the pub open? Do you serve food?"

"We are. We do."

"Great." I maneuvered past the bookstand, banging my hip into the freezer, and wedged myself into the pub section, where four high stools were squashed up against a counter. I perched myself on one, nose to nose with a Guinness tap. Enjoying the warmth of a mild June afternoon, I took off my jacket, wrapped it around the stool beside me, and sat my bag on top of it.

From the far end of the counter the man dislodged his belly and ambled slowly toward me.

"What can I get you?"

"What do you have?"

"Soup, toasted sandwiches, Tayto." Tayto are the makers of the finest cheese and onion crisps in Ireland, if not the world—a glorious institution.

"Yes, please," I said, suddenly realizing just how hungry I was.

"Right so."

The soup was vegetable, the sandwich was ham and cheese, and the Tayto were perfect. The barman and grocer was Martin. He joined me for the soup, and although he eyeballed me with curiosity he didn't ask me any questions. He was happy to chat about the weather and the size of supermarkets in Dublin.

"You wouldn't know where you'd be in those places." His

accent came from the back of his throat and rose and fell like an orchestra reaching its crescendo.

"I know. They can be large." With great satisfaction I put my spoon down and pushed away my bowl. I was full to the brim.

"Will you go again?" He looked at my empty soup bowl and stood to replenish it.

"I couldn't, honestly. Thanks, though."

"Tea. You'll have tea." There was no room for refusal. A pot of tea and a packet of chocolate HobNobs appeared from under the counter. I sipped and dunked happily, memories of David Hasselhoff and screaming paparazzi fading rapidly.

Martin coached the under-twelve hurling team, who were showing great potential, by all accounts, particularly a Sean Og, who was born with a hurling stick in his hand. The locals were trying to raise funds to buy the team a kit so they could compete in the nationals. There were pictures of them in a rainbow of colored T-shirts all over the shop/pub. I wondered why he was telling me about this, I wondered if he recognized me, if he was looking for money from me. I stopped myself. I couldn't and wouldn't allow myself to get suspicious of people. He probably told everyone about his team—he was proud of them.

"Will you be looking for a place to stay?"

Again the panic gripped me. Why was he asking? What did he know?

He sensed my anxiety. "I only ask because we've rooms above, and you've a look of uncertainty about you. Sometimes, when you're running, you're best to stand still a while."

I breathed deeply. That's all I wanted: to stand still.

"I'm only saying, there's a place up the road—Miles O'Brien runs it. He's four acres of pure rock out the back. Nothing will grow there for him, never has. I suppose you could go there if you wanted, but they say there are mice. But if you wanted a room here, my wife will sort you out grand."

"That would be great, thanks," I said, double-checking that my Visa card was in my wallet.

"You should stay till Monday, anyway. We do a chicken soup on Monday that would put hairs on your chest."

Mavis had a bosom that you wanted to run straight into and a behind that you wanted to look away from. She stared at me for a long time when she saw I had no luggage, no doubt wanting to know what brought a Dublin girl with no plans to the back end of Clare on a Friday. But, like her husband, she welcomed me and didn't question.

"Sometimes people just need to stand still," I said by way of explanation.

Happy with this diagnosis, she rubbed her hands together and led me upstairs, balancing carefully on each step as it creaked under the strain of her ample figure. She squeezed through the upstairs passageway and showed me to my room—well, she showed me five rooms and told me I could have whichever I thought best. Knocknamee was quiet at the moment, she explained, as she wiped a strand of white hair from her unwrinkled face.

I chose a room with pink rosebuds on the walls. It wasn't the biggest, but I liked the way the rosebuds didn't join up where the strips of wallpaper met—they were centimeters off from being a perfect fit. The imperfection made me feel right at home. I was going to be happy with Martin and Mavis.

22

I woke well rested and lay in bed looking at my rosebudded walls. *What now?* I thought.

I reached across the bed, grabbed my phone, and rang Lily to tell her where I was.

"What's it like?"

"Beautiful."

"I could come down? Take leave? Hide out with you for a while."

"Do you need to hide from Mr. Goatee? Is it any better?"

"It's worse," she sighed. "He's writing about me on a blog, pages and pages of stuff about my hair, my nose, my eyes."

"Weird."

"Tell me about it."

"I have a suggestion . . ."

"You do? Oh, please tell me. I'll try anything to get him off my case."

"Well, before I went to sleep last night, I asked out loud. It's a thing I've been doing, and it seems to work." I was sounding apologetic. "I asked: 'How can Mr. Goatee fall out of love with Lily?' And then I had a dream, and you were in it, and so was he. Well, I mean, it wasn't him—it was just a big goatee—but I'm pretty sure it was him. And there was a fairy, of course, because what else is going through my head these days? Anyway, the fairy was holding a stick and cutting it between you, but the stick had some lilies wrapped around it. I don't know if that's just because of your name or if there's something else. Then the fairy turned counterclockwise three times. Don't ask me how I know it was counterclockwise, but it was—you know how in dreams you just know things? And you have to say, 'This is broken.'"

"Kate, I'll try anything. I'll happily try this."

"Okay. Sorry it's a bit odd."

"This whole situation is odd—I need to get rid of him. Anyway, are you sure I can't come down to you?"

I appreciated the offer but said I wanted some space. I had some things to figure out.

"How's Fiona?" I asked.

Lily paused. "She's not great. The board of directors have put her on a formal warning. She's kept her job for now, but she says they're muscling her out and not giving her any work to do because they don't trust her. They want her to quit."

"What will she do?"

"I don't know. That's part of her problem. All she's ever known is work. If she didn't work, what would she do? Like, think about it, Kate. I can't remember the last time she even talked about a guy, let alone kissed one."

"I know, but she always says she doesn't have time."

Lily sighed. "Maybe if she quit her job she'd finally have time for the other things in life."

"Like men?"

"Well, yeah. Men and holidays and yoga."

"Yoga?"

"Oh, I don't know."

"While I think of it, I know you hate cats, but can you ask Fiona to call into my flat and feed Mister Snoop Doggy Dogg?"

We chatted for another little while until Lily had to go into a meeting. I hung up. Dad rang. He and Mam had been at some awards ceremony the night before. They were now officially D-list celebrities, which secured their invites for pretty much every opening or closing event that had a red carpet in Dublin. Dad had stood on the sidelines taking photos while Mam danced with Liam Neeson. Now she was sleeping off the excess champagne—it didn't agree with her.

"He was a great dancer, love. Had that whole cha-cha-cha thing going on. And you know how your mother loves to dance. Handing her over didn't bother me in the slightest."

I told him where I was.

He was surprised and a little bit worried. "Do you have enough money? Your mother and I can be down in a couple of hours to keep you company."

"No, Dad, honestly, I'm grand. I want a bit of a break from all the madness. Anyway, don't you have a shoot for the self-tanning gel?"

"We do, but sure, we could get Harry to reschedule. We'd much rather come down to you."

"Ah, no. You'll enjoy it. Have a good time. Show off your fake tan." I laughed down the phone at him.

"I'm half orange. But they're paying good money for it. Are you sure you don't want us?"

"Sure."

"I'll tell you, have your bit of a break and we'll head straight to Knocknamee after the shoot. It'll only be a few days."

"That sounds great."

"Now call if you need money or a chat or anything."

"I will, Dad." I hung up. My phone buzzed again. No such thing as peace and quiet. Fiona.

"Kate, we're on our way down in a day or two."

"What, Fi? What about work?"

"I quit. Can you believe it? I'd just had enough of them. It's like I woke up this morning and every inch of me said quit. I listened to my gut instinct, like your fairies said to do. And I did it. I quit. I rang my boss—I knew she'd be at work on a Saturday—and quit. Just like that! God, it felt good."

"Oh, wow!"

"I know. I never thought I'd do it. But it feels amazing." Fiona was talking at a hundred miles an hour. "I feel free, Kate. I should have done this years ago. I've saved some money, so I can take time to figure out what I'm all about."

"You sound really happy."

"I am. Ecstatic." She took a deep breath. "And myself and Lil fancy a road trip to Knocknamee. We haven't done one in ages. Load the car up with cider and crisps, get the tunes pumping loud—it'll be mighty *craic*. And Kate, you need us. Stop pretending you don't."

I did. I knew I did.

"Give us a couple of days to get sorted. We just have to make up a few good lies for Lily's work, and then we're on our way to the wild west. If you catch any fairies, shove them in your handbag and hang on to them until we get there."

"Thanks, Fi. And do you think you guys can bring me some stuff from home, some clothes, jeans, a few tops, my laptop?"

"Yeah, of course, and, Kate, this'll all be fine. This witch shit, these fairies, these Steps—they'll all be fine."

I hung up, smiling, delighted they were coming and thrilled Fiona sounded so happy. I stretched. Now what?

The smell of bacon sizzling gave me my answer. Up and at 'em. I put on yesterday's clothes, washed my face with soap and water, and tied my hair back into a loose ponytail.

Martin was stooped over a frying pan in the kitchen. Smoke billowed up to the ceiling. Mavis was clinking teacups and pouring steaming water into a blue teapot. She was humming quietly to herself.

"Morning," I announced cheerfully.

Martin turned around with a smile. "'Tis yourself."

"You'll be wanting tea." Mavis reached for another cup.

"Can I help?"

"Would you go on with that? Sit in there, now. Martin'll have the breakfast ready in a minute."

I sat down at the kitchen table, watching their easy, well-practiced routine.

"I thought I might do some sightseeing today. Is there anywhere you'd recommend?"

Mavis placed the teapot in front of me and started to pour. "An Trá Bhán is always popular with visitors—you could go for a dip? Or you could climb to the top of Devil's Bit. You can see forever from there. Or there's the old ruin."

Martin shook his head furiously. "Sure, why'd she want to go there?"

"Sometimes people are interested in that kind of thing."

"Well, she's not," he said sternly. Martin placed a mountain of fried food on the table, and was just about to sit when Mavis threw him a look. "Toast. I forgot toast." He retreated back to the toaster. "Did you come by car?"

"No. I didn't drive."

"Well, then, she can't be going to An Trá Bhán."

"How far is it?"

"Six miles, but it's a tricky road."

"She could take Colm's bike." Colm was their son. He was studying accountancy in Dublin.

I loved the idea of taking Colm's bike, but stayed quiet until they'd agreed on it themselves. Which they did, eventually, saying it needed a bit of fresh air to keep its wheels turning.

Two hours later, with a pencil sketch of the area and a muddled set of directions, I had mastered the crossbar on an oversized racer and was battling the hills all the way to An Trá Bhán. The uphill pushes were exhausting and the freewheeling downhills exhilarating. Not one car passed me as I spun around the back roads of Knocknamee, admiring the varying shades of green that tumbled in on themselves: the fields, the trees, the bushes all fighting with the road. The sky was freckled with clouds, and the summer sun shone on me and the open road.

An Trá Bhán was a white sanded beach that swept majestically for miles and melted into the ocean like the head of a pint of Guinness. The sea flapped with great urgency and intention, frothing, at the cool, frosty beach. There wasn't the shadow of another person, or the footsteps in the sand of those who must have walked there before me, my ancestors. As I admired this unchanged landscape, I knew I was looking at the same view, crunching the same sand underfoot as they had.

I walked for over an hour, enjoying the peace and stillness. And then the happiest thing happened—it felt like a dream— and my heart overflowed. Bounding up the beach, heavy paws flying, ears flapping, and gray curly hair rippling in the wind, was Setanta. It was a healthy, robust Setanta, much happier than the last time I'd seen him slumped weakly in Hugh's arms and practically foaming at the mouth. I couldn't believe it. The west of Ireland: hadn't Hugh said they were heading back to the west? Wasn't the west home? Where was he? Where was Hugh?

Setanta recognized me immediately and threw his big paws onto my shoulders in a loving embrace. All was forgiven, by him, at least. I struggled to keep my balance under his weight but eventually had to give in. I fell to the sand, his nose on my nose, licking my face. Laughing, I pushed him off and rolled away, conscious of the sea inching toward me. I turned my head to see a familiar pair of mucky hiking boots. A giant hand appeared, and a shocked-looking Hugh smiled down at me. Our eyes locked. Lost in his gaze, I took his hand and heaved myself up. Setanta bounced around us.

"You . . ." Hugh stopped, and his face exploded into a giant smile that stretched from one end of An Trá Bhán to the other. "Where did you come from?"

"I think I just ran away," I admitted.

"This is so strange."

A dark-haired couple were approaching us. Setanta knew them and in a few strides he'd encircled us all.

Hugh turned to the couple and then looked back at me. "Kate, this is my brother, Niall, and his wife, Aisling. They've got a place near here."

I moved forward and shook their hands, noticing that Niall had the same gray eyes as Hugh but looked a bit older— mid-thirties, maybe. Aisling jumped forward to kiss my cheek, her straight brown hair getting caught in the wind.

"Are you from Knocknamee, Kate?"

"No. Dublin. I guess I'm just visiting. It's beautiful here. I'm staying in Martin's B and B in town."

"Ah, Martin. I know him. We've had friends stay there when our house got too crowded with guests."

"You're from Dublin and you know my brother?" Niall looked at me quizzically. "You're a friend of Long Hugh's?" He turned to Hugh and laughed. "I thought you hated Dublin people!"

"Long Hugh?" I chose to ignore the Dublin comment, knowing it to be true.

"On account of the height, not any other part of his anatomy." They all laughed; a family in-joke.

"We worked together. Well, kind of, but not really." Hugh looked at his shoes.

"We just love it here. There's something special about this place," Niall said, his face glowing.

Setanta started to bark, anxious to keep moving.

"Well, any friend of Hugh's is a friend of ours." Aisling smiled at me, revealing straight pearly-white teeth. "Will you come for dinner tomorrow night? We're going all out, with a pig on a spit. A few friends are calling around. God, you're not a vegetarian, are you?"

I shook my head.

"That's set, so. You'll come, won't you?"

I wanted to, I definitely wanted to. This lovely, friendly couple, Setanta, handsome Hugh—he couldn't still hate me, could he? I looked over at him to see whether it was okay.

He flashed me that million-dollar smile. "Come if you want."

Hardly a glowing invitation. *Damn him*, I thought, *I'm coming anyway*. "I'd love to, thanks for asking."

Aisling scribbled down their address, some directions, and all three of their phone numbers. We said good-bye and I carried on along the beach, still enjoying my walk but now with an excited, nervous feeling bubbling in my stomach. *Breathe in the air*, I thought. *Breathe it in.*

23

Back at my rosebudded HQ I flicked on my phone with great trepidation. Every time I turned it on I was opening the gateway to the outside world, and I wasn't sure I wanted to.

Jim: "Yo, babe, wondering where you at? We're playing a gig Saturday, would love you to come?"

I hit delete.

Matthew: "Kate . . . I'm so sorry. I just . . . I'm so sorry."

Delete.

Matthew: "Kate, I'm sorry. Where did you go, anyway? You just ran out of here."

Delete.

Colin: "Kate, I apologize for anything I might have said to offend you. I really didn't mean to. I panicked. Call me back."

Delete.

Matthew: "Call me."

Delete.

Mam: "Hi, love, how's Knocknamee? Your father says I'm not to disturb you, but I couldn't help myself. Hope you're doing OK. Love you, pet, call me back."

I went downstairs to the grocery store–pub, mistakenly swinging my handbag around, just millimeters from creating a baked bean avalanche.

Martin was hunched over the countertop, reading a newspaper. "Tea?"

I shook my head. I fancied something else: atmosphere, ambience. There I was, miles from home and yet feeling strangely at home. My worlds were beginning to collide in Knocknamee, and I had to wonder why. Why had I ended up here? What cosmic forces were at play? I was sure that it had to be related to the Red Hag and that I owed it to her and to me to see if I could uncover more about her past. Who knew where the past could lead me?

"I might go for a walk up the town. Admire the view."

I walked into O'Donahue's pub, three doors up, promising myself I'd buy a postcard of the view. O'Donahue's was a dark pub with a scattering of knee-high stools and small round tables dotted with beer mats. There were four old men perched at the bar like budgies, dipping their heads in and out of their Guinness. A heavyset woman with rosy cheeks stood chatting to them from behind the bar.

I bought a pint of Guinness. *"Sláinte."* I mumbled the Irish word for "cheers" quietly to myself.

I chose the table in the corner, conscious of being there alone, and glanced around to see who else was there. A very drunk man was slumped in the opposite corner, speaking and swaying softly to the audience in his head.

Then a chilly gust of wind blew into the pub. The door banged shut, and the room froze for a nanosecond as all eyes turned.

Only I recognized her. Maura Ni Ghaora. She glided, catlike, across the room. Sitting opposite me, she ran her hands over her straight hair and clawed at a gold brooch on her neck.

"Maura. How did you . . ." I whispered.

"I thought I could assist you, and the fairies, in your quest," she said in a low purr.

"How did you know I was here?" Her presence made me nervous. I still hadn't been able to prove anything, but I was almost certain she was involved in a cult, a cult that dabbled in the dark arts. Her motives were sinister, I was sure of that now.

Maura ignored me. "As I explained previously, we are always interested in Knocknamee. It's a gateway to the fairy world."

Tír na nÓg, I thought.

"I'm researching the Red Hag and life during those times to understand her connection to the fairies." Maura leaned in so close to me I could see the glue on her false eyelashes. "We're getting close." Her breathing quickened, and for the first time she seemed to be showing an emotion—excitement.

She removed her gray cashmere jacket, revealing a cream lace blouse. "It's always helpful to speak to local people, to try and build up an image of the past. Often history lives in their current stories and lives."

I nodded in agreement. If I could, I should keep her onside.

Anyway, there was no way anyone in Knocknamee would speak to Maura. She was too different, too strange. I decided to play along with her. "Is it likely there'll be any stories?" I asked. "I mean, really, the Red Hag died over one hundred and thirty years ago."

"Given she was a witch . . ." Maura paused and looked at me. "It's likely she left a legacy. Her story will be here." She looked around the pub. "It'll be here."

"How will you find out?"

"I'll talk to people. I'll do it quietly, see if they'll open up to me."

I shrugged, remembering she was a journalist: she'd be used to getting things out of people. And just because I found her odd didn't mean everyone else would.

Maura produced the brown leather folder in which she kept the Steps. New pages had been added to it. "These are some notes, archive information about the era. Postfamine, 1850 onward, was a difficult time in the west of Ireland."

My face scrunched up. I felt guilty. In my head, the history books ended around 1852. I never thought about life after the famine, what it must have been like to pick up the pieces in a place where all that was left were ghosts of the past.

"Knocknamee, this tiny little spot, lost fifteen hundred people in the famine. That was almost two-thirds of the town's entire population. After the famine, the poverty was immense." Maura's fingers, gloved in cream leather, were flicking through her notes. "No money, no land. Just graves and emigrants. Times were hard. For example . . ." She pushed a piece of paper under my nose.

It was a record dated 18 April 1849, from a workhouse in Limerick.

There were 120 applicants, of whom 52 were children, many of whom were evidently in the last stage of starvation. Provisions were available for 83 applicants only. Thirty-seven applicants were rejected.

"It's awful."

"Back then, people were worried about the basics: food and shelter. And the church—they believed in the church—and, Kate, they believed in fairies. They really did. The other world gave them hope. Same as it gives me hope, gives everyone hope."

"Everyone?" I thought I'd stick my neck out. "Maura, the group that you're with . . ."

Her eyes widened.

"What do they want?"

"The same as anyone wants." She eyeballed me.

"Love? Happiness?" I questioned.

"For eternity."

"And you think the fairies can give you this?"

"We know the fairies have it. I doubt they'll give it to us. But we're willing to get it by any means possible."

That veiled threat again.

"Me? Am I one of those possible means?"

She looked at me and smiled thinly, probably debating whether or not to answer truthfully. "Maybe, but you're not the only one—or way."

I shivered. I felt scared. Her threats, the way she constantly insinuated that she knew a lot more than she was giving away, frightened me. Something told me I shouldn't let my guard down around her. I put on my game face and forced a laugh. "And there I was thinking I was special."

"You are. There is a connection, but you're not unique. They've done this style of crossover before. There are many ways to contact them to try and enter their realm."

"Is that what you want to do? Has anyone done it before?" I asked cautiously, unsure how much I should press her.

"Maybe, we don't know. We think so."

"And these people that you're with, this group, they all want the same thing?" I knew I sounded nervous.

"And they'll stop at nothing to get it." Her face hardened, and I was left under no illusions as to what she meant. This woman who liaised with gangsters, the media, and politicians was determined to get her way.

The drunk in the corner must have heard us talking about the famine, because his mumbles turned into a song, a low, deep tune. He sang with his eyes shut and his mouth wide open, revealing the two yellow teeth in his head.

> *Pale mothers, wherefore weeping—*
> *Would to God that we were dead;*
> *Our children swoon before us,*
> *and we cannot give them bread.*

"Do you think the villagers here know about the Seven Steps?" I said out loud to no one in particular. "About everything that's going on?"

"Well, there's no more media circus around you, is there?" It was the way she said it, the tone of her voice.

"You? You stopped the paparazzi?"

"Let's just say they're on hold temporarily."

Who was she? How could she do these things?

"Remember, Kate, you can trust me."

I nodded, pretending to agree, too scared not to placate her. But I knew I could never trust her. Aside from the fact she creeped me out, she seemed far too connected to dangerous people for me to want to have any dealings with her.

I looked at the drunk in the corner and the men at the bar, who were probably in the same positions they'd occupied for years. The Seven Steps and the fairies weren't having an impact on their life one bit. Not yet, anyway. That would happen soon enough.

24

A stranger in a small town will never know the rhythm of the place. A stranger will always cause an eyebrow to raise or a throat to clear. There is a language, a code built into the locals that a visitor cannot translate. When Annie drummed her fingers on the bar in O'Donahue's pub, the Guinness drinkers knew it was half an hour until last orders and someone had better organize a taxi for Dermot Flynn, because he was too drunk to walk and she wouldn't be the one to turf him out. When a dark cloud hung over the Devil's Bit, it meant not rain but an icy wind from the ocean that would make tears stream from your eyes. When Johnny Logan, the town mayor, rubbed his crooked nose, he'd put a bet on the horses, and if his mouth twitched, the odds were long. It was common knowledge that Sarah Mitchell was having an affair with Billy the pig farmer, but no one discussed it. It didn't spark idle banter out of respect for her poor long-suffering husband, who everyone knew was a good man. Everyone went to mass on Sundays, even though at least half the congregation thought religion was a load of old nonsense, but just in case, just in case, they were there every Sunday. And just in case, Billy the pig farmer wouldn't farm the land in the fairy ring in his back field, even though, Lord knows, he could have done with the extra acreage. And just in case, the schoolkids spun three times when they saw a lone magpie, and just in case, a voice turned into a whisper when fairies were mentioned.

From what I could gather, Maura wasn't having much joy. That afternoon in the pub she'd bought drinks for anyone who looked thirsty and tried to coax or coerce conversation from them. They'd talk forever about the village, the prices of things, the noise of Dublin, but when she mentioned the Red Hag, pints were drained, jackets buttoned up, and the conversation was over. Word quickly spread around the village that the woman from Dublin was asking questions about matters that were best left be.

Maura called me from her hotel in Ennis and specifically asked, in that rather abrupt manner she had, if I had visited the old ruin.

I was choosing to keep my enemy close, so I told her I'd seen it from the road, which was true. Since I'd arrived, I'd ridden past every hedgerow, every gap in a field, every corner of Knocknamee, but I hadn't entered the old ruin. There was something about it that gave me chills—a dark, hollow feeling.

"It has something to do with her, doesn't it?" I asked Maura.

"Well, nothing that anyone has said, since no one will speak to me. But the song—do you remember the song, that little tune I uncovered? 'She's left her big house on the hill'? That could be it. It dates back to 1840, the same era."

I remembered that the old ruin had looked very grand for a witch. Built of gray stone and still threateningly tall, it had been, back in the day, whenever its day was, a large, imposing building that must have loomed over the town. Now it stood exposed to the wild ocean winds and unprotected by the mountains that turned a cold shoulder to it.

"It's more likely to have been an English landlord's, who

probably owned the land around here and all the tenants on it. But I thought I'd ask if you knew it. There's no other building here that could fit those words."

"Who owns it now?"

"I don't know. It's vacant."

After that conversation, I decided to go and investigate for myself. It was about time I uncovered some of my own heritage. After all, I'd fallen in love with Knocknamee, and I wanted to know more about my ancestors. Had they loved this sleepy little village, too, I wondered. I certainly couldn't trust Maura Ni Ghaora to visit the ruin and report back to me. I couldn't trust her with anything, and while the ruin seemed threatening, my curiosity outweighed my fear.

I decided to take a walk on An Trá Bhán beforehand to blow away the cobwebs. The cold salt air was bracing and walking on the sand exhilarating.

"I'm going to the ruin, I'm going to the ruin," I repeated over and over to myself to try to put myself at ease. It didn't work. I froze. "I'm going to the ruin." Suddenly, it was as if I was encased in a block of ice: my feet sank heavily into the sand, my shoulders snapped into a tense spasm and I could have sworn my heart stopped. I felt a tremor through my body, a shiver that turned into a shake. Soon my whole body was trembling, convulsing into spasms, out of my control. I broke out in a cold sweat. Those weren't black spots before my eyes but smoke clouds, blinding me. I felt weak. A tight pain shot across my chest. I couldn't breathe.

As quick as it started it was gone. The moment had passed, the ice had melted away. I shook my head back, feeling strong again. It was something to do with that ruin. The thought of it made me freeze, made me physically react. What was up there? For once, I wasn't going to shy away from my fears. I was going to dig deep, be brave and face them. Feel the fear and do it anyway. Isn't that what they say?

I left the beach still trembling, more from shock than anything else. Then I climbed onto Colm's bike. I was going to the ruin.

I meandered up a twisty hill, pausing to catch my breath, fiddling with the bike's gears.

I don't know if I expected there to be a gate, or a plaque, or some type of landmark to the old ruin, but there wasn't anything. When I got to the top of the hill, I parked at the side of the road and climbed over a fence and stood in a green field like thousands of other green fields all over the country. The wind pushed the grass in all directions.

I crossed my arms over my middle, aware that I was still trembling. *It's so cold*, I thought. What was this place? Why was I reacting like this?

I circled the old ruin. Four walls still stood, propped up by the remnants of what once must have been a very grand building. The gray stone was covered in moss and ivy. Grass and bushes grew at the foot of the walls.

There was a doorway under a shelf of gray rock. I was so cold my arms were shaking and my teeth were chattering. I blew into my hands and tried to stamp my feet, but I could hardly move them for the cold.

I shuffled through the doorway into a large bricked room with an earthen floor. Once upon a time it may have been grand, but now, open to the sky, it just looked sad. A huge fireplace filled one wall, with a high chimney rising above it.

As I stood before the fireplace I began to burn up. I was roasting, in fact. I unbuttoned my jacket and took it off. I felt my cheeks flush and my feet start to sweat. A smell of heavy smoke filled my nostrils. Once more I was struggling to breathe. I stripped off the woolly jumper I'd bought in Martin's shop two days earlier, but still the heat was unbearable. I leaned on a wall, trying to cool myself against the cool stone.

On the far side of the fireplace, there was a narrow enclave. Stones were laid out in a circle, and a few cans of Dutch Gold lager were scattered around. This was where kids gathered to drink and hang out, I figured, eyeing the cigarette ends and joint butts. There was graffiti scrawled on one wall, most of it in black marker: "The Red Hag lives on," "666," "Devil walks," "Dylan and Nessa." There were other scrawls, words, half words, pictures. Kids' stuff, really.

I was sweating. Those smoke clouds were obscuring my vision, and I felt weak. My legs couldn't hold me. I hugged the wall—I had to get out. The walls were falling in on me. My chest was tight—I couldn't breathe with the smell of smoke. I was drowning in smoke. Choking. With what felt like my last bit of strength, I pushed myself back through the door.

A sharp blast of icy air smothered me. I fell onto the grass, face-first into a bunch of yellow dandelions. Smelling their freshness, I started to feel alive again. I could breathe. I filled my lungs and my head cleared.

There was something very strange about that ruin and about my connection to it. Why had I felt like I was choking? The smoke clouds, the heat? What had happened in there?

I was in no form to go to a social dinner that evening, especially one with Hugh Delaney and his rude attitude. Although there was something about him, I had to admit. Infuriating, yes.

Handsome, yes. Mysterious, definitely. I'd been thinking about him a lot. No, that didn't sound quite right. Not a lot, but he had been creeping into my thoughts, in spite of my now 24/7 fairy addiction. I disliked so many things about him. His work, for one—I mean, who the hell works in porn, except drug addicts and sex traffickers? It was what Mam would describe as a definite no-no. His personal hygiene left a lot to be desired, too— what was with the filthy boots, and hair that looked like a comb never went near it? And he'd been so rude to me, belittling my work, accusing me of trying to kill Setanta, and not thinking I was pretty enough to be the face of his porn site. (Obviously I didn't *want* to be the face of his site and would have turned it down immediately, but surely it's nice to be considered to have porn-star potential. Maybe? Oh, who knew!) All I knew was that Hugh Delaney still infuriated me. So I decided that, because his brother and his brother's wife had been so friendly and I didn't want to appear rude, I'd call in, claim I'd just eaten, have a quick drink and then leave. I'd ignore Hugh Delaney as much as I could within polite company.

I rode Colm's bike out to Niall and Aisling's. When I knocked on the door to their thatched cottage, it swung open by itself. A little boy in a pair of SpongeBob pajamas hurled himself down the stairs toward me before tearing off, through to the back of the house. I stepped in, nervous that I was in the wrong house, and squeaked out a feeble hello. A second boy in SpongeBob pajamas appeared. He was smaller than the first, with matted dark hair and rosy cheeks. He banged into my legs and proceeded to run to the back of the house, too. I dutifully followed and, after snaking through a small kitchen, was led by the noise of conversation and low guitar strumming to the back garden.

Multicolored Chinese lanterns hung from trees and washing

lines, illuminating a courtyard, the centerpiece of which was a large wooden table creaking under the weight of salad dishes and wine bottles. There were maybe fifteen people scattered around drinking, all smiling and talking, some dancing. The SpongeBobbed kids raced wildly around the group with Setanta in tow.

A giant pig was strung and skewered over a fire. Hugh Delaney hovered over it, patiently turning the spit. Every now and then he stopped to wipe his brow and sup on a beer. His cheeks were red, but he looked like a natural cook enjoying the sizzle.

"Kate, Kate!" Aisling, dressed in a green halter-neck dress, beckoned me over to a makeshift bar at the far end of the courtyard. She dipped forward to kiss me hello. "So glad you could make it. Look, Niall, Kate's here." Niall dipped in for a kiss, too. "Hugh will be pleased!" he said.

"Yes, of course. Thanks for having me." *Hugh will be pleased? Really? Why?*

"Now, what's it to be? I make the best cocktails you'll ever have. Spent four years as the best-tipped cocktail waitress in New York, and it had nothing to do with these." She ogled her cleavage.

I laughed. "What about a Long Island iced tea?"

"Easy." Aisling set to work throwing bottles together and clinking ice cubes, and then slid a cool glass into my hands. "Enjoy. Come on, I'll introduce you around."

There was a flurry of names, handshakes, and kisses. I learned that most of the people there lived in Galway and were down to party with Aisling and Niall in beautiful Knocknamee. This was their country home. They lived and worked in Galway, too, but let their hair down in Knocknamee every summer. I chatted and meandered, but my plans for ignoring Hugh failed as the crowd moved and I found myself backed up at the spit with only a pig or Hugh to talk to.

"Aisling'll get you sozzled on those things." Hugh pointed at my glass with a giant barbecue fork. "I stay away from them." He took another long gulp of his beer.

I nodded, suddenly feeling a bit tongue-tied and uptight, in spite of his relaxed demeanor.

"Funny banging into you like that." He flashed a look at me that I couldn't decipher. Accusing? Happy? Confused?

"Weird." I sounded like a soft-spoken mouse.

"Aisling said the universe is trying to bring us together."

I snorted loudly and rather abruptly shouted: "Hardly!" I quickly put my head back into my drink.

"Well, I'm glad I met you again . . ." He chewed his lip pensively.

"You are?"

"Yes. I wanted to apologize. I'm sorry about the way I spoke to you when Setanta, well, you know . . ."

I nodded.

"I just panicked. I'd never seen him like that. I was so shocked. And I took it all out on you. I'm sorry. It was very unfair of me." He looked at me earnestly, hopefully.

"You know, I didn't give him that chocolate. I would never hurt him. I don't know how he got hold of it."

"Thank God he's okay. Look, accidents happen." He laughed and gestured toward the pig. "Case in point. Old Percy here got hit by a tractor a few days ago. We did everything we could to save him, but there you go. Accidents happen."

"Percy?"

"Percy. He's been with me for three years. I have a farm about five miles from here. Just a small place, a few animals. Nothing fancy, but I love it. I love growing from scratch, and I love the animals. Nothing like a fresh egg in the morning." And he got that look again, the look of peace and happiness.

A farmer. Well, now, that made sense. The mucky boots, the dirty hands, and the choked-up expression in the city . . .

"I could see you as a farmer all right." I smiled at him. "You seemed a bit uncomfortable in Dublin."

"Ha, that's putting it mildly. Can't stand the place. I can't breathe there, and the people, Jesus Christ, they'll tell you black is white to get money out of you. Nobody talks straight. They're all pretending to be someone they're not, better than they are. Nobody just *is*." He was silent, then raised his hand to his brow. "Ah, no! I've done it again." Enunciating his words slowly and clearly he said: "Not—all—Dublin—people."

"A clear case of foot-in-mouth disease?"

He shook his head. "You must think I'm an awful eejit, Kate."

"You definitely have your moments." I raised my eyebrows, noticing how his whole body had turned toward mine. All that was separating us now was Percy.

A shout came from within the house. "Long Hugh, would you ever carve up that pig? We're starving!"

"On its way," Hugh shouted. "I'd better get carving," he said quietly to me. "Poor old Percy. He does look delicious, though." He winked at me before putting his head down and raising his knife.

My heart fluttered, and finally I admitted to myself that I was attracted to Hugh. The truth was, he was gorgeous. There was something sweet about him, and he could cook, and I knew there were muscles under that shirt.

I went and sat at the table, deciding to stay for dinner and maybe a chance to talk to him again. I had that bubbling feeling of expectancy, those butterflies of attraction, where every look and every gesture might mean something. The way Hugh smiled and looked around the party—was he looking to catch my eye? I felt my back straighten and flicked my hair, wanting to look my best in case his gaze rested on me. Meanwhile, Aisling kept dealing out the cocktails.

Percy was finally served up to much cheering and delight, and the table congratulated Hugh on his cooking.

He bashfully waved away their praise. "Percy did the work, not me." He raised his glass. "To Percy."

The table raised their glasses, and everyone oinked as cheers. We all tucked in, and I watched as Hugh clambered into his seat and did his best to fold his long legs in under the table. He smiled to himself, reaching for a plate and some bread. I wondered if he'd look toward me. I felt myself preening. But his gaze didn't budge from the food in front of him.

"Yoo-hoo!" A strong Galway accent echoed from the house. "Only me!" A tall, glamorous blonde in high heels, red lipstick, and Chanel No. 5 teetered into the back garden, balancing a Marks & Spencer's lemon meringue pie on her false nails. "Hope I've made it in time for dessert," she said before air-kissing Aisling. She made a beeline for Hugh, planted her lips on his cheek, shimmied in to sit beside him, and placed her hand on his knee. "Hugh, so sorry I'm late," she cooed.

Hugh looked around the table and then back to his plate.

He had a girlfriend. Of course he had a girlfriend. I should have guessed he had a girlfriend. And a glamorous one at that, a gorgeous blonde. I didn't care, of course I didn't care. Only I did. Goddammit, I cared.

I didn't stay much longer after that. Disappointment doesn't need to be extended into extra time. I made my excuses to

Aisling and crept down the side of the house, avoiding Hugh at all costs.

I gave myself a stern talking-to on the bike ride home. I was repeating all my previous mistakes. I hadn't learned anything from the Jim debacle. I had wasted so much time on him, and I was not going to do that again. Realistically, Hugh Delaney wasn't even attracted to me. He had said as much with the "natural" comment to Marjorie. The fact that I was finding myself attracted to him was my own fault and had nothing to do with him. He hadn't done anything to encourage me. He'd apologized to me for being rude—that was only a mannerly thing to do— and he'd asked my advice about the logos because he was confused, not because he fancied me. Anything I felt had all been in my head. He didn't feel anything. He was attached. I was being really foolish—I needed a reality check. The last thing I wanted in my already complicated life was a romantic complication. Men caused too much heartache and disappointment, and right now I had enough disappointment in my life. I needed to be on my own. To focus on who Kate McDaid was. To focus on witches and fairies, and to sort out my real-life mess, not the fantasy mess I was concocting in my own head. Decision made. Game over.

25

"Why would I talk to you?" The scrawny teenager hopped off the wall. He extended himself to his full height and stretched like a stick of chewing gum. Dylan—probably named after Matt, not Thomas—was wearing a gray cotton tracksuit, hood up like the grim reaper, and had the distracting habit of putting his two hands down the front of his trousers.

I was due to get the sixth Step the next day. My head was still fuzzy from the dinner with Hugh, and I was trying my best to concentrate on my Red Hag fact-finding mission. I hadn't heard from Maura—she might have given up on her own Red Hag mission and gone back to Dublin.

"You don't have to." I rummaged in my handbag and produced a can of Dutch Gold lager. I cracked it open and watched the head fizz over. With a slight grimace I took a sip. He eyed me enviously.

"Do you want one?"

Martin had told me where the teenagers usually hung out at night. At a wall. Like all teenage walls, it was the site of drinking, smoking, snogging, bragging, and mitching off school—you know, the skills that will set them up for life. Four equally scrawny boys and two girls watched me suspiciously from the wall.

"I've got another six of these in my bag."

"So."

"Tell me what you know about the Red Hag and they're yours." All those years of watching cop shows had helped me embrace my inner chief superintendent.

"I don't want your cans. I can just nick them off me da." He started to laugh, wobbling his neck. The rest of the group knew to laugh with him.

"I'm just trying to find out some information on the Red Hag. If you help me, maybe I can help you. Maybe I could get your picture in the paper? Would you like that?"

"Sure, then the guards'll know where I am." The group erupted into laughter.

This felt like a dead end.

"I'm just looking for some information. What do they say about her here? What's the local legend? The old ruin—was that her house?" I was looking desperate, I knew, letting my guard down in front of teenagers.

"I'm not telling you nothing or she'll come back and put a spell on me. Whooooo-hooooo." He waved his hands around.

"Is that what they say here? That she'll put a spell on you?"

He was mocking me. I sighed and kicked the ground with my ballet pumps, which were looking tired after four days in Knocknamee.

"I'll go." I turned around and walked three steps before looking back at them. "Oh, here, keep the bloody cans. I don't know how you drink this stuff. It's disgusting." I pulled the sixpack out of my bag and handed it to a small girl with pink stripes at the front of her fringe.

"Thanks."

Defeated, I walked back to my bike.

I heard a shout. "I'm going to see if she has any cigarettes." There was a scamper of feet. The girl with the pink stripes raced up behind me. I turned. Her brown eyes darted around uneasily. "There's an old cottage about two minutes up the road on the left. I'll see you around the back at the shed in ten minutes."

I breathed in sharply.

"Do you have any cigarettes?"

I shook my head.

"Ah, well. Ten minutes, yeah. And keep quiet about it."

I nodded, agreeing to whatever this fourteen-year-old wanted.

Ten minutes later, I was outside a cowshed, huddled around the neon glow of my mobile phone.

The girl was Nessa. "Dylan won't tell you any of this stuff because he doesn't know it. He wouldn't let on, though." She'd found a cigarette and was sucking on it furiously.

"Is that why you wanted to meet me here? Away from him?"

"Ah, no, it's just easier, you know. Not worth the hassle. My granny told me all about her, the Red Hag. She used to sing creepy songs about her, and when I was bad, Granny would say the Red Hag was going to come and get me. But you, I know you." She pointed at me. "I read the papers. I've seen you. They wouldn't know, Dylan and them, they wouldn't read the papers. But you, they call you a witch, or a what? A 'spiritual guru.' I can't remember all the stuff, but that's right, isn't it? Is that why you want to know about the Red Hag? Are you trying to find her spell book or something?" She laughed a smoky wheeze.

"No, I'm related to her. I just want to find out more about her."

"Jesus Christ. Is that those Steps? The fairy Steps? Holy God."

She produced another cigarette and lit it off the end of her first. "Father O'Brien'll go mental."

"I'm just trying to find out about a dead relative."

"It's mad. You're famous and everything."

"Hmm."

"And you're here in Knocknamee."

"Hmmmm."

"There's no grave. Did you know that?"

"Yeah, I'd heard . . . What else do you know about her?"

"Only bits, you know, that you'd hear in school and stuff. She was really bad, like, really bad." Nessa looked at me. "Sorry."

"That's okay. She was a very distant relative."

"They say she put spells on everyone. That whole family, the O'Donnells, they all walk with a limp, and they say it's because of her. That they wouldn't pay her for a cure, so she cursed the whole family . . ." She exhaled dramatically. "Forever."

"Is that what she did? Cured people?" I inched forward excitedly.

"No. She was evil. She didn't help people."

"She wasn't evil. She was just a bit of a mad old woman," I said, unsure why I was defending this very distant relative.

"No. She was evil. Once she stopped all the cows in the town from producing any milk until she got money. All of them, and back then, like, people didn't have stuff, you know, didn't have money. They needed milk and stuff. To live, like."

"Did she live in that old ruin where you and Dylan wrote your names?"

"I'm sorry about that, I am. I should never have gone out with him. He said he'd treat me like a princess. Like hell he did. All I ever got out of him was a pack of cigarettes. One pack. Not worth it."

I nodded in agreement. Dylan hadn't seemed worth it.

"But, yeah, that's where she lived. Looking out over everyone like Lady Muck. Casting spells from her castle. She still haunts the place."

"You don't believe in fairies, do you?" I had to ask.

"Nah, it's a load of shite."

I sighed with relief. What a sensible young girl.

"But I still wouldn't step into a fairy fort. Dylan did. He says he slept a night in one for a dare, and look at the state of him now. His face has been riddled with acne ever since."

I nodded.

"I've heard worse things about the fairies, like, a lot worse than acne. They can be really mean. My granny's sister was struck dumb by them. Couldn't talk or nothing. It was because she blocked a fairy path or something. I wouldn't mess with them."

"But you don't believe in them?"

"No. But you never know."

I sighed. This was exhausting.

"Do you know anything else about the Red Hag?"

"She'd red hair, ginger, like you. That's why they called her the Red Hag. And the auld ones, sometimes they say they hear her singing to the sea, out on An Trá Bhán, and it means a boat is going to sink. But that's a load of shite, because boats never sink out this way."

"Is there anything else? Do you know anything else about her?" I was grasping at straws.

Nessa shook her head.

"Thanks for your help."

She looked at me shyly. "Can I have your autograph?"

I reluctantly scribbled my name on the back of her cigarette pack.

"Do you, like, go out with that guy from Red Horizon? He's massive, he is."

"Jim? I know him, yeah."

"God, he's gorgeous. Is he a great kisser? I'd say he's a great kisser. He'd buy you more than a pack of cigarettes, I'd say."

I shook my head, unsure how to answer, wondering if Dylan wasn't such a bad catch after all.

26

Step number six came by FedEx to Knocknamee. I was in the B and B, sipping on a cup of milky tea and wiping chocolate HobNob crumbs off my jeans when it turned up.

Seamus MacMurphy had called earlier that morning and told me to expect it. I'd planned to do what I'd done for the last five Steps: read it and post it on spacemonkeys.com. But then I read it and my heart dropped.

Step Six

Rise up and dance and swing and howl
and hoot and drink and play,
Knock back the whiskey, redden your cheeks
and cavort from night to day,
Take hand in hand and twirl around,
your joy will grow more joy,
Tell a joke and play a trick on every man and boy.

Let your doings be full of goodness,
and happy and merry and free,
May your heart swell at the sound

of the fiddle and the slap of every knee,
The world has so much to offer,
with the good times laid within,
If it goes unused we'll be watching,
and believe it is a sin.

So rise up and dance and swing and howl
and hoot and drink and play,
We fold you up in these wise words
from our lair in Knocknamee,
Live by the essence of what we give,
and our faces you will see,
Listen with care to the next one coming,
we can unite for eternity.

Knocknamee. Why did they have to mention Knocknamee? Why now? Knocknamee was obviously such a special place to the fairies, but I'd never have thought they'd want to publicize their relationship with it.

I didn't want to publish it. It would open the floodgates—I knew the power of these things. This would put Knocknamee on the map. Knocknamee, a place that shouldn't be on any map, that should remain a hushed, idyllic secret.

I felt sick—I couldn't be responsible for this. It could destroy the village. I couldn't publish this.

I dug deep into my pocket, plucked out my phone, and rang Seamus MacMurphy.

"Seamus, I don't want to publish this one. I'm nervous."

"Okay."

"Okay? What do you mean, 'okay'?"

"I can't influence your decision."

"But can you give me legal advice?"

"That I can do."

"What happens if I rip this up now? If I never publish this?"

"Well, nothing. You won't inherit the estate."

"I don't care about the estate." At least, I didn't think I cared about the estate. I was so confused. That's why I'd started all this, and now everything just felt so out of control, and all I wanted was to have my old life back, my old simple life, and no estate was going to give that back to me.

"Well, then."

"So that's it. I can just rip it up and all this will be over."

"You can rip it up."

"Okay. Bye."

"Bye."

And I knew what I had to do. I just had to tear it up. My hand hovered over the paper.

But I didn't. I didn't rip it up. I called the one person who I knew would give me good advice, the one person who had been involved in this since the beginning.

"Kate, thank God you called. I've been so worried about you. I'm so, so sorry about everything."

"Look, Matthew. I don't want to talk about that now. I really don't."

"Okay, but you should know that I'm so sorry. I've just been beating myself up over it. I'm so stu—"

"Stupid. Yeah, you are. But that's not why I need to talk to you."

"Is it the shoot? Is that it? It went so well, Kate! You wouldn't have believed what happened. The Hoff—"

I cut him off. I was dying to hear about the shoot, but I had to figure out what to do about the sixth Step first. "Just listen for a minute."

I read out the Step and explained to Matthew about the beautiful little hideaway of Knocknamee.

"You know what these Steps'll do to a place like this."

Matthew was silent for a long time, thinking. "You have to publish it." I wasn't expecting that answer. "If you don't publish this, if these Steps end now, there'll always be a mystery about them. People will always wonder: What were the last two? What was the final message? You'll just make them even more popular."

"Like a cliffhanger." I could see his point, even though I didn't like it.

"And you know what else? They're going to find Knocknamee eventually. They won't even have to dig that hard. How many towns boast a Red Hag? I think Knocknamee was put on the map when the first Step was published. We just didn't know it at the time."

"I suppose." I felt defeated. "It's pretty amazing that Simon and the Anoraks haven't figured it out yet."

"They'll find it eventually."

I sighed heavily.

"I'm sorry. You sound like you've really fallen in love with the place."

"I have, and I'm so scared I'm going to ruin it."

"Kate, I'm sorry."

"I know."

"Really, really sorry."

"I've gotta go." I hung up—I wasn't ready for the apologies.

Martin had mentioned a town mayor. I felt like I should warn him before I pinpointed Knocknamee to the world.

Johnny Logan was a third-generation mayor. His grandfather had created the position, his father walked straight on into it, and Johnny was dismantling it. When I knocked on the door of his office, a small prefab building with wobbly walls that was attached to the side of a house, Johnny opened up absentmindedly and waved me in. A small radio attached to his ear was blaring out the tinny sound of the racetrack. Johnny's back was huddled over and his left hand was clenched into a tight fist. He had a long, crooked nose, a tight mouth, and a full head of shiny blond hair speckled with gray. His shirt was rolled up to his elbows, and his tie was hanging loose at his neck. As the buzzing on the radio reached a crescendo his knuckles turned white and his back stooped more.

"Feck it, anyway," he spat, slamming the radio on the table. He flicked it off and started to pace the area behind his desk. "Feck, feck, feck!"

I coughed in that annoying way people do to try to get someone else's attention. The fake cough.

"Yeah, yeah. Sorry about that. Sit yourself down there." He looked angrily at his desk. "How can I help you? Can I get you a cup of tea? Sure, you'll have tea." He pottered into a tiny room at the back and I heard him flick on a kettle.

He was looking a bit more relaxed as he put a cup of strong tea in my hand. "If you want sugar, just shout. There's some in the back. I don't take it myself. Keep it for visitors." He hugged his own cup, nodding to himself and to whatever conversation was going on in his head. He seemed very distracted.

"Thanks for seeing me. My name is Kate McDaid."

"Right, yeah. You're a Dublin girl, staying in Martin's place?"

You can't hide in a small town. "That's right. I don't know if you've heard of me at all?" I wasn't really sure how to explain myself. He looked at me blankly. "Have you heard of the Seven Steps?"

"I've been a bit preoccupied with business the last couple of weeks, so if it's a recent thing I probably wouldn't have. Is it a business you're in?"

There was a laptop on his desk. I pointed to it. "Do you have the Internet on that?" He nodded. "Put my name in and see what you get."

He looked at me suspiciously. "Are you famous?"

"Just see what you get."

He pried open the laptop and tapped into Google. Then his mouth hung open and his eyes were on stalks. "That's you!" He pointed at the screen. "And you're here. That is very funny." He stared at me. "What is it you are? A spiritual guru? What's that?"

"Well, I'm really not. It's all been a bit of a misunderstanding." I proceeded to tell him about the past six weeks, top-line details only—he didn't need to know about David Hasselhoff or Red Horizon.

"Well, I never!" He looked dumbfounded. "Never, ever. And here you are."

"Here I am."

As he leaned forward across his desk, his eyes narrowed and his crooked nose twitched. "Why?"

"Well . . ." I felt a flutter of butterflies in my stomach. I had a feeling that this wasn't going to go down well, that I was about to launch a rocket into this man's perfect little life. I already felt guilty.

"This is the sixth Step," I said, my eyes downcast as I handed him the slip of paper.

He slid back on his chair and studied it intensely. "What does it mean?"

"I dunno."

"Right, right."

He seemed so relaxed I wondered if he'd read it right. "Did you see the part about Knocknamee?"

"I did, yeah."

"The thing is . . ." I took a deep breath. "When this gets published, it puts Knocknamee on the map."

Like a Jack Russell, he cocked his head keenly to one side, listening hard.

"Once this is out there the floodgates will open, I'm guessing. I mean, I don't know for sure, but I'd imagine you'll have people from all over the place falling in on you here. You see, there's an interest in it all. People think they're like the steps of the universe or something. They're not." I looked at him intently.

He nodded, gauging it as the correct response.

"They'll see Knocknamee as a clue, as a piece in the puzzle." I had a flash of the Anoraks almost crying when they read this last lesson. It would be the best day of their lives, and judging by the blogs multiplying in cyberspace, there were other Anoraks out there who would feel the same. "They'll come here in their droves. They'll ask questions."

"Droves, you say." He started drumming his fingers on his upper lip.

"They'll ruin it. There'll be paparazzi, journalists, TV cameras. Knocknamee will be a hot spot."

"Droves."

"And they'll ask questions." Well, really, I had a question I wanted to ask, and I wondered if Johnny Logan, the town mayor, might have a few answers.

"What'll they be asking?"

"They'll be asking about the Red Hag. The Steps are her legacy."

"That auld witch. This is her doing?" A smile unexpectedly broke across his face. "Strange how things work out. She was almost the ruination of the town, and now she's going to be the makings of it."

I sat forward, hungry for information. "What do you mean, ruination?"

"Ah, I dunno, that's what they say." He stood up and started to pace the room again, rubbing his hands together.

I waited patiently for the big reveal, the story of the Red Hag.

"We'll have to call a town meeting, let everyone know. Martin only has the five rooms. We'll have to get an exterminator in to get rid of the mice in Miles O'Brien's guesthouse and open that up. We'll erect some type of a platform, a stage, at the foot of the town. We'll stop the traffic on the main street." He swept the room with his arms, his eyes wide with excitement. "I'll make speeches. I'll have to polish the mayor's chain. Knocknamee will be on the map. Oh, the money we'll make out of this!"

"Well . . . I mean . . . ." Oh, this wasn't going according to plan at all. "Surely you don't want crowds down here?"

He looked at me, wide-eyed. "Crowds? With money? This will be the making of us." He pumped his fist in the air with great determination.

"They'll wreck the place." This was all backfiring on me. By trying to protect Knocknamee, I could accidentally become its ruination. "They'll ruin this quiet little spot."

"Nonsense. Quiet never made money. It's great news."

"Okay . . . I guess," I said, somewhat defeated. It was his town. He was the mayor, after all. He must have known what he was doing.

"So you haven't published this yet? It's not out there?" And he rolled his eyes from side to side, indicating "out there."

I shook my head.

"Would you mind holding off until I tell everyone?" He puffed his chest out with importance, like a canary. "When you're going into battle, it's best to be prepared."

It was all over—my cover was about to be blown. I wondered if Martin and Mavis would look at me in the same way. If I'd become a freak, a witch, a whatever, in their eyes, too. I sighed. There was no backing out now. "So long as it goes out before midnight, it's okay."

He smacked the wooden paneling on his desk with great gusto and, grinning from ear to ear, proclaimed: "Let's gather the troops."

27

Johnny Logan ran up and down the village like a hare out of the traps. He knocked on every door and announced with a statesmanlike tone that there was a matter of grave importance that the people of the village needed to discuss. As town mayor, he declared that all businesses were to shut for one hour and all villagers were to attend a meeting at the town hall.

Martin and Mavis were surprised: in all their years they'd never heard of an impromptu town meeting. While they knew Johnny Logan was an excitable fellow (they agreed it was normally around the horses), they were curious to see what all the fuss was about.

By four o'clock the town hall was filling up nicely. Inside, the air was dusty—the place was usually only used for Christmas pageants and basketball matches for the local school when the rain was too heavy to play outdoors. Blue plastic chairs had been set out in perfect lines, and as villagers filed in and took their seats, their footsteps on the wooden floor echoed long and hard.

Everyone was straining their necks and whispering among themselves, trying to guess what it could possibly be about. Sitting in the second row, I heard Annie from O'Donahue's, who was behind me, tell Mavis that she had a bad feeling. When she'd woken up that morning her joints were sore, she said, which she knew meant rain. But she'd also had the strangest dream about her father that night, who'd been dead for forty years, and he didn't look one bit happy. "Leave 'em be," he kept saying, and then there was Johnny Logan leapin' around like a headless chicken. No, she didn't have a good feeling about this at all.

I whipped around several times waiting for Maura to make an appearance, but there was no sign of her. She must have gone back to Dublin, I thought, relieved.

Johnny had sworn on his dead mother's grave, God rest her, and assured me 100 percent that I wouldn't have to say a word, that he'd carry the meeting and give the villagers the news. He'd changed into his weddings and funerals suit, dark gray with a thin blue pinstripe running up it, and his cheeks were flushed as he took to the stage. Up there, his back poker straight, he looked about five inches taller. I sat stooped over, chewing on my fingernails.

Johnny cleared his throat dramatically and took a sip of water. "Thank you all for coming," he said in the lilting accent of Knocknamee that I'd grown so fond of. "Many of you will be aware that we've had some Dublin visitors over the last few days." I assumed he was referring to Maura and me. "And they've been very welcome indeed. Very welcome." He nodded in my direction. "One of those visitors came to see me today. Kate. Stand up, Kate. Let them have a look at you."

Reluctantly, I rose to my feet, smiling bashfully and wondering just how likely it was that I'd get away with not having to talk to the crowd. "Kate's a bit of a celebrity in Dublin."

He said the word *celebrity* slowly and clearly. You could tell he liked the way it sounded coming out of his mouth. I heard people shifting in their seats, edging closer to get a look at me.

"You may have heard of the Seven Steps." He paused, waiting for a reaction. He didn't get one. "Well, if you have the Internet at home, and Billy, I know you do, I'd advise you to take a look online and you'll see what I'm talking about."

"She's like really famous, like really, really famous," Nessa, the teenager with the pink stripes at the front of her hair, shouted from the back of the hall. She was sitting beside Dylan, whose hood was so far over his face he looked like E.T. "Those Steps are like the new bible or something. Everyone, and I mean everyone, is talking about them."

"Thank you, Nessa." Johnny looked uncomfortable with audience participation.

A deep voice piped up from behind a pillar. "So what are these Steps?"

"Well, there's only been five of them so far, and they're all kinds of everything. They're quite nice really, mainly about appreciating nature. They're just nice little messages, you know." Johnny Logan's smile overreached, exposing more gum than teeth.

"Who from? Does she write them?"

"Well, no, and this is where we come into play. Em . . . em . . . Well, the thing is, em . . ." He fumbled in his pocket and produced a packet of cigarettes, fingering the edges of the box nervously.

"The thing is, you see, the Steps are big news. And, you see, in the new Step, Knocknamee is mentioned." A few hums and haws rippled around the hall.

"Why would we be mentioned? Have you been at the whiskey again, Johnny?"

The town hall erupted into laughter. Johnny's shoulders dropped as he relaxed a little more.

"Would you be away with that, Sean. Sure, I'll read it to you and then we can have a discussion." He cleared his throat, unfolded the piece of paper I'd given him earlier that day, and read out the sixth Step.

When he'd finished, his eyes darted nervously around, looking for a response.

"Are we to be famous because of these Steps talking about Knocknamee now, Johnny? Is that what you're saying?"

"I think we might."

"Well, Fidelma, you'd better clear a space. I'll be looking for a haircut," an elderly man with a head as shiny as a polished strap shouted.

Fidelma waved him away. "And God knows—sorry, Father . . ." she apologized.

A tall, skinny, white-haired man dressed in black with a priest's collar was leaning against a wall away from the crowd, anxiously looking around the room. He nodded distractedly in acknowledgment.

Fidelma went on. "Someone needs to take a look at Jimmy's beard. He'll shame the village."

The place erupted into one loud chuckle as Jimmy stood up, proudly fingering a mass of tangled whiskers. "If you come near me with the clippers, Fidelma," he said, "I'll take them to your husband's regions."

Wiping away tears of laughter, Fidelma stood tall. "If that's the case, Jimmy, I'll see to you this afternoon." Good-naturedly, Fidelma's husband stood to take a bow, and the crowd burst into applause.

Johnny held his arms out as wide as his smile, gently trying to hush the crowd.

"What is it, Johnny? What is it you want us to know? I don't see how this has anything to do with us really." Annie from O'Donahue's sounded cross. "I've got a pub to run. I don't have time to be here laughing at the bald fellows. We do enough of that when the Guinness flows."

"And she's off, the auld party killer," someone in the back whispered loud enough for everyone to hear.

"You're right, Annie, you're right. It's a little more complicated than Knocknamee getting pinpointed. You see, the Steps, they don't come from Kate here." He pointed at me, and it felt like I'd been pierced with an arrow. "They, em, they were left to Kate by her great-great-great-grand-aunt, a Knocknamee resident." Johnny fell silent, tightly gripping his pack of cigarettes.

"Well, she's a local girl, now, I suppose. Isn't that grand?" Martin piped up with pride.

Slowly Johnny shook his head. "Now, folks, this can't go down wrong, and you have to remember it was all a long time ago, and aren't we a modern world now, and we don't believe in any of the nonsense . . ." He started to chew his bottom lip with a look of confusion on his face. "It turns out the Steps—well, the great-great-great-grand-aunt—well, it was the Red Hag, and she got them from the fairies."

There was a hushed silence. A quietness that you could grab by the fistful. I stared straight ahead, studying the grain of the wooden floor, my nostrils suffocating in dust. I couldn't look around me. What had I done? What was I doing to this village?

Annie, with her bolshie forthrightness, was the first to speak. "These Steps. Are they from her, then?"

"She got them from the fairies." Johnny spoke so quietly, the creaking of ears straining to hear was more audible.

A number of people rose from their seats and, pulling on their jackets, hurried toward the exit, shaking their heads and muttering.

"Stop!" Johnny shouted. "You can't leave. We have to deal with this as a community."

Heads turned.

"This type of thing is best left be, Johnny. You know it as well as the rest of us."

"Why would you bring this out now? Why?"

As if a Chinese firecracker had fizzled on my seat, I suddenly popped up. "It's me. This is all my fault."

People stopped in their tracks and turned to listen to the unfamiliar Dublin accent.

"You see, I inherited these, and I just thought it would be a bit of a laugh. I didn't think anything of it. I didn't think anyone would pay any attention to them. But the thing is, they have. People really like these Steps. They think they're special.

"I don't know who the Red Hag was. I know I'm related to her, but she lived over one hundred thirty years ago. I'm sure everyone here has a few skeletons in their closet—mine has just become public knowledge. I want you to know, from the bottom of my heart, I didn't mean, I don't mean, for anyone to get upset by this, for this to damage your beautiful village or for any cross words to be spoken."

"Well, why publish this at all?" Annie stepped out of the exit aisle and carefully sat down. She was followed by three of the others.

Johnny descended from the stage and signaled to me to take his place. "They'll hear you better up there," he whispered.

Cautiously, I stepped into position, gripping the sides of the polished mahogany stand. I took a deep breath. I would be fair and honest, as the village had been to me. "I originally published the Steps for an inheritance. When I publish all seven Steps, I inherit something—I don't even know what. It seemed like a good idea at the time. It was just a bit of fun. But it has escalated. Now it's out of my control, and, honestly, it's not going to make any difference if I publish this sixth Step or not. Knocknamee is going to be found. I can't believe they're not here yet, the followers of the Steps. Not many villages have a Red Hag in their history. They won't have to do much digging to get here. At least . . ." I couldn't help but sigh at my attempt to look on the bright side. "At least, this way, we can all be prepared."

"So it'll happen whether or not you publish this Step?" Annie asked.

"Yes, I believe it will."

"What can we expect?" Johnny Logan shouted, with a glint in his eye.

"TV cameras, photographers, fanatics. They'll all land here pretty soon after I post the Step online." I clenched my jaw. "They'll probably be looking for me. They think I'm, well . . ." I was struggling to get the words out. I stared over their heads, focusing on a blue-and-white statue of the Virgin Mary that was catching shadows in the sinking sunshine. "They think that I've inherited some type of powers, that I'm some type of spiritual person." I took a deep breath and scanned the room, looking as many people in the eye as I could. "I'm just a normal girl from Dublin who got caught up in a big mess." I hung my head.

Annie rested her hands heavily in front of her. "Well, if they're coming, they're coming. There's not much we can do about it." She nodded her head into her chest.

"That's it." Johnny punched the air excitedly and muscled me off the stage. "I don't think anyone here in this town wants the Red Hag dug up. But do you know what I think? I think we use her to make money. To change the shape of Knocknamee forever." He wiggled his fingertips.

"You and your money, Johnny. You never stop." Annie sat back down.

"That's right. And folks, they say there's a recession coming. Shouldn't we make hay now? Who knows what tomorrow will bring? And come on now, Annie, don't tell me you wouldn't say no to more business in O'Donahue's."

"I wouldn't say no, I suppose."

"And Miles? Think of all the customers you'll get in the B and B. Martin, your place will be through the roof. You can double your prices. And Vinny, you could use your van to do tours of the town." He balled his fists and held them high above his head. "The eyes of the world will be on Knocknamee. Let's not disappoint."

A clap slowly started, rising gently into applause, until eventually all hands were red raw from beating against each other. All except those of the priest, who remained silent, his face in his hands.

28

I had a small audience when I visited the Internet café later that evening. A handful of villagers formed a C shape around me as I typed out the sixth Step and uploaded it to spacemonkeys.com. The villagers were looking at me differently now, considering my ancestry, but in a good way. I was one of them. I wasn't one of the "Dublin visitors" anymore. I was a Knocknamee local.

"So now what happens?" Martin was bent over the back of my chair, peering at the screen.

"Well, it's gone live. It's out there."

"Amazing, isn't it?" Martin furrowed his eyebrows in concentration.

"How quickly will people know about it?" Mavis had forgotten her glasses, so hadn't been able to read the screen and follow the action as closely as Martin.

I hit the Refresh button. "They already know. Look." As I had predicted, messages were appearing immediately on the blog. Feeding in live.

"Amazing." Martin pointed at the screen. "Who's that?"

Greggius_08: knocknamee is in county clare, west of Ireland.

"I dunno. I don't know who any of these people are."

"Do they know you?"

"Some of them think they do, I suppose."

Annie had agreed to open the pub for one hour later than usual that night. Only one hour, she'd stressed with all the authority of a school principal. Everyone had agreed that was all they'd stay for and wasn't it awful good of her to leave the pints flowing for the extra sixty minutes. "And would a few of them be free, considering the gravity and trauma of the day?" Paddy, the postman, had asked, sticking his neck out with a mischievous glint in his eyes. Annie's face had gone red and her cheeks had puffed out in anger. "Paddy, if you think I'm staying open for the good of my health, you're sorely mistaken. It's raising the prices I should be doing."

And so, after the sixth Step was posted, we traipsed en masse into O'Donahue's pub, with a great thirst on us.

All conversation and heads turned quickly to me after the first round was poured. I spoke as truthfully as I could, giving as much information as I had. I wasn't keeping any secrets. There was a lot of wise nodding into pints. Sean Lalor stroked his beard pensively and Dermot Flynn, drunk again and in the same position he'd been in the previous nights, released a low rumble of a sound that gradually turned into a song.

> *Mary, we searched long and far,*
> *For the wails of famine to be gone,*
> *But love for us will never be,*
> *The crown has taken our hearts and run us down.*

I tapped my foot with the beat and marveled at how the whole pub seemed to know the song and crept into it with a throwaway word or a hum.

When the song was finished, I waited a respectful amount of time before speaking. "The thing is," I said softly, "I don't know much about her. I'd like to know more."

I noticed a moment, a heartbeat pass among them. Dermot spoke first to the others. "'Tis only fair."

They nodded in agreement.

"What we know has been handed down from our parents and their parents before them." He leaned forward and looked me straight in the eye. "She was a witch, and she wasn't a good woman."

"I gathered as much, yeah."

"She ruled this village with cruelty." He took a long sip of his Guinness.

"She ruled this village? Like the town mayor? Like Johnny?" Whenever I'd thought about the other Kate McDaid, I'd never ever considered she might be in a governmental role.

He threw his head back and breathed heavily out his nose. "Johnny has his faults, but he's nothing like that. No, she was a different kettle of fish. She was a young woman after the famine. Some have her as a great beauty that could cast spells over men. She had red hair like yourself—that's where she got the name. It sets you apart, the hair." He stopped for another drink, and I felt very self-conscious about my curls, falling over my shoulders like a deep red blanket.

"But the potato famine, oooh." His face creased into lines of pain. "The village was ravaged. There was death everywhere—oh, the misery of it! The people had nothing. They had no roofs over their heads because the English landlord, Phillips . . ." He curled his lip in disgust. "He burned them out. They had no land to call their own, no coins in their pockets, no food in their belly, and no whiskey in their mouths. Babies died in their mothers' arms and the stench of death was everywhere. The people fell

down on their knees and prayed with all their might to God. And
He never answered them. He never lightened their load. For four
years the potato crop failed. They never knew that life could be
so cruel, that God could do this to them. So they turned their
backs on Him and the church. They looked to the pagan gods,
who were here long before the church." He lowered his voice and
leaned in closer to me. "They asked the fairies for help."

I leaned in.

"Kate McDaid had been taken, you see, as a child. The hair,
you see, they had their eye on her. She was a beautiful child
and she could sing, and the fairies, they love music. What they
wouldn't do for a tune."

There was nodding and short grunts of agreement.

"So they took her, as was their wont. They were so enraptured
by her voice and her pure spirit—they say she had a pure soul as
a child—that they took her for seven years. Anyway, as is their
way, they never send a mortal back to the mortal world without
a gift from theirs. You can say what you want about the good
people, but they're fair, they're always fair."

There was more nodding and louder grunts of approval.

Annie expertly balanced a tray of pints as she made her way
across to the table. Setting it down, she silently distributed a
drink into each open hand.

"So, on hearing the people's cries for help, they gave her a
gift—the gift to heal the sick, man or beast. And because of the
famine and the people being in dire need of help, they gave her
an extra gift—the gift of spell making. She could cast spells on
anyone and anything. They wanted her to give the famine people
hope. But they warned her, oooh, they warned her." His voice
rose to a song. "She could not take money for her gift. They cannot abide greediness. Cannot abide it."

I was enjoying the drama, the singsong quality of the tale. The fire was crackling easily in the corner, the pints were slipping down smoothly, and we, Dermot's engrossed audience, sat with fixed stares, nodding in time to the beat of the story.

"So when the people, the starving, poor people in the last days of the famine, asked the fairies for help, they handed Kate McDaid back. She was about seventeen at the time. Gave her back to the people with her gift for healing and spell making, to do good by the people of Knocknamee. But she got a taste for it, for the money. And the darkness and the blackness crept into her. And she was worse than any Englishman had ever been to this village. Until she got paid, she put spells on the cattle so there was no milk, made the children sick, dried up the land until it was almost bare rock. And when she was paid, the sun would shine, the grass would grow, and buckets of milk would over-flow into the mouths of infants. She did dealings with the devil, there's no doubt about it."

"Tell her what happened then," Annie piped up from behind the bar, where she was busy pouring the next round.

"Well, they say the fairies got angry with her. Stopped her spells from working and her potions from curing. Left her a mad-woman, up in her big house, trying to get back into their favor, and the favor of the villagers. But neither side would have her." Dermot sat back and drained the end of his pint in one swift gulp. He raised his empty glass and nodded in the direction of Annie, calling for a refill.

"So how did it end?"

"We don't rightly know. She hadn't been seen for a long time. And then there was a fire in the old house. But you wouldn't know. History tends to overlap and the dates get all in a muddle."

"What a story!" I said, shivering at the memory of the old ruin.

"It's not a story, girl. Different times, different creatures." He winked at me.

I nodded solemnly with understanding.

"How did she know spells and potions?" I asked cautiously, aware of how my personal knowledge of spells and concoctions was springing up out of nowhere. "Did she have a book or did she just know things in her head?"

"Well, no one knows for certain. Biddy Early—have you heard of her?"

The good witch from Clare, with the crystal-ball Bottle. "Mmmm." I shrugged my shoulders at Dermot.

"She was over in Feakle, about ten miles from here, was alive the same time as the Red Hag. She had the gift, too, given to her by the fairies. But they were so different. She did nothing but good with her gift—cured the sick and never took a penny for it. But she used a Bottle, a dark-blue Bottle, like a crystal ball, I suppose. She could see into the future with it. They say she'd look into it and she'd know everything about you instantly. But the Red Hag didn't have a Bottle, she didn't have foresight. I don't know how she knew her spells."

Maybe the Red Hag just knew things, like I just knew things. "And the Bottle. Now it's . . ."

"No one knows. Some say it ended up in the bottom of a lake, thrown there by a Catholic priest. Some say the fairies came and took it back. Maybe the Red Hag got her hands on it. Others say it's buried with Biddy Early. No one knows for sure." He supped on his pint. "They would have known each other, the two witches. Some say they were taken at the same time, went to the same fairy palace, and then rose out and took different paths."

I nodded, thinking that a fairy palace sounded like an English boarding school for young ladies. "Thanks, Dermot. Thanks for telling me this."

He smiled at me. "I suppose everyone should know about their relatives, good or bad."

I had one last question for him. "So the Steps? Did you ever hear of them before?"

"No." He shook his head seriously. "I've never heard anything like that before."

If I'm honest, I felt a bit disappointed. I was hoping he'd have another story for me about Steps and fairies and high kings of Ireland, and between us we could tease out the truth. The thing was, six weeks earlier, when I'd sat in the solicitor's office and heard for the first time about the other Kate McDaid, I'd been 100 percent convinced that she was a mad old woman, that she'd been hearing voices in her head. Now I was beginning to wonder. This woman had a story, a real story. She was a legend.

For a few moments we all looked into the tops of our Guinness, lost in thought.

And once again, seizing the silence, Dermot Flynn piped up. He was drunk now, so the song kicked off loud and mid-chorus. It was a much livelier tune than earlier. I couldn't stop my foot tapping and my head bobbing. Annie started to do a small jig at the corner of the bar, grinning from ear to ear and daintily crossing her feet in front of each other. She looked as light as a feather, in spite of her heavy build.

"The fairies want us to have a good time? Sure, that's what we'll do. Isn't that what we've always done in Knocknamee? Isn't that why they made their home here? Git the fiddle out there, Dinny, would ya?" Dermot shouted across to a young man, who immediately stuck his head in a bag and produced a well-polished fiddle that he snuck under his chin. And then the fun really started. We rose from our seats and hopped and leaped around the room, looping arms for a spin with wild abandon. We bumped and swung from each other. Dizzy and rosy.

It must have been hours later, when my hair was damp from sweat, my cheeks ached from smiling, and I felt like I'd danced my toes off, that there was a loud rapping on the door. Everyone turned anxiously to Annie, who nervously looked at her watch. It was three in the morning. Her extra hour had turned into four.

She jabbed her finger at the room. "If it's the guards, I'll hang yis all."

The rapping got louder and more intense.

"I'm coming, for crying out loud. Is it a fire or what?" She jangled her keys and threw us another threatening look before cautiously opening the door just wide enough for her nose to poke out.

There were mumbles.

She closed the door again and looked over at me. "It's for you. Some fellas in anoraks."

It was starting.

29

Overnight, the stillness of Knocknamee had become a swirling rainbow of color. Tents had been pitched on every postage stamp of green space—tents as blue as the sea and as orange as the fiery sun, some with flags of stars, circles, and stripes. The sea of tents stretched for miles, to the outskirts of Feakle, to the shores of An Trá Bhán and halfway up Devil's Bit, like Skittles scattered on a mountaintop. Cars were knitted like Lego pieces, exhaling petrol fumes, sandwiched cheek to cheek with no room to inhale. Elbows jutted out of stopped-car windows, demanding attention. Anoraks of many colors, zips, and buttons paraded the main street, and strange accents and languages punctured the air. Pink, freckled, yellowed, black hands hung on to pages of maps, lessons, and clues. Everyone was joining up the dots and filling in the blanks.

Drake Chandler's fans arrived in their droves, all greasy hair, tight jeans, and cardigans with holes at the wrists. Their eyeliner was so liberally applied they looked like snowmen with lumps of coal for eyes. United in grief, their search for fairies was not out of curiosity. Instead, they were looking for confirmation that their hero, their leader, their inspiration, had not died in vain, that there was a reason for his passing, and that his death ultimately had meaning.

The media came, too, of course, by the angry truckload. Shiny vans with large logos pasted onto the side, tripping over cables and wires and large lenses that whirred like small dinosaurs. Reporters with plastic hair and hollow cheeks smoothed down their pastel suits and cleaned their oversized teeth with their tongues. They, too, were joining up the dots and filling in the blanks. They'd be staying until the seventh Step was published, hoping beyond hope that some fairies might appear.

The village was heaving, coughing, and spluttering. Every plug was sparked up with extension wires that hung out windows from first-floor bedrooms and led into TV vans. Queues snaked endlessly to use one of the two computers in the Internet café.

Annie had run out of pint glasses within hours and had to get Vinny to drive to Ennis to buy more. The foreigners drank slowly, she noticed, so there was never enough time to wash and reuse their glasses. Martin's shop had sold out in the first half a day, and he'd had to do the same, sending Vinny and his van to Ennis to restock. Then he raised his prices.

Dermot had sketched out a map of the town, highlighting local points of interest, and printed it up with the help of a photocopier. He was charging two euros a sheet and had cleared a cool thousand euros by the end of the day.

With the smell of money everywhere, even hooded Dylan had stubbed out his cigarettes and left his cans of Dutch Gold to lead small groups around the ruin. His tour included details of what the Red Hag ate for lunch, and the original site of her direct phone line to the devil.

Nessa had agreed to let Dylan be her boyfriend again. Dressed as the Red Hag, in a black shawl and a red headscarf, she was jumping out at people.

"Make hay while the sun shines." Johnny Logan was popping his head into every business on the main street to repeat his mantra while he rubbed his hands together. "We'll make a mint yet," he'd say with a wink out the door.

Johnny had his own ideas. He was building a stage at the entrance to the village. It was nothing too fancy—more of an elevated platform made out of wood. He told me he saw it as the focal point of the village. He was planning to make speeches from it, dressed in his mayoral garments, including his big town-mayor chain. "With all these cameras about, I should get a haircut," he said.

I'd decided to stay on in Knocknamee, and not try to outrun the carnival on my doorstep. First, I was certain the fiesta would follow me wherever I went. And secondly, I knew—call it coincidence, the fairies, cosmic alignment, heebie-jeebies, whatever you like—that Knocknamee was where I was supposed to be for the final Step. I had only days until the final reveal, and I was counting down just as much as the Anoraks.

Unbelievably, amid all the hurly-burly, I was managing to keep a low profile. And while the media knew I was in Knocknamee, they didn't know where. The locals, the lovely, lovely locals, remained tight-lipped. And so far no bribes, no offers, no pushy reporters, and no threatening words had managed to extract any information that revealed my whereabouts, and neither had Maura—in fact, I hadn't seen Maura in a while. But I knew my time was limited. I knew there'd be a slip, deliberate or accidental, and soon fingers would be pointing and I would be a witch once more: black hat, broomstick, and toothless.

I was spending a lot of time in the B and B and was starting to feel a bit claustrophobic, probably because I was excited about the girls coming soon, too. So I jumped at the chance to do something normal, something that involved getting out for a bit. Well, that and because the text that came through was from Hugh.

> Hey sorry i didn't get a chance to say bye at dinner. You left early, hope it wasn't my cooking. Was wondering if I could ask you a favor? I'm struggling with work in from the agency and need a second opinion. Dinner in return? Hugh

I agreed because, first, I wanted to get out; secondly, Hugh clearly had no idea what was happening in Knocknamee and who I was supposed to be; thirdly, I liked working in advertising and working was a nice normal thing to do, something that didn't involve fairies or witches or mystical steps; and, finally, I'd get to see Hugh one more time.

I knew I was going to see him in a platonic way—he wasn't asking me on a date. While the old me might have read into that text that it was potentially a date, the new hard, fast, steely, and never-to-have-her-heart-broken Kate knew that this was a working meeting. Not a date. Anyway, he had a girlfriend and he was not interested.

I was so confident it wasn't a date, I didn't even put any makeup on. Barefaced, in a pair of jeans and my slightly itchy woolly jumper, I put on Colm's helmet, confident it would disguise me, and cycled over to the Olde Punchbowl, a pub about five miles from Knocknamee where Hugh and I had agreed to meet. He'd suggested Knocknamee at first, but I'd quickly put a stop to that, telling him I'd like to see some more of the countryside.

Inside the Olde Punchbowl, Hugh was hunched over beside a log fire, cradling a pint of Guinness, his brow furrowed. Somehow he looked anxious. He saw me enter, shot up, and lurched toward me to kiss my cheek. Then he began to rearrange the furniture, mumbling about not knowing where I'd like to sit and would I prefer the window.

I sat down opposite the fire, stretched out my hands to warm them, and smiled comfortably at him. "This is perfect."

"A drink?" He clapped his hands together. "What's it to be, then?"

As he walked to the bar, he looked tense across the shoulders. *He must be worried about work*, I thought.

I looked around. The Olde Punchbowl was small and dark, walking a fine line between cozy and dingy. Candles flickered, and tuneless eighties pop music played in the background. There were maybe four other people in the bar—a couple and two old men—all drinking with an air of serious intent.

"I brought the menu." Hugh thrust a plastic card in front of me. "I've never been here before. I thought we could go to that bistro in Knocknamee, but that's cool that you wanted to go somewhere else. It's just, I don't know if this place is any good." He was talking at a mile a minute, and tiny beads of perspiration freckled his forehead. That's when I noticed that he was clean—well, at least not scruffy. His dirty blond hair was coiffed into something resembling a style, he'd shaved and his skin looked clear and tanned. His dark green shirt was ironed, his light blue jeans were spotless, and he was wearing a pair of shoes that weren't covered in mud. I must have looked a bit shocked, because he asked if I was okay.

"Yeah. You're, em . . ." I nodded my head up and down at him. "All scrubbed up."

His whole face turned a shade of purple I hadn't known existed, and he self-consciously rubbed his hands on the front of his shirt. "Ah, you know, got to make an effort now and again."

I laughed, thinking that the glamorous blonde was obviously doing a number on him.

I don't know if it was the heat of the fire, the fact that this was a nondate and therefore there was no pressure, or that the drinks were sliding down easily, but I began to relax. We fell into an easy conversation that was only interrupted when he raced to the bar to refill our glasses. We chatted about everything. I learned that he'd been born and still lived in Lisnawee, a small town about five miles from Knocknamee. He and his brother had lost their parents in a car crash about ten years earlier, and now it was just the two of them, plus Aisling and his mischievous nephews. He was thirty. He'd had Setanta for six years, but he also had forty other animals on the farm, including geese, sheep, and a few cows, one of which he was particularly fond of and which he described as "an auld pet." He employed a few people on the place to keep it ticking over—he was hoping to free himself up a bit more the following year to travel and see the world. He said he hadn't been anywhere and felt it was time he did, which was why he was looking to properly brand his business in the hope of investment or maybe even a takeover in the future.

When he started talking about his business, I remembered why we were there. We'd been chatting for well over two hours by that stage.

"Work!" I sat up out of my chair. "Don't you want to talk to me about work?"

He waved his hands in the air, shaking his head. "Don't you worry about that. We haven't even eaten. What am I like? Jesus. What'll it be, m'lady?"

"What about some good old-fashioned fish and chips?"

He grinned at me. "I couldn't think of anything more perfect."

A while later, when our plates had been licked clean, I decided to broach a delicate issue. "So . . ." I leaned forward, my hands practically touching his knees. He leaned toward me. "Your business? How did you actually get into such an industry?"

He rested back into his chair and spoke calmly, more serious. "Saw a space in the market, needed to make money, and wanted to be able to work from the farm. I started it about five years ago, and we're doing well. Really well, Kate."

I shook my head, still feeling a little unsure how comfortable I would ever be with the porn issue. "But it's porn!" I blurted out. "It's gross."

He threw his head back, looking shocked. "It's not porn! Did you think I worked in *porn*?"

I nodded. "You do, don't you?"

"What? Oh my God, what you must think of me!" His brow furrowed into a worried V. He looked at me, confused. "No. Of course I don't work in porn."

"Your website? It's a porn site, isn't it?" I leaned forward anxiously.

"No. Are you mental?" He shook his head in disbelief.

"But I—"

"I had no idea. Porn, of all things. No wonder you couldn't stand to be in the same room as me."

"What?"

"That day in the agency. You couldn't run away from me quick enough."

I didn't know if it was the heat of the fire or me, but I could feel my temperature rising, remembering that meeting in the kitchen.

"I don't understand. At work that's what you're known as. 'The porn guy.'"

"'The porn guy.' Brilliant, that is brilliant." He was laughing hard now. "So they think I'm some kind of pimp. I should get one of those MTV cribs, a fur coat. I'd look massive in a fur coat."

I was confused. "Hang on a minute. Are you saying you *don't* work in porn?"

"No. I mean, I guess I could see how it could be lost in translation, but, no, I run a discreet site." He wiggled his index fingers in the air as quotation marks around "discreet."

"Discreet? Isn't that porn?"

"Nah. We sell products that people are too embarrassed to buy in the shops, like men's hair dye, foot fungus cream, or denture paste. One of our bestsellers last year was a tonic for women with thinning hair, and, now that I think of it, condoms. We always sell a lot of condoms. I guess that might be the porn thing."

I was so confused. I'd had visions of him peddling smut. I'd gotten him wrong.

"Now that you say it, though, we could always throw in a few blue movies. There's definitely a market for it." He smiled at me.

I must have looked really shocked and confused.

"I'm joking. You wouldn't want to get mixed up in that kind of stuff. Especially in business. It could lead down lots of dark alleys."

"Wow. I should probably apologize. I think I had you pegged all wrong. I'd heard differently. In the office, I . . ." *Marjorie*, I thought. Now it all made sense. Marjorie had deliberately misled me. She was unbelievable. So manipulative. She wanted to run the account without any interference, and she probably had her eye on Hugh, too. What had she called him? Repulsive. When he clearly was anything but. Porn was the perfect cover. It would deter input from anyone else in the company. Quite smart, really.

"Sorry I'm not more of a shady character. I'd probably be a lot more interesting."

"Don't worry. My life is a little *too* interesting, at the moment."

He looked at me quizzically, but I waved it away, really not wanting to get into my current magical mystical situation.

So Hugh wasn't the confident porn guy I assumed he was. Unfortunately for my crush, though, he was just lovely, easy company, full of smiles, and so attractive.

I snapped back into reality. "So now that I know what your industry is, do you want to show me the work you're struggling with?"

He produced pages of ad treatments. Some worked; some didn't. We sat and reviewed and debated the pieces. Well, I debated the pieces—Hugh just agreed with everything I said, occasionally chipping in with "I thought that was a load of bollocks" about various executions. In the end we agreed on a style and format.

"This is your winner. It's really strong. It'll work across all mediums. This one I'm excited about. This will take you places."

He just stared at me, his stormy gray eyes holding fast on mine. My heart was pounding. "You really know your stuff."

"It's not rocket science, you know." I eyed him teasingly. "Or like working in the UN."

He put his hands to his face. "Oh God, I'm bloody useless." He hung his head. "I just panic, you know, and I say the wrong things."

"I should have known you weren't a porn guy. You would have been a lot smoother."

His cheeks were flushed and he looked embarrassed. "Oh, look, I'm sorry, em . . ." He looked toward the door, as if he wanted to bolt. "I've no filter. It just comes flying out. I suppose I didn't understand the work that you do, how hard it is. I haven't been able to make head nor tail of it. I don't want to make a mistake—it's important to the business—but it's all gibberish to me half the time."

He looked flustered, and hearing him backtrack was kind of amusing.

"But, in my defense, you don't talk like the other people in your work do. What you say makes sense. It's clearer. I don't know what they're saying half the time. It's bollocks. They just talk for the sake of talking. I'd prefer it if they just told it like it is, you know. Don't try and romance me. The way you talk, Kate, that's what I like."

"Shoot from the hip."

"That's what I do, too. I shoot from the hip."

"It's funny, I never used to. I guess I'm more confident now. I dunno. I've started to trust my instincts more."

"You should. You should trust your instincts."

And then we looked at each other, and suddenly we both seemed embarrassed and started to shift awkwardly and look around the pub, at the door, the fire, the empty glasses in front of us. It was as if we'd had a confessional moment, a heartbeat of intimacy, and now we didn't know what to do with ourselves.

The bell rang for last orders, relieving the tension.

"Would you like another one for the road, or do you just want to leave?"

"Another one would be great."

Hugh wanted to cycle with me back to the B and B five miles out of his way, there and back, so really ten miles. I appreciated the gesture but knew he'd get an eyeful of the tents and the commotion at Knocknamee and then the questions would start. I told him that I was fine, and that he was a bit drunk and wobbly to be escorting anyone anywhere. We both were. It was a clear night, chilly, and the moon was out. All was quiet. Hugh had parked his bike by a bench, and walked toward it, stretching his legs, then turned to me.

"I think I might be a bit saddle-sore in the morning by the time I get home."

He stood in front of me, his sheer size dwarfing me. A moth flew between us, and its fluttering filled the silence. I studied it with the dedication of an entomologist. It chose to settle on Hugh's chest, and I found myself staring at it in the moonlight, watching it rise and fall with his breathing. He licked his lips, and finally I met his gray-eyed hopeful gaze. He moved his face closer to mine, and I smiled up at him. He bent his head forward. And he kissed my cheek. "Thanks for all that tonight. It was great."

"Thanks for dinner."

He lingered. "Right, I'll be off on my bike now."

But he didn't move, and neither did I. We both stared at each other, acres of silence between us. "Right." Snapping himself out of the moment, he quickly turned, jumped onto his bike, and pedaled off, shouting: "Good night, Kate McDaid. Sleep tight, Kate McDaid!"

30

The disguise was a stupid idea, but I thought it might work. I'd bought from Martin a green anorak that was the color of a damp field, with a maze of buttons and zips, hidden pockets and hoods, and a sturdy pair of hiking boots, something Frankenstein would wear. For the final nail in the coffin, I got Vinny to pick me up a wig in Ennis. It was cheap, scratchy, and dark brown.

So I was one of them now, but at least I'd be able to step outside the door. It was depressing, though: I had to pretend to be a female Frankenstein to leave the house. Would I ever get back to being the old Kate McDaid? I wondered.

I already knew the answer to that. Because there'd been a shift, and the old me was gone. There'd be no *Kate McDaid Part 2: The Revenge,* the "I'll be back" part. There was a change in me, and I wasn't quite sure what it was, or how I would deal with it, but I knew my old life was gone.

With the wig on, I looked like Barbie's sick cousin, the one who got mangled in the plastics machine and never got near a sun bed. My synthetic hair crinkled like a packet of crisps to the touch, and the electric hum it gave out was causing dogs nation-wide to cover their ears and whimper.

But the disguise was working. So two days after my dinner

with Hugh, I zipped up my anorak and tightened the bolts on my Frankenstein boots. I was going for a walk to visit a fairy fort—Martin had told me that Billy the pig farmer had one on his land. It was a good distance out of town, and he'd deliberately kept it under the radar of the Anoraks, not wanting to have them traipse all over his potato crops.

Fairy forts are supposed to be an exit and entrance to an intricate system of roads that crisscross under the ground and that fairies travel on. The roads are protected with spells and magic. The forts are like a keyhole into their world. That's why you're never supposed to enter one unaccompanied; that is, without a fairy.

I walked for forty-five minutes until I reached Billy the pig farmer's land. His back field hosted the fairy fort, a perfect circle of high stones, each the size of a small car, with a lot of gnarly gorse bushes that had locked onto the rocks over the years. The actual circle was smaller than I thought it would be, but the rocks were larger—much too large for little people to be heaving around. There was no leprechaun there counting his pot of gold.

So now what happens? I wondered as I circled the fort like a one-legged swimmer. "Do I think I'm going to see a fairy or something?" I said to no one in particular.

The hills in the distance were trying to blow off some gray clouds that were threatening to rain on them and me. The clouds scooped out some raindrops and heavily plopped them on my head.

I should step inside, I thought, zipping up my anorak.

Knowing that I wasn't superstitious but admittedly a little bit more than curious, I stomped right on in there, past the rocks and gorse bushes into the middle of the circle. At that moment the heavens opened and rain spilled down. Standing there in the center of uneven clumps of grass, surrounded by a circle of misshapen rocks, I didn't feel like it was magical, like a gateway to an intricate system of fairy roads. It didn't feel like I was breaking an unwritten law. And yet I was. I was doing the unspeakable, standing in the middle of a fairy fort. But I hadn't been struck down, a magic wand hadn't been waved at me, and I still had all my limbs intact.

I shrugged. *It's just a collection of old rocks*, I thought. And suddenly the very idea of being scared of standing in a fairy fort amused me. *Superstitious nonsense*, I thought. I started to jump up and down on the spot, waving my arms around like an Indian performing a rain dance in a low-budget Western. "Helloo, fairies! I'm here! Come on out and play." I felt the wig plastered to my face. "Yoo-hoo, fairies!" I was laughing so hard now, I thought I couldn't breathe. I whipped my wig off and began whirling it into the air, shaking my own hair free at last. "God, that feels good," I said aloud. I kept pounding out my rain dance—somehow, thumping the ground relieved me of my own frustrations of the last few weeks. Jump, thump, stomp: the rhythmic beating felt therapeutic. The dancing felt good, the jumping, the thumping, the stomping.

And then it happened. The magic. As I raised my giant Frankenstein boot in the air to exit the fort, I felt a tight squeeze across my stomach, like a band had wrapped around me. I was being pulled back into the fairy fort. Like a tug of war, I pulled forward, heaving myself outward, but something or someone was tugging at me with more force than I could combat. I tried to step out again. My foot hung in the air. I leaned back to regain my balance and then pushed with all my strength. Just as quickly I was rocked back into the fort. Winded, I fell and landed on my back in the center. The ground was soggy from the rain. I struggled to my knees and stood upright again. With gritted teeth I swung around, spinning, and screamed into the rain. "Let me leave!" I shouted. Then I marched with steely determination to the edge of the fort. "Let me leave!" I shouted again, before closing my eyes and raising my boot. I felt a gentle push on my lower back, and I stumbled out of the fort.

I spun around to see who had pushed me, and I heard him, loud and clear. "Spoilsport."

I looked for him in the shadows. There was no one there. But I knew who was there. I just couldn't see him, but he was there—my fairy friend, Paudi O'Shea.

It all came back and it was real. It wasn't something from a dream or from my imagination. It, *he*, was a part of my childhood. He'd been my imaginary friend, and he wasn't Paulie, like Mam remembered. He was Paudi, the fabulous Paudi O'Shea. We'd played in my back garden, climbing trees, singing songs, dancing, playing, hurling, and laughing—more than anything I remembered the laughing. And I remembered his face: he had a grin that wrapped around him, apple-shaped cheeks that filled up when he laughed and eyes as green as the hills of Knocknamee. And he was small: not put-in-your-pocket small, but smaller than me as a child—maybe the size of a large dog. He wore bright-colored jackets in blue or purple with shiny gold buttons as big as his hand.

It was Paudi O'Shea who gave me my fairy name. He'd popped up in my dreams and whispered ideas to me. He was always looking out for me, even now I was grown up. I felt giddy and excited to see him again. Well, I couldn't see him, but I knew he was there in the fairy fort.

I spun around wildly in circles with my arms flung out, around and around. Paudi O'Shea was there! I was ecstatic. He was here in Knocknamee! My heart was leaping out of me with happiness. "You're here! You're here!" I shouted into the fort.

I skipped and ran through the fields. Somehow it felt like Paudi O'Shea was hopping along beside me, telling me to wait, like he did when I was a girl. *Those forts are magical,* I thought, *magical.* Paudi O'Shea was my wonderful secret, and I was going to keep him that way, for a little while, anyway. I ran for as long and as far as I could, until the village was safely in my sights, and then, when my wig was back in place, I smiled and skipped the whole way back, feeling like there was a second heart beating in my body.

✦   ✦   ✦

Martin knocked softly on my door and dipped his head inside. "Kate, there's a Hugh Delaney downstairs to see you. Will I send him up?"

Hugh? What was Hugh doing here?

I nodded and quickly ran to the mirror to straighten out my hair and fix the gray V-neck T-shirt I was wearing. I looked tired, so I pinched my cheeks to put some color into them, an old-school trick I'd seen in a film once.

I heard Hugh noisily enter the room and turned around. He looked angry. His face was red, his brow creased, his mouth downturned, and his nostrils flared. The room immediately shrank in size. He held up a fistful of newspapers and waved them wildly.

"Is this you?"

I knew he'd discovered the clippings, the press, heard the drama, seen the tents, maybe even read the Steps on the Internet.

I took a deep breath. "Hi, Kate, nice to see you. How are you? I'm fine, Hugh." I slowly pottered over to the chair on the far side of the room and sat down. Calmly.

His breathing was heavy. He pursed his mouth. "It *is* you."

"Lovely weather we're having. Mild for this time of year," I continued in a singsong voice, deliberately ignoring his posturing, waiting for him to calm down.

"Jesus, Kate." He stomped over to the window and stared out of it.

"Whenever you're ready to calm down, you can sit down," I said, sternly, eyeing him.

He paused, exhaled deeply, and physically shrank a few inches. Slowly he walked to the side of my bed and sat down, still tightly clutching the papers in his hand.

"What the hell is this?"

"This? This is my life right now."

"They're calling you a freak."

It stung, the way he said it.

"Why the hell didn't you tell me?"

I shrugged. I knew he probably deserved an explanation. "I just wanted to be me. You've no idea how mixed up everything has been. I'm exhausted, avoiding it. I don't know why I didn't tell you. Maybe because of this—how you'd react."

He shook his head. "You don't trust me."

"I don't know you to trust you."

"I . . ." His eyes widened and his mouth hung open. "I'm sorry. I didn't mean to fly in here at you. I just . . . I read these things, and I thought I knew you, but now I don't know."

I sighed. "You still know me. I don't know who that person is that they write about."

"Is it . . ." He paused to study my expression. "Is it true?"

I nodded. "Some of it, definitely. I'm trying to understand it, but, yes, some of it's true." And so I started telling him what had happened, and I told him everything. Told him about meeting my fairy again, about making stupid mistakes with Jim, about knowing spells, about the paparazzi hunting me down, about Maura creeping around and threatening me, about how I was scared, really scared, but also weirdly happy. I didn't even notice when he moved and sat beside me and put his arm around my shoulders.

"I'm hoping it's nearly over, but I'm not sure," I said. "It's only another four days until I get the final Step. I think that will be the end then."

He squeezed me tightly. "You've managed to hold it together. I would never have guessed you were going through something like that."

"Until now." I laughed, shaking my head.

"Well, I'm glad I get the real Kate McDaid. You know, the no-bullshit Kate, the shoot-from-the-hip Kate." He gently tucked my hair back behind my ears. His expression was kind. And then precisely at that moment, he changed. Thrusting his hands into his jeans pockets, he leaned away from me and his face hardened. "I should go."

"What? You just fly in and fly out, do you?"

"It's just . . ." He looked around the room.

Annoyed and frustrated, I responded deadpan. "Just go." I crossed my arms firmly across my middle. What was it with Hugh Delaney and how he never ceased to cause my blood to boil at one stage or another?

He stood up. "I left Setanta in the car. There's something I have to do. I'll, em . . ." He looked around the room. "Give you a call."

I shrugged at him, trying to calm my anger. *Go, Hugh Delaney, go. Go back to your glamorous blonde and your normal life and stop confusing the hell out of me.*

31

The carnival arrived late Saturday evening, with lights that flashed as brightly as Times Square, outshining the stars in the navy sky of Knocknamee. The lights promised endless entertainment: wheels of fortune, bumper cars, mountains of pillowed cotton candy, waltzers, a giant big wheel, and a gaggle of gypsies peering into crystal balls and turning tarot cards.

Johnny Logan admitted to me that he was annoyed with himself for not having thought of it sooner. He should have gotten the gypsies in a long time ago—wasn't that what people were interested in? The carnival was paying him 10 percent of all profits, so he was happy enough, just as long as none of those tigers escaped.

A few of the gypsies were claiming to be me or another descendant of Kate McDaid. Four of them had rinsed henna into their hair and hung signs saying THE REAL KATE MCDAID outside their caravans. All four were making money. The Anoraks stood patiently in line, gossiping among themselves about the Steps. I slid past them, wig on and my own anorak zipped tight up to my neck. I had already played and lost three rounds of darts, taken one stomach-heaving spin on the waltzer, and had almost gone on the big wheel before I chickened out, convinced that it was about to roll down the hill of its own accord. My disguise was holding up well. All around me people were clutching photos of Kate McDaid, yet there hadn't been one quizzical look or prolonged stare. I was blending right in.

Fiona and Lily were due that day. They'd called me excitedly from the road, singing songs at the top of their lungs, ecstatic to be out of Dublin and hitting the road. It had only been a week since Fiona had quit her job, but it felt like a year, and I was dying to see them. I'd booked them into Martin's B and B.

Matthew had arrived in Knocknamee, as I knew he would—not in a psychic way, but in a best-friend way. He was staying in Miles O'Brien's B and B, along with some of the more stubborn mice who refused to be exterminated. Over a toasted sandwich at Martin's, Matthew apologized until he was blue in the face. I forgave him—I'd forgiven him a long time ago. He finally filled me in on the shoot. David Hasselhoff had managed to get another day to shoot the Starshoot ad, and, according to Matthew, it looked really good. It was kitschy and retro, but it worked. And the best news of all was that we had both been promoted. I couldn't even believe I still had a job, but Matthew just rolled his eyes and explained that Colin had put me on stress leave. My job was there, I'd been promoted, and somehow, in spite of all the madness, we'd made a good ad. This had been exactly what I'd wanted only a few weeks earlier. This had been my dream. And now, with all that had happened, now that I had my fairy, now that I knew about my connection with the other world, the promotion, the job, and chocolate bars seemed like they belonged to another life, a faraway life. Things were changing.

After lunch, Matthew and I wandered down to O'Donahue's for a pint. It was six deep at the bar. There wasn't a pocket of air. With the keen eyes of an experienced publican, Annie spotted me from behind a pyramid of pint glasses. She was keeping her cool and managing to stay in control, in spite of the shouts for Guinness all around her. She threw me a ginormous and unsubtle wink, shouting *"fan"*—the Irish word for wait. Then, picking up two full pints she'd just poured, she came out from behind the counter and moved with great ease through the crowd.

"You'll be wanting seats," she said, eyeing Matthew up and down.

"Ah, it's grand, you're busy. We'll go for a walk or something," I said.

"You'll do no such thing."

Annie turned to two large men who were speaking a harsh language that may have been Swedish. They were sitting on low stools, crouched uncomfortably over a small table. "You two. Out. You're barred."

The men furrowed their blond eyebrows in confusion. "But madam, we are drinking," one said.

"Out." Annie motioned toward the door.

"We're paying customers."

"Well, I don't like the look of yis. Get out."

They rose up off their stools and hovered over Annie like strong, blond oak trees. "Madam, we paid many euros."

"Tell the guards. Get out." She jutted out her jaw defiantly.

They stood still, rooted to the spot.

"Do I need to call security?" she spat back, unfazed by the sheer bulk of the men.

"No. Come on, Sven." They lumbered toward the door, defeated.

"There you go now." Plonking the full pints down, she cleared the table, then set the three stools around it. "Give Paddy a shout whenever you want another. I've got him behind the bar. I think he's drinking more than he's serving, but if he can manage to stay

upright for the rest of the night, I'll have him back tomorrow."
She turned around and melted into the crowd.

Embarrassed, Matthew and I slowly slunk onto the stools, trying to remain as inconspicuous as possible.

"Thank God she's on our side," Matthew whispered. He took a sip of his Guinness, eyes down, too scared to look in Annie's direction.

I scanned the pub for a familiar face. The crowd seemed to be enjoying themselves, nursing pints and deep in heavy discussions. There were a lot of pens being waved, maps highlighted, and pages of what I guessed were the Steps being studied. These people were giving over a lot more time and effort to the whole thing than I was. I wondered how far they were getting, if anyone had cracked anything yet. I didn't see any locals—they'd all been budged out.

One group seemed to be more animated than the others: they were crouched lower, and you could sense the intensity of their conversation by the tightness of their shoulders. They were also the only people who, apart from me, had kept their anoraks on, in spite of the stifling heat of the pub. Their shoulders seemed to rise and fall as one, as they breathed in and out. Suddenly they uttered a collective "Ooooh!" It sounded like a eureka moment and they all slowly eased backward so their faces became visible. It was them! The Anoraks. The original Anoraks. I covered my face immediately. Even though I felt more confident with the wig in place, I knew this group of Anoraks were particularly thorough. But I had to admit that, in a very strange way, I was a little bit happy to see them. Maybe even more than a little bit. They'd been on this journey with me—albeit theirs was a much more unusual and potentially psychotic journey—but, still, they had been there from the beginning.

"I must be getting homesick. I'm kind of happy to see them."

"Who?"

I cocked my head toward the colorful corner. Matthew snapped his neck around. "Aren't they the Anoraks?" He looked shocked.

"The original crew." I could hear pride creeping into my voice.

"And here they are in Knocknamee." He rubbed his eyes. "They followed you down?"

"They followed the Steps down."

"This is nuts, isn't it?" He looked at me and slowly shook his head.

"Nuts."

"I mean, all these people believe in these Steps. They think there's a message. They believe they're going to reawaken the fairies. Nobody doubts it. They believe there's truth in it."

"Well, you did, too. For one moment." I didn't want to share with him what I knew. I wasn't ready to tell him that it was true, all of it was true. That there were fairies and spells. That the Anoraks were right.

"I know. I suppose I just got caught up in it. I think I always like to believe in the possibility of other things. But I really didn't mean to put you on the spot like that, Kate. I'm so . . ."

"Sorry, I know."

He furrowed his heavy eyebrows.

"No, I mean, I get it, kind of." I started to scratch at my wig. The heat of the room was making it itch. "And if this wasn't me, if it wasn't happening to me, maybe I'd really get it. You know, people believe in healing, in angels, in God—all kinds of things that aren't tangible. And I think the Steps are easy to believe in. There's a message—bang—every week. And now there's a place, and yeah, I get it, there's a leader. A reluctant leader." I gave out a half smile.

"Parched." Matthew licked his lips and sipped from his pint.

"Matthew . . ." It was a bit of a long shot but worth asking. "Have you ever heard of the Hellfire Club?"

"Yeah, the cult group in Dublin?"

"Do you know anything about them?" It was a hunch. Dad had mentioned that Liam McCarthy had been rumored to be involved with them. The signet rings, the interest in the other world—there was a chance that this was the group that Maura was affiliated with.

"A bit. I think it started up in around the 1700s. There's an old ruin that used to be some English landlord's grand estate. It was built on top of a cairn, you know, a mass grave. So it was always rumored to be haunted, and then it burned down a couple of times, so they gave up trying to rebuild it. Small groups of people used to meet there for satanic worship. They used to sacrifice animals—horrible stuff. But it's all rumor, really. There are YouTube videos of people playing with Ouija boards up there. It's kind of infamous."

I shivered at the memory of Mister Snoop Doggy Dogg trying to attack Maura. Could there be something in it? Could he have been trying to protect me? Could he see that she was involved in the dark arts?

"Infamous but not current? I mean, this stuff doesn't go on nowadays, does it?"

He looked at me and frowned. "What are you talking about, Kate?"

"The dark arts, contacting the other world: it doesn't happen anymore, does it?"

"Look around you, Kate. You're leading a whole group of 'other world' followers."

Oh God, I thought, *he's right*. If I was involved in this, I had

every reason to believe that Maura and her band of ancient politicians and powerful people were equally involved. But why? What
did they want?

"Wait until I tell you." Matthew leaned forward and slapped
my thigh. "You know the old ruin near here? There's a well close
by—I don't even think it's actually in the same grounds—but
this lot doesn't care." He was laughing. "They're getting water
out of the well and saying it can heal people."

"What?" I shouted, a little too loudly, judging by the number
of heads that spun back to see the commotion.

"I swear to God. I couldn't believe it. They're drinking the
water and putting it directly onto whatever is broken or sore. It's
just crazy."

"Are many people doing it?"

"The path up to it looks pretty well worn."

"Is it free?"

"No. People are handing over euros like you wouldn't believe."

"Are they stupid or greedy?" I said, not expecting an answer.

"I knew I recognized you."

Standing over the table was the biggest Anorak of them all.
Simon. He was staring at me. "It's Kate McDaid." Simon's voice
trembled and his eyes popped so far out of his head they looked
like they'd fall out. He began to whisper the same thing, trance-
like, over and over again. *"Tá tú laoch. Tá tú slánaitheoir."*

"What's he saying?" I asked Matthew.

"You are our hero. You are our savior."

Ah, fuck.

"Come on, let's go." Matthew stood up and started guiding
me to the door.

Nowhere was safe anymore.

32

Fiona and Lily arrived late that night, all rosy-cheeked and gasping for a drink. Mavis showed them upstairs to their room, a yellow, 1950s-style marital room with twin beds and hints of Doris Day and Rock Hudson.

There were now seven guests staying at the B and B, all followers of the Steps. Martin and Mavis had rented out every room, including their own, and had been sleeping on a blow-up mattress under the kitchen table. It was playing havoc with Mavis's knees, but they thought it was a bit of an adventure, so they didn't mind too much.

Normally I had breakfast in the dining room. I'd duck in late and, hiding behind my wig and a book, I'd eat my honeyed porridge and nobody would take any notice—no one in the B and B knew who I was. But now that I'd been discovered by the Anoraks, I was worried I'd be recognized. So I breakfasted early, with Martin and Mavis, huddling over the multifunctioning kitchen table well before the other guests had wiped the sleep from their eyes.

"So the good news is . . ." Martin poured some steaming tea into a mug with ITALIA '90 on the side. "With the extra money we've earned and with a couple of donations from people, we've now enough to buy a kit for the under-twelve hurling team. The post office is going to sponsor us." He was beaming with pride. "I can't wait to see the lads out there in their green and gold." He started to tear up. "I've waited a long time for this."

Mavis looked up, smiling. "It's because of you, you know? He'd never have organized the money, otherwise. But all these extra people in the village, the extra money. It's great stuff, altogether."

I blew on my tea to cool it down. "Well, at least something good is coming out of these Steps," I said into my cup.

"There's a lot of good out of these. Look at all the money in the village now."

I made a face. It wasn't all good. The beautiful wild purple and yellow flowers on the pathway to the foot of Devil's Bit had been trampled into the ground. Slimy gray wads of litter clogged up the stream that ran into the Shannon. There were bonfires on An Trá Bhán every night, which weren't cleaned up, leaving cans and cigarettes and half-eaten sausages poking through the golden sand. Johnny Logan was said to be considering widening the main street so there'd be more room for cars and vans to pass through. It would mean straightening it out, losing its soft curves and character, but maybe that's what money meant to Knocknamee.

"Money doesn't buy happiness." I knew it was a cliché, but I couldn't help myself.

"Well, it'll buy new kit." Mavis got up from the table and began to busy herself with the eggs.

"Look what money did to the Red Hag." I'd been thinking a lot about the old witch these last few days. I still had so many unanswered questions.

"That's true. But sure, aren't we wiser now than they were then?" Martin said with a wink.

I couldn't answer him.

I went upstairs and gave the girls a wake-up call by jumping on their beds.

"It's too early! What time is it?" Fiona pulled a pillow over her face. "I don't work. I haven't had a lie-in in years. Let me enjoy it."

"I don't use a clock because the fairies told me not to, remember?" I laughed.

Lily sprang out of bed, her blond hair haywire and stuck to her pink pajamas. "Your spell with Mr. Goatee—it worked! I felt like a maniac waving that stick around, but it doesn't matter, because it worked. He doesn't even like me anymore, let alone obsessively love me." She dropped her voice, serious now. "Kate, you can do spells."

I stopped jumping and sat uneasily on the bed.

Fiona sat up. "Anne-Marie's baby sleeps like a dream now, after she did all that stuff you said. Although he does sleep a lot. She says he nearly sleeps too much. He's pretty much asleep around the clock."

"Oh dear, that doesn't sound good."

"She asked me to mention it to you. To see if you had any other ideas."

"A little bit of basil in his milk and heavy woolen socks will have him back to normal." I shrugged apologetically. "I do seem to know things I shouldn't, if that makes any sense. But I'm not getting them quite right. I think I need more practice."

Lily sat beside me and put her arms around my shoulders. "Don't stress, hon. We think it's going to be great. We talked about it on the way down. Think of all the things you can do with this: spell books, love potions—well, proper ones. Maybe you can win the lottery out of this somehow. Who knows? It's so exciting!"

I shifted uncomfortably, chewing on my fingernails. "Look,

I think it's weird. It's freakish. I don't know what it is, yet. I just know that I know a few things. Spells, I guess, but that might be all I know. I don't even seem to know them fully. I'm getting them half right. Anyway, that might be the end of all I know—bits of spells."

Fiona leaned out of her bed and reached for my hand. "Well, if it's over, it's over, and if you're a freak, you're *our* freak. We wouldn't have you any other way."

I smiled. "You two are big saps."

"We know," they said in unison.

"Now, please, can I go back to sleep? It's only half-eight or something ridiculous. I'm enjoying my new life." Fiona collapsed back onto her bed and repositioned the pillow over her face.

"Wait for the big news, Kate!" Lily paused dramatically, smiling. "Fiona has a crush."

I must have looked really shocked, because Lily slyly pinched me and raised her eyebrows. I'd never known Fiona to have a crush on anyone. I tried to act nonchalant. "Really? Who?"

"One of those anorak guys. The head one. What's his name, Fi?"

"Simon. He's so cute. I met him when I called around to your flat to feed Snoop. Your boss has taken him back, by the way. His son's allergies have cleared up."

I nearly fell off the bed. Simon? Cute? But it was Fiona, who never liked anyone, so I had to be supportive. "Really?"

"We just started talking. He was out the front, dropping a book or something off at yours, and, God, I don't know." She blushed. "We seemed to hit it off. At least, I think we did. Maybe he feels differently. But I really liked him. He seemed really sweet and . . ." Misty-eyed, she trailed off.

I smiled. "This is brilliant!"

Fiona bit her lip nervously and then threw her head back onto her pillow. "I don't know. What if he doesn't like me?"

"Trust me, Fi. You would be a catch for him."

Lily snuggled down into her bed. "I'm going back to sleep, too, Kate. Half-eight: it's too early to be awake. Just twenty minutes more—that's all I need."

"Whatever." I started to leave the room. "You just can't cope with this country air, you city folk. I'll see you two after lunch." I shut the door behind me.

"You're as popular as ever." Matthew was sitting on my bed, rifling through piles of newspapers.

"Me? Or 'me, the spiritual guru'?"

"Spiritual guru. You should read some of these."

"I don't want to."

"Seriously, look at these headlines: 'The Humble Spiritualist,' 'Modern Witch Teaches Modesty,' 'Is Kate McDaid the Irish Dalai Lama?' And that's only the Sunday papers. The daily ones are off the scale. Who's, em . . ." He rummaged through some pages, flicking wildly. "Anita O'Herlihy?"

I had to think long and hard. "Oh, yeah, she was in my Spanish class at school up to third year. Blond girl."

"She sold a tell-all about you in school, but she did it with her clothes off. Check it out."

I had to look away: there was Anita, who'd clearly blossomed since third year, naked except for a strategically positioned Spanish book. "God!" I sat down. "Never thought I'd see that. What else is there?"

"Another article by your friend." Matthew pointed at an *Irish Times* article by Maura Ni Ghaora.

"Eugh." I sighed. "I don't think I could bring myself to read that one. She was here, you know."

Matthew raised an eyebrow.

"Doing research on the Red Hag, creeping around, asking questions. She didn't seem to get very far with the locals, so I'm pretty sure she's gone back to Dublin now."

Matthew handed me another newspaper. "This paper is doing a cartoon series of you. Cute pictures."

And they were, although I felt my hair was not as frizzy in real life as they'd drawn it.

"Sooo . . ." Matthew tugged awkwardly on his nose. "I kissed someone."

I perked up. "Someone? Off the Internet?"

He shook his head.

"A stranger?"

Another headshake.

I slapped my thighs in delight. "It's someone we know, isn't it?"

He nodded, blushing.

"Brilliant. Oh my God, is it work?"

Another nod.

"This is great! Lots of people meet their partners at work."

And so began a name-guessing game that could only lead to Rumpelstiltskin as I listed off all likely contenders to much headshaking.

"This is ridiculous," I said after the three-hundredth name. "I've gone through everyone in the building who I know, and I know everyone you know. Who is it?"

He took a deep breath. "Don't judge, but I like her. Marjorie."

"Nooooooooooooooooooooo! But she's *Marjorie*."

"I know. We had a few drinks after the shoot—after her crazy episode."

Memories of Marjorie flailing around on the ground, trying to conjure up a spell and screaming "abracadabra" suddenly sprang to mind.

"We just ended up kissing."

"Ahhh! You were drunk!"

"Maybe the first time. But not the second, third, or fourth time."

"She's your girlfriend."

"We're drifting that way, yeah."

Somewhere between looking sheepish and embarrassed, there was a flicker of delight in Matthew's eyes. I suppose Marjorie was a bit of a catch, if you could forget the fact that she was also a bit of a pain. I was still sore at her for having deliberately misled me about Hugh. What was it with my friends and their unlikely romances?

"She's not as bad as you think she is. She's actually really sweet." He grinned, looking happy.

"Okay, great." I didn't really know what to say, but I knew enough to stay quiet and never judge a friend's romantic choice. Matthew looked happy, which was all that really mattered.

That afternoon Matthew, Fiona, Lily, and I took off on a hike. We were a happy little troupe. Dressed in my disguise, which now included a huge pair of Jackie Onassis sunglasses for good measure, we ducked and dived to avoid the Anoraks, despite Fiona's protests. I really enjoyed getting out into the countryside, breathing in the fresh air, feeling the soft ground beneath my feet, and letting the wind ruddy up my cheeks. It felt invigorating.

We spotted a handwritten sign flapping in the breeze for "The Magic Well" and went along to see it in action for ourselves. Instantly, I could see the appeal: perched on top of the hill, the well looked like something from a nursery rhyme, with circular gray stone walls and a little roof. I could imagine Jack and Jill playfully dipping their pail in and out.

We stood about halfway up and watched as an orderly queue of people silently shuffled up the hillside toward it. Maura was there—so she wasn't in Dublin after all. She was weaving in and out of everyone, trying to strike up conversation—fishing at the well. When people reached the well, they opened their mouths, shut their eyes, and crossed their hands in front of them as though they were about to receive holy communion. Then Vinny the van driver, with an air of reverence and caution never seen in his van driving, used a large silver spoon to drop a few drops of water into their mouths.

A few other enterprising individuals had set up stalls selling bottles of "Magic Well Water." They were charging six euros for a tiny tumbler of the stuff—who knew whether they contained water that actually came out of the well or water from a kitchen tap.

I can't say I was shocked when I spotted Garda Fitzgerald in the queue. Nothing surprised me these days. He seemed very serious. His look was one of intense concentration. He was out of uniform, but his wide-eyed Cavan stare was unmistakable. I wondered whether he had any news on my bike.

Garda Fitzgerald was not alone: he was chaperoning a group of five men, all with a similar look of serious concentration. Occasionally one would lower his hands to his crotch protectively. Garda Fitzgerald must have shared the spell with them.

Matthew nudged me. "Look at the crotch grabbers."

Lily giggled and we watched as the people in front of and behind them inched farther away. It looked as if, having been cured of their problem "down there," they were being extra protective and careful with the crown jewels for fear of running into any more difficulties. I could only guess they'd come to the magic well to say thanks to the fairies for keeping everything in working order.

"Oh, it's too funny." I thought I might collapse with laughter.

Fiona pointed at a dark figure in the distance, loitering near the top of the hill. "Is that a priest?"

I strained my eyes to see. It was Father O'Brien, dressed all in black with his white collar peeping through. He appeared to be shaking his head and muttering something to himself.

He must hate this, I thought. From what I'd heard, Father O'Brien was respected and liked in Knocknamee. He was a fair man, a good man. He didn't judge, and Martin told me he was easy on the penance in confession. But whenever I'd seen him during the past few days, he'd been jumpy, irritable, and bad-tempered. He was one villager who didn't seem to be enjoying the Steps.

33

"Oh, baby, you and me, our hearts are singing."

What?

"Siiiiiiiiiiiiiinging . . ."

What was going on? I rubbed my eyes and pushed back my duvet. I'd been having a sneaky afternoon nap.

". . . the songs of you and me."

The guitar strumming was getting even louder. I marched over to my bedroom window, parted the pink curtains, heaved the window open, and stuck my head out to see what all the commotion was about. Jim was on the street outside. His leather jacket was zipped up tightly, and an ocean-blue scarf was tied in a sloppy knot around his neck. He was playing a guitar, and his face was firmly cocked in the direction of my bedroom window.

"We can make it together so long as we siiiiiiiiiing . . ."

His eyes were closed, and he was wallowing in a Stevie Wonder head movement.

". . . our songs of love . . ."

There were three people with him: a cameraman, a sound man, and a tiny woman who I guessed was the director. They circled him, observing, preening, coaxing.

". . . looooooove."

I moved my elbows onto the windowsill and rested my chin on my hands, listening. A spattering of Anoraks gathered around Jim, pausing momentarily to enjoy the song, looking at the camera with confusion and eventually fumbling in their pockets for change for the busker.

More intense guitar playing followed. Jim's face creased up in pain, and he jutted out his chin and gritted his teeth. Finally he opened his eyes as he strummed the final chord. Silence.

I shouted down to the top of his head, "I thought you'd turn up. Surprised it took you this long." And quickly I ducked back and peeped out from behind the curtains, realizing I probably shouldn't have stuck my head out like that. The Anoraks were everywhere.

He stretched his neck upward, and his wide grin enveloped me and the whole village of Knocknamee. "Kate!" He threw his arms out.

"And cut. That was perfect. Good work." The elfin director slapped her hands together to emphasize a job well done. The cameraman unburdened himself of his heavy equipment. His large sound boom, looking like an oversized ear cleaner, toppled slowly to the ground. The tops of their heads converged together until Jim broke free and looked up at me again.

"Kate, are you over this shop? Can I come in?"

"Why not? It's a free country," I shouted back with as much sarcasm as I could muster. I threw on a pair of jeans and my now slightly grubby woolly sweater. I didn't care what I looked like— this was typical Jim to turn up with a full TV crew and do this dramatic serenade.

I marched heavily down the stairs. As I reached the bottom I heard conversation in the shop.

"Is that so?" Martin's tone was thick with skepticism.

"Yeah, we have the number one single and all the love and glory that goes with it, hey?"

"Well, I've never heard of you."

"I bet your kids have."

"Hmmm. And you're a friend of Kate's?"

"We go wa-a-ay back, man."

"I'm surprised at that."

"I wasn't always a number one rock star."

"I didn't mean you."

Martin wasn't bothering to hide his disapproval, but it was apparent that, as always, Jim was oblivious to it anyway.

I burst through the shop door, anxious to put a stop to the conversation.

"Babe, you look awesome." Jim crossed the shop floor in two strides and threw his arms around me. I pushed him away, aware that the embrace was probably for Martin's benefit.

"Maybe we can get a cup of tea? Martin, would that be okay if we move to the pub area?" I stood tall and gestured toward the four stools at the far end of the bar.

Martin sighed heavily. "Well, I wouldn't normally be open for another twenty minutes," he said, tapping his wrist, "but I suppose, seeing as it's tea and not alcohol, that'll be fine."

"Thanks."

"There'll be no alcohol, mind?" I'd never known Martin to be anything but friendly and hospitable, and I was surprised to see him bristling and suspicious. Jim and I sat up on two barstools. Moments later, Martin slid two mugs of tea in front of us before retreating to the far end of the counter, where he shook out the local newspaper and pretended to read it.

"So, Jim, how are you?" My aim was to be polite and ladylike and to get it over with as quickly as possible. Jim looked good, though, in spite of the cold sore living on his mouth.

"Amazing. My life is just amazing."

Martin rustled his newspaper.

"Did you see that crew out there? True. Life. Story." He paused for effect. "My story, Kate. My crew. National television." He sneezed loudly and held a tissue up to his nose, which I noticed was rubbed raw.

"Is that . . . ?"

"They follow me around, trying to get inside my head, which they'll never do, but I can pretend. I'm a good actor. They come to band practice, photo shoots, all of it. Red Horizon is going to crack the States off the back of this. That's why I just had to come here. You know, it makes sense. The song, Knocknamee—it makes sense to come here with the crew."

It was always his career. "So all that singing outside, all that was for the cameras?" Why did I even ask? I knew it was for the cameras.

"Yeah, good bit of drama, wasn't it? It was the director's idea. I think we really nailed it, too.

"And the band is doing great. I mean, I think we're really coming into our own, creatively, although we're going to do a Burning Cradle cover, probably 'The Depths of My Despair.' People have been comparing me to Drake Chandler pretty much all my life, so it makes sense, you know? And this whole fairy thing, it ties in. A lot of those emo kids, the black-eyeliner crew, are finding solace in our music since Drake Chandler passed to the other side. We're working on a new sound, a bit more electronic, New Agey . . ."

He slid into a world of beats and musical influences. I listened as he rambled on, enjoying the view but not the volume, studying his gorgeous profile and following his hand as he slowly flicked a chestnut-brown curl from his eye.

My mind started to wander, and I began to feel annoyed at myself. I'd wasted a stupid amount of time on this guy, imagining and creating scenarios in my head that were never real, thinking his winks, his hugs, his smile meant something they didn't. I'd had groupie sex. I laughed at the relief of finally understanding it all. He had completely played me.

"Everything'll be in my documentary. Everything's filmed. They're following me around twenty-four/seven. They have complete editorial control—I've handed it over for the sake of art."

I looked at him suspiciously. "This? Now? Are we being filmed?"

"Just don't look out the window." He grinned. "The director doesn't like it when you look straight into the lens."

I swiveled my stool around. There they were, like The Three Stooges, with a camera pressed up against the window.

I shook my head. "I don't want to be filmed."

"Yeah, yeah. Have you signed the rights to someone else?"

"No. Look, I don't want to be filmed. You never asked me. You just presumed. You've done nothing but take liberties with me." I was getting angry.

Jim looked confused. "Well, you'll just have to sign a release form."

And then I had an idea. A hell-hath-no-fury-like-a-woman-scorned idea. "They're filming everything, yeah?" I stood up.

He smiled, delighted. "Do you want to go out and talk to them? God, they'd love that. That would really give an edge to the show. Yes." He started muscling me toward the exit. I shook off his hand and swung open the shop door.

"Hi," I shouted, giving a big dramatic wave to the camera crew. They were on me in a nanosecond, whirring and hovering.

Jim sidled up and, preening in front of the camera, placed an iron-clad arm around my shoulder. I bristled uneasily under his grasp.

"So, you two?" the elfin woman inquired. "It must be so great to be back together?"

Jim grinned, exposing every tooth, and slowly exhaled. "Hey, we're just good friends."

I stepped forward, shaking off his embrace, and looked directly into the camera, smiling and trying my best to sound breezy. "Well, of course we're just good friends. What else could we ever be? But I'm so happy and so lucky to have such a great gay friend. You should try taking him shoe shopping—he's a wonder. And I just hope one day he'll find Mr. Right. He's a catch, boys." Then I spun on my heel, throwing a pale-faced Jim a look of ultimate triumph. He wouldn't be having groupie sex for a long, long time.

I slammed the shop door behind me, beaming. "Martin, I'll have another cup of tea, please."

Martin busied himself making tea, then laid it down in front of me and studied my expression.

It was glum. Staring into my milky tea, I knew in my heart of hearts that the only person I would have liked to appear outside my bedroom window was Hugh Delaney. But it looked like that was never going to happen.

34

I was a prisoner by my own hand. My whereabouts had become common knowledge, and now a crowd was keeping vigil outside Martin's. People were sitting cross-legged in the street staring fixedly at the building. There were hundreds of them—it was a blur of colors, an ocean of faces. Occasionally they'd sing in a dull chant that rose to a roar in the chorus. Sometimes they sang pop songs, Coldplay, the Eagles, a lot of Burning Cradle, good solid guitar songs. At other times, they switched to Irish traditional music.

Simon and the Anoraks were front-row contenders, mesmerized and rooted to the spot, staring, swaying, chanting, waiting. There was a spot at the front of the shop where people were leaving gifts. Simon had left a copy of *Witchcraft for Dummies*.

Peeking out my window on Sunday morning, I noticed the crowd was having a bit of a party, dancing around an impromptu campfire. It wasn't a party that I, or anyone with any degree of sanity, would choose to attend, but if you'd just escaped from five years' solitary confinement in a prison and had to burrow through sewage tunnels with a little spoon that you'd fashioned from your prison wall, you'd probably be happy enough to be there.

Matthew was going back to Dublin that day. He had to work.

He phoned to say good-bye, he didn't fancy battling through the Anoraks. We made plans to meet in Dublin the following week when this was all over. It felt strange that the end was in sight, that the next time I saw Matthew this would be over, that there would be no more steps.

Father O'Brien had sent for me. That sounds biblical, doesn't it? Sent for me. He sent a schoolgirl, Hannah, who was also an altar girl, to Martin's with a note for me. Martin sent her off with a packet of crisps for her trouble and then peered over my shoulder to read.

> Please come to the church vestry at 4:15 this afternoon.
> There are some matters I'd like to discuss with you.
>   Father O'Brien

Lily and Fiona wanted to come with me. I think it was the vestry that got the better of them—to be invited into the inner sanctum of a church was terrifyingly exciting. All those doors that you'd peered at during mass through the years and wondered what went on behind them. They got into a fit of schoolgirl giggles imagining what could be in there, all the priests' dresses, holy water, and gold staffs. I shook my head and laughed at them, and promised them a full report afterward.

I had to shimmy over a garden wall and race through back gardens to avoid the crowds out front. I felt like I was on my way to the headmaster's office. That feeling fizzled in my stomach—that I was bad, that I had done something really bad and now I was in big, big trouble.

So I was nervous as I stepped up to the side door of the church and knocked loudly on the heavy oak panel.

"Enter," a stern voice called from inside.

I pushed the door open a crack. "Hello, Father. It's Kate McDaid," I said meekly. "You sent for me."

Father O'Brien shot out of his chair, which was a large wooden throne with wine-velvet upholstery. "Kate, yes." He came toward me and shook my hand. Black rings circled his eyes, and his face was pale, the skin pulled tight like a soccer ball. He looked around his room, flustered. "I'd offer you a cup of tea, but I'm afraid Mrs. Regan isn't here, and I'm a bit useless in the kitchen."

"Oh, that's fine. I just had a cup, anyway."

"Right, right," he said distractedly. He moved toward the window, nervously wringing his hands.

I looked around the room. Dark wooden cabinets with tiny keyholes lined three of the walls. Draped over the furniture were heavy linens with shiny gold embroidery. Two large, imposing candlesticks dominated a table, and an enormous bookcase was groaning with old books, all stacked with neat precision.

Father O'Brien gestured toward an uncomfortable-looking wooden bench for me to sit on.

"It's busy in town today," I said as I sat down.

Father O'Brien didn't reply—he was fixed to the spot, staring out the window, almost in a trance.

"Father, it's busy in town today," I said more loudly this time, before following up with a cough.

He turned sharply toward me, his eyes staring straight into mine. "We have to talk."

"Okay," I said, nervously watching as he paced the room.

"I . . ." He stopped, took a breath, and walked on. "I've had a letter from my bishop." He said *bishop* slowly, with caution, assuming that the very word would instill as much fear in me as it obviously did in him. "He's very concerned—very concerned—about these Steps."

"Really? Why?" I couldn't understand why a bishop would be remotely bothered.

"Thou shalt not put false gods before me."

"Oh." No one had ever quoted a commandment to me before. "Well, it's not really, I mean, there's no god here. They're just—"

Father O'Brien wasn't listening to me. "The pagan belief in fairies is flawed on so many levels. We thought we'd got rid of all that nonsense. But now, all this hysteria has developed with these messages from beyond the grave." He'd worked himself up into a frenzy, and his face was red and angry. "You're meddling in things you do not understand."

"Look, Father, I—"

"It's going higher than the bishop, you know. Cardinal Lysaght in Dublin is holding a meeting with his superiors today. This could go all the way up. All the way."

"Oh, come on, the pope isn't going to be interested in a little village in the west of Ireland. He has bigger fish to fry."

Father O'Brien shook his head furiously. "No, no, no. Look at Knock, Medjugorje, Lourdes. What happened in those little villages had huge consequences for the church and the faith of millions of people everywhere."

I felt myself frown involuntarily. I hadn't heard of Knock, Medjugorje, or Lourdes since primary school. They'd been inconsequential towns in Ireland, Bosnia, and France that were catapulted to fame after the Virgin Mary was said to have appeared there. I was pretty sure she'd had her hands joined in prayer and was crying, presumably over the inhumanity of it all, and not due to sunscreen in the eye or a loose eyelash. Religious apparitions had always felt a little bit classist to me: they seemed to happen to poor people or orphan children with no shoes and no hairbrush.

Nobody commuting to their nine-to-five job in a sharp suit with a leather briefcase ever saw the Virgin Mary while downing a skinny cappuccino.

"But Father. You can't compare Knocknamee to those places. There's no miracle here."

"You tell that to the people outside. They're looking for one. But they're not looking to the church to give them one. They're looking to you."

I put my head in my hands. I felt off-center, as if the air had been sucked from my body. "I never meant for any of this."

"Maybe you didn't," Father O'Brien said with sudden kindness in his voice. "But the fact of the matter is, it's here now, and we need to work out how to deal with it." He sat back on his throne, then muttered to himself: "We have to take a stand; we have to take a position."

"I mean, Father, I'm as much in the dark about all of this as you are."

He sat bolt upright in his chair and arched his head toward me. "So you've had no—how do I put this—feelings? Unusual intuitions or sensations?" He narrowed his eyes. "Are you telling me you've had no dreams?"

"What?" I almost fell off my seat. "What are you talking about?" How could he know?

"Well, the Steps and the letter from the Red Hag do point to your having certain abilities—special abilities?"

"But Father, you just said they're a load of nonsense."

"I never said that."

"I don't understand. How can you think I could have powers? You? You're a Catholic priest."

"So you've had no visions? None?"

"None." I shook my head, knowing that lying to a priest would get me into an awful lot of trouble. But I couldn't tell him. How could I trust him?

"Well." He turned his mouth downward, lost in thought.

"Father, please." I softened my voice. "This isn't fair. How could you think"—I nearly said *know*—"that I have powers?"

There was a flicker in Father O'Brien's left eye, and I could tell he was having an internal battle, deciding whether or not to tell me something.

"Please, Father, if you know something, be fair: tell me."

He sighed heavily. "If I tell you something, you have to promise me it stays here, in this room. You have to promise not to talk to your journalist friends about it. You don't talk to anyone."

I was intrigued. I nodded, nervous about what he was going to say.

"The Steps, these Steps." He lifted his head and looked at me. "I've seen them before."

"But how? I'm the only one who . . ."

He raised his hand and I knew not to interrupt him again.

"Fifty years or so ago, I came here fresh out of the seminary, a young man full of ideas and enthusiasm for my vocation. The retiring priest at the time, Father O'Connell, had also served here for over fifty years. He was a good and pious man. We were here together for about a year while Father O'Connell introduced me to the parishioners. We'd say mass together and he gave me time to familiarize myself with the people, with this beautiful village here in Knocknamee. It was near the end of our year when he told me about the Steps, when he warned me just as he had been warned by his predecessor."

I couldn't believe what I was hearing. My Steps, the Steps, had been read before, had been seen before.

"Father O'Connell had inherited the parish from Father

Creane, who had served here since 1866. Father Creane was by all accounts a stern man—back then it's fair to say that priests ruled their parishioners from the pulpit with an iron fist. There was a lot of fire and brimstone and intolerance. We've moved on quite a bit since then, and we all try to be compassionate and more understanding. During Father Creane's first few years in the parish, there was a lot of trouble. It was twenty years after the famine, and the community was slowly rebuilding itself. The church was still working to regain its place in people's lives. During the famine people had turned their back on the church—they couldn't believe in a god who would hurt and starve them. Even I can see how people could question their faith during tough times, times harder than we could ever even imagine. People had turned to other forces for help—pagan forces. They'd asked the fairies for help. I suppose you've heard a lot about them since you've been here?"

I nodded, interested.

He backtracked. "I mean, they're superstitious nonsense, most of these pagan beliefs. Legend has it that this witch, your aunt, was given to the people by the fairies to ease their suffering. Look, I don't know whether or not she was a witch. I do know that records show she was denounced from the pulpit. That Father Creane called her a witch in a mass, told the parishioners to turn their backs on her, that she was never going to help them. I know she was supposed to have taken their money and gotten greedy and caused a lot more hardship in the village."

Even though I'd heard this before, I was eager to hear any fresh information and didn't want to disturb his flow of thought, so I was doing my best to keep my mouth shut.

"Eventually—and I don't know the ins and outs of it—people came back to the church. It was after your aunt was gone, after she'd left the village."

"Or died," I interjected.

"Maybe." He rubbed his nose, looking anxiously around him. "But I digress. You want to hear about the Steps. Before she died or disappeared, she came to Father Creane. Now, you can imagine that wasn't a great meeting: here's the woman who, in his eyes, turned all his parishioners away from the church and then treated them badly and filled their heads with pagan beliefs of fairies and witchcraft. And she was coming to him for help. I'd say he laughed at her from here to Carlow."

"She wanted help? From the priest?"

"The people of Knocknamee had had enough of her. They didn't believe her anymore, so they wouldn't listen to her. They saw her for what she was: that she was just interested in her own well-being and gain. But the thing was, she had a message she wanted to give to the people. She'd been asked to reawaken, as she put it, the fairies."

"And the message? It's the Steps?"

He nodded. "She asked Father Creane, who had the ears of the parishioners, for help. She asked him to tell the people the Steps." Father O'Brien rolled his eyes to heaven. "Can you imagine? The insanity of it. As if Father Creane was going to help her spread her pagan ways. It didn't make any sense!" He shifted uncomfortably in his seat, like he was sitting on a prickly cactus. "Well, Father Creane said no. She begged and pleaded with him, and she gave him the Steps, all seven of them, in the hope that he'd slip them into his sermon. Which, of course, he was never going to do, and he told her as much. But she kept at him, trying to wear him down. Eventually, so they say, she put a curse on the church, and on him."

"What kind of a curse?"

"His health deteriorated rapidly. He was a young man at the

time and he took to walking with a stick. His back was curved, and he was never without a cold or a flu. And the church itself, well, even to this day there are holes in the roof that we've patched and repatched and even reroofed and still the rain comes in. It's strange, is all. Father Creane had the fear of God in him, there's no doubt about it. After she'd cursed him and the church, she disappeared. You wouldn't sleep easy with that haunting you, I'll tell you. He had the Seven Steps, but he didn't know what to do with them. He couldn't destroy them—he was too scared. He knew about the fairies and their potential, but he couldn't be seen to be believing in them. Still, he knew."

"So, Father Creane, he believed in fairies?"

"Yes, I think he believed there were some other forces at work. He really was scared. Priests . . . we're asked to believe in a lot of things—the devil and demons. So for some of us a belief in fairies—it's not such a leap." Father O'Brien looked sad. "He probably should have given the Steps over to the bishop, but I think he was frightened. So he locked them away. Here. Hoping they'd never reappear again. He told the next priest about it, who then told me."

I was looking around the room to see where they might be hidden. "You didn't destroy them?"

"No, I suppose I just forgot about them. I never thought it would be an issue. I never thought they'd arise again, because they weren't real until you . . ." He looked at me for a long time. "You're the key to the completion of these Steps. Because you can get people to believe in them. Without you, they don't work. I didn't know that until now."

"I don't understand. What do you want me to do about it?"

"Stop it. Stop it now. Tell everyone that it was a hoax, a cry for help, that you made them up yourself, that there was no witch and there are no fairies." Here was a man hanging from the edge of a cliff by his splintered fingernails. "Stop it."

"No." I was startled by my own response. I'd never spoken to a priest like that before. I'd never even considered speaking to a priest like that. Something had come over me. I don't know if it was the brazen schoolchild in me, or the shock of being told what to do by a man who didn't know anything about me, but I wasn't having any of it. These were my Steps. This would be my decision.

"Please."

"No. It's nearly over. There's only one more Step."

"Please." His hands grabbed the sides of his chair. "I'm begging you."

"No."

His face was flaming with anger. "But look what you've done! Look what you've created! A false god, a false religion!"

"I haven't created anything. This has evolved. People *like* this, they're happy with it." And I was happy with it. Since I'd remembered my fairy, Paudi O'Shea, I'd felt a warm and fuzzy sense of happiness and completion. What harm could possibly come from that wonderful joy? And surely if I could, I should share it.

"I'm begging you."

"I don't understand. You've seen these Steps. They're harmless. This will all blow over."

"Please."

Now I was suspicious. "Is there something else?"

His shoulders stiffened.

"It's the final Step. There's something about the final Step, isn't there? You've read it. You've seen it. Show it to me. Where is it?" I stood up and started frantically looking around the room. "Where is it?"

He shook his head. "Please stop this."

"Where is it?"

"Will you stop if I show it to you?"

"No. How can I stop this? Why would I stop this?"

He stood up, looking weak. "The final Step is not harmless. It's an awakening. It changes everything." He hung his head and shivered. "Follow me."

Stooped, he turned his back and walked toward a heavy wooden door. Grasping the iron handle, he heaved it open. He looked back at me nervously. I nodded and walked behind him. We entered the church, and I watched as he shuffled up the marble steps of the altar, silently blessing himself. I stood back, not sure whether to follow him. He waved his arm for me to proceed, and my thirteen years of Catholic schooling caused me to genuflect and bless myself before stepping up. Father O'Brien dropped awkwardly to his knees behind the altar and slid back a large green mat. He patted the stone underneath. "It's here. It's here," he whispered, under his breath. There was a wobble and the stone shifted gently. Father O'Brien slid his fingers around it.

I bent forward instinctively as he gritted his teeth and his face turned puce with the strain of pulling the stone back. "Can I help?"

But just as I spoke the stone came free. Father O'Brien flew backward, falling clumsily. I moved forward and stared into the black dusty hole. I caught a glimpse of a tin box.

"Stand back!" Father O'Brien jumped to his feet. "This is for me."

Surprised by the aggression in his voice, I edged away, keeping an eye on the box. Father O'Brien dipped in and pulled it out before rubbing it anxiously. "This, em . . ." His face creased with worry, and he placed a heavy hand on top of the altar to steady himself. "These are the Steps."

He flipped the box open toward his chest, and I noticed his

hand tremble as he pulled out pages of clear waxy paper. He studied one, and then handed it to me. It rustled between us as if caught by a breeze. It was the first Step. The same inky spidery script weaved its way across the page.

"It's the Step. It's the same handwriting."

He sighed. "You believe me?"

"I'm looking at it. It's true."

"Well, look, look." Father O'Brien was animated now. He moved toward me lightly; his breathing had quickened. "They're all here, all of them."

He started to push other pages into my hands, all bearing Kate McDaid's handwriting. They were the same Steps I'd received from Seamus MacMurphy. Father O'Brien was smiling. His eyes looked bright. "You see? They're here."

I nodded, unsure why his mood had changed and why he seemed so excited now.

"So, promise me you won't publish the seventh one. You won't even read it. You'll end this now." His face was inches from mine. He was clutching a piece of paper that must have been the seventh Step.

"No. This ends when the seventh Step is released." I looked at the page in his hand.

"No. You don't understand. This will bring you no peace. This is just the beginning for all of us. If you publish this," he said, looking straight at me, his face brimming with anger, "if you tell them what this says, then this, all of this . . ." He threw his arms wide open, embracing the church. "All of this is over."

"I don't . . . Let me read it."

He shook his head. "If you read this, if you publish this, it ends."

"Exactly. It ends. I'm publishing this final Step and then that's it. Game over."

"Trust me." He stumbled back a step. "I beg you to do the right thing. This is bigger than you."

"What? How? You have to tell me."

He shook his head again.

"I get the final Step tomorrow. I'll know what it says then," I said.

He winced.

I started to walk out of the church. "I'm not stopping this," I shouted over my shoulder.

"She didn't disappear . . ."

I spun around and stared, open-mouthed, at Father O'Brien.

"She didn't just disappear." Ashen-faced, the priest was resting his hands on the corner of the altar.

I walked back toward him to hear what he was saying.

"They burned her out. Burned her out of house and home and . . ." He swallowed dryly. "Burned her with it."

"The old ruin?"

"They set fire to it one night—it was Halloween. They wanted to be rid of her. It was a witch hunt."

I nodded. I knew this was true. It explained what had happened to me when I was at the ruin. I shivered, remembering how I'd felt the heat and smoke of the fire. There was no doubt that memories of the Red Hag's terrible death lingered there. They'd burned her the day after she'd written her will. She must have predicted it. She must have seen her own death.

"They succeeded. She burned to death up there." He shook his head.

"Who were they?"

He lifted his head. His face was like stone. "The villagers, led by Father Creane."

A religious man led a witch hunt? I was shocked. "That's

barbaric! He was a priest." I didn't know whether that was a state-ment or a question.

"Priests are human. Humans are scared of the unknown and can react in frenzy, rage, or fear." Father O'Brien sighed heavily. "Kate, what you're dabbling in is the occult, the other world. It brings an evil with it. You may think there's no harm in this, but, trust me, this final Step could be an awakening to the other world. Do not upset the natural order of God's earth. Put an end to this now. Never publish that final Step."

"Okay. Thanks, I think, Father," I answered dry-mouthed. I felt so confused. If Father O'Brien was telling the truth, if this seventh Step was going to "end it all," what did that mean? What could that mean? End the church? Or worse? What could be worse? And why would he say not to upset the natural order? Weren't the fairies part of the natural order?

Maybe Father O'Brien wasn't telling the truth. Maybe he was just trying to frighten me. Maybe it was about the Catholic Church. Maybe he was just scared because he'd kept the Steps from the bishop. Maybe he was worried he'd be defrocked and he'd lose his extensive wardrobe of gold trimmings and floor-dusting capes. I wouldn't know until I read the final Step. I couldn't even think about the "what ifs" until I read it.

I left the church feeling more confused than I'd ever felt in my life.

35

Fiona and Lily had gone to mass. I hadn't wanted to go, and I was glad I hadn't when they told me the blow-by-blow of what had happened. Father O'Brien had read a letter from the bishop to the parishioners. The bishop called the Steps an unnecessary evil, a cult of unchristian values, a nonsensical school of thought that had been developed from pagan beliefs and which was emphatically not condoned by the Catholic Church. The bishop said that these Steps, and any supporters of these Steps, were not Christian.

That stung. No matter what your beliefs were, Christianity was a part of being Irish—it was in our makeup.

Father O'Brien had apparently looked pale and hung on to the sides of the pulpit for support, swaying weakly under the burden of the message. He paused for a long time at one point, and the girls thought he might have been having second thoughts about whether or not to proceed, but, really, they knew he didn't have a choice. His orders came from the bishop and he had to follow them. So he denounced me. He said I was creating a religion and erecting a false god. He gritted his teeth and pointed at his parishioners, repeating the commandment that he'd recited to me earlier that day: "Thou shalt not put false gods before me."

He spoke of the corruption, greed, and sudden drive for money he saw in Knocknamee. He asked everyone to stop: to stop promoting these Steps; to stop running tours to the ruin; to stop selling water at the well; to stop talking about widening the main street or extending the circus into the back field; to stop talking about witches and fairies; and to stop listening to Kate McDaid.

The church pews had creaked noisily as people shifted uncomfortably.

And then, Lily said, the craziest thing happened as the sermon was interrupted. I suspected that no one had ever interrupted a sermon during the fifty years Father O'Brien had been in Knocknamee, so when Annie from O'Donahue's rose to her feet and coughed for attention, it appeared that he just thought she was ill. She wasn't. When she had his attention and everyone else's, she spoke loud and clear. "Father, I am a religious person— you know I am. We all are. But we're not putting any false gods before anyone. None of us here are spooning well water into us, or bathing in the nude at An Trá Bhán. Not one villager is going to see the psychics from the circus. That's what the tourists are doing. And let them at it, I say."

There was a rumbling of approval. "Let us make some money out of this. God knows, times can be hard here, and money will make all our lives a lot easier. Don't tell us to stop. I never thought I'd say it, but Johnny Logan is right. We should be making hay while the sun shines. We're paying no heed to the fairies, or to any false gods. We're making a bit of money."

"Money is also a false god, Annie," Father O'Brien replied, apparently looking like he was still in shock from being interrupted.

"That's rich coming from you, Father, a man who works for the richest organization in the world," Annie spat back. And with that, she had picked up her handbag, slung it over her shoulder, muscled her way out of the pew, and left the church. Others followed, silently padding after her. Some nodded to the pulpit as they passed, saying "Sorry, Father. I need the money." Others made no excuses, barging out and slamming the door after them.

A skeleton congregation remained, nervously eyeing one another as they waited for Father O'Brien to take the lead and tell them what to do. He didn't. He remained fixed to the spot, gripping the pulpit and breathing heavily, looking stunned that this could have happened to him.

Johnny Logan, who was sitting in the front pew, beside the girls, got up from his seat and walked to the altar. He held out his arm and gripped Father O'Brien firmly across the shoulder, whispering into his ear quietly. Then he led the priest slowly toward the vestry.

Father O'Brien followed Johnny, muttering to himself. "It can't happen. She can't do it. She can't."

Denounced. I'd been denounced. It felt so final, so severe. It wasn't that I was particularly religious, but I've always believed that, at its heart, the church had compassion and understanding. But now it had shown none of that, and I was angry. I didn't know what the seventh Step was, but it was undoubtedly something Father O'Brien believed would shake the foundations of the church, and he was going to do everything in his power to stop it and me.

Of course, in reality, all he'd done was give the Steps more publicity. He'd added me to a grand list of fornicators and rebels that included Sinéad O'Connor and Henry VIII. But without the lofty powers to behead anyone, it didn't feel like much fun. And why would I agree to stop the Steps when he wouldn't share the final one with me? I needed to see it to decide. I admit I was feeling scared. Father O'Brien had read it and had denounced me. In his eyes, it was the most extreme thing he could possibly do to stop the seventh Step being published. What did it say? What could possibly drive a man to take such an extreme action? I couldn't imagine.

I was starting to feel sick with worry. I'd lost my appetite, my nerves were fraught, and I was constantly distracted.

Part of me was really annoyed that this had been my journey, that the fairies couldn't have picked someone else, that it was me who had to have her life fall apart. I was angry at them. I didn't want this path, and maybe that's why they wouldn't speak to me.

I felt removed from my friends. It was great having their support in Knocknamee, but I knew they couldn't understand what I was going through. *I* didn't understand. I wasn't like them anymore. I wasn't the person I had been.

Nevertheless, in spite of all the madness, I was feeling stronger. There was something in me I hadn't felt before, a fire in my belly. Maura caught the brunt of the *new* me when she cornered me at the B and B. I'd thought I was rid of her as I hadn't seen or heard from her in a while. She had been deep in her investigation, or so she told me.

"We'd like you to attend a gathering tonight." Maura tried her best to smile calmly, but it was clear she was excited about something.

I was immediately suspicious. "We?" I pushed for more information.

"I know you're curious about us. Why not see firsthand what we do?" She looked nervous, and bubbles of perspiration appeared on her top lip.

"Are they here? Your group? In Knocknamee?"

She nodded.

"The Hellfire Club?" Why not ask her straight out? What was she going to do?

She threw me a condescending smile. "That title was abandoned a long time ago. But some of us are descendants of the original group, yes."

"And what do you want? What are you trying to achieve?"

She smoothed her hair, which I was now convinced was a wig. "The same as everyone: love and happiness forever."

Forever? "For eternity?"

"You're smarter than you look, Kate. We could use you. It's in your interest to come along tonight."

Tonight. The night before I got hold of the final Step. I shook my head. "I don't know what your intentions are, but they're not pure. I will not attend this gathering or any other gathering that you put on." I felt a rage bubbling up inside me. I would not be a pawn in whatever game they were playing.

"Are you sure?" She narrowed her eyes, all pretense of niceness disappearing. "You can come willingly or by force."

Finally she was showing her true colors. Something told me her connection with gangsters and murderers was not in the recent past. "Don't threaten me, Maura. Have you forgotten who I have on my side?"

She smiled weakly. "Don't misinterpret me, Kate. Of course the fairies are on your side. But there are people, other people who will insist you attend tonight."

Other people. I laughed to myself. "I'm not going, Maura. You can carry out your satanic worship or whatever it is you're up to alone."

I stormed off, back upstairs to my room.

That afternoon there was a light tapping on my door.

"Come in!" I shouted, assuming it was Martin.

I didn't expect him.

He stood in the doorway breathing heavily, his hands behind his back. He seemed nervous and agitated.

I froze.

My heart started pounding through my chest. What was he doing here?

He stepped forward and, with a look of determination, swung his arms out from behind his back and produced a massive bunch of flowers, blue and yellow and green, and thrust them toward me. "They're from the farm."

I nodded, shocked. They were beautiful.

"I . . ." Hugh was breathing very fast, as he closed the space between us. There was no time, there were no thoughts. There was only now, this moment. He leaned toward me, holding my face in his gaze, and gently moved his mouth toward mine.

We found each other and got lost in a kiss. His arms wrapped around me and held me with a ferocious intensity. I was locked in. It was an embrace of apologies and certainties.

Our lips parted and he pressed his forehead on mine, our eyelashes fluttering against each other. He moved his hands to my face and kissed me again. Softer, sweeter. I fell deeper and deeper into him.

He pulled back and whispered my name softly.

"I had a full speech worked out." He locked his arms tighter around me, his lips on my ear. "But when I saw you, I lost the words." His cheek was pressed against mine.

I nuzzled into the nape of his neck. "What were you going to say?"

"To tell you that you're the loveliest thing I've ever set eyes on."

I smiled into him.

"I say the wrong things all the time. I don't mean to." Delicately he brushed his lips over mine. "I'm a fool around you."

I inched slightly backward. "That day in the office, when

Marjorie pulled me into the meeting room. You said I was too 'natural-looking' for your site . . ."

He pulled back and looked straight into me. "Other women wear tons of crap to pretend to be someone they're not. You are just who you are. You don't hide behind anything."

"But still not the look for your site?"

"Hair-thinning products and condoms? Are you joking me? We're not good enough for you, Kate."

And he started to kiss my face, his hands racing through my hair. My whole being was straining, yearning to be lost in him.

I pulled back again. "The blonde? Who's the blonde?"

"A friend of Aine's. They've been trying to set me up with her for a long time. We went out a few times. I wanted to make sure she was out of the picture before I came here. That's why I left the other day. I needed to talk to her. She's no one, Kate. She's not you."

Another deep kiss.

Again, I pulled back.

"Aren't you going to let me kiss you?" He laughed, his nose pressed on mine.

"One more question. What if I'm a witch?"

"We'll deal with it. You are who you are."

I squeezed him tight. Finally. Finally. He was here.

36

There's a moment after sex that I like best. When you are spent. After you have yelped and laughed, and moaned and heavy-breathed all over each other. After every inch, crevice, and nook of your body has been kissed and caressed lovingly. After you've tickled and nuzzled and run your fingers over the soft skin of your lover. After you've trailed the freckles and moles on his back with the tips of your nails, and smoothed the tops of his thighs with the palms of your hands. After you take that last breath, that deep, salty, sweat-infused breath into his chest, and collapse wholly beside him, when your exhausted body crumples down beside his. When you can just about muster up the energy to lace your fingers together, to let the electric sensation linger between you and sigh a contented, peaceful, happy sigh. That. That's my favorite moment.

That evening I snuck out via the back garden wall of the B and B, hopped on Colm's bike for a few miles, parked up, and went for a stroll down a country road. It felt wonderful to be out in the air. I was grinning and shivering in happiness. I was in a love haze. I felt full up. My emotions were bubbling over but I was uncharacteristically mute. All I could do was smile full-toothed, eyes-closed, deep-breath smiles. I closed my eyes and breathed in the memory of that moment with Hugh that afternoon—the completion of it, the wholeness.

Typically, when one part of my life starts to work out, another part usually goes horribly wrong. So one minute I was daydreaming about the touch of Hugh's skin while I vaguely wondered why a car was driving so close to me, and the next I woke up in the middle of the night, tied to a tree in a dark field.

It was inexplicable, at first. My head felt heavy, my legs damp. I moved my hands to balance myself and found them tied behind me. My shoulders ached from the restraint. It was dark, cold. I was outside. The wind howled around me, the leaves on the tree thrashing back and forth. The air smelled of damp grass. I licked my lips. My mouth was parched and I craved a glass of water. Where was I? What was going on? My head pounded and my heart was racing. Suddenly I was rigid with fear. I went to shout out but couldn't make a noise. *Help*, I thought. *Help*.

My eyes became accustomed to the dark. I scanned the shades of black, trying to distinguish any shapes or shadows. Everything felt alive and moving. I pulled on my arms again, trying to wriggle free, but I was tightly secured.

Far away, but it was so difficult to judge distances, I heard a rumble—it sounded like the wind at first. Whistling low. But it became louder and moved closer. I saw a low ember bobbing— not just one, many. Five, ten, fifteen, more and more. Moving in a line like stars in the night. The whistling became a hum, which in turn became music. It was a chant; people were chanting. The stars were candles flickering, and they were coming closer. Now I could see them in the candlelight, people dressed in red robes with peaked hoods. How many? Thirty? It was hard to tell. They walked in perfect single file until they'd formed a perfect circle. It was then that I knew where I was: Billy the pig farmer's field. I was looking at the fairy fort, and the Hellfire Club were about to perform one of their rituals.

The chanting grew louder and louder, a rhythmic, trance-inducing theme. Then it stopped and there was silence. That's when I became really scared.

A man's voice bellowed through the darkness. He spoke in Irish, and I couldn't understand him. Then a woman's voice broke into a haunting song, and the lyrics caught on the wind and rode through the empty fields and wastelands of Ireland. The melody was heartbreaking. Her voice channeled death and misery, and mothers' tears and broken hearts.

I was mesmerized. The chants returned and the robes started to sway from side to side. The man spoke again. Out of the shadow of darkness a large man appeared beside me. Suddenly I found my voice and I screamed, louder and harder than I'd ever screamed before in my life. As I screamed, I wriggled and writhed like a wild animal, trying desperately to get away from the man. "Help!" I cried. "Help!" I prayed to God that my screams would carry and someone would hear me cry. But the chanting just grew louder.

The man crouched down near me. He was large, dressed in a red robe, and it was difficult to make out his face. "Kate, I don't want to hurt you. That's not what this is about. Calm down." I didn't recognize his voice, which was deep.

I started to cry. "What is this? Who are you? What are you doing with me?"

He started to untie my hands, but kept a firm grip on my shoulder. I could feel the bruises from his handprint appearing. I was so paralyzed with fear I wouldn't have been capable of escaping anyway. He pulled me to my feet and dragged me toward the fairy fort. With a great deal of force, he tripped and pushed me past some of the robes and threw me into the center.

Now I could see that they were all standing outside the fairy fort and I was the only one inside. I was trembling, but then I realized where I was. They couldn't know what I knew, that I was safe in the fairy fort, that the fairies protected me. Nothing could happen to me there.

Somehow, I started to regulate my breathing and take in my surroundings. I scanned the circle. All cloaked in robes, hoods heavy over their faces, the figures chanting around the fairy fort were impossible to identify. Each one held a candle, prayer-like, in their hands. They were swaying from side to side, and their chanting was getting louder and faster. They were working themselves up into some kind of frenzy.

Reaching fever pitch, they started to stamp their feet. I stared at them wondering what was going to happen. The man spoke again, shouting into the circle, in English this time. "Open the passageway—do it for the girl."

The fairy fort? The passageway? Where did they want to go?

"You have one of our members. Let him show us the way."

The chanting was getting so hysterical, the circle almost levitated.

At last I made out what they were saying. "Brick! Brick! Brick! Brick!"

They believed the fairies had taken Brick, the gangster? But why would they take him?

I tried to concentrate really hard. What could I remember about Brick? He'd been last seen at Liam McCarthy's wake. What had Maura said about wakes? That the fairies attended them. Had they struck up a deal somehow? Had Brick accompanied the fairies to their homeland? To Tír na nÓg? Perhaps that's what the Hellfire Club believed.

Now the chanters were dancing. Their robes began to slip and I saw glimpses of white hair, bald heads, wrinkled skin, frail bodies. These people were all old. Really old. They wanted a passageway to Tír na nÓg, the land of eternal youth. And they were trying to please the fairies by offering me as a gift. But they didn't know that the fairies already had me where they wanted me.

"STOP!" I screamed at them. They weaved past each other like bees on a honeycomb. "The fairies won't take you to Tír na nÓg. Brick is probably dead, or in the south of Spain."

I ran around the inner edge of the circle. The members of the Hellfire Club appeared almost drugged, their eyes glassy as if they were on a hallucinogenic trip.

Maura, I thought. *Which one is Maura?*

Then I found her. Maura's wig had come off, and thin, white wispy hair peeped from under her hood. She had no gloves on and her hands were gnarly and covered in liver spots. She was ancient.

I grabbed her by the shoulders and shook her to wake her. "Maura! This is madness. The ground isn't going to open up. Tír na nÓg isn't going to appear!"

"Kate!" Maura, suddenly lucid, focused her eyes on me. "Isn't it wonderful? We're going to live forever, Kate! Forever!"

"You're crazy, Maura. You're all crazy."

I didn't need the fairy fort to protect me. I could outrun these old people. In fact, I could out*walk* them. I didn't know how they'd managed to get my there, but they wouldn't be able to stop my leaving. I broke through the circle just as some of the men were starting to disrobe. They'd worked themselves up into such a fever, no one even noticed.

I glanced back over my shoulder. The Hellfire Club members were now dancing naked, their frail, white bodies luminescent in the darkness. They hopped and skipped around the fairy ring, emulating children in that carefree land of youth they so desperately wanted to be part of.

I ran, faster and faster, and as I ran, the sound of their chanting became softer and softer, until it was not much more than a hum. And then silence.

37

As soon as I was back safe and warm at Martin's, drinking tea with a shot of whiskey in it as prescribed by Fiona with chocolate HobNobs from Lily, I rang Hugh. He came as fast as he could. He stormed in, held me close, and then threatened to kill every member of the Hellfire Club. He tried to convince me to tell the police, but I just shook my head. What was the point? They *were* the police, the government, the media. What could the local guards do against them? We were best off leaving them alone, and, anyway, I felt I was free of them. They were people near the end of their days looking for another option. However they'd planned to use me to coerce the fairies to take them to Tír na nÓg, it hadn't worked.

I had a sleepless night, full of horrible visions of the Hellfire Club and the goings-on at the fairy fort. Now, lying exhausted on my bed, I could hear more chanting, this time outside my window. "Kaayyyyy-ate! Kaayyyyy-ate." Today was the day. Outside, the chants had started at daybreak. They were low and rhythmic, and as steady as a drumbeat. The crowd were bobbing their heads in unison. Like a heartbeat. The bright lights of TV crews were blinding, and the busy chatter of reporters deafening. Helicopters scattered around the sky like the throw of a die, zooming and hovering, the noise of their engines threatening and intimidating. Mam and Dad were due in at one that morning.

Hugh had left early, to feed the animals. I knew the girls were out for an early-morning walk, so I asked them to swing by and pick up Colm's bike. It was actually more of a morning stalk than a walk. Fi was on the Anorak hunt. I made my way downstairs, only to discover that Martin had shut the shop—well, he'd actually barricaded the door.

"Just in case," he said when he saw my look of surprise.

Hanging off the edge of a kitchen chair while Mavis made him breakfast was the spindly frame of Seamus MacMurphy. He stood tall and extended his arm for a handshake when I appeared. "I hope you don't mind my delivering this in person. I was passing through en route to Galway, and thought I'd pop in and see what all the fuss was about. You've really put this place on the map."

I shook his hand and sat on the far side of the table. Seamus MacMurphy was excited. "I mean really, it's on every TV station. RTÉ news have live coverage running all day. It's like a royal wedding." His eyes were racing, and his voice was high-pitched and shaky. "It's just amazing, you know. In a little tiny way I'm part of this whole thing. Our little law firm is part of all this attention. Amazing."

Mavis plonked a gigantic plate of fried food in front of him. She looked at me, nonplussed by all the excitement. "Will you have tea?"

"I'm grand, thanks."

"Ah, you will, yeah," she said, ignoring me and moving toward the teapot.

"So, em . . . what happens now?"

"Well, I have the final Step here if you want it?" Seamus had lost the excited tone in his voice—he was back to business. He rummaged in his pocket and produced a sealed envelope that he slid across the table to me. "I tell you, I was nervous coming through the crowds there, carrying something like this. I should have got myself a bodyguard."

"Thanks." I picked up the envelope and, staring at the wax seal, ran my fingers over its sharp edges. I couldn't tear my eyes from the envelope. This was it.

Father O'Brien's words echoed through my mind: "This brings an evil." I should have felt relieved, that this *was* the end. But what if it was different? What if it did start something? For everyone, not just for me? What if it was an awakening? Was I ready for this? Were *we* ready for this?

Father O'Brien was the only person who had read the seventh Step. Could I believe anything he had to say? I gripped the envelope tighter, unaware of the chatter around me. Shivering slightly, I hugged my arms around me to warm up.

"And the estate. As soon as this is published, you'll get the estate."

"I wonder what it is?" Mavis piped up before quickly excusing herself. "Sorry, love, it's not any of my business. It's your business."

"I have the box in the car."

"The box? The estate is a box?"

"Well, I don't know what's in the box. It's been sealed for a hundred and thirty years. You'll be the first to open it."

I'd never thought the estate would turn up in a box. It felt like an anticlimax: all this for a box. Seven weeks earlier, the lure of an estate had enticed me. An "estate" had sounded awfully grand—it sounded like it could be like a lottery win. It definitely had sounded like money. It had conjured up images of tweed jackets, springer spaniels at the heel, and hunts on horseback that ended with quaffing champagne. It had implied adventure, but now whatever was in that box was inconsequential compared to the journey that had changed everything for me. There were fairies in my life, spells in my head, and a gorgeous man in my bed. The contents of the box were irrelevant.

"So will you just be posting it online as you've done before?" Seamus asked, interrupting my train of thought.

"Yeah, I will, yeah. Fiona brought my laptop with her, I'm all set."

Seamus nodded carefully. "So you won't go out there?"

"No. I'm going to stick to what I've been doing. I just have to publish it, right? I don't need to promote it."

"Absolutely. Whatever you choose."

Did I need to do something different? I didn't want to.

"So, what does it say?" Seamus licked his lips, hungry for the envelope and its contents, and not the fry going cold in front of him.

"She doesn't have to tell you anything," Mavis spat out protectively. She heaved her heavy frame into a chair and daintily started to munch on some shortbread biscuits.

I felt my breathing quicken and pushed myself away from the table. My throat felt dry. "I might just go up to my room and, you know, take a minute." I clutched the envelope and started toward the door.

"Sure, off you go, not a bother," Mavis shouted after me, oblivious to the fact that I was shaking violently.

Upstairs, the dull beat of the chants outside echoed around my room. I crawled into bed and pulled the duvet over my head, hoping that the heat would stop my body trembling. But it was fear, not cold, that I was shaking from. What if? What if? What if? Exhausted, I started to cry. This envelope was the end or the very beginning.

Just open it, I thought. *Open it*. But I couldn't. Instead, I stared at it. It wasn't just what Father O'Brien had said. All the people outside, they believed; Father O'Brien, he believed; Maura and the Hellfire Club believed. And I believed. I believed in fairies.

I took a deep breath. *Stay strong*, I thought. With my heart in my mouth I broke the wax seal on the back of the envelope and lifted out the wafer-thin paper. It was covered in the same spidery, inky scrawl as the previous Steps.

My hand was shaking so badly the words jumped. I placed the paper on the bed. *Steady now*, I thought. Then I read it. And I read it again. And once more.

Stillness swamped me. Dark shadows flickered around the edge of my vision. I was aware only of my heart pounding in my chest. "Oh dear God."

I felt as if my very self was being pulled out of me. My shoulders collapsed and I sank backward, washed over by a weakness. Breathe, I had to breathe, to concentrate on breathing.

It was different this time. It was all different. Father O'Brien had been right.

What had I done? I'd been tricked, tricked by the past, tricked by Grand-aunt Kate and tricked by the fairies. I'd accepted them too easily. I'd accepted their promise of innocence, never questioning that there might have been a darker force or real evil at work.

This was all my fault. I'd reintroduced them to the living world. Enraptured by their playfulness, I'd been lost in the idea of them, and never heeded the warnings. They'd disappeared generations ago because they were meant to disappear. That was their journey. They shouldn't have been here now. This was not their time.

The final Step was their battle cry. The fairies were ready to emerge from the shadows and release an unholy yell, and it would start a fairy war between the believers, led by the fairies, and the nonbelievers. This was payback for the nonbelievers not respecting nature: the fairies would send them under the earth. And then the fairies would reclaim the natural world and reign supreme. Hellfires and dark forces fueled their crusade. As soon as I published the Step, it would start.

I had been their pawn.

Father O'Brien had been right. The final Step would end all this; humanity as we knew it. I couldn't let that happen. It had to end now. I had to stop it. But how?

I rolled into a tight ball and squeezed my eyes shut. What was I to do? *What am I to do? What am I to do?*

I couldn't release it. I couldn't put that evil into the world. The chants outside drummed heavily inside me. All those people out there wanted to know what the final Step was. They'd traveled from all over and turned their lives inside out in the hope of glimpsing a fairy. They were fanatical: if I didn't release the Step, they'd never release me. I'd be followed and persecuted for the rest of my life. They wanted an answer and I had it, but I couldn't give it to them.

I couldn't publish the Step. But I couldn't *not* publish it, either. Maura and her cronies had tried to abduct me. What could a crowd of fanatics do? They could turn on me, become an angry mob. Who knew how far they'd go for the fairies? At that moment, I felt a genuine fear for my life. Anything could happen.

Could I tell them there was no final Step? Would they believe me? No, that would never work. They were too invested. They'd spent their lives looking for it. But there had to be a solution. Every problem had an answer—I just needed to figure it out. *Start at the beginning*, I thought, *and follow this through.*

And so I pulled out the original letter, and the six previous Steps, and I reread them, and then I studied them, I pored over them, every nuance, every rhyme, the syntax. And I wondered what I could do. How could I cheat the fairies? How could I go up against them? I needed to play them at their own game. I needed a trick.

Nobody knew what the final Step was, except for Father O'Brien and me. Not even Seamus MacMurphy knew. What if I forged it and made something up? What if I made it look and sound like the other Steps? Would that satisfy the believers? Would they fall for it? And how would I know that I'd succeeded in fooling everyone if I just posted it online?

And what would the fairies do to me when they realized I hadn't completed their task? What hideous fate would lie in store for me? What would their plan for revenge be?

I went to the laptop and stared at Google. I had an idea. I didn't know if it would work, but it was all I had. I typed in "W. B. Yeats" and waited for his poetry and musings to appear. The language he used was in keeping with the fairies'. And then I set to work rewriting the final Step. It would be my version, with a little help from Mr. Yeats. It was my biggest challenge as a copywriter to date.

Hours later, I emerged bleary-eyed and asked Mavis to get Johnny Logan on the phone. The only way I'd know if my fake

Step had worked was to see a reaction. I needed to see their faces—I needed a crowd. I'd deliver this one personally.

Johnny Logan would help me gather the masses, and I'd look them in the eye and, hopefully, finish it all. And no one would ever know the truth. No one would ever know how close we'd come.

38

I couldn't see when I stepped outside the door four hours later.
The lightning bolt of flashlights burned straight into my eyes. I
stumbled backward and felt Hugh's hand on my shoulder, firm
and warm.

I was petrified. I had made my decision—I felt that this was
my only option, to come face-to-face with these people and lie to
them, but what if they didn't buy it? I'd never been a good liar.
I'd never been a good actress. They might see right through me.
And what then? Exposed and vulnerable, there was only one of
me and thousands of them. Would they believe me? Could I end
this? Would the fairies let me? I was eaten up with nerves. I shoved
my shaking hand into the pocket of my jeans, where the fake Step
was folded up neatly. I clutched it: this had to work. With a deep
breath I muscled forward. The crowd heaved toward me. "Kayyyy-
ate! Kayyyy-ate," faster, louder, panicked. Like a brick wall they
pushed through firmly, swiftly moving into me. Suffocating me.
I ducked my head and attempted to torpedo through, catching
zips and colored anoraks in my peripheral view. I tried to bulldoze
onward, but was getting nowhere. I was penned in and pushed
backward by a sea of anoraks. "Kayyyy-ate, Kayyyyy-ate."

My heart knocked heavily in my chest. Hugh's arm slipped

down around me, holding tight. We couldn't move in either direction. I felt heat rise through my cheeks, and my lungs tighten. We were stuck and the walls were falling in.

"Lads, lads!" A thick Cavan accent shot through the crowd. "LADS!" it shouted with more force. "She needs our help! This way." Elbows, fists, and bums jutted awkwardly in every direction. And then suddenly there was space and I could breathe. I creaked my back up straight and stood tall to see what had just happened. Circling me like a swarm of bees protecting their queen were the crotch grabbers.

"Garda Fitzgerald!" I shouted in shock. "What are you doing?"

"Making sure you get wherever you need to get to. Isn't that right, lads?" There were five of them. They were all out of uniform, but I knew they were guards from their tight haircuts, suspicious glares, and practiced walks of men on the beat—confident and slow. They circled me as an invisible shield, and no one dared pass through.

"Thank you, thank you!" I shouted to them all, anxious to be heard over the din of the chants.

"Well, you helped us . . . well, some of us." And the circle turned to a rather overweight, embarrassed man whose left hand was hovering over his crotch, scratching awkwardly, while his right hand beat back the crowd.

"Right, right. Sometimes I get the spells right and sometimes I don't. Sorry it didn't work for you," I said, equally embarrassed.

"Maybe next time," the guard said, still scratching. "Now come on, lads, let's go."

They cleared a path for me and I began to walk. Hands were hungrily clawing through the circle trying to touch me. Faces, eyes, pleading, begging for me, crying, shaking, whimpering, "Help me, Kate! Tell me what to do!"

Hysterical screams. "She looked at me! Ahhh, ahhh, she looked at me!"

I fixed my eyes firmly ahead, over heads and faces. I would not look at anyone. I couldn't let them see into my eyes. I couldn't crumble. I had to stay strong on the outside at least. I needed to try my best to end all of this. I would not let the fairies win. I would not be the one to start a fairy war.

Johnny Logan's plywood stage was straining at the center, like a stretched toffee bar, under the weight of all the activity. Green, white, and gold streamers and balloons hung tightly in the breeze. A row of white plastic garden chairs lined the rear of the stage. I saw Mam and Dad on them, both looking orange, and Johnny, who was wearing his mayoral robes and chain for the occasion.

Red Horizon were onstage. Jim was clinging to the microphone and looking pained as he tried to overcome the din of the chants to sing out "The Seven Steps," their number one hit song.

A roar from the crowd announced my arrival. My shield opened up and created a passageway at the foot of the rickety plywood steps up to the stage.

I turned back to Garda Fitzgerald. "Thank you."

He nodded firmly. "We'll wait here for you." And with military precision, my bodyguards formed an orderly row.

I grabbed hold of the railing, feeling the wood splinter in my hands.

Hugh released himself from me. "Do you want me to go with you?" he whispered in my ear.

I shook my head. I needed to do this on my own. I couldn't have Hugh trying to defend me, if the crowd turned. I needed to face them alone. Hugh had no idea what I was about to do. No one did. This was my decision and had to be my responsibility.

"I'm okay, I'm okay," I repeated to myself as I slowly walked up the steps. I felt like I was approaching the gallows. My legs were shaking so violently I had to stop to briefly lock my knees to steady myself.

This has to work, I thought, *this has to work*. There was an excited roar in the crowd, which bounced through it like a Mexican wave. The sense of anticipation was giddy—there was a high. A feeling they were about to witness a moment of greatness. They shuffled from foot to foot, anxiously inching closer to me, a powerful wall of people excitedly repeating my name. Thousands of eyes followed me, swallowed me up. *What if this doesn't work? What if they don't believe me?*

"Kate, Kate! This is for you." A tiny voice somehow cut through the crowds, just above a whisper but still I heard it. It was Simon the Anorak. A pale hand reached through the banisters. "For luck." He held out a cluster of four-leaf clovers.

I took them and shook his hand, touched by the gesture. "Thank you, Simon."

"It's Larry Watersprite."

"Sorry. Thank you, Larry Watersprite." I half smiled. I'd need more than a fistful of greenery to get me through this.

On seeing me onstage, Red Horizon disbanded immediately. Only Jim stood grinning, one eye on me, one eye on the crowd. Johnny Logan shot out of his chair and bulleted toward the microphone. He tried to grab it from Jim, who had stopped singing but greedily clung to it and cleared his throat. You could hear the phlegm catching. He kissed his lips to the top of the microphone, and softly he whispered, "Before Kate gets here—" When he said my name, the crowd flew into shrieks, deafening roars. Jim's whispers were overpowered, but I could just make out, "—just in case she says anything, I'm not gay. I've nothing against gays but I'm not gay. I love girls."

Johnny wrestled the microphone off him. He went pale and swallowed loudly. He said something about things being "Cool, man, cool," and slowly stumbled to the back of the stage into the arms of Red Horizon's leather-clad crew.

The noise of the crowd was thunderous. "Kate McDaid!" I could see the words coming out of Johnny Logan's mouth but I couldn't hear them. Johnny looked toward me, held his palms up to the sky, and shrugged. What could he do? I walked over as steady as I could and took the microphone stand from him. I looked Johnny in the eye and thanked him, knowing that I was going to try to do the right thing for him, for all of them, and, hopefully, for me.

I stood and breathed. Still. *Breathe.* I looked out at the crowd, people stretched as far as I could see, becoming gray dots on the horizon, blending into the distance. Arms waved frantically, and the shouts, oh the shouts, they pumped into the vibrating air. I noticed Fiona and Lily standing in the front row. They gave me two thumbs-up and a nervous smile. "Good luck," Lily mouthed. I watched as Simon the Anorak muscled through the crowd to stand beside Fiona, the top of his head just reaching her shoulder. I saw her smile at him, nervously, before she coyly bit her lip and looked to the ground, blushing.

This was it. This was my final moment. I was on a razor edge. Either they'd accept the fake Step and that it had come from the fairies, or they wouldn't and I would be outed as a liar and these thousands of fanatical people could get angry, very angry, at me. It was a risk, but it was one I felt I had to take, whatever the consequences.

I held my arms out in front of me and waved them up and down. "Shhhh, shhhhhh," I said into the mic, like a teacher shushing a belligerent class. "Shhhhhhhhhh," I said for even longer this time, closing my eyes, concentrating hard on the feeling of silence. I stood and waited. And eventually it came, a pure stillness. There was not a shuffle, not a breath, not a chatter of teeth or a tear from the eye. There was no sound.

"Thank you." My voice erupted like thunder. I stood back from the microphone, shocked by the noise I'd just made. Then I leaned into it again. "Thank you for your silence, and thank you for listening to what I'm about to say."

I took a deep breath. It was now or never. *Please let this work, please let this work.* The eyes of the world and the fairy world were on me. I had to do it. I had to stop them.

"The last seven weeks have been a long journey for me. Me, the messenger, which is all I've ever been. These Steps have never been my story to tell. The experience has been an awakening in many ways. I've discovered truths about myself, the values I hold dear and the people I love. They have made me look at nature with new eyes and respect. I understand now that every piece of this world is a piece of me and of you.

"Many of you have had similar experiences over the last few weeks. These Steps have caused all of us here today to ask new questions of ourselves, to look for answers we'd never before searched deeply enough for. How many of you have questioned the order of life since these Steps have appeared? How many of you have looked at the world differently? How many of you have looked at the past differently? By being here today, by asking these questions, you're already finding answers."

I felt a slight tremor in my hand as I reached for the paper in my jeans pocket. I took a breath. *Don't crumble, not now.*

I cleared my throat. "And that is what the seventh Step says." I began to read.

O human friend, we brought you hope,
and brought you into light.
It was within you from the start,
to make you shine and make you bright,

Now you know that we are here,
you know that we are true.
We've taught and watched and
worked our words of wisdom upon you.

Every Step of ours, we saw you read
and learn and play.
And all along we wondered,
if we're among you here to stay.
Alas, we learned, not this time,
you mortals are not ready,
Yet we shall come again when time is old
and good and steady.

We will look into the eyes of children yet to be,
And one day, they and we will
share the skies and share the sea,
Till then, cherish nature, still, o human friend,
Until the years come when we breathe life into this end.

My eyes raced around the faces in the crowd. *Please work, please work, please work.*

There was a hush, a stillness. They were watching me.

I'll smile, I thought. *I'll smile, and maybe they'll copy me, maybe they'll feel good about the final Step.* I puffed out my chest and grinned the widest grin I could muster up. Silence. And then there was a crack in the crowd, and a man's deep voice shouted out, gravelly and loud, "What are you smiling about?"

There was another shout, even louder than the first. "So that's it, then? Where are the fairies?"

Another one was more aggressive. "Where are the fairies?"

The crowd heaved and seemed to bear down on the stage. I took a step back, scared. I could see red faces and furrowed brows. In the distance, there were fists pumping in the air. They were angry.

"This is bullshit!"

"Where are the fairies?"

I panicked. Had I got this completely wrong? Had I misjudged the crowd and written the wrong thing? Would they only be happy if they saw a fairy?

"We want fairies!"

"Come out, come out, wherever you are!"

"Back off!" It was Garda Fitzgerald. He was screaming back at the crowd. He turned to face the crowd. "You heard what she said. We're not ready. The fairies aren't ready to meet us yet. Not until we are."

A few heads nodded in agreement. A murmur rippled through the crowd. "We're not ready."

"Bullshit! I'm ready!" came an angry shout from the back.

"No, you're not."

"If you were ready they'd be here."

"We're not ready."

Garda Fitzgerald said it again. "We're not ready."

There was a collective sigh from the crowd, an air of disappointment, but I could sense a change: they seemed to be accepting the message. They weren't happy, but seemed resigned to the fact that there would be no fairies. Heads were bobbing, shoulders seemed to fall, fists unclenched, and red faces calmed. They eased back and away from the stage. I felt myself relax. This might have worked. They might have bought it.

People turned to each other, looking confused, mouthing the words "We're not ready" to one another. *We're not ready*, I thought. *Say it. We're not ready.*

There were grunts of approval and agreement.

It was working. My fake Step was working. I felt my heart quicken as I watched the crowd slowly move away. They were disbanding.

A few of the more optimistic were not giving up.

"I'm going to hunt them down."

"I'm still going to try and find them!"

Some people looked pleased; others, not so much. But either way, it was over. They seemed to have accepted the Step.

They filed off, occasionally looking toward me, waving half-heartedly. Uninterested in me. Some now and again shouting *thanks* up at me, as an afterthought.

The original Anoraks came close. Simon smiled and nodded confidently, punching the air. "Cheers, Kate! I get it now. I really get it. We're not ready, we may never be ready." He looked to Fiona, who was stuck firm beside him, and they both smiled shyly at each other and slowly started walking together away from the crowd.

I relaxed and smiled. I'd done it. I'd beaten the fairies at their own game. They wouldn't win this time. The relief was overwhelming. I watched happily as the road cleared and the cobblestones reappeared. Cables and cameras were reloaded into shiny vans and all the Anoraks shuffled off, unzipping as they walked.

Mam and Dad, looking like stained floorboards, were clapping proudly. They stood up and hugged me, squeezing me so tightly I thought I'd never breathe again. "We're so proud of you! You were wonderful."

"It's the end of your media careers." The words fell clunky out of my mouth. I felt numb.

Mam threw her head back, laughing. "Sure, we'd a great time while it lasted, but we always knew it would end. And you know what? It was getting a bit boring. The novelty was wearing off. I tell you, Wanda Simpson is having a bridge night in the Duck and Dog tomorrow, and I can't wait for a nice glass of sherry and some good intelligent conversation."

Dad looked at me uncomfortably. "I've really hated wearing these leather trousers."

"Kate." Hugh threw himself around me, leaning back to brush my hair from my face. "You were amazing. I'm so proud of you."

"Kate." Mam grabbed my arm hurriedly. "What about Jim?"

I nodded my head over to where Jim was looking lost at the crowd. "He was never a goer."

Hugh hung his arm off my shoulder and we started to climb down from the stage. There was no need for bodyguards this time. The place was calm.

A loud beep came from up the road. Seamus MacMurphy hung out the window of a red Ford Cortina, waving at me.

Telling the others I'd be right back, I walked toward him.

"Sorry for the beep," he apologized. "I've got to get on the road. The traffic is going to be terrible, you know."

"That's grand."

"The final Step is published all over the Internet already. You've got a couple of thousand hits on YouTube." Leaning over to the floor of the passenger seat, he awkwardly bundled up a small wooden box and passed it through the open window to me.

"The estate?" I asked.

"It is, yeah." Then he winked, revved up the engine, and, waving a long arm out the open window, was gone up the Galway road.

I rested the box on my knee. It wasn't heavy. I ripped open the brown paper packaging around it and looked inside. It was a bottle, like a beer bottle, only blue. A stained blue bottle. I knew immediately what it was. This was the famous blue Bottle that Biddy Early had used to see the future. This had been a gift to her from the fairies. It was the lost Bottle. The Red Hag must have got her hands on it somehow. Maybe she stole it from Biddy Early on her deathbed. Maybe Biddy Early gave it to her in the hope she would redeem herself. It was meant to have powers of foresight, a type of crystal ball. It made sense that the Red Hag wouldn't let it disappear—its powers were too valuable. She would have done anything she could to get her hands on it. This might have been how she'd seen me coming.

I covered the box over, unsure what to do. The only person I could speak to, the only person who would understand, was Father O'Brien. He knew the truth. I had to talk to him.

I walked back to my parents and friends and told them there was someone I had to see. Then I headed up the village toward the church, happy, for once, not to draw a crowd or attract pointing fingers.

I banged firmly on the vestry door.

"Father, it's me, Kate," I shouted.

"Oh dear Lord, come in."

He was sitting in the same throne-like seat. He looked smaller than before. His face was in his hands and he was crying, his shoulders shaking. He looked up. His eyes were red-rimmed and fat tears rolled down his cheeks.

I moved over and knelt at his feet. I lifted my arms and hugged him tight, feeling his head rest heavily on the crook of my neck, his body trembling with sobs.

"Thank you, thank you."

"I didn't have a choice."

He sat back and wiped the tears from his face. "Thank you."

"Honestly, Father, I did it because I didn't know what else to do."

He took my hands in his and shook them. His skin felt papery and cold. "You're a good person. You did the right thing."

Father O'Brien knew the truth. He'd read the real final Step, and he knew that what I'd read out was fake. That I had averted a fairy war.

Father O'Brien held the real final Step in his hand and waved it, heavily. "The fairies will be angry with you. You know that?"

"I know. I'll suffer repercussions."

He took a deep breath. "It was too much to ask of you, to let them release their battle cry. To start their war."

I nodded, agreeing. The Seventh Step, the real Step, asked for me to lead a crowd of true believers of Celtic blood to a fairy fort. To bring gifts of whiskey, milk, and music and to repeat a *beannacht*, the Irish word for blessing, until they appeared. And they *would* appear. I knew with absolute certainty that they would have appeared. They'd have crept out from the rocks, crawled down from the trees, brushed away the shrubbery, and been among us—the mortals living with the immortals. The invisible world visible. And then they would have let loose, they'd have started their fairy war. They'd have hunted down nonbelievers and thrown them under the earth, promising an eternity of damnation in the fires of hell. How could I have let that happen? How could I have shaken the very foundations of our existence? Our reality would no longer be. I couldn't have done it. I couldn't have lifted the veil.

"The world isn't the way we've always thought it is," I said.

"I know, I know." Father O'Brien sniffed back another tear and attempted to straighten himself.

I felt my own shoulders crumble with the weight of the responsibility I'd been given. "I need to sit down." I moved over to the other side of the room and sank into a chair.

Neither of us spoke for a while as the enormity of the situation sank in.

"You will destroy the final Step," Father O'Brien said very clearly, breaking the silence.

I sighed. "Even if I destroy it, it doesn't change anything. I have the power to reveal an invisible world." Saying these words out loud gave me shivers. Goose bumps raced up my arm. "The seventh Step gives me absolute proof that the fairy realm runs parallel to our world, and Father, I . . ." I heard my voice crack. I took a breath. "I can flip the switch. I can make their world visible to ours."

"I know."

I knew that. I just had to say it out loud. I had to see his reaction. I had to know that I hadn't gone mad. That this was real.

"This would be the biggest event in human civilization—are we ready for it? We have no idea what this would mean for the human race. We have no idea what we might be unleashing if we took this Step. How is all this possible?"

Father O'Brien shook his head heavily. "Your aunt had an insight. She understood the fairies, listened to them, and unraveled their mysteries. It was as if she knocked on the door. But you, you can open it, you can unleash them." He took a deep breath.

I nodded. "I wonder, though, Father. Do people have a right to know? Why should I keep this to myself? This is bigger than us, than just two people."

"No, Kate. This is an unknown world. Humanity has enough struggles. We don't need to introduce fairies to the world."

And suddenly I started to laugh. I couldn't help myself. I had a vision of fairies in our day-to-day lives: a leprechaun as a bank teller, an impish fairy working in the local coffee shop making a mean mocha. Would we interdate? Imagine the online dating profiles: "I like long walks on the beach, basic spells, evil tricks, and my favorite singer is the banshee." It's all too absurd. It would never work.

"Let's just try and put this behind us now," Father O'Brien said. "Leave the fairies in the shadows. I'm just happy it's over."

I knew what he said made sense. I knew I'd done the right thing by not starting a fairy war.

"I'm here, Kate. If you need someone to talk to. I'm here."

I smiled. I think that was the nicest thing anyone had said to me in a long time. "Thanks."

I stood up and straightened my back. "I should go. Look after yourself, Father."

"Kate." He stopped me. "What about you and who you are? What will happen now?"

I shrugged, thinking of what Hugh had said to me: *You are who you are.* "I'll have to figure it out. I can't hide away, I can't waste my magic, but I can't do this again, this circus. I'll have to figure something out. Maybe I'll read that *Witchcraft for Dummies* book, get myself trained up. Invest in a cauldron and some stick-on warts for my nose."

I ran my hand through my hair. A cobweb of red hairs came free at the root and tangled around my fingers. *That's unusual,* I thought. That had never happened before. Could my hair be falling out? Would I be investing in more cheap wigs?

I knew the fairies would try and seek revenge because they didn't get their way. I had to be prepared for payback. Maybe that was going to be my hair. Could I get comfortable with head-scarves and hats?

In all of it, in the madness where I saw reality bend, the fairies had lurked in the background, their world untouched. They were willing to disrupt ours, to bring evil with them, to lift the veil. But I'd stood in the way of the mighty fairies and stopped them. Somehow, they only had themselves to blame.

I had to trust that I'd made the right decision, and I had to trust that I could battle through whatever revenge they had planned for me.

Father O'Brien smiled and looked exhausted as we said good-bye. "Remember, Kate, I'm here. You may need me."

I smiled, thinking that if I did need him in the future, if I was to battle against the other world again, it would be on my terms, and I might need an ally.

39

"And the winner is . . ." The MC swept the room with a smile as he reached into the gold envelope. "F & P! For Starshoot!"

Matthew jumped out of his seat and punched the air with his fist. Beaming, he spun back and threw out his hand for me to take. I shook my head and mouthed "You go."

Bouncing up to the stage, Matthew bear-hugged the MC and said "Woop woop!" into the mic. This was F & P's fifth award of the night, and the third for the Starshoot David Hasselhof ad. It was the most we'd ever won at the Irish Advertising Awards. The whole table was drunk, swaying and singing. We'd toasted and drunk to everything we could think of. Colin had proposed the last one—"To all the people who load the photocopier at F & P. Thank you, we couldn't have done it without you"—which was greeted with huge applause and another round of champagne.

Matthew plonked himself back onto his seat and leaned in to give Marjorie a kiss. Those two were going strong. "Three awards for Starshoot! Can you believe it?"

My phone buzzed with a picture message. Laughing, I showed it to Matthew—Dad on a camel, looking very uncomfortable. Despite Mam's outrageous spending, they'd managed to save some money from their celebrity days and were now traveling everywhere and anywhere. They kept me updated on Facebook and sent through photos, including some I didn't need to see of them half naked in a Jacuzzi in North Africa. Mam referred to herself and Dad as the "Born Again Flashpackers."

Matthew has lost most of the weight he put on during the campaign, but it's going to be short-lived. Three days ago, the Little Prince marched into the office with a new brief: Dinojellies. Matthew's eyes lit up and he absentmindedly patted his belly as he told me how he'd requested a box of free samples.

Colin asked me back for the awards. I'd left F & P eight months ago. I couldn't get back into the rhythm of working, and besides, I have a new calling that I need to explore.

My friends are doing great. Lily is on the hunt for a husband. She's taken on the ten commandments of a new dating book and is sticking to them religiously. They're pretty quirky. The fourth commandment is to always wear high heels, and the first is "If you want him to marry you, don't sleep with him." She's struggling with the celibacy part but loving all her new shoes.

Fiona and Simon (I'm not allowed to call him Simon the Anorak anymore, just Simon) are completely smitten with each other. She loves his conspiracy theories on just about everything, and melts into smiles when he's around. He still has his anorak, but in a strange way it's grown on me a bit—he looks well in it. The Anoraks themselves have disbanded and gone back to normal life, but I'm sure they're just waiting in the wings to jump on the next fad—I've heard that aliens are going to be big next year. Fiona is weighing up job offers. She says she's ready to go back into the workforce, but with a better life balance and probably a smaller paycheck.

No doubt you saw Jim on the cover of *Rolling Stone* magazine, twice in six months. Red Horizon's album went to number one in twenty-seven countries. Last I heard, Jim had moved to L.A. He's still single.

I never heard from Maura again. Her articles still appear in *The Times*, and she's still as connected as she ever was. I assume that the Hellfire Club is still raging and that they're still looking for a way into Tír na nÓg. In a way, as mad as they are, I admire them. At least they haven't given in to old age. They won't be found walking up and down beachfront promenades sucking on sticks of rock candy or pouring their pensions into support stockings and blue rinses. They're still raving on, filling in the wrinkles with Botox and squeezing bunioned feet into stiletto heels. Good luck to them.

I became yesterday's news very quickly. Some celebrity got caught having an affair with a footballer, and within hours I was forgotten.

For me, the last twelve months have been all about accepting who I am. Kate McDaid, sometime spell maker, sometime copywriter, full-time girlfriend, part-time gym member.

My hair did fall out. All of it. I'm as bald as an egg. It was a shock, at first, but I'm used to it now. I have drawers of fancy wigs—I've upgraded from my acrylic number from last year—and I experiment with different styles: pixie cuts, romantic curls, blond, brunette, afro. I go all out. Hugh doesn't know who he's going to come home to from one day to the next.

I know that was a trick played by the fairies. The other trick, if you could call it that, is harder to live with. I couldn't definitively say it was their doing, but a month after the final Step, I started to get terrible stomach pains, like knives shooting through me. The doctors ran a million tests, and while they couldn't find anything that could explain the stomach cramps, they did find that my ovaries were gone, that there was an empty space where they should have been. No ovaries. No children. The fairies have made sure that I'm the end of the line. I knew there would be repercussions—I'd stopped a fairy war—but this really did feel harsh.

I was miserable and angry for a long time. I was angry at the fairies and what they'd done to my life, for turning it upside down and shaking it out. I was angry that they'd tricked me with their playful words, seduced me with their pretend innocence. But slowly my anger has subsided. There are many ways to have a family, and I've realized that ultimately I'm the winner here—not the fairies. They didn't get what they wanted. I've kept the power.

After I left F & P, I packed up my Dublin life and rented a small cottage in Knocknamee. It felt like the right move: Knocknamee felt like home. But there was an adjustment period. Moving from the city to the country wasn't as easy as I thought it was going to be. I started to miss some of the things that would drive most people out of the city: the smell of rain on cement, the choke of car fumes, angry bus drivers who will battle like samurais for the correct fare, wobbly seats at the French cinema that smell like every day of their fifty years of service. I also missed late-night shopping under fluorescent lights, sushi bars, and delicious cocktails with expensive-sounding names. But it all balanced out, and Knocknamee has given me a lot more than alcohol options. I am still madly in love with this beautiful little spot.

Hugh hasn't officially moved in, but his bike, clothes, shoes, shaving gear, surfboard, and books have. I cleaned out some drawers and suggested he put his stuff in them, but he said they were much happier on the floor/chair/bed. I always lose the battle over the remote control, so TV viewing has been dominated by sports and political dramas with never-ending plotlines.

Hugh takes off his muddy boots at the door every evening and bursts through excitedly, bounding toward me, delighted that I'm here and delighted that our evening is beginning. I'll throw my arms around him and we kiss, smiling. I tell him he smells of the farm and he needs a shower, and he'll strip off in the kitchen and try to pull me in with him. I hope that we're still doing this evening dance together in forty years' time, that we are still so excited to see each other after a day apart.

Hugh is a master in the kitchen, which means that my jeans are a little bit too tight these days while he's perfecting pasta dishes. We've taken up running to counteract the weight gain and are regularly huffing and puffing down An Trá Bhán in the evening with Setanta in tow. After showers and stretches we flop out on the couch and into a bottle of wine. With Hugh, I am filled with happiness. He is my best friend, my love, my darling.

Not long after I moved to Knocknamee, the letters started arriving, and often people come to the door. I still don't know how they find me. Some are lost, distressed, hurt, out of love, out of pocket. All want help. The recession has taken Ireland firmly by the throat, and life has become very hard for a lot of people. The Irish bankers have played the country like a game of Monopoly, only to flip the board over once every house was mortgaged but just before the old boot got the chance to pass Go. Journalists have scrambled for vocabulary to describe the bleak state of the country: cheap cuts of meat, heavy blankets, and candlelight. Unemployment is on the rise, and basic necessities are getting harder and harder to afford. I wonder if it's because of this bleakness that my skills are so in demand. Like the Red Hag in the famine, I seem to be able to provide people with some hope. At least I try my best to.

So they come and sit on my Ikea furniture, sip on a cup of tea, and tell me their troubles: missing engagement rings, business worries, love affairs, and money—they always need to know if there's money coming down the line.

Sometimes people just need a friendly ear—they don't need an answer. But I try my best. I concentrate, sit still, and wait. And sometimes, I find the answers. I prescribe potions and lotions—treatments for obscure ailments. I keep track of the spells, now, write them all up in a large book. Hugh calls it my cookbook. I have to keep a record, because sometimes the spells pop in and out of my head so quickly it's a race to hold the pen. I still don't understand everything, but I'm trying and I'm learning.

I never ask for money. I don't want to go down the road the Red Hag traveled. But people leave donations: milk from their farm, a new set of shelves, an iPod.

The blue Bottle is still a mystery. Occasionally a clouded image appears and disappears, but invariably I can't understand it. I know it has power—I just don't know how the power will work for me, yet. I know it's been left to me for an important reason, and I'm sure it will reveal itself one day.

I see fairies a lot more clearly, now. They still hide from me, but I catch a glimpse. I know they're there, being mischievous, playing tricks, guarding us, and having fun. I listen for their messages, which come to me in my dreams, most of the time. I know they're still angry with me for not bringing them into the world, but I know I made the right decision. I don't regret that.

I don't know what the future holds for the fairies. Maybe there will be a time to lift the veil, to let the immortal walk with the mortal. But until then, I know that I'll keep loving nature and enjoying every beautiful moment in it. I'll keep having fun, and singing and dancing and laughing, just like they asked us to.

RELUCTANTLY CHARMED
AND FAIRIES

Thanks so much for picking up *Reluctantly Charmed*. It's my first novel, and it's been a labor of love, tears, and many cups of tea. I wrote it in my parents' front room in Dublin, their good room. I was given permission to use it as long as I promised not to eat or drink in there (I'm sure Hemingway never had to contend with a mother concerned about crumbs).

I knew I had a story, and I knew I had to get it down.

It all came to me in a roundabout way from my granny. William Butler Yeats, Walt Disney, and my granny believed in fairies. Granny O'Neill instilled the fear of God in her grandchildren with stories of fairies. Irish fairies are not cute little angelic creatures, but mischievous fellows with an evil glint in their eye who would put a hump on your back for singing a song out of tune. Granny came from a small farm and, as many of her generation did, grew up with the certainty of their existence and of their wrath if not appeased. As I got older and Santa and the Easter Bunny disappeared, the fairies remained. Fairies belonged to the grown-up world.

When she passed away six years ago, I was sad to lose that link to the other world—the maybe world and all the dreaming and possibilities of it. I started to investigate the folklore around fairies. I found hundreds of firsthand reports of encounters with the *little people*. There were recent articles and stories of road works and construction sites brought to a halt because of the threat of disturbing a fairy tree or fort. I found it hard to believe that modern Ireland was holding fast to these superstitious beliefs. There was something wonderfully romantic about it.

And I wondered . . . what if? As crazy as it sounds, what if there was something in it?

And so I found Kate McDaid, a modern, funny, cynical, regular city dweller, probably the antithesis of my granny in her twenties. Kate already had enough on her plate with romantic troubles, a hectic work schedule, and some off-the-wall parents. I chose her as the key holder to the fairy world and watched the story unfold.

Reluctantly Charmed is a story of magical realism. It's a story for anyone who has ever wondered *what if.*

I really hope you enjoyed it.

Ellie O'Neill
2014

ACKNOWLEDGMENTS

Thanks to my sisters, Niamh and Cathy, who have been my biggest cheerleaders on this long journey to publication, my first readers, my best friends, my harshest critics and biggest supporters. You have pushed and pulled *Reluctantly Charmed* in the right direction.

Jacinta di Mase and Catherine Drayton, who have shown me great leadership and advice. A big thank-you to the team at Touchstone New York for taking a punt on an unknown author. I am deeply grateful to you all, particularly Miya Kumangai, Maria Whelan, and Linda Sawicki. Thanks to all at Simon & Schuster Sydney, in particular Roberta Ivers, Larissa Edwards, and Anna O'Grady. Thanks, too, to Jude McGee and Elizabeth Cowell.

Thanks to William Butler Yeats, part of whose poem "The Stolen Child" has been reproduced in *Reluctantly Charmed*. I would also like to acknowledge the authorship of the epigraph used at the beginning of the book: "The world is full of magic things patiently waiting for our senses to grow sharper." For me, it was a perfect summation of Kate's journey, and while historically the quote has been attributed to Yeats, it can't be substantiated by the poet's literary estate. A quote that is very similar has been attributed to English author and playwright Eden Phillpotts, where the word "universe" is used in place of "world." In any case, I acknowledge both writers for their eloquence.

To the fairies, for allowing me to peep under the veil of this world into theirs to share this story and encourage magic to bloom.

And to Joe and Cian, my happily ever after, forever and ever my men.

ABOUT THE AUTHOR

ELLIE O'NEILL took the long way around. She sold spider catchers in Sydney, flipped burgers in Dublin, and worked in advertising in London. All the while, she had that niggling feeling she had stories to tell. So, at thirtysomething, she made the brave leap and moved back in with her parents to get the job done. Swapping the dizzy disco lights of London for their suburban Dublin house, she scribbled away, knowing that there was something about Irish fairies she needed to share with the world.

Then, most unexpectedly, Ellie fell madly in love. The only catch was that he lived in Australia. True to form, she couldn't ignore the magic and followed her heart to Oz for what was supposed to be a long holiday. Five years later, Australia is home to Ellie, her Joe, and their fabulous baby (with an Irish name no one can pronounce). They live in Geelong, and Ellie is currently working on her second book.

TOUCHSTONE READING GROUP GUIDE

Reluctantly Charmed

ELLIE O'NEILL

When Dubliner Kate McDaid turned twenty-six, her goal for the next year was to get a promotion at work. Focused on a pay raise and a new job title, she certainly never expected that her twenty-sixth year would bring her fame and attention beyond anything she could imagine—or want. It begins when a mysterious letter arrives inviting her to attend the reading of the will of Miss Kate McDaid. What seems at first to be an obvious mistake will soon turn Kate's life completely upside down when she is named the sole beneficiary to the estate of her great-great-great-grand-aunt of the same name. The catch is that the estate will only be revealed after Kate publishes a letter and a series of seven poems that her ancestor has bequeathed to her. Curious—and a little amused—Kate agrees, and decides to publish the poems online. And so begins a frenzy in Ireland and around the world as each of the "Seven Steps" brings followers closer to a world beyond ours, a world with fairies and witches and the promise of eternal youth. As the messages gradually become more sinister with each step, Kate is faced with the decision of whether or not to see them through. Could the fate of humanity be in her hands?

Filled with humor, romance, building suspense—and of course a little bit of magic—*Reluctantly Charmed* makes us think about the things we believe in and ponder what may exist just beyond our detection. It charms from page one, and is a debut to be devoured without any reluctance.

FOR DISCUSSION

1. On page 32, Matthew says, "Some of that stuff is kind of nice. Thinking that there's something else out there, that maybe it isn't just this." Do you agree? How do you feel about the idea that it could be "just this"? Do you think it's possible in today's modern world to believe in an "other world"?

2. Kate and her parents have very different approaches to dealing with the sudden fame and publicity they receive from the Seven Steps. What do you make of their reactions? Who would you act like in a similar situation? Or would you take a totally different approach?

3. Drake Chandler's suicide note mentioned fairies. Was it a coincidence—or something more?

4. On page 89, Kate decides to keep following the steps. She acknowledges that she likes to stay on top of trends: "If people are talking about it, I'm going to try it." Are you also quick to try out the latest fads, or are you more of a wait-and-see type? Do you think you would have been likely to start following the Seven Steps if everyone else around you were talking about it?

5. Kate had an imaginary friend as a child that she later remembers and realizes was one of the fairies. Have you ever had a childhood memory suddenly come back to you? Do you think it's possible to hold onto childhood beliefs, like fairies, in adulthood? What were the magical things you believed in as a child?

6. "A stranger in a small town will never know the rhythm of the place. A stranger will always cause an eyebrow to raise

or a throat to clear. There is a language, a code built into the locals that a visitor cannot translate" (p. 250). Does this notion of a small town ring true with your own experiences? Have you ever been an insider or an outsider in a small town?

7. Do you think it was right for the people of Knocknamee to try to profit off the attention that the Seven Steps brought them? Should they be "making hay while the sun shines" (p. 347), as Annie put it, or do you agree with Father O'Brien that cashing in on the attention is worshipping money as a false god?

8. Compare and contrast the characters of Hugh and Jim. How did your feelings toward each of them evolve throughout the course of the story?

9. Kate handles the truth about her ancestor the Red Hag fairly well. How do you think you would feel if, like Kate, you found out that you were the descendant of someone who was considered evil and murdered by his or her contemporaries?

10. Do you agree with Kate's decision not to share the real seventh Step? What would you have done in her position? Should she still have inherited the blue bottle even though she didn't actually do what the will required of her?

11. What do you make of Kate losing her hair? Discuss the symbolism in her supposed punishment from the fairies.

12. Kate's journey with the Seven Steps changed her. She felt distanced from the people closest to her because no one could really understand what she was going through. She acknowledges, "I wasn't the person I had been" (p. 349). Discuss the ways that Kate changes and evolves throughout the story. Have you ever had an experience where you came out feeling like you were no longer the same person?

ENHANCE YOUR BOOK CLUB

1. Every year on Kate's birthday, she has dinner with her parents at the same Italian restaurant and they recount the story of her birth: "It's a redhead!" Do you have any specific birthday traditions in your family? Or funny stories that you tell every year for the occasion?

2. Have you thought of what your fairy name might be? Go around the group and try to come up with a fairy name for each member of your book club.

3. What childhood beliefs have you held onto in adulthood?

4. At the end of the book, Kate says, "I'll keep loving nature and enjoying every beautiful moment in it. I'll keep having fun, and singing and dancing and laughing, just like they asked us to" (p. 387). Not everything in the Seven Steps was manipulative. What can you appreciate from them? Pick one or two of the more positive aspects from the fairies' instructions and try following them.

5. To learn more about fairies and Irish folklore, visit the website ireland.mysteriousworld.com/Mystery/Folklore/FairyTales/, or pick up a copy of W. B. Yeats' *Fairy & Folk Tales of Ireland*.

A CONVERSATION WITH ELLIE O'NEILL

You've said this story came to you in a roundabout way from your grandmother. Do you think she truly believed in fairies?
I really don't know—I'd love to be able to ask her that. She may just have been erring on the side of caution. My granny was a for-midable woman who shed her rural upbringing with delight and made a very modern life for herself in Dublin. She always wore a fur coat, had her nails polished, and worked when it wasn't the thing for a woman to do. But there were traditions from her upbringing that she was never able to shake, and one of them was talking about fairies. Her childhood was colored with stories of the nasty tricks the Little People had performed. I touch on this in *Reluctantly Charmed*—how sometimes it's hard to lose child-hood beliefs, that often there's a niggle of doubt about something you heard as a kid. But did she truly believe? I don't know.

Do you believe in fairies? Or in magic, or the existence of something beyond?
I choose to believe in the possibility of them. I hope there's magic out there, that karma exists, that there's some great puppeteer in the sky pulling strings to make wonderful things happen. I have that dream, but I'm also a realist—bills need to be paid, bones get broken, feelings get hurt, life can be really hard . . . but maybe because life can be hard we need to believe in magic even more!

What kind of research was involved in the writing of this novel? Was there anything particularly interesting that you came across while researching?
I read a lot of books (shocker: *Writer in Reading Scandal!!!*). I

was living in Ireland while I was writing, and so I spoke to a lot of people to hear their stories and get their opinions on fairy lore, which was ridiculously good fun. William Butler Yeats was probably my primary source of inspiration from a literary point of view; I fell in love with his idea of fairies. His poems and his imagery of Ireland is really breathtaking.

Folklore is fun—its very nature as an oral tradition leaves everything in a gray area. There's a lot of wiggle room for truth and fact, and that's part of the appeal. It's good old-fashioned sci-fi!

Is Knocknamee a real place? Or based on one? Have you ever been anywhere like it?
It's fictitious. Sorry! But there are plenty of places like it in the west of Ireland. Little pockets of heaven are there, just waiting for you to stumble across them at the turn in a road.

How do you think you would personally handle fame and media attention, like Kate had to?
I am a bit—OK, a *lot*—celebrity-obsessed. I read my show-biz blogs and magazines, check out the fashion, discuss the romances. I love the crazy world of selfies and surgery. But could I handle being in it? Probably not. I am happy to remain a voyeur, with no fan clubs and all of my own wrinkles.

If you had the chance to go to Tír na Nóg and live in the land of eternal youth, would you?
Imagine—a world with no wrinkles, no creaks in your back, no aches and pains? Amazing. Just think of the money you'd save on creams alone. The only problem with Tír na Nóg is that once you're there, you can never leave. And as exciting a prospect as it

is to still be raving well into my nineties, I wouldn't want to be without my family.

Why do you think the Irish make such good storytellers?
Have you ever walked away from an Irish person and thought, *Well, they really didn't have much to say for themselves?* You see? It doesn't happen. The ability to chat is in our DNA, and somewhere along the way we learned that a beginning, a middle, and an end, with maybe a few jokes and some bad language thrown in, might get you a pint in the pub and win you a few friends.

Are there any particular writers or works that inspired your interest in writing a story of magical realism?
I read a broad spectrum of genres. A good story is what appeals to me, whatever the backdrop.

What has been the most exciting part of the publishing process so far?
I remember when the contract came through—I was five months pregnant and literally shaking from head to toe in disbelief and thinking that all this adrenaline couldn't be good for the baby! It was surreal, after countless rejections, to suddenly have a contract in front of me. I was dumbstruck by it all.

What's up next for you?
I'm working on another book and running after a toddler, so life is pretty full and busy right now.